RUGGED SPLENDOR

"Why do you do that?" she demanded.

"Do what?"

"Snarl at me all the time!"

The Stetson's wide brim shadowed his eyes, but she knew he was looking at her. "Do I?" he asked after a lengthy silence.

"Yes." Silver felt close to tears.

He leaned over and placed his index finger beneath her chin, forcing her head back until she was looking into his face. She expected another surly reply or perhaps even an unconcerned shrug—certainly not his tender response.

"I'm sorry, Miss Matlock. I think you deserve better." And then he leaned low and gently kissed her lips.

RUGGED SPLENDOR

ROBIN LEIGH

AVON BOOKS ◈ NEW YORK

AVON BOOKS
A division of
The Hearst Corporation
105 Madison Avenue
New York, New York 10016

Copyright © 1991 by Robin Lee Hatcher
Published by arrangement with the author
Library of Congress Catalog Card Number: 90-93407
ISBN: 0-380-76318-4

First Avon Books Printing: March 1991

AVON TRADEMARK REG. U.S. PAT. OFF. AND IN OTHER COUNTRIES, MARCA REGISTRADA, HECHO EN U.S.A.

Printed in the U.S.A.

RA 10 9 8 7 6 5 4 3 2 1

Prologue

Masonville, Colorado
May, 1873

Jared Newman stopped his pinto gelding in front of the lone saloon of Masonville. The bright May sun glared down on the tiny town. Silence reigned along the main street. Nothing stirred; there wasn't even the hint of a breeze.

Jared glanced up the street, then back the way he'd come. If he hadn't been through this same spot just three days before, he would have thought it a ghost town. Not a single person was in sight.

He removed his battered Stetson and raked his fingers through shaggy dark hair, then stepped down from the saddle. He hit the hat against his pant leg a few times, sending up a cloud of dust. He was bone-weary and hot, and his temper had seen better days.

"Get down, Peterson. We could both use a drink."

His prisoner quickly obeyed, sliding to the ground, his hands tied in front of him.

With a jingle of spurs, Jared ushered Lute Peterson through the swinging doors of the Mountain Rose Saloon. The narrow room was dimly lit and musty-smelling. Two men, a circle of smoke lingering above their heads, glanced up from their game of cards, their faces expressing their mutual disinterest in the two strangers. A scantily garbed blonde lounged against the bar. The moment she saw Jared, her mouth turned up in a broad smile of welcome. Behind her, the bartender slowly swirled a white cloth along the bar's hardwood surface.

"Move," Jared said in a low voice, then followed behind Peterson as they approached the bar.

"What'll it be, stranger?" the bartender asked.

"Whiskey. Two." He tossed four bits onto the counter.

The woman sidled closer. "Haven't seen you in here before. Where you headed?"

Jared turned his head to look at the woman. Ample white breasts nearly spilled over the bodice of her purple dress. A generous dusting of powder and rouge had been applied to her angular face. At one time, she might have been attractive, but life had left its mark around her eyes and in the cynical corners of her painted mouth.

"Denver," he responded reluctantly. He wasn't in the mood for idle chatter.

He tossed back his head and let the whiskey burn its way down his throat. It was rotgut, as he'd suspected it would be, but he didn't much care. He was tired and thirsty, and he still had a ways to ride before nightfall.

"You a lawman?" the woman asked, jerking her head toward Peterson.

"Of a sort." He tossed another coin onto the bar. "I'll have more of the same."

"You look tired, mister. Maybe you oughta stay here tonight." She leaned closer, smiling an invitation. "I've got a room of my own with clean sheets."

Jared caught a whiff of her cheap cologne and barely contained a grimace. "Sorry. I'm in a hurry." With a shake of his head, he turned his back to the bar. "Where is everyone? The town looks deserted."

"Big do today," the bartender said as he poured the golden liquid into Jared's glass. "Town's leading citizens have got a gal gettin' married. Just about everybody's at the church."

"But not you?"

The blonde at his elbow laughed sharply. "Do we look like the type to get invited to a church weddin'?" She snorted.

Jared shrugged, then looked toward Peterson. "Let's go. We've got a long ride before dark."

Jared stopped right outside the swinging doors of the saloon, his prisoner at his side. He squinted, allowing his eyes a moment to adjust to the bright sunlight, then turned and looked up the street one more time. Not a soul in sight.

"Why don't we spend the night here?" Peterson asked, his voice an irritating whine. "I'm too tired to go any further."

"We're not staying, so mount up," Jared ordered, his ill temper growing by the minute.

If this lousy little town had a sheriff, he wouldn't still have to ride into Denver to turn Peterson over to the law and collect his reward. He could be done with the miserable coward. For two days he'd listened to the short, bespectacled Peterson whining about his innocence, claiming he'd been framed, swearing he'd never touched his employer's daughter. Jared was sick to death of it.

As he stepped toward the horses, his hand on

Peterson's elbow, he glanced in the opposite direction, then stopped dead in his tracks.

A vision in white satin and pearls, her long lace train dragging on the dusty planks of the boardwalk, the girl raced toward him. As he watched, she jerked the filmy white veil from her head and sent her ebony hair cascading down her back as she tossed the offending veil into the street. She was obviously the bride the bartender had mentioned, the daughter of Masonville's leading family. He couldn't help wondering what had caused the girl to flee the church in such an agitated state. Maybe she'd gotten a case of cold feet.

They must be very cold to send her running through the center of town in her wedding gown, he thought. He couldn't stop an amused grin from creeping into the corners of his mouth.

Suddenly, she seemed to become aware of him. She paused, and her eyes lifted to meet his. Silvergray set in an arrestingly beautiful face, they were awash with tears. He felt an unexpected urge to offer some sort of comfort.

Then he heard an indignant oath as those same bewitching eyes sparked with anger. If he stood in her way a moment longer, he had no doubt she would run over him in a fit of rage. Instinct—and a touch of self-preservation—made him quickly step back toward the saloon wall, jerking Peterson after him. His prisoner's head hit the boards with force.

"What's the matter, bounty?" Peterson whined. "You trying to kill me before we get to Denver?"

The gray eyes widened just a fraction more before she swept past them in a flash of white, disappearing moments later around the next corner.

"Whew . . ." Jared let out a long breath, still

staring down the sidewalk in the direction she'd fled, feeling slightly winded by the near-encounter.

"Maybe we could use another drink." Peterson rubbed the back of his head with his bound hands.

Jared tugged down the ragged brim of his Stetson, the bride quickly forgotten. "Mount up," he snapped. "We're going to make Denver before nightfall it if kills us both."

Chapter 1

Tension gripped the small parlor as it had the entire house for days. Silver Matlock sat on the edge of the settee, staring at the carpet, her hands balled into tight fists in her lap.

"Are you telling me we're going to lose the store, Gerald?" her mother asked, her tone incredulous.

"The store. Our house. Everything."

"But that's impossible. We couldn't be . . . *impoverished.*" Her voice shook with horror at the notion. It was too incomprehensible to be believed. "Gerald, we helped build this town. We . . ."

Gerald Matlock ran a hand over his balding head. "No, Marlene. It's not impossible. Without that money, we're ruined. We've been spending more than the store brings in for too long now."

"You mean *I've* been spending too much."

Her father didn't acknowledge or confirm Marlene's statement. "Selling that land was to have paid off the mortgage. Now there's nothing left to fall back on."

Silver looked up as her father, his shoulders slumped in untold weariness, left the room. She swallowed the lump in her throat.

"This is your fault, Silvana," her mother said

as she turned suddenly toward her eldest daughter.

"We don't know he robbed the store," Silver protested, but there was little conviction in her voice.

Marlene didn't even seem to hear. "I warned you about him. I told you not to take up with a gambler. Heaven knows, it was bad enough having a spinster daughter, but you should have had enough brains not to agree to marry such a man. And then to be left at the altar in front of everyone . . ." She threw up her hands and turned away, sweeping toward the front parlor window. "I'll never be able to lift my head up in town again. We're a laughingstock because of you."

Silver listened in stoic silence. After all, what could she reply? It was true. Her mother had protested when Bob Cassidy began his whirlwind courtship. She had declared his profession a dishonorable one. But after years of hearing that no man would ever want to marry her, either because she was too tall or too outspoken, Silver hadn't been able to turn him away. She'd wanted to prove, just once, that she was desirable and attractive. That someone could love her.

Silver rose stiffly. "I'm sorry, Mother."

"Sorry!" Marlene spun around. Her dark blue eyes flashed with fury. "Sorry won't save our store and our home. That man stole everything. Do you understand? Everything."

"We don't know he did it," Silver repeated.

But she knew in her heart that he had. Wearing the expensive white gown her mother had insisted upon (the dress Silver hadn't wanted, the one which had kept Denver dressmakers working round the clock for days, the one that had cost a small fortune and increased their debt), Silver had watched the church pews fill with nearly every person who lived within a half-day's ride. And while she watched the guests arriving, Bob had emptied the mercantile safe and then taken everything of value from throughout their home. Their money. Their jewelry. Everything.

Worse yet, he had taken the last shreds of her pride.

Bob Cassidy had ridden into town four weeks before and begun his pursuit of Silver within days of his arrival. He had made her dizzy with his professions of undying devotion. He had swept her away with flowers and attention. How could she have turned down his proposal of marriage, the only proposal she'd ever received? For once, just once, she'd had the chance to prove to her mother that she wouldn't die an unwanted spinster, that someone could love her, just as she was.

But even that had been a lie.

Silver felt the threatening sting of tears but firmly blinked them away. She had no time for crying. They were a useless waste.

"I won't let you and Papa lose the store because of me." Silver raised her chin.

Her mother's only response was a mocking laugh as she turned her back upon her daughter once more.

Stiff resolve straightened Silver's spine and lifted her head high as she left the parlor, retreating quickly to her father's office at the back of the mercantile. She knew she would find him there.

Elbows braced on the desk top, Gerald's head rested in his hands. Papers were still strewn across the office floor, just as they'd found them three days before.

"Papa." Silver's fingers brushed the back of his neck. "What can I do to help?"

He raised his head to look at her, and she felt the lump forming in her throat again. He looked years older than he had just a week ago. The creases around his eyes had deepened; his round jowls sagged. His brown eyes mirrored the hopelessness in his soul.

"There's nothing any of us can do, daughter. We sold everything we could to meet the mortgage payment. I was going to take the money to Denver after the wedding. That's why it was in the safe." His hand lifted to gesture toward the store. "All that remains is on the shelves."

Silver touched the necklace hidden beneath the collar of her dress. "I still have Great-grandmother's locket. Perhaps . . ."

"It would never be enough, Silver. Thank you for offering, my dear, but you keep it. It was your great-grandmother's gift to you." He patted her hand which now rested on his shoulder. "Your mother doesn't mean to be cruel. She's just never been able to accept that I'm only a simple merchant. She's always wanted so much more than I could give her."

"Perhaps the sheriff in Denver can find . . ."

Gerald sighed as he shook his head. "Sheriff Cooper's done what he can to find Bob. Besides, even if he were found, we've no proof he took the money. No one saw anything. The store was empty. Anyone could have broken into the safe. Mattie says Bob left the boardinghouse the night before and never returned. It doesn't look like he was even in Masonville when the store was robbed."

She'd heard her father's words before, but it didn't change what she believed in her heart. Silver knew Bob had taken the money. She was the one who had brought him into the store. She was the one who'd answered all his questions. She was the one who'd shown him where the safe was and how the books were kept. She'd thought at the time it was because he wanted to help her parents in the mercantile after they were married. He'd said he would give up gambling as a profession. She'd thought he was interested in the store because he cared for her. What a fool she'd been.

Perhaps Marlene was right about her after all.

"There's got to be some way to save the store, Papa."

He patted her hand once again, but there was nothing more either of them could say.

Jess Owens rose from his desk as the attractive young woman was shown into his office. She was surprisingly tall, taller than he was, and slender as a reed. Long black hair curled about her shoulders in attractive clusters. Her eyes were a beautiful shade of gray, almost silver, surrounded by thick black lashes. She made him wish he were single, four inches taller, and twenty years younger.

"Good afternoon, Miss Matlock. Won't you please be seated?"

"Thank you, Mr. Owens." She settled onto the deep leather chair, her hands folded in the lap of her pink gingham dress. "Thank you for seeing me on such short notice. I arrived in Denver only today."

"You're traveling alone?"

"My sister and her husband live here," she replied.

"I see. Well then, what is it I can do for you?"

"Mr. Owens, your bank holds the mortgage on my parents' home and business in Masonville. Matlock Mercantile."

He waited, one eyebrow lifting in encouragement for her to proceed.

She glanced down at her hands, then looked

up at him again, her chin raised just a fraction more, almost defiantly. "Mr. Owens, my parents' store was robbed a few days ago. All the money in the safe was taken. And the note for their mortgage is due next week."

"I see." He swiveled his chair around and rose, then walked to his office door. "John," he called to his clerk, "bring me the Matlock file. Matlock Mercantile, Masonville." When he turned around, he found her anxious gray eyes watching him. "Why haven't your parents come to speak with me, Miss Matlock? Were they harmed in the robbery?"

The young woman shook her head. "They don't know I've come. My father would be very unhappy to know I've taken it upon myself to do so. He's a proud man, Mr. Owens. He doesn't like to ask anyone for a favor." She leaned forward, the fingers of one hand gripping the edge of his desk as her eyes pleaded with him. "It's my fault the store was robbed. You see, I was to be married that day and everyone was at the church. And when we came back, everything was gone. If they hadn't been at the church, it wouldn't have happened."

Married? Yet she was still *Miss* Matlock? Curiosity pricked Jess Owens, but he restrained the desire to ask more questions. "That's hardly a reason to take the blame, my dear."

The clerk entered the office and laid the requested file on the banker's desk, then unobtrusively slipped out again.

"Excuse me, Miss Matlock," the banker said as he slid his glasses up his nose and opened the file. He studied the papers and ledgers thoughtfully. The note was, indeed, due next week, and it was a good deal of money. If what the girl said were true, they would be foreclosing on the house and mercantile in short order.

"Mr. Owens." She had risen from her chair. "Please don't take their home. Papa has worked so hard. He's poured his life into that store. If you could just forgive the note . . ."

It was interesting that she asked the favor only for her parents. Never once had she called it "her" store or "her" home. Not even "ours." It was always for her parents. It struck a chord in his usually reserved banker's heart.

Jess Owens stood and removed his glasses, dropping them on the open file. "I'm sorry, Miss Matlock. I can't disregard the note. It's a large sum of money. It wouldn't be fair to the bank's depositors."

Her lovely face paled. "*How* large, Mr. Owens?"

"I'm afraid I can't divulge that information to you."

Her right hand drifted to her throat; she lifted a small gold and diamond locket toward him. "Would this cover the amount? It's a real diamond, Mr. Owens. It belonged to my great-grandmother."

At that moment, he wished he could grant her request. She made him feel like a thief just because he was doing his job. "I'm sorry," he repeated, adding in a subdued tone, "Miss Matlock, the note is for over seven hundred dollars."

He watched the color drain from her face and knew she'd never imagined the sum could be so high. To her, it might as well have been ten thousand.

The banker coughed, clearing his throat, then said briskly, "I can grant your parents an extension on the note. Say, ninety days?"

"Ninety days," she repeated in a whisper.

He stepped around his desk and touched her arm. "I'm afraid it's the best I can do." He saw her resolve strengthening, watched as she drew herself up straight, causing her to look down upon him.

"Thank you for your time, Mr. Owens, and for your help. We'll have the money here in ninety days." With that, she turned and left.

Jess Owens stepped to the window and lifted the blinds to gaze down upon the street below. He watched her leave the bank, saw her pause for a moment on the sidewalk. The breeze caught her ebony hair, raising it from her back. Her pink dress wrapped itself around her long slender legs. Her hand moved to her throat, fingering the tiny locket, then she dropped it inside the bodice of her dress, turned, and walked resolutely away from the bank.

"I'm afraid your father's right, Miss Matlock. There's no evidence that Bob Cassidy had any part in the theft." The sheriff leaned back in his chair and looked up at her. Slate-black eyes studied her. "I've known your father ever since I came to Denver and I like him. I wish there was some way I could help, but there really is nothing I can do."

Silver felt the small knot in her stomach twist but withstood his gaze with as much aplomb as she could muster. "But Sheriff Cooper, I know he—"

"Several people saw your fiancé leave town the night before." She could hear the frustration in his voice and imagined what he must be thinking of her. "I'm afraid we've no call to put out a warrant for his arrest."

"I see." How desperate she must look in his eyes. The deserted woman.

The chair squeaked as Sheriff Cooper rose from it. "I wish I could help you, Miss Matlock."

"Thank you, sir."

The walls were closing in on her. She had to get out before she made a complete fool of herself, before she began begging him to do something. She had to hang onto what little self-respect and dignity Bob Cassidy had left her.

"Give my best to your father," the sheriff called after her as she hurried outside.

She scarcely heard him.

"Silver, whatever are you doing here?" Sapphire exclaimed as she opened the door wider.

"I needed to get away for a few days. May I come in?"

"Of course." Her sister, immediately sympathetic, grabbed her arm and pulled her into the parlor of the tiny house. Sapphire hugged Silver and kissed her cheek, then drew her toward the sofa. "You should have let me know you were coming, Silver. Dan got word that his mother is ill. He left this morning for Missouri. If it's serious, I may be leaving too."

"Oh, Sapphire. I'm sorry to hear—"

Just then, the baby began to cry, and Sapphire turned toward the cradle. Silver settled onto the sofa as she watched her sister lift the fussing infant from his bed. Holding him close, she rocked from side to side while her hand supported the downy head near her shoulder.

Silver couldn't help envying her younger sister. Sapphira Matlock Downing was everything Silver was not. She was petite, barely five feet tall. It seemed she was born knowing what was right and proper for a young lady to do, what she should say, how she should behave. Her brown hair was always perfectly coiffed, her dresses always neatly pressed. At seventeen, she had met and married Dan Downing, an apprentice studying under the guidance of the renowned veterinarian Emmett Peasely. Now, just two years later, she was already the mother of two and as deliriously happy and in love as the day she'd married Dan.

"Little Dan is hungry," Sapphire said, disrupting Silver's thoughts. "I'd better go feed him."

"Please. Stay here. I don't mind."

"Well, I . . ."

"Please," Silver said again.

"I suppose, since you're my own sister . . ." Sapphire settled onto the rocker and unbuttoned the bodice of her dress. Before long, the baby was suckling noisily at her breast as she gently rocked back and forth in the chair.

"He's so beautiful," Silver said wistfully.

"Mmmm." Her sister smiled, her expression both maternal and mysterious.

For several moments, both young women simply watched the infant boy nurse. The house seemed to be filled with love and safety. Silver felt herself relaxing for the first time in days.

Sapphire was the first to break the mood. "How's Mother? She was so angry at the church when we left."

Tension crept up the back of Silver's neck. "She's still angry."

"Have you . . . have you heard from Bob?"

"No. And I won't."

Sapphire's pretty brown eyes glittered. "I'm so sorry, Silver. He—"

"I don't want to talk about him," she replied quickly. The last thing she needed right now was pity from Sapphire. Sapphire, the perfect sister. Sapphire, her mother's favorite, the example of what Silver should be but wasn't. As much as she loved her sister, she didn't want her pity. "There are worse things happening at home than . . . than a change in wedding plans."

"What is it? What's wrong? Is Papa ill?"

Silver shook her head, then told Sapphire about the robbery and the bank note. "The banker's given us an extra ninety days," she ended, "but I don't know what good it will do. There's no way to raise any money, no matter how much time we have."

"If Dan were here, maybe he could think of something. I'll give you whatever—"

"No, Sapphire. You barely have enough to get by on now, what with the two babies and Dan still an apprentice. That's no solution. I'll just have to go home and do what I can to make it easier on them. Poor Papa," she added. "Mother will never let him live this down."

She didn't want to think about the things her mother would continue to say to her.

Silver leaned against the headboard of her bed, tucked in a small room at the back of the Downing home. She wished there were a window she could open for a fresh breeze. Perhaps then she could sleep. As it was, her head was filled with a tangle of thoughts.

She'd been thinking about Bob again, wondering why he'd bothered to court her so carefully just so he could rob a store. Had he ever cared for her, even a little?

Or had *she* ever cared for *him?* She grimaced, not wanting to face the answer to that question. She hadn't loved him. She'd known that all along. And, in all honesty, she'd liked him less the longer she'd known him. Sometimes, he'd seemed to be laughing at her, mocking her and her family just a little. And other times there had seemed to be a rage, barely controlled, just beneath his smooth exterior. But her height hadn't mattered to him, and he hadn't seemed to notice when she said or did things wrong. He'd liked to steal an occasional kiss while they stood on the Matlocks' front porch. He would tell her how much he longed to make her his wife, how much he wanted to make her happy. She'd believed him. Perhaps because she'd wanted to believe him.

Her cheeks grew hot as the sting of humiliation returned along with the memory of her wedding day. They'd waited for him for two hours. She'd heard the whispers, seen the laughter in their eyes. Too tall, too gawky, too clumsy. An old maid. A spinster.

How she hated Bob for reducing her to such humiliation. He'd played her for a fool, then compounded it by stealing from her parents. She couldn't let him get away with it. She had to find him. Somehow she had to get back not only the money he'd taken but some of her pride as well.

Suddenly, she remembered her madcap race away from the church, and the way she'd nearly run into those two men outside the Mountain Rose. She'd looked up and there he was, towering over her. Then he'd stepped back, pulling the man with the bound wrists with him.

What's the matter, bounty?

She could hear the sarcasm in the prisoner's voice even now.

You trying to kill me . . . It wasn't enough that she'd been humiliated in front of the whole town. Even complete strangers had been witness to it. A bounty hunter and his prisoner. He'd been laughing at her beneath the ratty brim of his hat. She'd seen him. That man had been laughing . . .

"Of course!" she exclaimed aloud, sitting forward, her eyes wide. "Why didn't I think of it before?"

A bounty hunter. She would pay someone to find Bob, and who better than a bounty hunter, someone who spent his life tracking criminals. If the sheriff hadn't any proof that Bob was the thief, if he couldn't issue a warrant or even try to find Bob Cassidy, then she would hire someone herself.

She fingered the locket. It was all she had, but if it would find Bob, if it would get the money back, she would gladly sell it. Surely, it would be worth enough for that.

Tomorrow she would find herself a bounty hunter.

Chapter 2

Jared Newman leaned back in his chair and let his gaze move over the customers in the restaurant. His mood was black, and it didn't help to think about his lack of money.

Lute Peterson hadn't been lying. He was a coward and a whiner, but he hadn't harmed his employer's daughter. By the time he'd brought Peterson in, the girl had fessed up. Heaven only knew why she'd lied about the fellow in the first place.

But the whys didn't amount to a hill of beans. Nor did it put any money in his empty pockets.

After breakfast, Jared would have to head for the sheriff's office and check on the wanted posters. It galled him. If he could have collected on Peterson, he'd already be back on the trail, looking for Cass.

Unconsciously, Jared rubbed the old bullet wound in his shoulder. *Cass.* The name always stirred a hatred in his belly, a hatred that would only be assuaged when the man called Cass met his death. Jared had sworn his life to bringing in the killer, and he would hunt him until the day he died, if that's how long it took.

With the scrape of wood against wood, Jared pushed back his chair and got up from the table.

The morning was wasting away. He'd better get
to the sheriff's office.

The sheriff shook his head slowly. "I've told
you before we don't have any reason to bring him
in, even if we did find him. Besides, if you think
he's a thief, you should count yourself lucky he
left without marryin' you."

"I understand why *you* can't do anything,
Sheriff Cooper, but *I* still want to try."

"It's a blame fool idea."

Silver stood her ground. "Why? If the law
won't go after Bob, why shouldn't I hire someone
to do it for me?"

"Do you know what kind of men spend their
lives tracking criminals for the money it will bring?
These aren't country gentlemen, Miss Matlock.
Most of them aren't much better than the men
they seek."

Silver remembered the bounty hunter outside
the Mountain Rose. Just the thought of his eyes
unnerved her. She could believe that a man with
such eyes was capable of anything. She shivered
and pushed such thoughts aside. "I don't care,"
she said stubbornly. "Not if he can do the job.
Now will you or won't you give me the name of
someone who can help me?"

The sheriff shook his head again as he returned
to his desk. Placing his knuckles on the desk top,
he leaned toward her. "Listen, little lady, I'd like
to oblige you, but—"

Her nerves stretched to the limit, Silver's control burst. "Sheriff, I'm no *little* lady." She almost
spat the words at him. "If I have to, I'll do it
myself. I'll run an ad in the paper. I'll do whatever it takes." Her voice was shaking. "I *will* find
Bob. I will!" She hated the note of desperation
even she could hear. But she *was* desperate.

"All right, Miss Matlock," he said with a sigh. "You go on back to your sister's. I'll see what I can do for you."

Silver's voice was subdued as she replied, "Thank you."

"Sure . . . Sure . . ." He waved her away, still shaking his head.

Silver stepped out of the jail, her eyes cast down upon her clasped hands. How long would it take? she wondered. How long before she could find Bob and get back the money? There was so little time. So little time.

She turned and began walking toward Sapphire's.

"Mornin', Coop."

The sheriff looked up as Jared stepped through the open door. "Jared, what are you still doin' in Denver?"

He shrugged. "Looking for work." He straddled a nearby chair and leveled his gaze upon Rick Cooper. "Got anything for me? I'd just as soon stay in the area if I can. I've got a gut feeling Cass is still someplace close. I can't take a job that'll take me off to Texas or back east."

"Why don't you give it up, Jare? Go back to Kentucky where you belong. It's been six years, my friend."

"He's out there. I'll find him."

"You could walk by him on the street and not know it."

Jared's jaw tightened and his eyes narrowed. "I'll know him." He didn't want to talk about the years of failure. He just wanted enough money in his pocket so he could take up his search again. "Do you have anything for me or not?"

"Well, I . . ." the sheriff began, opening his desk drawer. Then he stopped speaking. Slowly,

his eyes lifted toward Jared. "I think I might have
something after all. I'm not sure what kind of
money's bein' offered. Might not be much, but
you'd be helpin' out some deservin' folks if you
took the job."

Jared frowned. He didn't much care for the way
Cooper was looking at him. But a job was a job.
"I don't need much as long as I can eat. How do
I find out about it?"

The sheriff rose from his chair, a half-smile
turning up the corners of his mouth. "Let me
check on it. I'll get in touch with you. Where you
stayin'?"

"The Golden Glove till tomorrow." Jared got
up too. "Then on my horse, I guess."

"Need a loan?" Cooper asked, his hand already slipping into his pocket.

"No thanks. Just see what you can do about
the job."

The sheriff nodded as he pulled on his hat.
"Stick around the hotel."

"I'll be there."

Back on the street, Jared watched the lawman
walk away. He liked Rick Cooper. Always had.
Their paths had first crossed back in '69 when
Jared brought in the Lansing brothers, ostensibly
for their crimes of cattle-rustling and bank robbery. He'd listened, along with Jared, as the two
men begged for mercy, swearing they'd had
nothing to do with Katrina's gruesome death,
promising they knew nothing about Sam Black's
friend. They'd known him only as Cass, they said.
They'd sworn they never knew his last name or
where he came from. They'd said they had ridden
with him just a few days before they parted company. Ridden with him just long enough to kill
Jared's mother and father and sister.

Three years before, Cooper had stood beside

Jared when the Lansing brothers were hanged. Over two years later, it had been Cooper who first told Jared of the brutal murder in Texas that had led him to Ted Harrison, the grieving widower who would pay dearly for the capture of his wife's killer. The offered bounty was the one chance Jared had of ever regaining what he'd lost so very long ago.

Jared tugged on his hat brim as he swiveled on his boot heel and started walking in the opposite direction. Cooper had got him thinking about Fair Acres again, about going home. With it came a sharp sting in the region of his heart. Until he found Cass, there would be no home to go back to. The bastard had taken it from Jared as surely as he'd killed the Newman family and stolen the past six years of Jared's life.

"Jared Newman's room, please."

The clerk looked up from the register. "I beg your pardon, miss?"

"Mr. Newman. Which room is he in?"

His eyes moved from Silver's face down to the bodice of her dress, then back up again. An unmistakable smirk was causing his mouth to twitch. "You want me to send for him?"

She wasn't so sheltered she didn't know what he was thinking. She had had enough humiliation and condescending looks this past week to last her a lifetime, and she wasn't about to take it from this clod behind the counter. Silver impaled him with an icy glare. "I need to see the gentleman in private. What is his room number?"

"Two seven," he replied after a quick glance at the book. "Top of the stairs to the left."

"Thank you."

She wasn't as confident as she looked. Sheriff Cooper had warned her that this Newman fellow

wouldn't take on a job for nothing. He was a
bounty hunter by trade, and he took the jobs that
would make his time worthwhile. She knew she
didn't have the kind of money he would ask for,
although she hadn't admitted as much to the
sheriff. But Jared Newman was the only bounty
hunter the sheriff could—or would—recommend
to her.

"Remember," Sheriff Cooper had said just before leaving Sapphire's house, "there isn't a warrant for Bob's arrest, and you can't go accusing
him of theft just because he left town the day before the wedding." He hadn't meant to be cruel,
just honest. Of all the people who were laughing
at her, Rick Cooper wasn't one of them. "There's
no law against tryin' to find him, but you can't
haul him back against his will. You understand?"

She understood, all right, but she knew Bob
was guilty. She would prove it somehow—either
before or after she brought him back to Masonville.

Room twenty-seven.

Silver paused before the door, her stomach
twisted in knots. Whatever happened in the next
few minutes, she had to convince this man to help
her find Bob Cassidy. No matter what she had to
say, no matter what she had to do. If she failed,
she failed everyone. And she was so tired of failing.

She knocked.

Before the door was entirely open, she recognized him. Couldn't it have been anyone but him?

With his boots on, he was easily five inches over
six feet. She was instantly aware of his alert
stance, like a cougar about to strike. It frightened
her, made her want to turn tail and run. He was
handsome, but she wasn't certain if it was his
looks or something much deeper—something

dangerous and uncivilized—that made him seem so.

"May I help you?" he asked. His voice was deep, with the hint of a Southern drawl. His polite question seemed at odds with everything else about him.

"Mr. Newman?"

"Yes."

"Sheriff Cooper sent me to see you."

His eyes—hazel eyes, flecked with gold and green—drifted down the length of her. She felt disrobed by the thoroughness of his perusal. The sheriff's words returned to taunt her. *Most of them aren't much better than the men they seek.* Just what was this man capable of, and what was she doing here?

His gaze met hers. It was an unrelenting look, sparing her nothing as he lifted a questioning eyebrow. "Coop sent you?"

She raised her chin in a show of courage. "It's business, Mr. Newman. May I come in?"

"Please do." He stepped back from the door and motioned her in with a sweep of his hand.

There was little more in the hotel room except for the bed and a rickety-looking chair. She wasn't sure where she should sit, and so chose to stand. She heard the door close behind her. When she turned around, she found him leaning against the wall, watching her with hooded eyes.

She hid the shiver that swept over her, but she couldn't deny the fear she felt. Just what was this man capable of? How could she think to trust him? She'd trusted Bob and where had it gotten her? But this man . . . this man . . .

Unable to bear the full impact of his penetrating gaze any longer, she dipped her head down, then studied him through a fringe of dark lashes. A dark, close-trimmed mustache rode his upper lip, and she could already see the shadow of his beard beneath his bronzed skin. One corner of his mouth turned up slightly, but it wasn't a smile. It was a sardonic, disdainful look. Not toward her, she suspected, but toward the world in general. He was tall and lanky, yet there was no mistaking the hard muscles beneath his shirt. A gun belt rode low on his slim hips, double holsters strapped to his thighs. The leather was worn and shiny. How often did he draw his guns? How many men had he killed with bullets once worn in that belt? Once again she pictured a stalking mountain lion. She felt oddly drawn toward the aura of danger surrounding him, which frightened her even more.

Trying hard to ignore her fear, she spoke quickly. "Mr. Newman, I want to hire your services."

"My services?" His lip curled even more, and she knew he was mocking her.

Her reply stuck in her throat. She couldn't bear to confess she'd been jilted, not when he already found her amusing. And she knew—even more now that she was standing here in his presence than when the sheriff had warned her—that he wouldn't take a job for nothing. This wasn't the type of man who did something out of pity or the goodness of his heart. Well, that wouldn't stop her. She just wouldn't tell him about the robbery. He needn't know everything. He only needed to find Bob.

He stepped away from the wall. "Just what services did you want from me, miss?"

Silver bristled but did her best to keep her irritation from showing. "You *are* a bounty hunter, aren't you?"

He nodded.

"I have someone I want you to find."

She had the most unusual eyes he'd ever seen. More silver than gray, fringed with thick smoky-black lashes. Round, wide, intelligent eyes that sloped upward at the corners. Ebony hair, thick and glowing with blue highlights, tumbled around her shoulders. Her nose was long and narrow, her cheekbones high, her skin like fine porcelain. Her mouth was a delicate shade of pink, the full lower lip glistening with moisture as she ran the tip of her tongue nervously across it. A thrill of anticipation swept through him.

He guessed her to be twenty, perhaps a year or two older. She was tall, only a couple inches under six feet, slender and willowy in build, and she was braced as if waiting for someone to hit her. It was obvious she didn't want to be there, was probably even afraid of him. Yet there she was. She had courage, despite her fears, and he admired her for it.

"Just who is it you want to find, Miss . . ." He let his voice trail away in question.

"Matlock. Silver Matlock."

Silver. Like her eyes. He could spend a lot of time looking into those eyes.

Jared mentally shook himself. "Why don't you have a seat, Miss Matlock, and tell me about this missing person." He picked up the chair from against the wall and set it in the middle of the room. Then, without waiting for her to follow his direction, he crossed to the bed and sat down himself.

She was still standing. "I need you to find my fiancé. He . . . he failed to show up for the wedding. I'm afraid something may have happened to him."

Was this one of Coop's bad jokes? He'd said he was looking for work, but this wasn't exactly what

he'd had in mind. Finding missing bridegrooms
with cold feet just weren't up his alley. He
scowled at the young woman.

"Mr. Newman." She sank onto the waiting
chair. Her hands were clenched tightly in her lap.

Beautiful hands. White with long, tapered fingers. His mother had always said hands could tell
a lady. And it must be true, he thought as he
looked into her lovely silver-gray eyes. Silver Matlock was every inch a lady, from her shiny black
hair to the hem of her pretty blue gown.

"Mr. Newman, please help me find my fiancé."

Jared shook his head. "I'm sorry. This just
doesn't sound like the right job for me."

"I can pay you very generously. Not now. I
won't pay until after you find him." She pulled
something from her pocket and held it out toward
him.

Instinctively, he reached forward and allowed
her to drop it into his hand. It was a delicate gold
chain with a diamond-studded locket.

"It was my great-grandmother's. It means a
great deal to me. You may keep it until you find
Bob, then you'll get your money. You may set
your price."

She wasn't joking. He knew when something
was important to someone. She treasured this
locket far beyond its material worth, and she was
willing to risk it to find this missing Bob. She must
love him a lot. Whoever he was, Bob was a lucky
man and a fool for leaving.

"I'm sorry," Jared repeated, this time standing
while he returned the locket to her cupped hand.
"It's not what I do. But I hope you find him."
He headed for the door, intent on opening it and
showing her out.

She jumped to her feet. Her fingers closed

around his upper arm. "Please, Mr. Newman. Please don't turn me down."

Jared turned, his entire body made taut by the very nearness of her. The color had drained from her beautiful face, and her silver-gray eyes were misty. He could feel the warmth of her touch through his shirt sleeve. She seemed delicate, fragile, and a long-forgotten urge to do something chivalrous and gallant intruded upon his determination to refuse her.

Her fingers tightened their grip on his arm. "You don't understand, Mr. Newman. I *must* find him. I *must* find him right away." Her voice rose with the sound of desperation.

Who was he kidding? He couldn't help her. He needed some quick money so he could start looking for Cass again. He couldn't go soft for a pair of pleading silver eyes or a pair of soft, white hands or a mouth that begged to be kissed.

Damn! He was going to make Coop pay for this. He didn't need this kind of work, and he needed an hysterical female in his room even less.

"Why do you want to find him, Miss Matlock?" he asked, making his tone deliberately cruel. "If he doesn't want to marry you, isn't it better you know that now? Let him go."

She released him and stepped back as if he'd struck her. The distraught look on her face made him feel a bit guilty, but he wasn't about to apologize. He wanted her out of there, and nothing she said or did was going to change his mind.

"I'm pregnant, Mr. Newman," she whispered. "I must find him."

She hadn't planned to say it. It had just slipped out. And what else *could* she have said? The robbery had left the Matlocks without any substantial funds, and knowing that, no bounty hunter was going to help her. He certainly hadn't been interested in her locket.

But a baby! Where on earth had such an idea come from? Good Lord, wouldn't her mother fall down in a dead faint if she knew to what depths Silver had sunk?

Suddenly aware of the silence in the room and of Jared's studious gaze, Silver sat down on the chair once more. Quaking inside, she lifted her chin in an unconsciously proud pose. She'd told him she was pregnant, and she wasn't going to change her story now. It had, at the very least, caused him to pause before he threw her out.

"I desperately need your help, Mr. Newman. I don't have anyone else to turn to. I don't . . . I don't know where Bob has gone or why he didn't come to the church that day. The sheriff says he's not in Denver, but if Bob knew I was going to have his baby, I know he wouldn't desert me."

It became surprisingly easy to let one lie follow another, and she was warming to the role. Not that she didn't feel true desperation. She did, but not for the reason she wanted him to believe.

She lowered her eyes, then dared a glimpse at him through smoky-black lashes. She had never seen such a closed, blank expression in her life. She had no idea what he was thinking, what he was feeling. Was she going to fail after all this? Had he no heart, no ears to hear her plea? What kind of black-hearted scoundrel was he?

She'd failed. She knew it. She supposed that was her punishment for telling such monstrous lies.

Pregnant and unmarried. And he'd thought her a lady!

Yet as he watched her, saw the mixture of pride

and determination on her face, he knew she was still a lady. An unconventional lady, perhaps, but still a lady. He was almost sorry he couldn't help her.

"I know this must be difficult for you, Miss Matlock, but I'm just not the man for this job."

Silver rose slowly to her feet. Her eyes stared directly into his. As the silence stretched between them, he found himself wondering what it would be like to kiss that delicate mouth. Would she taste as sweet as he imagined?

Her gaze dropped to the floor. "I see. Thank you for your time."

As she walked past him, he caught a faint whiff of lavender cologne, a delightful, clean scent that he would forever associate with ebony hair and silver-gray eyes.

She paused at the door, her hand on the knob. "Mr. Newman . . ."

"Yes?"

She turned and looked at him over her shoulder. Her voice was low, her tone accusing. "Didn't you ever have someone you cared for who was in trouble, but you weren't there? Wouldn't you have wanted someone else to answer their cry for help?"

To Jared, it seemed as if Katrina was there in the room with him, her soft brown eyes reproachful. If someone had heard her cries, if someone had tried to help, perhaps she would be alive today. Perhaps he would still be living at Fair Acres with his sister and their parents. Perhaps . . .

Was it for Katrina's memory or for the beautifully troubled Silver standing before him? Only God knew what made him do it.

"All right, Miss Matlock. I'll help you. You tell

me where to find you in the morning, and we'll talk more then.''

He imagined his sister was pleased with his decision. He certainly hoped so.

Chapter 3

Silver paced back and forth across the cluttered confines of her sister's parlor. Each time she turned toward the entry, her eyes darted to the clock in the hall.

He's not coming.

He'd said he would be there at ten and it was already five past the hour.

He's not coming.

The sharp knock on the door caused her to gasp.

He's here.

She heard the soft tapping of Sapphire's shoes upon the wooden floor as she left the kitchen and hurried toward the front door. As her sister went past the parlor doorway, she cast Silver a worried glance, then moved out of sight again. The front door squeaked on its hinges.

"Mrs. Downing? I'm Jared Newman. I'm here to see your sister."

The sound of his voice caused her pulse to race. Silver stepped backward until she was stopped by the far wall.

"Silver is expecting you, Mr. Newman. Please come in."

She heard the door close.

"I'll take your hat," Sapphire said softly. "Silver is in the parlor."

He was so tall that his dark brown hair brushed the arch dividing the parlor from the entry hall. He made her feel small, and with her height of five feet ten, few men ever did that.

"I'll be in the kitchen if you need me," Sapphire said, her gaze locked on Silver. She didn't bother to try to disguise her disapproval. She'd thoroughly expressed her dismay when Silver had told her about Jared and how she planned to find Bob Cassidy with his help. Sapphire's feminine sensibilities had been outraged, but she'd been unable to change Silver's mind. With a shake of her head, she disappeared into the back of the house.

Jared glanced over his shoulder, watching Sapphire's retreat. Silver took the opportunity to study him once again. Her first impression hadn't changed. The sheer height and strength of the man seemed to fill the parlor. She felt as if she were standing on the brink of a precipice and felt an irresistible urge to lean forward for a better look.

He turned suddenly. His words were polite but not his tone. "Morning, Miss Matlock."

She straightened her spine. "Good morning, Mr. Newman." She wasn't about to reveal her own uncertainty.

"Have you thought about your proposition any further? Reconsidered, perhaps?"

Thought about it? She'd thought of nothing else. She'd been so afraid he would change his mind. So afraid he wouldn't come. Even now he could say he wasn't going to help her.

His mouth was set in a grim line, and his eyes . . . They seemed so remote, so emotionless. What kind of man was he? Did he ever *feel* anything?

Silver forced her hands to relax at her sides. She pasted what she hoped was a pleasant smile on her lips. "Won't you sit down, Mr. Newman. I'm sure we have many details to discuss before you can begin your search." She didn't wait for him to comply before sinking onto the nearest chair herself.

Jared chose a straight-backed chair near the parlor doorway. He braced his forearms on his thighs and leaned forward, watching, waiting.

"I wrote down all the things you asked about. A description of Bob, his habits, his work . . ." She let her voice drift into silence and felt herself blushing. It was a short list. It was embarrassing to admit how little she'd known about the man she was to have married. Especially to admit it to a man who believed her pregnant by her missing fiancé.

Jared reached out to take the paper from her. His hazel eyes perused it, taking much longer than the short notes required.

Silver found herself studying him once again. Yesterday, she had been aware that he was handsome in a rugged, ominous sort of way. Did he seem even more handsome today? His thick hair was combed back from his darkly tanned face, revealing a creased forehead and heavy brows. He had a strong, rather forbidding jawline, and the bridge of his nose was slightly crooked. Broken, perhaps, in a fight with some criminal?

Her gaze was drawn to his mouth. It was narrow, wide and . . . sensuous. She wondered what it would feel like to be kissed by a man with a mustache. An odd tingling sensation stirred and tightened her stomach as she realized it was *that* mouth and *that* mustache she wanted to feel.

She dropped her gaze, hoping to still the sudden racing of her heart. She found herself staring at his square shoulders and muscular arms. He was lanky but whipcord-strong. It wasn't something she could actually see. Once again she thought of the analogy of the cougar and its prey, and once again she felt a thrill of expectation mixed with a dash of fear.

Suddenly, she was looking into his harsh hazel eyes. "This isn't much to go on, Miss Matlock. This description could fit hundreds men in Denver alone. Gamblers are a dime a dozen out here."

"But *I'll* recognize him."

"You? What good will . . ." Jared straightened suddenly in his chair. His eyebrows shot up in surprise. "Wait a minute! You don't think you're going with me?"

"Of course I am." She couldn't understand why he was so taken aback. Surely he'd understood that she had to find Bob, and the quickest and easiest way would be if she went along.

"Miss Matlock . . ."

This was only their second meeting, but already she recognized that tone of voice. He was about to cancel their agreement. He was about to refuse her. She couldn't allow it. She couldn't go back to Masonville and watch her parents lose everything because of Bob Cassidy—because of her own stupidity. At least she didn't have to fake the tears in her eyes. She wasn't very good at the art of feminine wiles and could never have summoned them merely for show, but these tears were real enough.

"Mr. Newman," she said in a low voice so there was no chance Sapphire could hear, "you can't leave me behind. If you should fail to find Bob quickly, everyone will know about the baby. I couldn't shame my parents that way. The humiliation of a jilted daughter has already broken their hearts. My mother can barely speak to me as it is."

Jared found himself captured by the gossamer glitter of tears in her silvery eyes. He knew he should find his hat and get out now. But there was something about this girl—vulnerable, proud, scared, determined. A single woman, pregnant and deserted. Why did she make him think of Katrina? She wasn't anything like his sister, and yet . . .

"All right, Miss Matlock," he said, hardly able to believe even now that he was saying it. "It's against my better judgment, but you can come along. Do you have a horse? Can you even ride?"

"It's my one true accomplishment. I assure you, I'll be able to keep up."

There was one more chance that he could extract himself from this woman's problems. "We haven't discussed my fee."

Did her porcelain complexion seem to pale even further?

Silver lifted her slightly pointed chin, her entire body stiff and erect. "I told you, sir, that I will pay you whatever you demand should you find Mr. Cassidy. But there'll be no money until he *is* found."

He wasn't sure just what to think of her. Was she just naive or did she think he wasn't smart enough to learn the truth? Whatever the reason, she was lying to him. He knew about the theft, knew the Matlocks were in serious financial trouble, even knew there was a chance he might never get paid. It had taken him only a few minutes with Coop to learn that much. So why was she trying to hide the truth from him?

Perhaps Silver Matlock wasn't all that she seemed. Perhaps there was more to her attempt at manipulation than what appeared on the surface. He would have to guard himself against the guileless look in her beautiful round eyes and the soft curve of her mouth.

She was lying to him. That alone should free him from his promise to help her. He shouldn't feel honor bound when the woman was obviously trying to deceive him. He placed the palms of his hands on his thighs, preparing to rise. He would tell her he was sorry but he couldn't help her. He would tell her he knew about the robbery.

But before he could act on his decision, he sensed Katrina's presence once again and imagined her disappointment. He tried to ignore the feeling, tried to shove her image from his mind. He'd done hundreds of things through the years that she would have disapproved of. Why should she be haunting him now?

He glared at Silver. It was her fault for stirring up all the memories he'd been trying to forget. He was angered by his inability to tell her he'd changed his mind. Between her beautiful, pleading eyes and Katrina's insistent ghostly presence, he felt as if the choice had been removed from him. His anger deepened.

"We'll need some supplies for the trail," he snapped, then waited for her to explain just how she was going to pay for them.

"We can get whatever we need from my parents' store in Masonville. If we leave right away, we can stay there tonight and get an early start in the morning."

Jared rose from his chair. "Let's get something straight right now, Miss Matlock. I'm the one who'll decide when we leave and where we stay. If you can't live with that, you'd better stay here with your sister."

The plea for help vanished from her eyes. "I

assure you, sir, I know how to follow directions. You do your job, and I'll keep out of your way."

The look on her face was enough to warn him that she was neither docile nor passive. Promising to always obey without question was as much a lie as hiding the truth about the mercantile robbery.

I must be crazy, he thought as he stared down at her, but still he asked the question. "How soon will you be ready to leave?"

She was on her feet instantly. "It will take me only a moment to change and gather together the things I brought with me." Her look was pensive. "Where do you propose we begin our search?"

"Coop says he's not in Denver. Since your Mr. Cassidy's a gambler, I'll start with Black Hawk and Central City first. If I don't pick up any clues there . . ." He shrugged. As far as he was concerned, if he found no trace of Silver's missing fiancé there, the search would end. She would have to deal with her problems in some other way. *Besides*, he thought, trying to justify his decision to stop before he'd finished the job, *if this guy's a thief, wouldn't she rather face the scorn of having an illegitimate baby than be married to him for life?*

But he didn't tell her that Central City was as far as he intended to go. One day on the trail would probably be enough for her to admit defeat, and then he could wash his hands of this whole fiasco.

"I'll get my things. Excuse me."

Alone in the parlor, Jared strolled around the room, touching the small knickknacks, looking at the photographs on the mantel. It was a cozy room, warm and domestic. A home for people who loved one another. Jared felt out of place. Too many years . . . Too many memories . . .

He felt a slight tug on his pant leg and looked down. A towheaded toddler was staring up at him, his dark eyes wide and questioning, a smear of chocolate on his chin.

"Hello." He knelt down. "What's your name?"

The boy held out a cookie toward Jared.

"No thanks, buddy. You'd better keep it for yourself."

A rustle of skirts drew his attention just as Sapphire Downing, a baby in her arms, appeared in the parlor doorway. "Robert Gerald, what are you doing? You come over here right now."

The little boy scurried toward his mother and hid himself in the folds of her skirt, glancing back over his shoulder at Jared.

"I'm sorry, Mr. Newman. He slipped away while I was feeding the baby."

Jared stood, saying in a low voice, "He wasn't bothering me." Of course, he knew she didn't care if he'd been bothered by the boy or not. Concerned mothers didn't want their youngsters hanging around men like him. Men little better than the criminals they sought. Gunmen, bounty hunters, horse thieves were much the same in the eyes of respectable people. He should be used to it by now, but he wasn't.

"Where is Silver?" she asked, breaking into his thoughts.

"Changing. We're leaving for Masonville."

Sapphire moved toward him. Her brown eyes, not as striking as Silver's unusual gray ones but pretty nonetheless, stared up at him, her brows drawn together in a frown as she worried her lower lip. He returned her gaze, his practiced expression bland.

It was difficult to believe these two were sisters. Silver was tall and willowy while Sapphire was petite with a mother's generous curves. Silver had porcelain skin that blushed a bright pink in the apples of her cheeks when she was embarrassed. Sapphire's complexion was golden. Silver's hair, thick and wavy, was so black it gleamed with bluish highlights. Her sister's hair was a soft brown, baby-fine and straight.

And it wasn't just looks that made the two different. There was something almost poignant, something painfully lonely about Silver, while Sapphire wore the serene, confident air of someone who was loved and cherished. If anyone made him think of Katrina, it should have been the younger of the two Matlock sisters.

Jared made a mental note of all this in mere seconds.

"Mr. Newman . . ." Sapphire stopped, her look uncertain.

"Yes?"

"You . . . you will make certain Silver doesn't get hurt anymore, won't you?"

Something tightened in his chest. "I'll do my best, Mrs. Downing."

She reached out and touched his arm, then released it quickly. "I don't approve of what my sister is doing. I'm sure you can understand why."

Footsteps sounded on the stairs, and a moment later, Silver appeared. She was holding a small satchel and was wearing a gray riding habit, her hair tucked up beneath a matching gray bonnet. Her gaze darted between Jared and Sapphire, standing so close together.

"Mr. Newman tells me you're leaving with him," Sapphire said as she stepped away from him.

Silver nodded. "I'll need to borrow your riding horse. I'll have Papa return him to you right away."

"Keep him as long as you need." As Sapphire spoke, she moved toward her sister. "Are you certain you should do this?" she asked softly.

Silver hugged her. "I'm sure." She turned toward Jared. "I'm ready, Mr. Newman."

Silver's stomach was in an uproar and grew worse as they drew closer to Masonville. What was her mother going to say about Silver's scheme to find Bob? Marlene had barely spoken to her daughter when she left on the stagecoach for Denver. Would she have softened a bit toward her by now?

No. Marlene never approved of anything Silver did. This time would be no different.

She glanced at the man riding to the side and slightly ahead of her. His hat hid his face in shadows, but she could imagine the hard glint in his eyes, the stern set of his jaw. She was trusting so much to this stranger. Was she insane to do so? What did she know about him after all?

No better than the criminals they seek. A cold chill shivered up her spine. She had confessed to this stranger that she was pregnant out of wedlock. In his eyes, she must seem no better than a common saloon girl—or something worse. A niggling fear gripped her. What if he thought to use her in the same manner? She would be alone with him on the trail. If he thought her the sort to . . .

She looked away from him, trying to forget the hard edges of the man, but she couldn't escape the nagging questions. What would he do if he found out she was lying to him about the baby? He wasn't the sort of man to take it well, she decided quickly.

Her stomach tightened another notch. What if he should learn she had no means to pay him unless Bob was found with money? Would he continue the search when payment was in question? Of course not. No bounty hunter would take such a job under a cloud of doubt. Not one.

She stiffened her back. Then he couldn't find out. Not about the money. Not about the baby. She would have to make sure he never found out the truth.

She nudged the gelding's ribs and drew up beside Jared. "Mr. Newman?"

She thought his glance might have flicked her way, yet she couldn't be certain. Even this close, she couldn't make out his face beneath his hat brim. He seemed scarcely to move as his pinto cantered along the dusty road.

"I think I should warn you that my parents don't expect you. I . . . I mean, I didn't tell them what I was going to do."

This time his head did turn.

"And they . . . they don't know about . . . about the baby, so I would appreciate your silence about it."

He looked away without a word.

"Mr. Newman, stop!" Silver jerked back on the reins. Her gelding braced his legs and slid to a halt.

Jared spun his horse around, then jogged back to where she was waiting.

She gathered up her courage, silently damning the shadows that concealed his face, wishing she knew what he was thinking. "I need your promise that you won't say anything to them."

"I'm not in the habit of talking overly much."

She was counting on just that. "One more thing." She drew her diamond locket from the pocket of her riding habit and held it out to him. "This is yours to keep until I pay you for finding Bob."

"And if I don't find him?"

"Then it's yours for your trouble."

He gave his head a quick shake. "You keep it."

Silver leaned forward and grabbed his hand, turning it over so she could drop the necklace into his callused palm. "This seals our bargain, Mr. Newman. You *must* take it."

With the tip of his forefinger, he pushed his hat back on his head. Sunlight played across the strong angles and planes of his face. His eyes were staring at her in their normal enigmatic manner. "You're a stubborn young woman, Miss Matlock." He pocketed the locket in his shirt. "I hope you don't come to regret your decision."

Once again, fear shot up her spine. Her mouth tasted like cotton. Her throat felt dry. Something told her he might be right. She might very well regret her decision before this journey was done, but it was too late to turn back now. Come hell or high water, she was going to find Bob Cassidy, and this bounty hunter was going to help her do it.

She opened her mouth to tell him so, but he wasn't waiting for a reply. He turned his pinto up the road again and cantered away from her, never looking back to see if she followed.

Chapter 4

Jared dismounted and tethered his gelding to the rail in front of Matlock Mercantile. It had the same false-front facade as the other buildings on the main street, but it was freshly whitewashed, the store's name painted in wide black letters above the awning.

He studied the surroundings for a moment, then turned around, facing the store entrance where Silver stood waiting. She was nervous, but she was trying hard not to show it. She had smoothed her windswept hair back from her face and tied it once again with a ribbon. There was a fine layer of trail dust across her nose which he found surprisingly appealing. Her small pink tongue ran nervously along her lower lip. He thought of strawberries. Kissing her would be a sweet delight.

His jaw tightened as he pushed away that thought. Silver Matlock was definitely hands-off.

He stepped up onto the boardwalk, accompanied by the jingle of his spurs. As she turned around, her hand reaching for the door, he caught a light whiff of lavender. Burying his face in her hair would be like lying in a field of wildflowers.

Damn! He stepped into the mercantile with an angry scowl furrowing his brows.

Every spare inch of space was designed to hold merchandise. Display tables held bolts of fabric, cooking utensils, lamps, and other sundry items. Glass cases revealed sharp knives and a few pieces of jewelry. Dry goods and foodstuffs seemed to fill the shelves which lined the walls from floor to ceiling. The store had an air of prosperity. Could Coop have been wrong about the Matlocks' financial condition? But a closer look revealed the careful placement of items to make it appear the shelves were full when, in truth, the supplies were sadly depleted. Maybe Coop hadn't been wrong after all.

The woman behind the counter was short and slightly plump. Her honey-brown hair, sprinkled with gray, was caught in a no-nonsense bun at the nape. She wore a crisp white apron over a blue gingham dress. When she saw them, she folded her hands in front of the apron, her eyes narrowing, her lips pursing slightly.

"So, you've returned," she said.

Silver, standing in front of him, seemed to sway backward, as if the woman's words had been a physical blow. Then she stiffened. Her narrow shoulders were squared, her head held high. "I need to talk to you and Papa."

Her mother's eyes moved behind Silver to Jared. "May I help you, sir?"

"Mr. Newman is with me, Mother." Silver turned around. "My father's office is back this way," she said softly before winding her way through the maze of tables toward the back of the store.

Jared didn't move immediately. He met Marlene's disapproving glare with one of his own. The woman had unknowingly made it all the more difficult for him to extricate himself from Silver's problems.

He'd considered more than once during the ride from Denver how he would put an end to all this. The reason he'd gone to Coop in the first place was to earn enough money to hold him over while he continued his own private search. If payment for this job was in jeopardy, it was pointless for him to waste his time on it. Yet, just when he had decided not to follow through, Silver had given him the locket to "seal the bargain," as she had put it. He should have given the blasted piece of jewelry back to her and got out when he had the chance.

He still might have done so if it weren't for the disdainful look in her mother's eyes, not just toward him but toward her own daughter.

"Nice meeting you, ma'am." With a cocky tip of his hat, Jared hurried after Silver, catching up with her just as she arrived at the back of the store.

Gerald Matlock was a balding man, perhaps in his mid-fifties. He was seated behind a large desk. His faded brown eyes glanced up wearily as his office door opened.

"Silver!" His face broke into a smile. The weariness disappeared.

Jared was quick to notice the affection in the name, an affection which had been noticeably lacking in his wife's voice.

"Hello, Papa." She stepped quickly around the desk and dropped a kiss on his forehead. Then, turning, she looked toward Jared. "This is Mr. Newman. He's come to help me find Bob."

Her father frowned. "Help you . . ."

Silver's words came quickly after that. "Mr. Newman is a bounty hunter. Sheriff Cooper recommended him. We've come to get supplies, and then we're going to Central City. I've used Great-grandmother Johnson's locket for payment."

Gerald stood and held out his hand toward Jared, his expression still one of confusion and concern. "Please sit down, Mr. Newman. I think we need to discuss this matter further."

Jared took hold of the man's proffered hand. Gerald's grip was firm despite the tired slope of his shoulders. When their hands broke free, Jared removed his hat and settled onto a chair near the desk.

By this time, Marlene had joined them.

Jared's gaze moved to each party in the room, noting small clues to what they were thinking and feeling. They weren't a difficult family to read.

Gerald loved his daughter. Loved her more than his store and business. And Jared would wager he was an honest and fair-minded man. But he was also a beaten man. It showed on his face and in his posture.

Marlene Matlock . . . She was the sort of woman who loved only herself. She probably went through life with her nose constantly turned up in the air, as if to avoid smelling the little people around her. She wouldn't be the sort to approve of Jared or his profession.

His gaze settled on Silver. Tall and striking in her lovely riding habit, she was looking at her mother with the strangest expression in her silvery eyes. As if there was a little child hidden inside and she was pleading for something she knew would be denied her. It was that same sort of look that had gotten him involved in this mess in the first place.

I must be growing soft in the head.

But then she turned and looked at him, and he realized there was something much deeper about Silver. She might be vulnerable, but she had an inner strength which ultimately overcame it. She was caught in an untenable situation, yet she faced it bravely. He'd learned long ago that courage meant nothing unless one was first afraid of something. Grudgingly, he acknowledged his own admiration for Silver's fortitude.

Silver faced her mother once again. "I was just telling Papa that I've hired Mr. Newman to help me find Bob. We need some supplies to take with us, and then we're going to Central City. Bob isn't anywhere in Denver. Sheriff Cooper has looked. There's no point in arguing with me. I've made up my mind to do this. I've used Great-grandmother's locket to secure Mr. Newman's services. Once we've found Bob, then we'll pay him his usual fee."

"Good Lord!" her mother exclaimed. "Have you no sense at all? Isn't it bad enough that you try to make a gambler a part of the family? Now you're hiring a common gunman to track him down?"

"Marlene, please . . ." Gerald's voice was low. He turned his eyes upon Jared. "Mr. Newman, I think we need to discuss this matter as a family. Will you excuse us, please?"

"Of course." Jared rose and placed his hat back on his head. "I'll wait outside."

Before he was out of the office, he heard Silver saying, "I'm going to do this, and you can't stop me. I'm twenty-one and can decide for myself."

"You would give my grandmother's locket to that . . . that . . ."

Jared let the store door bang behind him.

Marlene was shaking all over. Her face was bright red, and she looked about ready to explode. "Do you know what people will say about you if you go with that man? For heaven's sake, Silvana, you would be traveling all alone, unchaperoned with him. All sorts of things could happen to you. Your reputation will be ruined."

"My reputation is already ruined."

Marlene looked toward the ceiling. "What terrible wrong did I ever do to deserve such a daughter? Why couldn't I have had two like Saphira? *She* at least knows how to behave. She had no trouble attracting a suitable husband."

"That's enough, Marlene," Gerald said.

"No, it's not enough." She turned angry eyes on Silver. "Just what sort of man do you think this Mr. Newman is? He hunts down criminals with his gun. He kills people for a living. Good Lord, even a gambler was better than this. Next thing I know, you'll be deciding to marry this . . . this . . ." She threw her hands into the air.

Silver took the hurled insults with silent resignation. When her mother seemed unable to say any more, she turned toward her father. "I have to do this, Papa. If I can find Bob and get back the money, we'll save the store and our home. I saw Mr. Owens at the bank. He's agreed to a ninety-day extension."

"He *what*?" Marlene exclaimed.

"Ninety days. I have that much time. I won't fail you." She touched his cheek. "I *must* do it, Papa."

Gerald took hold of Silver's hands and squeezed tightly. "All right, Silver. I doubt you'll find him, but I do understand your need to try."

"Good heavens!" Marlene spat. "You're as foolish as she is. No wonder we're about to lose everything we own. And now you mean to let that gunman take whatever he wants from our remaining stock without paying for it. Are we to starve as well?" With that, Marlene stormed out of the office.

Silver sank to the floor in a puddle of skirt. She

laid her head on her father's knee. She felt like crying but her eyes were dry. "Why does she dislike me so?" she whispered.

"She doesn't dislike you, my dear." He stroked her hair as he'd done when she was a child. "Your mother is a very unhappy woman inside, and she takes it out on those closest to her."

Silver wished she could believe him, but all her memories of her mother were ones of disapproval. Always she had failed to be the kind of daughter Marlene wanted.

Tall and skinny as a rail, Silver had been teased mercilessly by the children in school. Her father had told her the boys were jealous of her height and the girls were jealous of how pretty she was. The reasons hadn't mattered to Silver. She only knew she was different. So she'd spent her time reading books beneath the leafy shade of the mountain aspens or taking long rides on the pony her father had given her. On the route from childhood to womanhood, she had discovered that these two pursuits could set her free, take her to other places where she didn't have to deal with the disapproval of others or her own shortcomings.

Unfortunately, all the hours she'd spent reading had also filled her head with a lot of "ridiculous notions," according to her mother—notions Silver always managed to verbalize at the wrong moment. Her outspokenness had driven away more than one young man from the Matlock parlor. But how could she spend hours talking of dresses and bonnets and rose gardens when there were so many interesting things happening in the world, such as women voting in Wyoming Territory or the rapid changes occurring between east and west now that they were joined by the railroads?

In her mind, she ticked off all her faults. She was a lousy seamstress and a worse cook. She was too tall and thin. She spoke her mind at the worst possible moments. She was often a dreamer. She was too independent, and she lost her temper far too easily. She had no sense of style whatsoever, one dress being the same as another as far as she was concerned. And now, she was a woman who had been rejected in front of an entire town.

No wonder her mother disliked her so.

She lifted her head and looked up at her father. He loved her. He had always loved her, despite all her faults—despite her skinned knees and the grass in her hair and the torn skirts when she took a spill from her horse or a tumble out of a tree. He'd never minded that she wasn't feminine and coy and adorable like Sapphire. To him, she was beautiful.

She had to save the store for him. She had to.

The blonde's name was Doris. She was wearing the same purple dress she'd had on the first time Jared was in the Mountain Rose Saloon. He also recognized the cheap cologne that rose in invisible clouds, making his eyes water. A big difference from Silver's light lavender fragrance, he thought.

"Sure, I knew Bob Cassidy," Doris said as she accepted the drink. "He did plenty of card-playin' in here 'fore that hoity-toity Mrs. Matlock tried to reform him for her daughter. But I knew he wasn't ever gonna marry Silver. He was quite the debonair fella from what I seen of him." She winked as she leaned closer, offering a view of her generous breasts. "And I seen plenty of him. I mean," she whispered, "he was the sorta man who wants a *real* woman. You understand?"

"How long did he live in Masonville?"

"I don't know. One day's pretty much the same as another around this town. You tend to lose track of time."

Jared persisted. "A year? Two years?"

"Nowheres near that long, honey. Say, what's your interest in him anyway?"

"Just curious." He shrugged. "I'm a friend of Miss Matlock's."

"*You* are?" She hooted. Her gaze ran the length of him and back. "Honey, you need a real woman even more than Bob. A man like you can't be wastin' your time on some gal who spends her time with her nose pressed in a book. Silver Matlock wouldn't have the least idea what to do with you. Why do you think her fiancé took off the way he did?" She smiled suggestively. "But I'd know what to do."

Jared couldn't help thinking that Silver knew more than Doris gave her credit for, or she wouldn't be in the condition she was in. The thought made Jared irritable, so he cast it aside.

He would have liked to ask more questions about Bob and Silver and the Matlock family, but he felt certain he wasn't going to learn anything helpful, especially now that Doris was fingering his shirt collar and trying to tug him closer. Her eyelids were heavy, her gaze smoldering with unrestrained desire. She was the kind of woman who loved danger, and Jared was the kind of man who seemed to radiate it.

For just a moment, he considered her offer. All morning, he'd been all too aware of the luxurious waves of Silver's ebony hair, the pale pink of her mouth, her faint cologne, and the intoxicating glimmer of her silver-gray eyes. Perhaps a roll in Doris's bed would drive Silver from his head, and he could start thinking clearly again.

But after one more long look at Doris, he knew that was no solution. It wasn't this garish saloon girl that stirred his senses, making him want to protect her with one hand and ravish her with the other.

"I'll tell you what, Doris." He rose from the table, leaning forward and placing a finger under her chin. "You buy yourself a drink on me. I've got some business to take care of." He dropped some coins on the table.

"When you get ready, I'll be here, lawman."

There was a bad taste in his mouth as he stepped onto the boardwalk. Unbidden, he thought of his mother, of Katrina, of the genteel girls and women who had come calling at Fair Acres throughout his youth. If one of them came walking down the street right now, they would make a wide arc around him. He wasn't the sort of man a lady would associate herself with. He was a hired gun and had long since forgotten how to behave as a gentleman.

A strong longing assailed him. A longing for Fair Acres and all it had been to him. A longing for cool summer nights on the veranda, watching as the Thoroughbred horses galloped through the long, green grass in the fenced pastures. A longing for his mother's quiet wisdom and his sister's soft laughter. He could see them now as they'd been . . .

And then that picture was spoiled, replaced by the image of Katrina lying on her bed, her pretty brown hair cropped at the scalp, her eyes sunken in a bruised face.

An icy rage welled within him. What was he doing here in Masonville when Katrina's killer still roamed free? What did he care about a fiancé with cold feet and sticky fingers? He knew darned good and well that even if he found Bob there would likely not be any payment for his time and trouble, not if what folks said was true. He should be out looking for Cass instead of wasting his efforts here. So why didn't he get out now?

Because he kept feeling Katrina's presence, as if she were pushing him forward, as if she wanted him to help Silver Matlock even more than she wanted him to find Cass. And because whenever he looked into a pair of silvery-gray eyes, something in him seemed to give.

With an angry tug of his hat brim, pulling it low on his forehead, he spun on his heel and strode purposefully toward the mercantile. It was time he found out if he was to stay or to go. And he wasn't even sure which way he wanted it himself.

From the window of Matlock Mercantile, Silver watched Jared exit the Mountain Rose. Even from down the street, she could see the angry set of his shoulders. The man seemed always to be angry—when he felt anything at all, that is.

He faced the store and began walking swiftly toward it. She jumped back from the window, suddenly frightened by the aura of rage that encircled him and afraid he would see her watching him. Then she leaned cautiously forward once more, peeking through the glass at the handsome bounty hunter who was to be her companion in the days to come.

Was her mother right? Was the sheriff right? Was this man little better than those he hunted down like animals? Did he find pleasure in shooting another man for money? Somehow, she didn't think so. There was something about Jared Newman . . .

She moved toward the door and pushed it open

just as he stepped up onto the boardwalk. He stopped abruptly.

"Mr. Newman, if you'd like to tell my father what it is you think we'll need, he'll have it ready for us in the morning."

One eyebrow seemed to raise infinitesimally. "Your parents agreed for you to do this?"

"I managed to convince them."

"You didn't tell them you're . . ."

She felt the heat rising in her cheeks. "Please, Mr. Newman," she whispered. "Don't say it around here. People seem to hear things so easily."

He removed his hat, then raked his fingers through his shaggy dark hair. "You'd be better off staying behind. I'll be moving hard and fast, and you're not likely to find much comfort on the trail."

She gave her head a stubborn shake. "I'm going with you. I can take it if you can."

"You don't have the faintest notion what you're getting yourself into, Miss Matlock."

"I'm not a fool. What I don't know, I can learn."

He made a sound that was not quite a laugh. It grated on her nerves, and she had a strong urge to hit him. She thrust her chin up high.

"You're not going to change my mind, Mr. Newman. We have a bargain, you and I. I mean to stand by my part. Do you? Or are you entirely without honor?"

His face darkened as the scowl returned. His hazel eyes glinted with subdued anger. "All right, Miss Matlock. We'd better tell your father what we'll be needing."

Jared Newman hadn't understated when he'd said he didn't talk overly much. He hadn't spoken a single word since they'd left Masonville at the crack of dawn.

Silver had, at least, noted his look of approval when he first saw her that morning. Instead of her stylish riding habit, she was wearing a simple blouse and a soft leather skirt which was split for riding astride. Her mother, of course, was always horrified when she appeared in the outfit, but Silver had no intention of riding sidesaddle for what could end up to be days, maybe even weeks. But it hadn't mattered this morning how Marlene felt about her split riding skirt, for her mother had never left her bedroom. Only Gerald had been there to see them off.

Silver drew her thoughts back to the present. She had pulled her buckskin mare, Cinder, in behind the bounty hunter's pinto and the packhorse Jared led, and now her gaze fell upon the man's broad back. He rode his horse with the fluid ease of a man who spent much time in the saddle, his body flowing with the horse's movements rather than against them. His right hand rested casually on his thigh. She saw his head turn slightly to the left, then to the right, and she knew he was memorizing the terrain, watching for danger at every turn.

Danger must be a constant part of his life.

Who was Jared Newman? she wondered.

She had perceived a slight Southern accent in his voice. Nothing overpowering, just a hint. A soft, gentlemanly drawl. And there was something about the way he carried himself that bespoke of privilege and education. Not exactly what one would expect from a man in his profession.

Was there a Mrs. Newman somewhere? The question was strangely unsettling to her.

Jared slowed his gelding, allowing Silver to

draw up alongside. His head turned, and she could feel the power of his gaze upon her. It was a riveting look; she was helpless to turn away from it. There was no hint of a gentleman in those hazel eyes. They were harsh, probing, searching.

"You know Central City is just a shot in the dark," he said, his voice low. "He could be anywhere by now."

"I know. But I have to try. I'm willing to trust your instincts. You're the expert."

His eyes narrowed as he continued to stare at her. "And I hope you won't forget that fact the first time I tell you to do something, Miss Matlock. I let you come with me against my better judgment. The last thing I need is a woman tagging along, fouling things up, let alone a preg . . . one in your condition. I don't aim to take it easy just to suit you. You've hired me to do a job, and I mean to do it. But you'll do as I say, no matter what it is, or I leave you behind at the first town that's got a stage coming through. Do we understand each other?"

Silver glared back at him, suddenly angry. "Oh, I understand you perfectly, *Mr.* Newman. I told you before that I would follow instructions, and my memory is very good. I haven't forgotten a thing we've said to each other."

He was just like most men, she fumed. He expected a woman to be at his beck and call and to hop the moment he spoke. He thought she had no more brains in her head than a Christmas tree ornament.

Her ire quickly cooled. Could she blame him for thinking she was an empty-headed fool? Here she was chasing after a man who, as far as Jared knew, had done nothing more than change his mind about marrying a woman whom he didn't know was pregnant with his child. How had she ever gotten herself into this tangle of lies? Perhaps she should tell him . . .

But just then Jared's pinto shot forward, and Silver's thoughts of confession were quickly forgotten as she spurred Cinder into a canter.

Chapter 5

Black Hawk—and Central City above it—was a town built in a narrow draw between mountains rich with ore. While the gold rush days were past, the mines would still produce wealth for years to come, for those willing to work hard enough to find it.

It was early afternoon that same day when Jared and Silver rode into town. Raucous music and laughter spilled from a nearby saloon, and it was there that Jared reined in his mount and stepped out of the saddle.

"I'm going to get something to wet my whistle, then ask around." He glanced up at her. "You thirsty?"

Her response was automatic. "I couldn't go in *there.*"

"You're right. Your mama wouldn't approve."

"This doesn't have anything to do with my mother. I don't *want* to go in."

Jared shrugged. "Suit yourself." Accompanied by the familiar jingle of his spurs, he disappeared into the dim recesses of the tiny saloon.

Silver sat where she was, her ire rising as she considered his response. He was just trying to make her give up, to cry uncle. Well, she wasn't going to do it. What more damage could be done to her reputation, after all? Besides, they weren't in Masonville. Who would even know her here?

She hopped from Cinder's back and looped the reins around the hitching rail, then stepped toward the swinging doors of the Crow's Nest Saloon. With a flick of her hand, she tossed her thick black braid behind her shoulder and pushed open the doors.

Dense smoke formed a cloud above the tables where men sat playing cards. Scantily garbed women were scattered around the small room, some lounging against the bar, others draped over men in various degrees of intoxication. The tinkle and bang of an off-key piano sounded from a far corner.

Silver had never been inside a saloon before. Chaotic seemed the only word to describe the scene. It was noisy and smelly. She felt terribly exposed as several sets of male eyes turned upon her. She was rethinking the wisdom of her decision to enter when a tall, unshaven man rose from his chair and stepped toward her. He reeked of whiskey and was sorely in need of a bath.

"Hello, pretty lady." His arm went around her shoulders.

"Excuse me. I . . . I think I'd better wait outside."

His arm tightened. "Now, don't get your feathers ruffled. You must've come in for a reason. You just come on over here with . . ."

"Unhand the lady."

Silver's head jerked up, and her gaze collided with Jared's. The expression on his face was one of disinterest, but his words sent a chill down her spine.

"Ain't no call . . ." the man began.

Jared's eyes abandoned her for the man at her side. "I said unhand her."

The arm dropped quickly from her shoulders. "I didn't mean no harm," her assailant mumbled as he backed away.

Jared's fingers clasped around her upper arm, and she was whisked out the door. He didn't stop moving until they were sandwiched in between the buckskin and the pinto. He spun her toward him, forcing her to meet his chilling gaze.

"What in blue blazes did you think you were doing?" he demanded.

She pulled her arm from his grasp, rubbing the spot where he'd held her. "I decided I *did* want something to drink," she answered in a small voice. She didn't like the angry look on his face.

He glared at her in silence.

She lifted her chin. "Well, *you* were the one who *asked* me in."

"I asked if you were thirsty. I would have brought you something to drink if you'd asked for it."

"That isn't the way you made it sound," she shot back, her temper flaring.

Jared stepped closer, forcing her to lean backward to look up at him. She felt dizzy, and for the moment her anger was forgotten. She was so close to him she could see the dark brown circles that rimmed his hazel eyes. She could almost count the golden flecks that made them seem to flash with a light of their own. She noticed for the first time the spattering of dark red hairs in his mustache. She wondered if his beard would look red if he allowed it to grow.

"I don't care how it sounded." He enunciated the words with extreme care, his bland expression in contrast to the harshness of his voice. "My job is to protect you. Yours is to obey. You don't move unless I tell you to. You don't even *breathe* unless I tell you to. Do you understand me, Miss Matlock?''

Damn that blasted stone face of his! Silver thrust her head forward until they were nearly touching noses. ''If you think I'm going to quake and shrink over every little thing, you're sorely mistaken.'' The coldhearted miscreant!

Jared stepped back from her. If she'd expected to force him to reveal what he was thinking or feeling, she was disappointed. His expression remained as composed and blank as ever. Maybe he doesn't have a heart to feel with, she thought as she met his cool gaze.

''We've been over this before. You'll do as I tell you or I go on without you. It's up to you.''

Her retort lodged in her throat. She couldn't go back. Not without her parents' money. She had no choice but to obey. Reluctantly, she nodded.

''Come on. Let's put you someplace safe so I can do my job.'' Jared didn't wait for her. He swung into the saddle and led the way up the hill toward Central City, never looking back to see if she obeyed him or not.

Things would have been much easier if Silver Matlock had a photograph of her fiancé.

Jared leaned against the bar and let his eyes move slowly around the large gaming room of the Crystal Palace once again. This room held few similarities with the Crow's Nest in Black Hawk or the half-dozen other saloons he'd visited that afternoon. The owners of the Crystal Palace had made great attempts to make it appear to be something different than what it was.

Most of the men seated around the green felt tables were dressed in suits. Smoke from their cigarettes and cigars dissipated quickly as it rose toward the high ceilings. Chandeliers overhead and lamps on the walls bathed the room in light.

Even the women looked different, clad in colorful gowns which he supposed were copies of the latest fashions, their hair clean and shiny. They smelled lovely, too. No cheap cologne in the Crystal Palace. Of course, their looks didn't fool Jared. He knew they did more than just dress the room and encourage the men to gamble. He'd known too many of them not to recognize the cynicism hidden deep in their eyes. He only hoped they were more observant than those he'd talked to in other establishments.

"Excuse me, sir. There's an opening at one of the tables if you're interested."

He turned his head toward the silken voice. Her head came no higher than his shoulder. Her fire-red hair was caught in a mass of curls atop her head. Her off-the-shoulder gown revealed only a discreet glimpse of cleavage. Green eyes looked up at him while a friendly smile played across her pink mouth.

"If you would rather, we could sit at a table and talk," she offered.

"I'd like that."

She turned, the hem of her gown sweeping the shiny black-and-white tiled floor, and led the way to a table in a more private area of the room. She waited beside a chair until Jared pulled it out for her.

"You're not from around here," she said as he sat down across from her. Her eyes swept over him.

He didn't have a fancy suit in his bedroll, but he'd paid his dollar and a half for a warm bath and shave, and he'd changed into clean denims and a white shirt. He wouldn't pass muster for a wealthy, high-stakes gambler, but they wouldn't throw him out for being a worthless trail bum either.

He shook his head.

"My name is Claudette. And yours?"

"Jared."

"A pleasure to make your acquaintance, Jared." She paused, as if waiting for him to supply a last name. When he didn't, she continued, "What brings you to Central City?"

Jared studied her a moment, then made his decision. "I'm looking for someone. An . . . acquaintance of mine. There's a member of his family who needs him, and I promised to try to find him. I just missed him a while back in Denver and heard he was coming up this way. Name's Bob. Bob Cassidy. Bob's rather fond of a good card game. I thought sure I'd find him in a place like this."

Claudette shook her head. "We get strangers through here all the time. Most of them don't give their names."

"Well, let's see. I don't know if I'm much good at describing folks, but I'll try." Actually, he was very good at it. He could only hope Silver's description was as accurate as his would have been had he ever seen Bob. "He's about six feet tall. Blond hair . . ."

His words were interrupted by the appearance of a pretty brunette. "Claudette, come quickly. It's Felicity. She's awake."

Claudette was instantly on her feet. Her face was pale, her green eyes wide and haunted. "You must excuse me." With that, she was running toward the curving staircase leading to the second floor.

Jared saw the bartender step toward the edge of the bar and watch the two women disappear up the stairs. His hand clenched the cloth in his hand, and his jaw was set in frustrated anger. Jared's instincts pushed him out of his chair and toward the man.

"What's wrong with Felicity?" he asked in a familiar tone.

The bartender didn't even look at him. "You haven't heard?"

"No, I've been out of town for a while."

"Some murderin' son of a bitch tried to kill her. Don't know if she'll pull through."

It was a gamble, but he took it. "Why would anyone want to kill a sweet thing like Felicity?"

Now the bartender looked at him, but his gaze was still blinded by rage. "The world's full of sick people." He started scrubbing the bar with a vengeance. "If I ever find out who did this to her . . . She don't hardly have a face left, he beat her so bad. Cut off all that pretty hair o' hers and left her for dead . . ."

The man was still talking, but Jared couldn't hear him anymore. His eyes had returned to the top of the stairs. His blood was hammering in his ears. "What room is she in?"

The man fell silent as Jared's gaze turned back upon him.

"What room is she in?" he repeated, his voice low and threatening.

"You can't go up there, mister. Claudette, she—"

Jared leaned forward. "Tell me."

"She's in Claudette's room. End of the hall. But . . ."

Jared took the stairs three at a time.

Silver glanced out the window of the second-floor hotel room for the tenth time in the past half hour. Where was he?

Jared had deposited her in this cramped room

hours ago, telling her to stay put until he came for her. Her stomach was grumbling, but she didn't dare cross him again. All she needed was to make him so angry that he sent her packing back to Masonville.

Oh, how she would relish being able to tell him just exactly what she thought of him. He had no heart, no feelings. He certainly had no manners. If she weren't desperate, she would be the one to send *him* packing—and she'd bet her last cent he didn't have a home or a wife to go back to. No self-respecting woman would have anything to do with the likes of Jared Newman—no matter how handsome he was.

Handsome! He wasn't handsome. What had ever made her think, even for a moment, that he was? He was too rough, too hard, too dangerous, too . . .

She sat down again in the chair beside the bed. If only she didn't need to find Bob, she wouldn't be trapped in this miserable little hotel room. How had she ever gotten herself into this mess?

She closed her eyes, remembering too clearly how it had begun . . .

Bob Cassidy had stepped off the stage from Denver, wearing a black suit and a white shirt, his blond hair slicked back from his handsome face. Silver had just been returning to the mercantile after picking up some medication from the doctor for her mother.

His eyes, a piercing blue, had stopped her in her tracks. A slow smile lifted the corners of his mouth, then he swept his hat from his head and bowed at the waist.

Silver was left speechless. She'd never had a good-looking stranger—a tall one, at that—pay such attention to her. Gathering her wits about her, she nodded briefly and hurried around him.

He showed up at the Matlock home that same night, a bouquet of flowers in his hands. The next night he did the same, and the night after. He brought candy for Marlene and fine cigars for Gerald. He talked of places he'd been, and he told Silver she was the most beautiful woman he'd ever met. He took her riding and listened when she talked of things most men thought women knew nothing about. He didn't seem to think she was a foolish spinster. And when he proposed that very next week and Marlene objected to his profession, he quietly said he would give it up if Silver consented to be his bride.

She knew she didn't love him. Sometimes, when he looked at her and she saw desire—was it desire?—in the blue of his eyes, she was afraid. Afraid of what she saw there but unable to understand why. His kisses didn't stir in her what she thought they should. In the romantic novels she'd read, the heroines were almost reduced to swooning at the mere touch of the hero. She waited, hoping to feel those things.

She was twenty-one and had never received a single proposal of marriage. How could she have turned him down when he offered for her?

Silver jumped up from her chair and stalked to the window once again. Anger and shame roiled inside her, twisting her stomach until she thought she might be sick.

He had played her for such a fool. She should have guessed it. She should have known. She wasn't beautiful or interesting. She was just what her mother had always said—a woman no man would want.

She glanced down at the street below.

Maybe this Jared Newman wasn't as smart as she'd been told. If he was, he never would have believed she was pregnant with Bob's baby. He would have known that no man would be interested in the likes of her.

She might have been a pretty girl at one time, but it was hard to tell beneath the swollen purple and red mass of flesh. Short tufts were all that remained of her once-luxurious black hair.

Jared sat on the chair beside the bed, holding the girl's hand. It hadn't been easy convincing the protective Claudette to let him talk to the girl, but somehow he'd managed to do so.

He leaned forward, speaking softly but clearly. "My name is Jared Newman. I want to help find the man who did this to you. What can you tell me about him, Felicity?"

She could open only one eye. She looked at him with stark fear, then glanced at Claudette, standing behind Jared.

"It's all right, honey," Claudette encouraged. "I've got a feeling you can trust him."

"Can you tell me what he looked like?"

"I . . . couldn't see . . . his face. It was dark."

Jared glanced up at Claudette.

"She was attacked on her way home. Felicity doesn't stay here at the Crystal Palace. She and her little boy live—"

"Scar . . ." the girl whispered. "He . . . had a scar."

Jared's belly tightened. "What kind of scar?"

"On . . . his chest." Felicity closed her eye as a tear tracked down her bruised cheek.

Jared's heart pounded. He'd found him. He was here in Central City. Or had been.

"What did it look like?" He forced his voice to remain calm. "The scar, Felicity. Tell me about the scar."

"Shaped . . . like a . . . star."

Unconsciously, his fingers tightened around Felicity's hand. She groaned and tried to pull away, but Jared hung on. But he wasn't seeing Felicity any longer. It was Katrina's face he was gazing down upon, Katrina's battered and ravaged body.

A star on his chest. That's what Katrina had told him. That was all she'd been able to tell him in the weeks before she died.

"Mr. Newman . . . Jared, I think you'd better leave," Claudette said softly but firmly.

"Just a few more questions," he said.

"No," she replied. "I don't want you upsetting her anymore."

Jared knew he wasn't going to change Claudette's mind. He rose from the chair. "I'll be back in the morning."

Claudette followed him into the hallway. "Mr. Newman, why do you want to find this man? You're not from Central City. You don't know Felicity."

He rarely spoke of it. In all these years, only Rick Cooper had dragged the whole story from him. "My sister died the same way. I've been trying to find this man for six years."

"I'm sorry," she whispered. "If Felicity is stronger in the morning, you may see her."

"Thank you."

"Where are you staying?"

"At the Carlton."

"I'll send word to you."

Jared placed his hat on his head. "What has the sheriff turned up?"

"Not a thing. Seems there's not much interest in finding a man for raping and beating a saloon-hall girl." Her voice was bitter. "Whoever did it is likely long gone by now."

She was probably right, he thought. Cass

wasn't the type to take chances. He would have left Central City. But only a week had passed since Felicity was attacked in that alley. At most, he was seven days behind Cass, and this time, he wouldn't know Jared was on his trail. If only Felicity could give him some clue, something more to go on . . .

"I'll see you in the morning," he said, and walked away.

Chapter 6

He'd pushed all thoughts of Silver from his mind from the moment he learned about Felicity, but as he walked down the hall, he could see the light shining under her door, and he knew he couldn't ignore her any longer.

He paused outside her room. Obviously she was still awake, waiting to see if he'd learned anything. Only she wasn't going to like hearing what he'd found out. He would have to send her back to Masonville now. He couldn't go on looking for her fiancé when he was on the trail of his family's killer.

He rapped on the door. It opened quickly.

She was wearing a robe, her bare feet poking out beneath the hem of the dressing gown. Her hair tumbled freely over her shoulders and down her back.

For a moment he could only stare at her in mute appreciation. The cotton robe, blue-green in color, fell softly from her shoulders, like a high mountain waterfall. Her belt emphasized the narrowness of her waist and the ripe swell of her small, firm breasts. Soft and supple and inviting. She would fit well in his arms. He felt the beginnings of desire stirring hot within him.

Attractive patches of pink brightened her

72

cheeks as she returned his look, her expression both innocent and confused. Finally, the blush deepening, she whispered, "Did you find him, Mr. Newman?"

"No." He glanced up and down the hall. "May I come in? We need to talk."

She hesitated only the fraction of a second before stepping back, her hands gripping the edge of the door, allowing him to enter her room. Jared stopped in the middle, staying away from the window—and the bed—as he heard the door close behind him.

He looked at her again. Her silver-gray eyes watched him, filled with hope and fear.

Had he noticed before how beautiful she was? Had he noticed that her nose was aristocratic, narrow and long? Had he noticed how high her cheekbones were? Had he noticed the delicate arch of her slate-black brows or the sooty shade of her eyelashes, or how luxurious and thick her hair was when it tumbled free from her braid?

Yes, come to think of it, he had. That first day when he saw her in her wedding gown, he'd thought she was beautiful then. And he'd thought so every time he'd looked at her since.

The desire to pull her into his arms and kiss her had never been stronger. With only a step or two, they could be lying beside one another on the bed. He could be kissing her inviting pink mouth, tangling his fingers through her mass of shiny black hair. Lord, she was becoming an obsession!

But she was a lady. Despite the unfortunate predicament she found herself in, he knew she was still a lady. And she belonged to another man. Besides, he didn't need any more complications in his life. With great strength of will, Jared forced down his desires, assuming once more an air of cool control.

"Miss Matlock, I've been unable to uncover any word of your fiancé. I'm afraid it's hopeless. I think it's best if I put you on a stage for home."

Her face paled. "You can't mean it. You can't mean to quit so soon. You haven't even tried."

"The truth is I've had news of a fugitive I've been seeking for a long time and—"

"What of our bargain? You took my locket. Papa gave you what little money he could afford and all the supplies you asked for. Is it just because finding the other man will pay more? I told you to name your price." She stepped toward him, her voice rising hysterically. "You can't abandon the search now! There's so little time! I can't go back without finding Bob. I . . ." She clamped her mouth closed, and he saw the telltale glitter of tears in her eyes.

Why was it so damned hard for him to say no to her? He hadn't allowed anyone to get under his skin this way in years. He hadn't time to get involved in other people's lives. Just do the job, get paid, and get out. So why did the word *no* get caught in his throat now?

She placed her palm flat on his chest, her face turned up to his. Her pleading silvery eyes were awash with unshed tears. "Please, Mr. Newman. I can't go back until I find him. You must help me. You're my only hope."

Angered by his own helplessness against her plea, he snapped, "Why do you want to find him anyway? He stole everything your family owns. He left you standing in the church. Lord knows, he probably seduced you with lies. And you won't be able to pay me even if I *do* find him."

Silver fell back from him. Her cheeks flamed with color, and she lifted her hands to cover the flush of shame. "You know about the robbery?"

"Of course I know. I make my living finding out the truth."

Now the tears streaked her cheeks.

"Oh, hell," he muttered as he reached for the knob. "Why you go on loving a man who would steal from you is beyond me. Be ready in the morning *and* don't you dare leave this room. If I learn anything, I want to be able to ride out fast. I don't want to have to come looking for you."

"I'll be ready," she whispered, just before the door slammed closed behind him.

Silver lay awake on the bed. The mattress was lumpy and the sheets rough, but it wasn't the crude accommodations that caused her sleeplessness. It was the bounty hunter.

No matter how long she tried, she couldn't shake the feelings he'd stirred within her. Inexperienced she might be, but instinct had told her what Jared had been feeling this evening. She'd seen the desire in his eyes. What alarmed and surprised her now was her own desire for him to act on those feelings. She'd wanted him to kiss her. She'd wanted to be pressed close against that tall, lean body and experience the strength of his muscles as she was clasped in his arms.

She turned onto her back and squeezed her eyes closed. She would not think of him like that. She *wouldn't!* She had to be logical. Had to keep a clear head.

Before Jared had shown up at her door tonight, she had been wrestling with her conscience. It bothered her that she had told him so many lies. Wouldn't it have been enough to tell him she thought Bob was guilty of theft and that she had to get the money back? He would still need her to come along to identify Bob, especially since there wasn't a warrant for his arrest. She'd been

ready to confess everything the next time she saw
Jared.

But now she knew she couldn't tell him the
whole truth. He had taken the job knowing there
was little or no chance he would be paid for his
efforts. But why? Why hadn't he sent her packing? There was only one plausible explanation. It
was because she'd told him she was pregnant. It
was obvious he had taken pity on her only because he felt sorry for her. Now she knew she
couldn't tell him it was all a lie or he would surely
put her on a stage for home.

And *what* he must think of her . . .

With a jerk of the covers, she rolled over onto
her stomach. What did she care what Jared Newman thought of her? He was a bounty hunter, for
heaven's sake, not some parish priest. Who knew
what vile and lawless things he had done? She
was telling only a little white lie. And if he just
wouldn't look at her with those imperious hazel
eyes of his, even her little lie wouldn't bother her.

Jared was awake when a message arrived from
Claudette the next morning saying that he could
see Felicity now. In fact, he hadn't slept all night.
What with knowing he might be on Cass's trail
and thinking about a pair of pleading silver-gray
eyes, sleep had been a hopeless quest.

He hesitated only a moment outside Silver's
door, then hurried on. She could damn well sit
there and cool her heels until he was good and
ready. The amount of trouble that slip of a girl
was causing him was far more than he'd bar-
gained for. She'd gotten herself into this pickle
on her own, probably by looking poor Bob in the
face and letting those eyes tear up and . . .

Ruthlessly, he shoved Silver from his thoughts.
Right now, he had more important concerns.

Claudette met him outside the door of her room. "She wants to speak with you alone. If you upset her . . ."

He had no doubt that the young proprietress of the Crystal Palace would carry through with her unspoken threat. She would certainly make him pay dearly if he caused Felicity untoward stress.

Felicity was propped up on the bed by a number of fluffy pillows. A bright red silk scarf covered her head, hiding the hideous haircut from view. She looked stronger this morning, although Jared doubted she would ever be pretty again.

"Morning, Felicity," he greeted her, and offered one of his rare smiles.

Her returned smile was crooked, due to the swollen right corner of her mouth, and it didn't remain long.

Jared pulled a chair out from the wall and turned it so he could face her without being too close. He didn't want to make her feel threatened. "Felicity, I want to find the man who hurt you. He's done this before, and I want to make sure he doesn't do it again. But I can't find him unless you tell me more about him."

She swallowed and turned her head toward the window where morning sunshine was spilling through the curtains and onto the floor. "He . . . laughed a lot. Especially when he . . . when he was hurting me."

It was difficult to wait, to not ask more questions, but he had to let her tell the story in her own way, in her own time.

"He took me into an abandoned shed. He had a lamp, but it was behind him and . . . and turned low. I . . . I think his hair was yellow . . . or maybe it was just the lamplight. I . . . I don't know. I tried to see his face but . . . He hit me so hard I passed out. When I came to, he was . . .

he . . ." Felicity drew a ragged breath. "I just stared at the scar on his chest and tried to pretend it wasn't happening."

The room fell silent except for the ticking of the mantel clock. It was a silence filled with pain.

"When he was finished, he started hitting me again. He took out his knife and cut off my hair in chunks. I asked him why." She turned her good eye on Jared for the first time since she'd begun speaking. "I asked him why was he doing it. I wouldn't have told anyone. I've had men be . . . be rough before. Why was he trying to kill me? Why was he cutting my hair?" She stopped speaking and closed her eye.

Jared waited as long as he could. "What did he say, Felicity?"

Her voice was a breathless whisper. "He said once he has a girl, he doesn't want anyone else to have her. So he . . . so he makes sure they're so ugly that nobody wants them." Another lengthy silence followed. "*If* they live, nobody wants them. He didn't mean for me to live."

Jared's fists clenched.

Felicity stared at him. "Virgins were always better, he said, but I was just a whore. While they were burying me in Central City, he would be . . . Oh my God!" She reached toward him.

Alarmed, Jared moved to the bed and grasped her hand.

"He told me where he was going. He must have thought I was dying and couldn't tell anyone."

"Where, Felicity? Where was he going?"

"Nevada. He said he'd be hitting his own bonanza in Virginia City."

Silver's stomach growled and her head ached. She was so hungry that the mere thought of food made her mouth salivate. She'd been too nervous to eat breakfast before leaving Masonville, and she'd been too excited and jittery when they'd reached Central City to even think of food. Then she'd waited for Jared last night, expecting they would eat together, but of course, they hadn't. And after his threat to send her home, she hadn't dared disobey him this morning by leaving her room. He'd said to be ready to ride out, and she was.

She crossed the room to the washstand and poured water into the porcelain bowl from the chipped pitcher. She splashed her face, then dried it with a towel before regarding her reflection in the mirror. There were gray smudges beneath her eyes, evidence of her sleepless night, and her face was abnormally pale. She pinched her cheeks, trying to bring some color into them. It wouldn't do to have Jared think she was ill. He was just looking for excuses to be rid of her.

She jumped at the sound of a sharp rap on the door. It had to be him. Everything about him was abrupt and demanding, she thought as she went to answer it.

"We're leaving," he said without a greeting. "Meet me out front in five minutes."

Five minutes. No breakfast. Her stomach growled again as she watched him walk down the hall. Then Silver grabbed her saddlebags and bedroll and hurriedly left the room. She wasn't going to have him waiting for her, not even for a second.

As she passed the hotel restaurant, she caught a whiff of fried bacon and eggs and hot breads. She hesitated briefly and cast a longing glance toward the dining room filled with tables. Unconsciously, she pressed a hand against her stomach to stop its protest. She felt slightly light-headed.

She turned away and rushed outside for a gasp of crisp morning air.

Saddlebags slung over his shoulder, Jared stepped out of the hotel. Silver was already waiting astride her sleek buckskin mare. When she opened her mouth as if to speak, he silenced her with an intentionally angry glare. He wasn't ready to answer any questions yet.

He knew she would ask what he'd learned and where they were going, and he also knew he intended to lie to her. And why shouldn't he? She'd done the same. He was only giving her back a bit of her own. Let her think it was Bob they were following. Let him drag her across the country in a mad chase. Let her sleep on the ground a night or two. She'd give up soon enough, and then he would put her onto that stage and send her home. Better yet, it would be her own decision and he wouldn't have to try to deny her plea for help or face those blasted gray eyes of hers.

Damn Coop's hide! Jared had always thought the man was his friend, but would a friend have done this to him? He didn't think so.

He should have followed his intuition, he thought as he secured his saddlebags and bedroll behind his saddle. He should have gotten his stuff together and left this morning without a word to Silver. She wouldn't have had any choice then but to go home. That's what he should have done. So why had he listened to that damned nagging voice in the back of his head that said he couldn't do that to her? He'd left women behind before.

He cursed himself as he gathered the reins in his left hand. Without looking at Silver, he swung into the saddle and turned his pinto out of town. As soon as they were beyond the rows of houses and businesses, he kicked his gelding into a canter. He didn't bother to look behind him. It was up to Silver to keep up. If she couldn't, it was her problem, not his.

An hour later he eased back on the reins to rest his horse. Below the trail, a clear mountain stream tumbled over moss-covered rocks. He walked his horse for about ten minutes, then dismounted and led the animal down the gentle slope to the stream.

It wasn't until the pinto and packhorse had plunged their muzzles deep into the water that Jared turned and looked at his companion.

Silver wore a fine layer of dust on her face and clothes. Her large gray eyes stared at him with a waiflike expression. Her hat hung by its string against her back, and her thick black braid swirled over her right shoulder and lay between the valley of her breasts.

She didn't say one word and already he was feeling ashamed of his behavior. "I suppose you're wondering where we're going," he said, his voice little better than a snarl.

"Yes."

"I've got reason to believe he's on his way to Nevada. Probably Virginia City." Perhaps a trace of guilty conscience kept him from actually lying and saying it was Bob they were following.

"So far?" she asked softly, her eyes widening.

"It's not too late to go back."

She shook her head. "I'm not going back."

"We're talking a thousand miles, Miss Matlock, and we may not even find him when we get there. It may be a wild goose chase. If he *is* on his way there, he's most likely traveling by stage or train and will be there long before we are. But we don't have the option of traveling in comfort, 'cause you'll recall we're a bit short of cash."

Of course, it wasn't her fault they were short

of cash, he mentally conceded. She'd never pretended she would pay him anything until after Bob was found. And it wasn't her fault they weren't chasing her fiancé any longer, either. But that thought didn't improve his temper any. She was going to slow him down. If he lost Cass's trail because of her . . .

"I'm not going back, Mr. Newman. If we have to go all the way to Nevada to find him, then so be it."

Stubborn female. "Mount up. We've got a lot of ground to cover."

The hot May sun was relentless. She could feel trickles of sweat running down her back and beneath her arms. Her empty stomach seemed to have flattened itself against her spine. She'd given up wondering if Jared ever meant to stop to eat something. In fact, she forcibly kept her thoughts off food. It seemed a lifetime since she had last had a meal.

Hour after interminable hour, dust swirled up from beneath the pinto's hooves and into her face. Her eyes stung and her nostrils felt clogged with dirt. The trail ahead of them climbed steadily upward, undulating in the afternoon heat. The pounding in her head receded to a strange hum, and then her vision became blurred with riotous black dots.

"Mr. Newman . . ." she began, before she pitched sideways toward a pool of darkness.

Chapter 7

Strong arms supported her. She smiled, warmed by the unusual sense of security they provided.

"Silver . . . Miss Matlock . . ."

She struggled to open her eyes, then once she did, it took a moment for her blurred vision to clear. His face was mere inches away. Her cheek rested against his chest. She could feel the rhythm of his heart through his shirt. It was a comforting sound. Above him, a leafy aspen whispered in a gentle breeze, adding to her sense of peace.

"What happened?" she asked, confused.

"You fell off your horse."

He had a very interesting mouth. The lower lip was fuller than the upper. His mustache was neatly trimmed. His white teeth were straight, except for one near the right corner of his mouth. And then there was his forbidding jawline. It didn't seem quite so stern at the moment. What would it be like to kiss that mouth? She wondered . . .

"Miss Matlock?"

His eyes weren't cold and remote. They were filled with warmth and . . . and something more. Heat surged through her, and she felt a strange ache in her loins. Almost painful. Her pulse raced.

She closed her eyes, seeking to still the swirling sensations that swept over her.

"Silver? Look at me."

That soft, Southern drawl of his. So gentlemanly. So at odds with the hardened gunfighter she knew him to be.

"Open your eyes," he encouraged.

She obeyed.

"I thought I was losing you again. Here. Have a sip of water." His arm tightened around her back.

She liked the feel of his arms about her. She liked hearing his heart beat. She liked the look of his eyes and his mustache and his unshaven appearance and . . .

Silver sat up and pulled away from him, feeling ashamed. What if he could tell what she was thinking? "I . . . I don't know what happened," she stammered. "I've never fallen off a horse in my life." She took a few sips from the canteen. "At least, not like that, for no reason at all."

Jared shrugged as he stood up, towering high above her. "Sometimes ladies in your . . ." He seemed to be struggling for the right words. ". . . *delicate* condition . . . faint."

Because she read so much, Silver knew more about the intimacies between a man and a woman than was thought proper for an unmarried young woman. It embarrassed her to have Jared thinking she had behaved in such a manner with Bob. She couldn't quite imagine anyone wanting to do such a thing—except perhaps for the purpose of having children. Sometimes she'd been tempted to ask Sapphire about it, but she hadn't had the courage to do so. There *were* limits to Silver's outspokenness and inquisitive nature.

"Miss Matlock, did it ever occur to you that

you might . . . lose this child if you go on with me? If you don't want your parents to know, maybe we could find a place for you to stay until . . ."

This concerned man was a stranger to her. Since she'd first met him, he'd shown only irritation and anger toward her—when he'd shown any emotion at all. She wasn't sure just how to respond to him now. It made her feel strange inside. Was she about to faint again?

She rose shakily to her feet. "I know you think I'm foolish, but I must go with you. If that's a risk, then . . . then it's a risk I must take."

He shook his head slowly as he looked at her, but he still didn't seem to be angry.

With her stomach growling, she thought that now might be a good time to ask a favor of him. "Do you suppose we could *eat* something before we go on? It's been so long."

"We can't take time to . . ." Jared gave her a sharp glance. "When *was* the last time you ate?"

"Supper . . ." She hated to admit it, but she couldn't bring herself to tell another lie—at least not about this. "At my parents' house."

"That was almost two days ago! No wonder you fainted." The irritation was back in his voice again. "Why didn't you eat something at the hotel?"

"Because," she snapped back at him, feeling unfairly accused, "you told me not to leave my room. And you needn't shout at me."

"I thought you had enough common sense to eat. Do you expect me to do your thinking for you too?"

"You'd be the last person on earth I'd want to do my thinking for me. I don't want you to do anything for me except what you were hired to do. Not one thing."

His reaction was so lightning-quick, she had no opportunity to defend against it. His arms closed around her, and she was pulled against his long, lean body. A shock jolted through her at the touch of his mouth against hers. His lips were demanding at first, and then there was a subtle change. The pressure lightened. The kiss became a caress. Her knees weakened, and she pressed her hands against his chest to steady herself, afraid she would crumple to the ground at any moment.

As quickly as the kiss started, it ended. He set her away from him. Any trace of the friendly man she thought she'd seen moments before had disappeared. She quivered beneath his gaze as fear coursed through her veins.

"A gentleman would never have done that," she whispered, her throat tight.

Dark and threatening, he loomed above her. "I never claimed to be a gentleman."

This man was quite capable of anything. Anything! And she was helpless to stop him. She was alone in the middle of nowhere and helpless—against him and against her own reaction to him.

Jared muttered something under his breath as he turned away. He started toward the horses, tossing over his shoulder as he went, "Let's find a place to make camp. We've got only a couple more hours of daylight left anyway."

Fool female! Going nearly two days without food just because he told her to stay put. What kind of man did she think he was that he would make her go hungry in her room?

He uttered a low curse. He knew exactly the type of man she thought him. And he'd proved her right back there when he grabbed and kissed her against her will. But he couldn't have stopped himself. He might as well admit it. He'd wanted her almost from the first moment he saw her, and that kiss had only made him want her more.

A gentleman would never have done that. He grimaced. When was the last time anyone had mistaken him for a gentleman? Long before a boy had called him out on the streets of Dodge City and he'd been forced to return gunfire. Long before he'd seen a dozen men fall through trapdoors, stopped before hitting the ground by the looped ropes around their necks. Long before he'd started waking in the middle of the night with strange women in bed beside him, the room smelling of cheap cologne and stale liquor.

No, he was no gentleman, and he had no right to inflict himself on Silver. She had enough problems without him adding to them. She might be pregnant, but she was still a lady, still an innocent. It had taken only that one kiss for him to know that.

Jared glanced behind him. Silver's shoulders were slumped and her head was bent forward, but she followed doggedly after him without a word of protest. Poor thing. Wasn't it bad enough that she was saddled with a shrew for a mother and had been used and deserted by that gambling thief of a lover? Did Jared have to make her suffer more just because he was frustrated by how close he'd come to finding Cass?

Face facts, Newman. Cass doesn't have anything to do with this.

What was really bothering him was how much more he'd wanted than just a kiss—and how close he'd come to taking it. She'd tasted just as sweet as he had imagined she would. And she had fit against his body as if made for him. Just thinking of her exquisite face, the look of surprise in eyes turned suddenly sultry, made him throb with desire. Even now he wanted to stop the horses, lay

out his bedroll, and make love to her. He wanted
to gaze upon her tender flesh as firelight danced
over each swell and curve of her body. He wanted
to watch the flash of desire light her silvery eyes.
He wanted to hear her cry out with ecstasy, her
voice echoing in the treetops.

Damn!

He tried to pull his thoughts away from Silver
but was only temporarily successful. He thought
of the women who'd warmed his bed and assuaged his needs since the day he'd left Fair
Acres. Saloon girls mostly, willing to share their
bodies for an hour or two for some coins and perhaps a few kind words. He couldn't recall their
names or faces. He'd never stayed anywhere for
more than a day or two. He was always on the
move. Always searching.

It hit him then that his use of the gentler sex
was as degrading as the rest of his life. He lived
among the outcasts of society. He chased them
down and dragged them in, but he was more one
of them than not. There were no "ladies" in his
world, only women with tired souls and used
bodies.

Katrina . . . Why did he think of her so often
lately? His sister with her gentle ways and sweet
smile. Her whole life before her. Untouched even
by the hardships of the war, always hopeful for a
brighter tomorrow. So young. So damned young.
Just flowering into womanhood. Just beginning to
fall in love for the first time with the oldest Rollins
boy. Jared's father would have approved of the
union. Katrina would have been happy.

Jared had pursued the elusive, murderous Cass
for nearly six years, all the time trying—successfully
for the most part—never to think of his family.
He found the memories of his father and mother
and Katrina and his Kentucky home too painful.

But now it seemed that Katrina's image was always with him, haunting him, causing him to feel things he'd thought long since buried, reminding him of what he'd lost, the man he could have been.

And why did he have this insane notion that his little sister wanted him to help Silver Matlock? Was it just because she offered him a chance to help someone in trouble when there'd been no one to help Katrina? Or was there more to it than that?

He remembered the way Silver had felt in his arms as he'd lifted her from the dusty road and carried her into the shade of the whispering aspen. His sister's memory and all his other questions were forgotten as the desire to possess Silver burst through him. She was pregnant, she loved another man—and still he wanted her.

"We'll stop here," he called back to her, turning his gelding abruptly from the trail.

Jared chose a campsite in a copse of thick brush surrounded by aspens and scrub pines. A clear brook flowed past the site, the gurgle and swish of the water adding a pleasant melody to the crackle of the cook fire he set.

"Make some coffee and stir up some grub while I take care of the horses," he told Silver before walking away.

She started to protest but managed to bite back the words. She had promised to do as she was told, and he was just itching for an excuse to be rid of her. He'd made that abundantly clear.

While Jared rubbed down the horses, then tethered them and fed them some grain, Silver filled the coffeepot with water. She wasn't sure how much of the dark grounds to use, and she was determined not to ask Jared after the way he'd spoken to her. She stared at the pot for a while before pouring in a generous amount, then added two more healthy scoops for good measure.

The coffee on the fire, Silver opened a can of beans and slapped two pork steaks into a pan to fry. She hoped the meat—which had been packed in salt by her father—would still be good after nearly two days under the hot sun. She was sure this would be one of few meals when they would enjoy fresh meat. Hardtack and jerky were likely to be their normal fare.

Which was probably just as well, she thought, considering her limited skills as a cook.

She cast a surreptitious glance toward the horses and Jared. She wished his good mood would return. She wished he hadn't kissed her. Or did she? And then she wondered *why* he'd kissed her. He didn't even seem to like her. He was always growling at her about one thing or another. Why had he kissed her?

She touched her lips with her fingertips and re-membered once again that wonderfully frighten-ing sensation. As if all her nerve endings were exploding. Kissing him had been better than any-thing she'd imagined. Certainly better than the few times she'd allowed Bob to do the same.

Horrified to find herself confessing she'd liked Jared's unwanted advances, Silver pressed her lips together in silent denial. She was tired, that was all. And if Jared Newman ever tried to kiss her again, she would punch him a good one.

She grinned as she watched him working with the horses. Punching Jared Newman. Now there was a thought. Just like the time she let Oscar Freedman have it in fifth grade. She couldn't have been more than ten or eleven at the time, and Oscar was a year or two older. He'd been teasing her for days, calling her a scarecrow. She'd taken that well enough, but when he'd purposefully tripped Sapphire during a game of tag at recess, Silver had had enough. She'd waited for him after school and punched him square in the mouth.

Jared started toward her, and she realized suddenly that punching *his* mouth wasn't what she wanted to do with it.

"Coffee?" she asked as he approached the fire. Her hand shaking slightly, she held out a tin cup filled with the hot, black brew.

Jared accepted it and took a swallow. His hazel eyes widened in surprise, then he gagged and sputtered. "What's *in* this?" he demanded, his voice cracking.

"Coffee."

"Coffee? This would eat a hole clean through the leather of my saddle. How much did you put in here anyway? Didn't anyone ever teach you how to make coffee?"

One more insult and she *was* going to punch him. "If you don't like it, you can jolly well make your own coffee. You've been bullying and threatening me for two days just so you can get out of your promise to help me. Well, you're not going to get away with it. I'm here and I'm staying, and you're just going to have to make the best of it." Silver turned her back toward him and slapped some beans and a pork steak onto a plate. Turning around again, she snapped, "See if this won't put a hole in your belly to match the one in your saddle."

He gazed down at the charred pork and watery beans. "You might have told me you couldn't cook." His tone was accusatory.

Silver nearly choked on her rage. "Listen, bounty. I didn't sign on as your cook. You told me to fix supper and I did. Throw it in the fire if it's not to your liking." With an angry toss of her head, she filled her own plate and sat down on her bedroll, folding her legs beneath her. She refused to look up to see if he ate his supper or not.

Of course, he was right. She was a terrible cook. The coffee tasted like varnish, the pork steak wasn't fit to eat, and the lukewarm beans should have been left in the can. But she ate every last bite. Not just because she was half-starved, but because she wouldn't give him the satisfaction of seeing she agreed with his assessment of her culinary skills.

Damn Jared Newman anyway!

Outside the ring of firelight, Jared leaned against a tree, smoking a cigarette. He smiled as he remembered the way she'd told him what he could damn well do with his supper. It reminded him of the way she'd looked the first time he saw her, dressed in bridal white, stomping along the board sidewalks of Masonville and looking like she would kill the first person to cross her path. He realized now it was that same fire, that same energy she tried so hard to subdue, which drew him to her.

He watched as she loosened her thick braid and began brushing her hair, drawing the heavy tresses over her shoulder as she leaned her head forward. The ebony waves glowed midnight blue in the firelight. He imagined how that hair would look spread across a white pillowcase. He imagined the feel of it spilling across his bare chest as he cradled her in his arms, her head resting on his shoulder.

His muscles tensed, and he fought the urge to finish what he'd started earlier. She was another man's woman. He needed to remember that. He'd stepped out of line today. He couldn't afford to do it again.

Silver pulled a bottle of ointment from her saddlebag, then winced as she tried to reach the sore muscles of her upper back. He crushed his cigarette into the moist earth before walking across the camp. She looked up as he approached. Her hand stilled in midair. Her mouth was slightly open, her lips moist and inviting.

He quelled his rising desire. "Let me do that for you."

"No, thank you. I can do it myself."

"Don't be stubborn. I can see how miserable you are."

Her cheeks grew pink, her voice indignant. "I'm *not* being stubborn. I'm perfectly capable . . ."

"Here." He knelt behind her and took the bottle from her hand.

She glared at him a moment longer, then slowly the anger faded from her eyes, replaced by a puzzled expression. Finally, she turned her face away.

Jared slipped her blouse down just far enough to reveal the width of her shoulders. "Lift your hair," he ordered softly.

Silently—to his surprise—she obeyed.

He worked the strong-smelling liniment into her smooth white flesh, kneading the tense muscles. Her neck presented another temptation. He longed to lean forward and kiss it. Had Bob kissed her neck? Had he seen the gooseflesh rise along her arm in response? Jared's mood darkened at the thought.

He replaced the cap on the liniment bottle, then stood and started to walk away. He didn't know what possessed him to pause and ask, "What made you fall in love with him? Couldn't you tell what kind of man he was?"

She shook her head, eyes wide.

"Right. It's none of my business." He turned toward his bedroll. "Better get some sleep. We'll get an early start in the morning."

He unbuckled his gun belt, laying the weapon within easy reach. Then he dropped to the ground and pulled the blanket over his shoulders. He stared up at the sky overhead, heedless of his own command for sleep.

A breeze whispered through the trees, and in the distance a coyote's mournful cry rose toward the quarter moon. Silver-edged clouds skidded across the ink-black sky, occasionally passing a filmy curtain between earth and incandescent moon. One of the horses nickered, another snorted in reply. Familiar sights and sounds. No warning of danger.

"I don't know." Silver's soft voice floated across the campsite to him. "He said he loved me. I thought . . . I thought that was enough."

Jared tensed.

Her last words were barely audible. "I was such a fool."

He wasn't sure, but he thought the sounds of muffled weeping might have joined the coyote's late-night wail.

Chapter 8

Silver awakened to the scent and sound of frying bacon. She sat up, pushing her tangled hair from her face.

"Morning," Jared greeted her.

The sky was still pewter in color, the mountain air crisp and cold. It seemed a much better idea to stay snuggled beneath her blanket than to be awake at such a ridiculously early hour.

As if he read her thoughts, Jared said, "Better get moving. We're on our way as soon as we eat. Looks like we're going to have good weather again. Should be able to cover a lot of ground."

Silver nodded sleepily, then rose from her bedroll and stumbled off in the general direction of the stream. Perhaps she would feel human again once she'd splashed some water on her face. Then again, she doubted it. Her body ached from head to toe; at least two dozen pebbles must have found their way under her bedroll last night, and each one of them had chosen an unusually tender part of her anatomy to torture.

Silver had never been known for her sunny early-morning disposition. If she was left alone for fifteen or twenty minutes and allowed to wake up at her own pace, she could be relatively human. But pity the poor person who woke her and expected her to be pleasant. Sapphire's morning cheerfulness had always brought thoughts of murder to Silver's mind. She'd been considering some similar homicidal action toward Jared from the moment he said, "Morning," his tone implying that it was a good one.

Facing the cold mountain stream wasn't improving her mood any. She would dearly love a real bath. Her mother's pride and joy in the Matlock home was a separate bathing room, and she'd insisted that her daughters use it daily, as she did. Folks who knew probably thought it a silly extravagance, but Silver was only too happy to comply. She loved soaking in hot water, steam swirling around her face.

Now, covered with grime, she would have settled for a pan of warm water and a door to close behind her.

"Hurry up," Jared called, his voice intruding on her wishful thoughts.

With her back toward their camp, Silver unbuttoned the neck of her blouse and rolled up her sleeves. Scooping the icy water into her hands, she washed away as much dirt as possible from her neck, arms, and face. Next, she ran a hasty brush over her hair, then wove thick sections into one braid.

"Your breakfast is ready."

Why did he always growl every other time he spoke to her but sound so doggoned happy in the morning? "I'll be there in a minute," she retorted as she stepped away in search of a bit more privacy.

"Be careful you don't wake up any rattlesnakes."

She froze in her tracks. Rattlesnakes? The thought of stepping behind a tree, pulling down her skirt, and facing a rattler was not exactly an encouraging one.

Then she heard his chuckle. The filthy buzzard! He was trying to scare her, but he wasn't going to succeed. With a determined step, she moved on.

When she returned, she found Jared already saddling the horses. "Your food's cold," he said without looking at her.

"I like it that way." She sat on a log and began eating.

"A regular ray of sunshine, aren't you?" He chuckled as he turned to look at her.

Her eyes widened. He was *laughing* at her again! This two-bit, no-good bounty hunter had the nerve to *laugh* at her. This man—the one who couldn't say anything without snarling—had the gall to insinuate *she* was a grump? "I'm not along for pleasant company, Mr. Newman," she replied in her most contemptuous tone.

"It's a good thing." Traces of laughter lingered in the words.

It was all she could do not to throw her plate of food at him.

Jared turned his back toward her, smothering the fire with sand and dirt, then poured the last of the coffee over the coals before stirring them with a stick, making sure the fire was completely extinguished. "Time we were out of here." He glanced at her plate, an obvious hint to hurry her along. "I'd like to make Laramie by tomorrow."

"But Laramie is north. Why aren't we heading west?"

"I want to stay close to the rail line. That way, if he did go by train and got off anywhere along the way, we won't lose him. If we're lucky," he added. "Are you ready?"

Her stomach full and her face clean, Silver was

beginning to feel a little more civilized. Even his goading didn't seem so irritating. At least he seemed to know what he was doing. It made sense to Silver that they stay close to the rail line. She might not like the bounty hunter a great deal, but at least he had found out where Bob was going. If she didn't create any delays, they would find him and she could part company with Jared soon after.

She rinsed off her plate and cup in the stream, shoved them into a pack, then hastily rolled up her bedroll and tied it behind the saddle on Cinder's back.

Even as her sore muscles protested another day in the saddle, she couldn't help but smile at how speedily she had readied herself. As she settled her hat over her head, she glanced toward Jared, certain he would agree and offer a word of praise. After all, he'd been in a strangely good humor all morning, even if he had only spoken in clipped sentences.

But his hazel eyes were as remote as she'd ever seen them, his face devoid of expression. "If you take this long every morning, we'll never catch him." With that, he turned his pinto toward the road.

Silver followed him, thoughts of homicide reactivated.

Jared maintained a steady pace throughout the day, resting only when necessary for the horses. If he had the money to buy fresh mounts when needed, he wouldn't have rested even then. He'd learned long ago that he could go without sleep or rest for several days if the need arose.

He never asked Silver how she was doing. The only times he spoke to her were to say they were stopping or they were leaving. He kept expecting

to hear her voice a complaint, but she didn't. Not
one word. Not one plea to slow down or to stop
or to eat. He felt a grudging admiration for her
grit. She wasn't an I-give-up kind of person.

Nightfall found them within a half-day's ride of
Laramie, Wyoming.

After the horses were cared for, Jared started a
fire and made a pot of coffee. Aware of how
closely Silver watched his every move, he was
certain that the next time she made coffee, it
would be fit to drink.

He threw together a quick meal, and they ate
in silence, Jared covertly observing his traveling
companion. He was torn between guilt for mis-
leading her about the man they were actually following and irritation for the complications her
presence added to his task of finding Cass.

He cleaned the last bit of food from his plate,
then set the plate near the fire before leaning back
against a log and lighting a cigarette. He reminded himself that he didn't have time to waste
on feeling guilty. When a man lived by stealth,
making himself a part of the seamier side of life
where his prey dwelt, he told a lot of lies. So
why was this lie—one made by omission of facts—
bothering him? She'd lied to him first, he reminded himself.

He should have sent her home, whether she
liked it or not. He shouldn't be dragging her
across the country. He was following a murderer,
not some two-bit gambler. He could be placing
Silver's life in jeopardy. And there was the baby
to be considered, too.

How did a girl like Silver get herself into such
a mess?

He watched her rise from her bedroll and move
around the camp. There was a certain grace about
her movements. She held her shoulders straight,

her head erect. It was a proud, strong posture, and strangely contradictory with the hurt and insecurities he sensed beneath the surface. But then, there were many things about her he found contradictory.

She picked up the plate he'd left near the fire along with the other supper utensils and carried them to the stream where she washed them as best she could. When she returned, he noted once again the gentle sway of her hips and how slender she was. He wondered just when the baby was due. She couldn't be too far along or her reed-slender frame could never conceal it.

He said he loved me . . . I was such a fool . . .

He could imagine the sweet talk Bob had used to seduce her. Jared didn't know the man, but he knew the type. He'd taken an innocent, gullible girl and plied her with fancy lies. It made his blood boil just thinking about it.

But was he so different?

He was lying to her, too, letting her think they were following Bob when they weren't. By the time he found Cass and took him in for the reward, it would be too late to look for her fiancé. Silver's pregnancy would be evident to everyone by then. And he didn't want to think about the scorn she would have to live with then, not only from the townspeople but also from her own family. The little he'd seen of her mother told him she would be unforgiving.

Silver settled once again onto her bedroll. While she stared into the fire, she freed her hair from its braid. She slowly pulled the brush through it, removing any tangles, then wove the three thick strands together once again.

Jared watched, mesmerized by each movement. He hadn't ever realized how tantalizing the sight of a woman braiding her hair could be.

He tossed the butt of his cigarette into the fire, the action drawing Silver's gaze to him. Damn those eyes! They were the reason he couldn't send her away. He couldn't even think straight when she leveled them at him.

"Tell me about yourself, Mr. Newman," she said, breaking the lengthy silence.

"I'm not much for talking about myself."

"We're going to be traveling together for a while. It would be nice if we . . . well, if we knew each other a little better. Don't you think so?" She pulled her knees up to her chest and wrapped her arms around her shins. "Tell me about your home, where you're from." Her silver-gray eyes never wavered from his face.

When was the last time anybody had asked him such a thing? Something in the way she looked at him said she truly cared, truly wanted to know. It wasn't an easy thing to ask of him; he hadn't talked about himself in years.

"I'm from Kentucky."

She waited expectantly.

It had been a perfect boyhood. Green pastures and whitewashed fences. Mares and foals cantering through belly-high grass. Sunny afternoons spent swinging from tree limbs with his brothers and friends and splashing naked into the cold, clear pond surrounded by weeping willows. The shadowy barns filled with hay and straw and the pungent odors of dung and sweat. Fresh lemonade served in the shade of the wide veranda, his mother smelling of honeysuckle toilet water.

"You needn't tell me if it's so hard to talk about. I understand. Is that why you became a bounty hunter? Because you were so unhappy as a child?"

"What?"

She was looking at him with great tenderness,

as if she pitied him. "You needn't explain. I can imagine what it must have been like."

"Just what *do* you imagine?" he asked.

Silver shook her head, her cheeks growing pink. "I'm sorry. I shouldn't have said—"

"No, please. I really want to know."

"Well, I . . . I don't know. I suppose you were poor. What else could make you become . . . well . . . that is . . ."

"Become the sort of man I am? Is that what you mean?"

Her blush deepened. "Really, I . . ." Her voice faded as she glanced down at her hands, folded now in her lap.

He wanted her to know how wrong she was, that, at least at one time, he had been a gentleman. He wanted, if only for a moment, for her to see him as something other than what he was. "We weren't poor, Miss Matlock. The Newmans owned the largest horse farm in all Kentucky before the war. We raised Thoroughbreds."

"Really? I've always loved horses."

A little of the tension eased from him. "It shows. You ride very well."

"Papa gave me Cinder when she was just a yearling. I trained her myself. Mother was horrified. It was all right, of course, for a young lady to learn to ride, but it was terribly gauche for a 'Masonville Matlock' to actually *work* with the animals."

Jared couldn't help smiling at the emphasis she put on her name, tilting her nose up in the air as she spoke. He could just imagine her mother's attitude.

Silver leaned forward. "Did you help train your horses, too?"

"Everyone worked around Fair Acres. I mucked

stalls when I was little. As I got older, I learned to do it all."

"It must be wonderful to have so many horses, to be around them all the time."

Jared nodded. Image after image flitted quickly through his head. He hadn't talked about it in years, hadn't even let himself remember. It would be so easy now to just open up and tell her what his childhood had really been like. She seemed so willing to listen.

"What about the rest of your family? Do you have any brothers or sisters?"

He stiffened. *I did once.* "My family's dead."

Her voice was very low. "You have no one? I'm so sorry."

He shrugged as he turned his gaze toward the fire.

"Is that why you became a bounty hunter?"

It had been foolish to think he could talk to her about his boyhood, to even consider telling her what had happened to his family. Just revealing that he was from Kentucky and the name of his family home had been more than he'd told anyone in years. What was it about her that made him think he could tell her about himself?

"You'd better get some sleep," he said as he leaned back on his bedroll. "We've got another early start tomorrow." He closed his eyes, putting an end to her unwelcome questions.

"I'm sorry, Jared," she whispered from across the camp.

His belly constricted. He didn't want pity from her. He wanted things a bounty hunter shouldn't want from a lady.

So, the Newmans had raised Thoroughbreds in Kentucky on a place called Fair Acres. That was more than she'd known about him that morning.

She lay back on her blanket, staring up at the starry sky, and tried to imagine it. Fair Acres. It sounded beautiful. There was probably an enormous white house with pillars and a veranda and a sweep of green lawn and lush trees. And, of course, there were the horses, hundreds of them, galloping across rolling fields of green.

She imagined Jared riding a sleek Thoroughbred toward the house, then vaulting from the saddle as he reached it. He was wearing a dark frock coat and tight breeches that revealed the taut muscles of his thighs and shiny black boots that rose nearly to his knees. His dark hair fell across his forehead and he brushed it back as he took the steps up to the veranda three at a time.

A warmth started in her stomach and spread all through her as she realized where her thoughts were taking her. She was imagining herself standing on that veranda. She could see Jared gathering her into his arms and claiming her lips in a passionate kiss. He would whisper sweet words into her ear before carrying her through the open doors and up the sweeping staircase.

She closed her eyes and tried to quiet her shaking limbs. It was becoming all too clear that she was dangerously attracted to the bounty hunter. She shouldn't care about Jared's boyhood or his home in Kentucky or what had caused him to choose his profession. In a week or two, they would find Bob and then Jared would ride out of her life forever. He would never give her another thought. And why should he?

The throbbing in her backside returned. She grimaced but was glad for the distraction. She would rather curse him for dragging her across the country at breakneck speed than think of him holding her. She would rather feel the anger than the strange wanting he'd stirred in her soul.

She thought of her family's comfortable home, of her nice, soft bed with the smooth sheets and plenty of blankets. She thought of her mother's excellent meals. She even thought of her wardrobe full of pretty gowns. She had always taken her family's prosperity for granted. Never had she imagined a time would come when she couldn't bathe or change her clothes or eat when she wanted to. Papa and her mother were counting on her to save it for them. She couldn't fail them. She mustn't.

She hated the trail, hated being dirty, hated the ache in her backside. And she hated Jared Newman. He was heartless and cruel and surly, and she wanted to find Bob and go home and never see the bounty hunter again.

She hated him.

But as she drifted into a troubled sleep, she imagined once again his strong arms enveloping her and his lips claiming hers.

Chapter 9

Laramie had appeared on the Wyoming prairie almost overnight, a product of the Union Pacific Railroad, a "hell on wheels" town that survived after the rail crews moved further west toward their date with destiny at Promontory, Utah.

Silver guided her mare across the tracks beneath the shadow of the towering windmill and water tank. She wondered how long ago Bob had passed through here on his way to Nevada. And why was he going to Nevada? Jared had never told her why he suspected that was Bob's destination. In fact, he hadn't told her anything of what he'd learned back in Central City.

As they entered the main part of town, they rode past a hotel. Silver eyed it hungrily. A bed with real sheets and blankets and a soft mattress. What she wouldn't give for just one night . . .

It was tempting to use the money her father had secretly given her, the money she had pinned to the inside of her underdrawers. For an emergency, Papa had told her, and she'd known he'd meant for it to get her home should she change her mind about continuing the search. But since she had no intention of changing her mind, maybe it wouldn't hurt to spend a night in a hotel.

But what if Jared wanted her to turn her money over to him once he found out about it? Since she wasn't ready to do that, she reluctantly gave up the idea of spending a night in a hotel. Besides, they had a long road ahead of them. She might need something else far more than a soft bed before they were through.

Jared stopped his pinto in front of a restaurant in the center of town. *Mabel*'s, the sign read.

"You get something to eat," he told her. "I'm going to check out the train station."

"Shouldn't I come with you?"

His gaze was hard. "No." He leaned sideways in his saddle and dropped a few coins into her hand. "Be sure to eat. I don't want you fainting on me again."

Silver clenched her teeth, but she couldn't hold back the hot reply. "I don't have any intention of fainting again, Mr. Newman. I can manage just fine eating whenever you do. If you're not hungry, neither am I."

"I didn't say I wasn't hungry." His eyes narrowed. "Just do as I say. I'll meet you back here in a little while. Don't wander off."

He was treating her like a three-year-old, which inflamed her ire. She was tempted to act like a three-year-old in return. She itched to hit him. "I'll be here."

He didn't move, just watched with those intrusive hazel eyes until she couldn't stand it any longer. She turned her head away from him as she slipped down from the saddle, looping Cinder's reins around the hitching post in front of Mabel's.

As she stepped up onto the boardwalk, he turned his horse away. "I'll be back after a while."

Silver paused at the restaurant door and glanced over her shoulder. Jared was riding down the middle of the street toward the train station. It rankled her that he wouldn't let her go with him. Why shouldn't she? It was her fiancé they were looking for, after all. And why should she eat in a restaurant, spending what little money they had, if he didn't? She could manage as well as he on beans out of the can.

Just then she heard a feminine voice call out, "Jared Newman, as I live and breathe!"

Jared stopped his pinto, glanced toward the saloon he'd been passing, then jumped down from the saddle. A moment later, a strawberry blonde pushed her way through the swinging saloon doors and hurried toward him. She hugged him right in the middle of the street, and then he *kissed* her cheek, in plain sight of everyone, before she tugged him back into the saloon.

Her eyes wide, Silver continued to watch and wait. He'd said he was going to the train station to ask questions. He certainly couldn't be finding out anything about Bob in that saloon—with that saloon woman!

She waited for five minutes, her irritation growing with each passing second. That no-good, third-rate, womanizing bounty hunter! Just two days ago, he'd been kissing *her*, and now he was kissing some *hussy* on the street. He didn't even remember he had a job to do. At this rate, they never would find Bob. Well, if he wasn't going to do it, she would. Her promise to stay at the restaurant be damned! Silver remounted and hurried Cinder down the street.

Whitney's face glowed as her green-apple eyes perused him. "You haven't changed a bit, Mr. Newman. Still as handsome as ever."

"You're looking pretty yourself, Mrs. Culver. Where's Tom?"

"Over at the bank. He'll be back in a few minutes. Sit down. He'd have my head if I let you get away without saying hello."

Jared obeyed, sitting beside a green felt table, his gaze sweeping over the place. "What are you and Tom doing in Laramie? I thought you meant to stay put in Topeka."

"We hoped to," she replied, sadness entering her eyes as she sat down across from him. "But it just wasn't the same. Even though you brought in Henderson and cleared Tom of the murder charges, folks just couldn't seem to forget Tom had been in jail. He couldn't get another job and business in my little store never came back. So we sold it all and left." She waved her hand at the bar, her smile returning. "So, this is our new business. Fancy me, the owner of a place called the Red Dog."

He joined in her laughter. When he'd first met Whitney Culver, she had been the most shy, soft-spoken, and timid woman he'd ever known—or probably ever would know. She'd run a small millinery shop for the ladies of Topeka. When Tom had been accused of killing his boss at the livery stable, Whitney had been shunned by those she'd thought were her friends. But she'd known her husband wasn't guilty, and so she'd sought help. Fate had brought her to Jared.

"We're usually pretty busy by this time of day, but there's a funeral in town this morning so we closed down till tonight out of respect. The Red Dog's a popular place in Laramie. Tom runs the saloon and I handle the records and receipts. Tom doesn't want me down here much. Things can get a little rowdy some nights."

"I can't say that I blame Tom for keeping you

out of sight. You look radiant, Whitney. Maybe you should have owned a saloon before." Not being a man who was loose with compliments, he meant exactly what he said.

She blushed right up to the roots of her reddish-gold hair. "It's not the saloon. It's motherhood. Tom and I have a son." She hopped up from her chair. "Would you like to see him?"

"Well . . ."

Her green eyes pleaded.

"Sure. I'd love to." He let her lead him up the stairs to the small living quarters above the saloon.

"Who'd you say you was lookin' for?"

"He's my . . . my brother. His name is Bob Cassidy. I've just got to find him, and I think he must be heading west by train."

"Miss, lots of people travel through here . . ."

Silver leaned forward, gripping the counter that separated them. "Please try to remember. It would have to have been within the last week. He's tall, a little over six feet. Clean-shaven. Blonde hair. Pale blue eyes. Oh," she added, just now remembering, "he has a little white scar along the right side of his jaw. Right here." She ran her fingernail along her jawline.

"Scar, you say? And blond hair? Hmmm." The stationmaster rubbed his chin. "Come to think of it, I mighta seen that brother of yours. But not here. It was in town. At the Red Dog Saloon. That was it. Sakes alive. He was gamblin' pretty heavy a few nights back. Had hisself a pretty fair stake."

"Gambling?" she asked in a small voice. *What if he lost the money?*

As if he'd read her anxious thoughts, he said, "Oh, don't worry, miss. He come out a winner that night. I seen him leave the table."

"Is . . . is he still in town?"

The man shook his head. "No. Least not that I've seen of him. Might've left on the next mornin' train. He didn't look the sort to hang around a town like this. All duded up, you know. But I wasn't on duty that mornin'. You'd have to ask Yancy. He's my cousin. He takes the early mornin' shift most days.

"May I speak to him?"

"He's havin' his lunch right now. Be back in thirty minutes or so."

"Thank you." Silver turned away from the counter and stepped outside into the brilliant midday sun.

Excitement flowed through her veins, pumped by her racing heart. Bob had been there only a few days before. He'd been gambling with her parents' money—and he'd won. There was a chance he was still in Laramie. If they moved quickly . . .

Silver swung into the saddle and turned her horse back toward the center of town. Her excitement was quickly replaced by anger when she saw Jared's pinto still tied to the hitching post outside the Red Dog Saloon.

The Red Dog! That was where Bob had been gambling.

She dismounted and tied Cinder beside the pinto, then hurried through the swinging doors. Just as she did so, Jared and the woman he'd met earlier appeared at the top of the stairs, both of them smiling.

Silver stopped at the sight. The woman's face glowed, and for the first time, she saw what Jared looked like when he was happy. He'd been handsome before, but his dark good looks were devastating now. As she watched, he took hold of the redhead's elbow, prepared to help her down the stairs. There was something so intimate about the scene. Silver's stomach plummeted. Her breath came hard.

Jared's smile disappeared when he saw her. "What are you doing in here?" He turned toward the woman at his side. "Excuse me, Whitney." Then he briskly descended the stairs and approached Silver. "I thought I told you to stay at the restaurant."

Silver's anger flared. With a quick glance toward the woman on the stairs, she countered. "And I thought *you* were going to the train station."

"That's where I'm going now."

"You don't have to. I've already been. Bob was here." Again her eyes flicked toward Whitney. "In fact, he was gambling in this saloon just a few nights ago."

"How do you know?" Jared inquired, his hard gaze riveting her.

"Because I had sense enough to spend my time asking questions that would help. Not . . . not spending my time dallying with . . . with . . ." She couldn't say it. She felt herself growing hot with embarrassment.

"Sit down," Jared ordered.

She sat.

He turned toward the woman. "Whitney, we need some information from you."

Silver watched the woman called Whitney as she walked down the stairs and across the empty saloon. She was petite but well-rounded in all the right places. Her pretty hair was worn up; wispy tendrils caressed the back of her neck. Her attractive green dress was not as risqué as Silver would have expected from a saloon girl. In fact, it looked more like something Sapphire would wear to a ladies' church social.

And she was pretty. Very pretty. No wonder Jared had stopped when she called to him. Whitney was everything Silver had ever wanted to be. Her stomach tightened again.

Whitney's green eyes were assessing Silver as she neared the table, and the moment she arrived, she held out a hand. "I'm Whitney Culver." A delicately arched eyebrow rose a fraction as she waited for a like introduction.

Jared answered for her. "Silver Matlock. I'm looking for her fiancé."

Silver's gaze darted to him. He didn't have to sound so disgusted and contemptuous. She straightened her shoulders and returned her gaze to Whitney. *"We're* looking for my fiancé," she amended. "The stationmaster says he was at this saloon a few nights ago. His name's Bob Cassidy. He's tall and blond and *very* good-looking." She couldn't help herself. She'd added the "very" for Jared's benefit.

"I'm sorry. As I told Jared, my husband doesn't want me down in the saloon when there are many customers. And the baby keeps me busy most nights."

"Your *husband?"* The words came out in a whisper. *A baby?* Did she feel relief or disbelief? And why should she even care?

"Yes. Oh, Jared, here's Tom now." Whitney moved away from the table and grabbed the arm of a fair-haired man with a close-trimmed beard as he came through the swinging doors. "Tom, look who's here!" she exclaimed as she towed him closer.

The two men grasped hands.

"Jared."

"Good to see you, Tom."

"Jared needs our help," Whitney explained. "He's looking for someone he believes was here

at the Red Dog the other night." She glanced at
Silver. "Describe the man again, Miss Matlock."

Once again, Silver gave Bob's name and noted
his height, hair color, and eyes. "And he has a
small white scar on the jaw." She touched her
finger to her own face. "Right here."

"A scar?" Jared said, pulling her gaze to him.
"You never told me he had a scar on his jaw."

She shrugged. "I forgot. I'd gotten so used to
seeing it . . ." Her voice trailed away beneath his
censuring eyes.

The tense silence stretched out uncomfortably.

Tom cleared his throat. "Sounds like the
stranger that was here. Come in about three,
maybe four nights in a row. Last time was about
three nights ago. He was playing poker and winning pretty big. I figured he must've left town on
the westbound train. I think if he'd stayed in Laramie, we would've seen him again. He liked winning."

Silver's excitement returned, quickening her
pulse. They were close. Only three nights ago.
And Bob still had the money. If they found him
quickly, they could pay off the mortgage and save
the store and house and . . .

Jared didn't know whether he was glad to hear
about Bob or not. When he'd set off for the train
station, it had been more for show. So Silver
would think he was doing the things she expected of him. But he already knew where they
were going, and since no one who'd seen Cass's
face had ever lived, he was unable to describe the
killer to anyone. He couldn't ask folks if they'd
seen him. Unfortunately, the only clear trail Cass
had ever left was one of death and destruction.

He watched the color return to Silver's cheeks.
There was a gleam in her eye as she listened to

Tom. *Was* she still in love with Bob? He'd begun to believe otherwise, but now . . .

Jared swung his gaze back toward Tom. "What makes you think he took the westbound?"

"Only train that's been through since. They had some trouble with the tracks and had to cancel the eastbound that was due through."

Jared glanced at Silver once again. Perhaps they would get lucky and find Bob after all. Perhaps it would relieve him of some of his guilt for dragging her off after Cass instead of her fiancé. *If* they could find Bob and *if* Silver still wanted the scoundrel, perhaps he could be rid of her before long.

Perhaps. Only he wasn't so sure he wanted to be rid of her any longer.

Chapter 10

Perspiration beaded on Silver's forehead and trickled down the sides of her face and the bridge of her nose. Occasionally she raised a hand to wipe the moisture away, but it was pointless. It returned instantly.

It was nearly seven o'clock in the evening, and still the heat hadn't abated. And now they were riding into the sun. She squinted her eyes against the bright yellow glare.

Silver felt wilted and weary. Since leaving Laramie four days ago, Jared's pace had been relentless. She had no idea how much ground they had covered each day. Although she was curious, she hadn't the nerve—or the strength—to ask, and Jared certainly hadn't volunteered the information. In fact, he hadn't spoken more than a dozen words to her since they left Laramie.

She glared at his dust-covered back, sweat stains running the length of his vertebrae. He was trying to punish her, she thought. That's why he was driving them so hard. He was angry because she'd been the one to find out about Bob's whereabouts instead of leaving it up to him. He didn't even appreciate her help.

Or did it have anything to do with Bob? A quiver ran up her back as she remembered the way Jared looked at her every now and again. A sixth sense told her he wasn't as disinterested in her as he pretended to be. She remembered the way his mouth had felt against hers, remembered the betrayal of her own body as she responded to him. Perhaps his anger had more to do with what he wanted but didn't dare take.

Suddenly, Jared stopped his horse. He didn't turn to look at her until she'd ridden up beside him. "We'll leave the trail here. If Bob's on that train, there's nowhere along this stretch he's likely to get off anyway. There's a creek down that way about two, three miles. We'll try to make it before dark. Or do you need to stop now?"

She shook her head. "I can wait." Of course, she wouldn't have admitted it to him even if she did need to stop.

Besides, the idea of fresh water was infinitely appealing. The only water she'd seen for over two days had been what was in their canteens, two each, and they had to reserve that for drinking, not just for themselves but for the horses too. Jared had made it clear there wasn't even a drop for cooling their skin or bathing away the sweat and dust of the day's journey.

After days of riding through sagebrush desert, the endless country waving and cresting like a brown sea all around them, she was delighted to find the green oasis complete with trees and some hardy wildflowers. The creek was wide and shallow, bubbling up from some underground spring.

Jared didn't bother to dismount. "There's plenty of daylight left. I'm going to hunt up some fresh meat. I'll be gone . . . long enough."

She scarcely acknowledged his going or realized what he was saying. She had only one thing on her mind. A bath and a clean change of clothes.

With an economy of movement, Silver unsaddled Cinder and the packhorse and hobbled their front legs. She spread her bedroll beneath the pines, then took some clean clothes, a towel, and a bar of lavender soap from her saddlebags and headed for the stream.

The icy water was little more than just melted snow. Testing it with her toes, she gasped for air but refused to give up. She was going to have this bath if it killed her.

She heard a single shot fired in the distance. Supper! She had to hurry before Jared returned.

It was then she recalled his parting words. He'd be gone "long enough." He had known she yearned for a bath and had given her the privacy she needed. She didn't want to feel grateful to him for his thoughtfulness, but she did.

Quickly, she shucked out of her filthy clothes, tossing them onto the bank to be washed as soon as she was finished with her own bath. She knelt down on the smooth stones that lined the bottom of the stream and splashed the cold water over her bare skin, then lathered herself with the scented soap. It was no easy task to do the same with her thick hair, but she managed.

Feeling revitalized, she dried off with the inadequate towel and dressed in a clean leather skirt and a pink blouse. Then she scrubbed her soiled clothing and laid them across nearby bushes to dry. Finally, she sat on the ground and began combing the tangles from her hair.

Her thoughts turned instantly to the bounty hunter. Even in a moment of peace she couldn't escape him. Why was it so? He was ruthless, dangerous, hard as steel. It was more than the life he led or the guns strapped to his hips that made her wary. He frightened her, yet she was drawn to him.

She let out a sigh. There was no point in kidding herself. As irritating and coldhearted and frustrating as he was, he made her feel something that no man ever had before. She couldn't describe it. It was more than just a quickened pulse, more than just that look in his hazel eyes or the way his dark brown hair fell over his forehead. It was so much more than the roguish, lethal aura that surrounded him. More even than the way his kiss had made her feel. It was something intimate. Something . . . sexual.

What would it be like to have a man like Jared make love to her? No, not a man *like* him. What would it be like to have *Jared* make love to her? What would it be like to feel his hands on her skin as he slipped away her clothing? What would it be like to see his body, to touch him, to . . .

A strange frustration welled up inside her as she tried to imagine what the books she'd read had only hinted at. Somehow she knew it was so much more than she might expect.

Jared watched from the hillside. He'd taken his time returning with the rabbit but had still found her seated by the stream, her feet tucked under her as she drew the comb through her long ebony hair.

It was beautiful hair, thick and wavy. More than once he'd thought about how it would be to free the braid and run his fingers through the silken tresses. Had she let Bob do that?

His jaw stiffened and he moved toward camp.

Too often he found himself wondering about Silver and Bob, wondering when it was they first became lovers, wondering how often the man had gazed upon her porcelain skin, wondering about the soft curves beneath her blouse, wondering . . .

She turned her head, her wet hair hanging over one shoulder, her silvery-gray gaze meeting his. Her mouth was slightly parted. Surprise widened her eyes. Her cheeks were flushed. Her voice sounded breathless. "You're back."

"I got lucky."

She scrambled to her feet. "I'll start a fire."

He glanced down at her bare feet. They were long and narrow, her toes tapered. The skin was nearly translucent. He wanted to touch and hold them, to feel the smooth skin, to rub away the soreness. How could a pair of bare feet be so tantalizing?

He turned away from her before she could see the flash of desire in his eyes. "Make it quick. It won't take me long to skin this stringy jackrabbit."

He could just imagine the look in her eyes right now. She would be furious; she hated it when he ordered her around. Well, that was just how he wanted it. If she stayed angry with him, maybe he would be able to behave himself, to resist temptation. At the moment, skinning and cooking the game he'd shot was the last thing he wanted to do. And what he wanted wasn't the least bit gentlemanly or chivalrous.

Damn! He should have taken Tom and Whitney up on their invitation to stay overnight in Laramie. He should have found himself a woman to spend the night in his bed. That's all that was wrong with him. It wasn't Silver Matlock he wanted. Any woman would serve his purpose.

He tossed the rabbit onto a tree stump before returning to his pinto. He removed the saddle and rubbed down the animal, then led him to the creek for a drink. Finally, he hobbled the gelding and turned him free to graze on the green grass growing near the banks. That done, Jared stripped off his shirt and rinsed himself in the creek, slicking back his hair and scrubbing the dirt from his face and arms.

When he turned around, she was staring at him, her eyes focused on his chest. There was a sudden flare of color in her cheeks before she looked away, busying herself with gathering more wood for the fire.

Only once before had she seen a man's bare chest—and that only by accident. Bob had spilled wine on his shirt at supper and had waited in her father's office while Marlene removed the stain. When Silver had taken him the shirt, he had opened the door just wide enough for her to catch a glimpse. Bob's skin had been hairless, pale and smooth except for an ugly scar near his heart, with nothing remotely exciting about it. In fact, she had turned and fled quickly back to the family parlor, unnerved by something she'd seen in Bob's eyes when he found her looking at his half-clothed body.

Until now, she'd had no idea that a man's chest could look so strong and broad and . . . and beautiful!

She picked up another piece of firewood without thinking what she was doing. She was too busy remembering how Jared had looked, standing next to the creek, bare to the waist.

She'd never imagined hair on a man's chest before. At first it had looked strange to her, and then she'd realized it looked appealing as well. Jared's dark chest hair was nearly black. It spread across the upper part of his torso, then narrowed to a thin line that disappeared into the top of his britches. She wondered if it was soft to touch or if it was coarse and wiry. And there was the skin beneath, molded over strong chest muscles. His shoulders were so broad, his stomach so flat. What other surprises were still hidden from view?

Appalled by such thoughts, she felt her flush of embarrassment increase.

It was all this silence and the monotony of the journey. She was running out of things to think about and had far too much time to wonder about the man with whom she traveled. That's what was wrong. That's why she was thinking these outrageous things. She had to put a stop to her attraction to this man. She couldn't succumb to these traitorous feelings. Once they found Bob, she would never allow herself to give Jared another thought.

Steeling herself to face him, Silver returned to the fire and added the wood in her arms to the flames. Then she sat on her heels and gazed across the camp at Jared. He had finished skinning their supper and had skewered the meat for roasting over the fire. His eyes met hers as he stood.

"It shouldn't take this skinny thing long to cook through," he told her as he staked the meat on a makeshift tripod above the fire.

"No. It shouldn't."

He looked as if he might say something more, then suddenly he stepped back and spun away from her. His revolver was drawn before she realized what was happening. Fear paralyzed her.

"Hands up. Come out slow," he said in a firm voice.

A man appeared from behind the scrub pines, leading his horse behind him, his hands held away from the gun belt strapped to his hip.

"What do you want?" Jared demanded.

"Just come for some water, young fella," replied the scraggly-looking man. "Didn't mean no harm to you an' the missus."

Silver tore her gaze from the grizzled stranger, returning to Jared. From their first meeting, she'd sensed the dangerous undercurrents in this man, but never had she seen so clearly the deadly instincts that ruled him. In the flash of a second, he could take another human being's life. She shivered, glad it wasn't she who was staring down the barrel of his gun.

She glanced again at the stranger, his face white beneath his dark, scraggly beard. She sensed his fear and felt herself quaking with him.

Jared lowered his arm. "Where are you headed?"

"Denver. I been up to the mines in Montana, but now I'm goin' home."

Silver knew the moment Jared decided the man was harmless. It wasn't something he said or did so much as an infinitesimal change in his eyes, the relaxed muscles at the corners of his mouth.

A moment later he holstered his Colt. "My name's Newman. This is Miss Matlock."

Daring to move at last, Silver rose from her crouched position beside the campfire and looked once again at the stranger.

"Folks call me Smitty." He cracked a grin, revealing missing teeth on the right side of his mouth. His eyes flicked to the rabbit roasting over the fire. "I see you're about t'have your supper. Well, I won't be keepin' you. I'll just fill up my canteen an' be on my way."

Pity replaced fear as Silver noted the look of hunger in their visitor's eyes. "You're welcome to join us if you'd like, Smitty. There's not much, but we're willing to share."

"Well, that's right nice of you, ma'am. Don't mind if I do. I'll just wash up in the stream a bit. Can't be sittin' down for vittles with a purty woman without gettin' rid of the trail dust, now kin I?''

Silver returned Smitty's friendly smile, then turned toward the supply packs beneath a nearby tree. Jared was standing in front of her.

"Why'd you do that?" he whispered.

He was so blasted tall and standing so close she had to bend her head back to look at him. Her heart did a little jig in her chest. "Because he looked hungry," she returned, just as softly.

"Next time, you ask me first. Understand?" He stepped aside to let her pass.

Why *had* she done it? she wondered as she reached into the pack and withdrew the tin plates and eating utensils. Because, she suddenly realized, she didn't want to be alone with Jared—not because she feared *him* but because she feared herself.

Jared couldn't take his eyes off Silver. She was as beautiful by firelight as she was at any other time. Her eyes seemed a smoky gray rather than silver. The patrician lines of her face were sharpened by shadows. Her lips seemed fuller, sweeter, more inviting. His desire for her had been building for days, until he thought it might drive him insane.

"Well, folks, I thank you fer includin' me in your supper. It was right tasty." Smitty got to his feet. "Guess I'll move on."

"But it's too dark to travel," Silver protested.

"Silver's right," Jared said, shifting his gaze toward Smitty. He'd nearly forgotten the old man was there. "There's no reason you shouldn't bed down here for the night. We don't mind."

He couldn't believe he was saying it. What he really wanted was to be left alone with her, to hold her in his arms, to kiss the rosy smoothness of her mouth. What he really wanted was to see her naked in the firelight, to feel himself entering the silken sweetness of her body.

Which was exactly why he was inviting the old miner to stay. Maybe by tomorrow he would be able to get his thoughts back to where they belonged. He hadn't time to get involved with a female, least of all this one. Good lord, she was pregnant by another man! Had he sunk so low that he had no morals left at all?

"Well . . ." Smitty looked from Jared to Silver, then back again. "If you're sure I won't be underfoot, I sure wouldn't mind an evenin' of company. Gits mighty lonesome some nights."

"We're sure," Silver said softly.

Was there just the slightest quiver in her voice? Jared wondered. Was she inviting the old man to stay for the same reason he was? Could it be . . .

He stood. "I think I'll check on the horses." He swiveled on his boot heel and walked off into the darkness.

Silver lifted a hand and waved as Smitty rode toward the rising sun. The miner's chatter had gone on late into the night and had filled the awkward silence between Jared and Silver this morning. Or did it only seem awkward to her?

She turned around and glanced toward Jared as he kicked at the dying remains of their campfire. The muscles in her stomach tightened and she felt the now familiar thrill, the sense of uncertain danger.

"We should reach Green River City tonight. We'll get a couple rooms at the hotel for the night."

"Can we afford it?" She felt guilty for asking, knowing that she had some money secreted away.

"We'll make do."

She drew a deep breath. "Perhaps we should just take one room."

He turned his head slowly toward her. His eyes seemed dark and deadly.

"I . . . I mean, it would save money." She swallowed. "I could sleep on the floor if you want the bed."

"That won't be necessary, Miss Matlock."

"It's just—"

"Mount up," he snapped, his voice little more than a low growl.

Her anger flared. "Why do you do that?" she demanded.

He stepped up into the saddle. "Do what?"

"Snarl at me all the time!"

The Stetson's wide brim shadowed his eyes, but she knew he was looking at her. "Do I?" he asked after a lengthy silence.

"Yes." Silver felt close to tears. "I . . . I was only trying to help."

His spurs nudged the pinto up close to her. He leaned over in the saddle and placed his index finger beneath her chin, forcing her head back until she was looking into his face. She expected another surly reply or perhaps even an unconcerned shrug. Certainly not his tender response.

"I'm sorry, Miss Matlock. I think you deserve better." And then he leaned low and gently kissed her lips.

Chapter 11

Green River City, population two hundred and fifty, was much the same—although bigger than some—as any other western town built beside the Union Pacific rail line. It had its train station and mercantile, churches and saloons. There was a doctor's office and a jail and a hotel. There were the homes of merchants and settlers, large ones and small ones. And there was the street running through the center of town, spewing up a layer of dust with each passing horse and carriage, leaving everything the same dull shade of taupe.

Silver was relieved to reach the small town, was glad to enter the hotel room, happy to see the bed and washstand, pitcher and bowl. When Jared left her at the door, he told her to meet him in the hotel restaurant at seven, then said he was going to have a look around town.

She stepped over to the window and looked down on the dusty street below. Moments later, she saw Jared cross the street. His pace was unhurried, his strides almost catlike. He looked so totally unaware and unconcerned with what went on around him, yet she knew the opposite was true. He paused on the boardwalk, glanced quickly up the street, then entered a nearby saloon.

She wondered if he knew any pretty saloon owners in Green River as he had in Laramie. With a shake of her head, she let the lacy curtain fall back into place.

Throughout the day, she had been haunted by the feel of Jared's mouth upon hers. Even now she felt the tremble the touch had stirred within her. She'd never experienced anything like it before and was appalled by the rush of jealous anger she felt wondering about the saloon girls he might meet across the street, the idea that he might kiss one of them.

Her thoughts confused and troubled, Silver stripped out of her clothes and poured water into the washbasin. She cleansed away the evidence of the day's ride, then lay down on the bed. She closed her eyes and sought slumber, hoping to find escape from the strange longing that twisted her heart.

Doug Gordon's eyes lifted from his cards as Jared stepped through the saloon doors. There wasn't the faintest glimmer of recognition in them. Taking his cue, Jared moved off toward the bar and ordered himself a drink, then turned and leaned against the counter.

It didn't surprise Jared to find Doug in Green River. A Pinkerton detective during the war, Doug worked alone now, traveling the roads and rails as constantly as Jared and moving among the same class of people. Their paths had crossed often since Rick Cooper had first introduced them nearly four years ago.

Jared's eyes scanned the dimly lit saloon. It was small and narrow and obviously not geared toward the more affluent visitors or citizens of

Green River. The air smelled musty, and there was a coat of dust on the bottles that lined the counter beneath the small mirror behind the bar. From what Jared knew about Bob Cassidy, this wasn't likely to have been where he would come for a game of cards. But Jared had come to do his own card-playing, not to look for Bob. With any luck, he could make more than enough to cover the hotel rooms plus a nice meal for two.

As Doug collected his winnings, the two men grumbled, then rose from their chairs and left the saloon. Jared waited an appropriate length of time before picking up his whiskey glass and ambling toward the lone man remaining at the table.

Doug's black eyes glanced up as he shuffled the cards. "Care for a game, mister?"

"I might try a hand or two, if my luck's running right." He pulled out a chair and sat down. "My name's Stone. Jess Stone."

Jared nodded. "Newman. You from around these parts, Mr. Stone?"

"If you're smart, you're always just passin' through a town like this. I'm on my way back east eventually." He fanned the cards across the green felt, then scooped them up again. "And you?"

"Nevada. Virginia City."

Doug started to deal. "And what takes you there?"

"I'm following a star."

The detective's hand paused for a fraction of a second before tossing the next card. His gaze flicked around the saloon. When he spoke, his voice was low and guarded. "What makes you think so?"

"The last girl he tried to kill said that's what he told her."

"Did you get a description of him?"

Jared's fingers tightened around the whiskey

glass. "No. It was too dark for her to see much. Except for the scar. She saw that."

"Let's see your money," Doug said, his voice just a little louder as he pushed some coins toward the center of the table. Then, low again, "I wish I could be of help."

"Actually, maybe you can. There's another man. A gambler."

"Traveling with Cass?"

"No, but I think he's heading west by train. From what I know about him, he's a slick operator, popular with the ladies." Popular with one very particular lady, he thought as he threw in his ante.

Silver checked the watch pinned to her bodice. It was seven-thirty and there was still no sign of Jared. Maybe he had met up with a saloon girl after all. She motioned to the waitress. She wasn't going to wait for him a moment longer. She ordered a meal, being careful not to spend much of her hoarded funds.

She glanced down at her pink gingham dress, the only attractive item of clothing she'd brought with her. She hated to admit it, but she had dressed for Jared tonight. For some absurd reason, she'd tried her best to make herself look attractive. And he hadn't given her even enough thought to join her as promised.

"Evenin', miss."

She glanced up at the tall man of extreme girth who stood beside her table.

"I couldn't help seein' you was here by your lonesome, and I was thinkin' you might like a bit of company." He pulled out a chair and sat down. "My name's Winters. Will Winters."

She remained speechless as she stared at the man. He must have weighed two hundred and fifty pounds, at the very least. There were food stains on his white shirt just above his belt, and judging by the looks of his hair, it had been a while since he'd been introduced to soap and water.

Regaining her composure, she said, "You are mistaken, sir. I am not alone. My . . . *husband* will be joining me shortly." When he didn't move to leave, she added, "I'm sure you would be more comfortable if you found another table."

Winters's face grew blotched as he rose. His dark eyes glared hotly down at her. Silver raised her chin and returned his look, never wavering beneath it.

"Don't go thinkin' you're too good for the likes o' me, ma'am, 'cause you ain't." He turned away. "I'll prove it t'you," he muttered as he stalked away.

Silver drew a deep breath, then exhaled slowly. If Jared had been there, she wouldn't have had to deal with that odious fellow. Where the dickens was he?

Her food arrived, and she ate without tasting a thing. She was too upset with Jared. Where was he? she wondered again. Why hadn't he sent her word if he didn't intend to meet her there as arranged? Had he learned something? Was Bob in Green River right this moment?

She wished she understood why Jared treated her this way. There were those rare moments when she imagined he might even like her a little, but for the most part, it was obvious he would love to be rid of her.

Her eyes widened. *Rid of her.* Perhaps that's why he wasn't there now. Perhaps Jared wasn't even in Green River any longer. Perhaps he'd never meant to stay.

She rose from her chair and dropped her nap-

kin on the table beside her plate, her heart racing
with alarm. If he'd left her there, she would have
no choice but to go back to Masonville. Jared
would be smart enough to know that. She had to
find out.

The streets were deserted, the town quiet as the
mantle of evening settled over it. Silver hurried
along the irregular boardwalk toward the livery
stable.

Surely he hadn't deserted her. He didn't want
her along, thought of her as being in the way, but
he wouldn't just leave her. Surely he wouldn't.
She knew he was coldhearted, rude, even ruthless, but she couldn't help believing there was
something good inside him too. Surely she wasn't
mistaken about that. He couldn't be so cruel that
he would just leave her behind.

She lifted the bar that closed the livery doors,
then shoved them open. Light from the saloon
across the street spilled in from behind her, casting a yellow glow across the hard-packed dirt
floor. A horse snorted its objections at her sudden
intrusion. Another nickered. A third pawed at the
straw on the floor of its stall.

Silver moved quickly past each enclosure, looking for the familiar black-and-white coat. She
found the pinto in the far corner. He thrust his
head over the stall door at the sight of her. Letting
out a deep sigh of relief, she stroked his muzzle.

"I'm glad you're here, fella," she whispered.

His head bobbed, as if in agreement.

Feeling drained, Silver patted the animal's
neck, then turned and left the stable, barring the
door behind her.

Jared leaned back in his chair, glancing once
more at the cards in his hand, then wordlessly
pushed a silver dollar across the green felt sur-

face. His gaze shifted toward the man across from him.

"I'll see you." Another dollar joined those in the center of the table.

Jared lay down his cards. "Full house."

"I see your luck continues, Newman."

"At cards." He swept his winnings toward him.

Doug's mien was one of detached interest toward a stranger. His voice, though low, carried no inflection of importance. It was doubtful any of the few customers in the dingy saloon would care what the two card players were discussing, and his tone certainly invited no eavesdropping. "I could use your help, Jare."

Jared picked up the cards and shuffled them.

"I'm expecting a man through here in a day or two. There are men in Washington very anxious to meet and talk with him regarding some confidential documents which are now missing."

"Why Green River?" Jared asked as he began dealing.

"He's got family on a ranch north of town."

Jared picked up his own cards and fanned them in his hand.

"There'd be some money in it for you, my friend. Enough to buy a train ticket to Nevada."

"That's not much."

"But more than you have, right?" Doug chuckled, then motioned for another whiskey. "How about you?" he asked.

Jared turned down the offer. His head felt a little light already. "I need to get back to the hotel. I must be late as it is. What time is it?"

"Late?" One eyebrow raised. "Tell me about her."

"Who?" He leveled a gaze upon the man across from him.

"A man doesn't worry about being late unless there's a lady expecting him."

"You're not a bad detective—for a city slicker," he said softly, although there was no one close enough to hear his words. "Miss Matlock's the one who hired me to find Bob Cassidy, the gambler I was telling you about."

Doug's eyes widened. "She's traveling *with* you?"

"That's just how I feel about it," he answered gruffly. "But there were extenuating circumstances."

"I'll bet." Doug wore a knowing grin.

Jared didn't feel like arguing with Doug. Besides, maybe he was right. Maybe it was more than her plea for help that had persuaded him to bring her along. He certainly hadn't been acting like a man who'd taken pity on some poor female. It wasn't the thought of protecting her that plagued him night and day. He had to keep reminding himself more and more frequently that she was another man's woman.

"It was a pleasure meeting you, Mr. Stone." He emphasized the name Doug had given him earlier this evening as he pushed back his chair and stood up.

"You too, sir. I hope I'll see you again before you leave town." His eyes studied Jared. "Tomorrow, perhaps. I plan to take a ride out of town, look over some land. I'm thinkin' of goin' into ranching. Maybe you'd be interested in seeing it too."

Jared considered it a moment. If he could get enough money from helping Doug to pay their way to Virginia City, they could be there in just a couple of days rather than weeks. It seemed worth the delay. "I've thought of ranching a time or two. Maybe I will join you."

Doug's eyes registered his appreciation. "Good. Say about noon? I'll meet you at the livery."

"Noon it is. I look forward to it."

Jared stepped out into the still night air. The buildings across the street seemed a bit unsteady, swaying in the light evening breeze. He rubbed his eyes. It had been a long time since he'd allowed himself to have more than an occasional single drink. In his profession, he needed to keep his wits about him at all times. Maybe it was because he had been with Doug that he'd let himself indulge in the bottle of whiskey tonight. What he needed now was a hot meal and a good night's sleep.

He turned toward the hotel and began walking.

Chapter 12

Silver didn't see the man until she was almost upon him. Without a moon to light up the night, he was merely a large shadow in the darkened town. She moved to step around him. He moved in unison.

"Hello, pretty lady." His voice was deep, throaty. "What you doin' out all by your lonesome?"

It would have been hard enough to mistake his size, but his voice confirmed his identity. "Excuse me, Mr. Winters," she answered stiffly, keeping the sudden tension from her voice. "You're blocking my way."

"So I am, miss. So I am."

He acted with surprising quickness for a man of such bulk. He grabbed her arms and pulled her into the alley between two buildings, swathing them in an even darker curtain of night.

"You know, you weren't very polite to me this evenin'. All I wanted was a bite of supper with some pretty company. It wasn't too much t'ask of you. And you lied to me to boot. Tellin' me you got a husband. Don't you think I know how to ask a hotel clerk about you? You're travelin' with a man, all right, but you're not married. Don't even have the sense to give 'em the same last name for the registry. You think folks in this little town don't notice things like that."

She tried to remain calm, tried to keep the alarm from her voice. "Mr. Newman is escorting me to Nevada. He is in my employ. But that is no concern of yours, sir. Now, please be so kind as to unhand me and allow me to pass."

"You don't fool me, Miss High and Mighty. You're lyin' to me. I seen you with him when you come into town. I seen how you looked at him. You got no call to turn your nose up at me when you're sniffin' around the likes o' him."

"What are you talking—" she began, her voice rising in indignation. She felt the tip of a knife at the hollow of her throat and was quickly silenced.

"I don't think you want to make any noise," Winters threatened. "Now, you just behave and you won't get hurt."

Panic rose like bile in her throat. A scream began deep in her chest but was stifled by his mouth upon hers. His breath was hot and rank, and she feared she would vomit. A meaty hand mauled her breast, squeezing and pinching, pressing her even harder against the planks at her back. His body bounced against her in an ugly rhythm.

Winters slid his hand down her dress and began drawing up her skirt. Sheer terror gave her strength. Mindless of the knife, she shoved against his burly chest, tearing her mouth from his. "No!" The word came out strangled, barely audible, before the vile feel of him was upon her again.

The dull edge of the knife pressed against her flesh. "Behave yourself, little lady. Do ya hear me?"

This time, her voice was louder. "Help me! Please. Someone . . ."

His hand covered her face, smothering not only

her words but also her ability to draw air into her lungs.

"What's going on here?"

Winters spun away from her. She heard a grunt, then the sound of flesh hitting flesh. As the men grappled in the dark, Silver pressed herself against the building at her back, too stunned and afraid to move. It wasn't until she heard footsteps running away that she realized she'd recognized the voice of the man who had stopped her attacker.

"Jared?"

His reply was tight, breathless. "I'm here."

She moved toward the darker shadow against the dark ground. As she drew close, she heard the hiss of exhaled air.

"Are you hurt?" She leaned over him.

"Just my pride. What were you doing out here? Don't you ever think before you do something?"

His words felt like a slap in the face. She sucked in a quick breath as she straightened. Surprise kept her silent.

He rose slowly to his feet. "You were supposed to stay in the hotel."

She caught the scent of whiskey on his breath. Her eyes widened. Fury replaced surprise. "You dirty, no-good saddle tramp! You're drunk!"

He hadn't been looking for Bob. He'd been drinking in that saloon instead of dining with her. She'd been worried about him, and he'd never given her a thought.

"I hope you *are* hurt." She gave his chest a shove. "It would serve you right."

He'd gotten just what he deserved. Leaving her sitting alone in that restaurant while he cavorted in saloons—probably with a woman.

"Silver." There was that imperious tone of his again. "What were you doing out here?"

"I was looking for you, damn it. Did you think I *planned* to get dragged into a dark alley and . . . and . . ." A sudden sickness overtook her, and she had to stop talking and swallow hard. The last shreds of her courage vanished. Nothing remained but the remnants of her terror. If Jared hadn't come along when he had . . .

She began to cry. She fought against it, tried to choke back the sobs, but she couldn't seem to stop. Her whole body shook as tears flowed down her cheeks.

Jared's arms wrapped around her, and she was pulled against his chest. His hand stroked her hair while he waited for her to cry herself out. He felt so strong and solid and safe. It was so easy to lean into him, to give herself over to the comfort he provided. Within the shelter of his arms, she could forget her fears.

When the sobs subsided, he asked, "Did he hurt you?" One hand rose to her face, lightly stroking her cheek.

"No." Her voice was shaky. "I'm all right." She drew a deep breath, then whispered, "You came in time."

"We'd better get inside," he said at last. He placed an arm around her shoulders as he turned toward the street, drawing her with him.

She heard a sound, like a strangled groan deep in his chest, as he bent slightly forward. "Jared, you *are* hurt. What's wrong? Should I get a doctor?"

"No. Let's just get inside."

She slipped an arm around his waist. She thought his breathing sounded shallow and irregular. "I *should* get a doctor," she said as they began walking. "And I should send for the sheriff."

"No," he said again, more firmly this time. "I'll take care of this myself. Do you hear me, Silver?"

Stepping up onto the boardwalk outside the hotel, golden lamplight spilling through the lobby window, she could see him clearly for the first time. His face had an unhealthy pallor. He was pressing his free hand against his side. She could tell he was trying to walk straight, to not lean too heavily upon her, but he was only partially succeeding. He wavered as they passed through the open doorway.

"I really shouldn't have had so much to drink," he told her. "Whiskey's a weakness of mine, love. You might as well know it now."

His words were so unexpected, she paused and glanced up at him. She'd been so certain he was hurt, that he'd been injured while rescuing her from that wretched man. But he wasn't hurt. Only drunk.

The desk clerk looked up from his black book of accounts, glancing at them over the rim of his glasses. He frowned, then looked away once more.

"You'd better get me to my room," Jared slurred, "before I pass out in the middle of the lobby."

Once again, she'd been proven a fool. For one moment, she'd thought he was truly concerned about her. She'd thought she'd heard a note of caring in his voice. But instead it was merely the alcohol talking. She felt . . . betrayed. It would serve him right if she let him drop right then and there. He could lie on the lobby floor and rot for all she cared.

"Next time . . ." He had the gall to grin at her. "Next time, you'll stay inside where you belong."

That did it. She pulled away from him, and just as she'd suspected, he toppled to the floor.

"Find your room on your own," she snapped, fully intending to leave him where he was.

"Hold it, ma'am," the desk clerk interrupted. "He can't stay there. I'll have to call the sheriff."

Silver gritted her teeth. She couldn't have him put in jail, no matter how mad she was at him. Time was too short, too precious to be wasted.

Jared was already starting to rise. He swayed to the right, then teetered to the left before she caught his arm.

"Come on," she grumbled as she wrapped his arm around her shoulders, bracing herself against his weight.

She would get even with him some other time. God help her, she would.

He could feel the warm blood oozing through his fingers. He willed himself to stay erect as they neared his room next to Silver's. If she sent for the doctor or the sheriff, there would be questions he would just as soon not answer. He'd rather not call attention to himself. Not with Doug Gordon in town on a case, and not until he knew more about Silver's assailant.

Besides, this was personal. Very personal. The man had threatened Silver, and Jared wasn't going to let him get away with it.

Silver's forced assistance ended the moment they entered his room. Just as she'd done in the lobby, she slipped from beneath his arm, this time giving him a rough shove toward the bed.

"You mangy varmint!" she began. "I've had just about all I'm going to take from—"

"Silver." His voice was low and strained, and he was surprised she even heard him. "Close the door and light the lamp. Then get me some water and a towel.''

He closed his eyes, trying to keep pressure on the bleeding wound. He was fairly certain the knife had missed anything vital, but it was painful and bleeding hard. He heard the match striking, listened as she lifted the glass chimney, then set it back in place. There was a moment's quiet before he heard her sharp intake of breath.

''Oh, God! Jared, look at you.''

''The water and towel, Silver,'' he ground out. He sat up and struggled out of his shirt. Leaning against the wall at the head of the bed, he examined the wound in his side. The knife had made a clean entry and withdrawal. The hole was relatively small. He'd seen worse. He'd *had* worse.

He cursed himself for his own stupidity. He was a long way from being the bumbling drunk he'd portrayed for the desk clerk's benefit, but his senses had been dulled by whiskey. If not, he would have been alert to a weapon. He never would have stepped into that alley unprepared, not even in response to a woman's plea for help. He would have had his gun drawn and ready.

But it could have been worse, he reminded himself. He might not have come along when he did. He might not have heard her cry. He chose not to think about the consequences of that scenario.

Silver brought the water pitcher and a towel over to the bed. Her face looked pale in the lamplight. ''You should have a doctor,'' she said once again. ''You're losing a lot of blood.''

He shook his head. ''It's not as bad as it looks. Get me some bandages out of the saddlebags. And some whiskey. There's some of that in the saddlebags, too.''

"Haven't you had enough . . ." she began, then purposefully closed her mouth, stopping her protest.

"Yes, I have." He grimaced, then drew in a breath. He swallowed forcibly, his voice sounding gruff as he continued, "But it's not a drink I'm after. Just get the whiskey."

He didn't mean to sound angry at her, nor did he really blame her for what had happened tonight. She was looking for him, she'd said. So it was his fault she'd been attacked. She should have been safe because she *was* traveling with him, but he'd left her alone.

She'd done it to him again. She was making him feel guilty for things he'd said and done. She had him wanting to apologize. And he didn't much like it.

Apparently unaware of the turmoil she'd caused him, Silver worked quickly and silently, following his instructions to the letter. She helped him bathe the wound, then poured whiskey over it before wrapping a wide swath of white material tightly around his rib cage several times.

Jared was exhausted by the time she was finished. He lay back on the bloodstained bedding. "Thanks for your help, Silver." He took hold of her hand. Her slim fingers felt cool against his hot, callused palms. "Are *you* all right?"

"I'm fine. Really I am."

He closed his eyes. "You'd better get some sleep. Be sure to lock your door," he whispered as waves of darkness overtook him.

Silver waited until she was certain he was in a deep sleep before she went to the end of the bed and tugged off his boots. That accomplished, she pulled a light blanket over his lean body, covering his bandaged chest. Then she turned the lamp down and sat on the chair beside the bed.

She stared at Jared for a long time, noting the changes that sleep had brought to his features. The hard lines around his mouth had softened and the deep furrows above his brows, so noticeable when he was frowning at her, were smoothed away.

Unable to help herself, she leaned forward and brushed back the lock of hair that had fallen across his forehead. It felt unexpectedly silky. Next, she allowed her fingers to slid across his temple and down the side of his face. The day's growth of beard was prickly.

His mustache wasn't prickly. She remembered the way it had felt those times he'd kissed her. She'd found it surprisingly . . . pleasant.

She moved her hand to his mouth, tracing the curve of his lower lip. She could feel his warm breath on the back of her hand, a comforting sensation. He was all right. Thank God, he was all right.

She'd been so frightened when she turned and saw the crimson stain spreading over his shirt. She'd thought he would surely bleed to death before her eyes. But even in pain, he had remained calm, his voice commanding as he told her how to care for him.

What kind of man was he? He seemed so remote from everything—from her, from life, even from pain. At times she'd wondered if he could feel anything, if he even had a heart to feel with. But he wasn't like that. Not truly. Although she had sensed the underlying danger of the man, for some reason, she wasn't afraid of him. Not any longer. She didn't understand him, but she wanted to, very much.

Who are you, bounty? she wondered. *Who are you really?*

With a sigh, she sank back against the chair and prepared to keep vigil over him through the night.

Chapter 13

Jared resisted consciousness. It meant acknowledging the nagging pain in his right side. But a sixth sense told him the sun was already well up, and they should have been on the trail hours ago. No. Not the trail. He remembered it now. He was supposed to meet Doug at the livery at noon.

Determinedly, he opened his eyes. He was right. Sunlight filtered through the flimsy curtains at the window. He wondered what Silver was doing. Was she still asleep or was she, perhaps, having a look around Green River City? He doubted either was true. Not after last night's scare.

He turned his head, intent on rising. That's when he saw her. She was, indeed, still asleep—right there in his room. She was sitting up in the chair beside the bed, her arms folded on top of the washstand, her head cradled on her wrists. There were bloodstains on her pretty pink dress, and he knew she had stayed with him all night. Why?

As if she sensed a change, her eyes opened and she straightened in the chair. She looked at him. For a moment, she had that same sleep-dazed look she always had upon first arising. He liked the look. He always had. He imagined she would look like that after being thoroughly loved.

Then she smiled. Jared felt her gaze flow over him like warm honey. "You should have gotten some rest. What are you doing here?"

"I thought you might need something in the night."

He pushed himself up against the wall, wincing as he did so.

"I'd better have a look at you. The dressing must need to be changed."

"I'm fine." He shoved the blanket aside. The white wrap had only a small stain, the crimson blood now dried to a dark brown blot.

"Don't argue with me, Jared. You should have seen a doctor last night. What if you need stitches?"

"And are you going to sew me up if I need any?" he asked, a wry grin breaking the grim line of his mouth.

"I could if I had to." She was perfectly serious. "I watched Doc Fisher sew up Sapphire once when she cut her arm."

"Well, I'm not your sister."

Her voice sounded different—strained—when she spoke. "No, you're not." She didn't look him in the eye. "Now, let's get that unwrapped."

For some reason he couldn't quite put his finger on, he obeyed without further protest, leaning forward as she loosened the cotton bandage and unwound it until the wound was revealed. He caught a whiff of the lavender cologne she always wore. Her blue-black hair fell invitingly over one shoulder. Her fingers lightly brushed his skin, and suddenly he was imagining her touching him in other ways. The muscles in his abdomen contracted.

"I'm sorry. Did I hurt you?"

"No," he replied in a clipped voice. He wished she had hurt him. He wished he could feel the pain again. It would take his mind off the potent desire that filled him.

Her gaze lifted, meeting his. Her gray eyes widened, as if she saw something in his that alarmed her.

It should alarm her, he thought. It should scare her to death. If he had just a fraction less self-control, he would pull her down onto the bed this very minute and make love to her—slow, languorous love, exploring her body until he knew it better than his own. And he wouldn't give a thought to her fiancé and the baby she carried.

He swallowed. "Well, what do you thing, Doc? Do I need stitches?" He tried to keep his tone light.

"No. You're going to have a scar, I think. But it should be just a thin white line. Nothing much."

Jared grunted. "I've got others to match. They don't matter—unless a woman minds them, of course." He could so very easily have asked, Would you mind the scars, Silver?

She moved away from the bed, crossing to the window.

He watched as she pushed the curtains aside. Was he imagining it or did her fingers tremble? Was there a flush of pink in her cheeks?

"Bob has a scar," she said in a whisper.

Why did she have to bring him up now? Was it because she understood what he was thinking? Was she trying to keep Bob between them, to remind him that she wasn't free? "Yeah, you finally told me about it in Laramie."

"No. Not the one on his jaw. I'd forgotten about the other one until just the other day. I . . .

I only saw it the once when . . ." She shrugged. "I suppose it doesn't matter."

"Any description you can tell me matters. He might not always be gambling and winning so that folks notice him. What about the scar?"

Silver continued to stare down at the street. "It was quite large. White and pink and formed in an almost perfect star shape." She turned around, pointing to the valley between her breasts. "It was right here. I remember now that I thought it was ugly ."

Years of practice kept his expression blank, but inside, a rampant storm tore through him. He should have known. He should have guessed. What a fool he'd been not to figure it out before. Bob Cassidy. Cass. They were one and the same. He and Silver had always been seeking the same man.

And then he was smote by another revelation. Cass had been with Silver. He had held her, made love to her, sired a child that even now grew in her womb. Cass, that demented, murdering son of a bitch, and Silver.

He felt sick to his stomach.

He wanted to break something.

He thought he should feel repulsed by the knowledge that Silver had been with Cass, had allowed him to seduce her, but instead, he felt relief. Relief that she was still alive. Relief that Cass hadn't beaten and abused her as he had others.

The others . . .

So many others . . .

There was nothing in his voice to hint at his rage. "Tell me about Bob."

"I've told you everything."

"I don't mean his physical description or what

he does for a living. I mean about the man. Tell me about *him*, Silver."

Her alabaster complexion, always fair, lost all hint of color. There was a lost look about her eyes that gripped his heart.

"He wasn't like anyone I'd ever known before. The first time I saw him, he was wearing a fancy suit like you'd see in a city back east, I suppose, but not in Masonville. He had a way of talking . . . I don't know. So smooth. Kind of poetic. He brought me flowers and gifts all the time. He said he'd been waiting to meet a girl like me to fall in love with." Silver sat on the chair near the window and returned her gaze outside. Her voice was soft. "There was something *rich* about him. I don't mean money. *He* was golden. His hair and his skin. He had such refined hands."

Jared had always thought he would know Cass on the street if he ever saw him, but his image had been so different. He'd imagined him as dark and coarse and heavy, perhaps unshaven, always unkempt. An equal with the Lansing brothers.

Refined hands. Refined hands upon Katrina, beating and cutting her. Refined hands on Silver, removing her clothes and . . .

"I never admitted it to anyone, but sometimes, he frightened me. He'd be telling me he loved me, and yet . . ." She swallowed, and he saw a glimmer of unshed tears in her eyes. "I know now I was just a diversion while he was in Masonville. Maybe he only chose me because of my parents' store. Or because I was so naive. I'd never had a beau before." She paused, then added, "I'm so ashamed."

What would it do to her to know the type of man Cassidy really was? Jared asked himself. Nausea twisted his gut.

She turned toward him, straightening in the

chair, sniffing back the tears. "I should have known he didn't love me. Mother always told me no man ever would. I'm too tall and unattractive and . . . and unconventional. I should have accepted that and learned to live with it." With a little shake of her head, she rose and came toward him, her expression completely businesslike now. "We'd better get another bandage on you before you move and start bleeding again."

Jared grabbed her hand as she reached for the bandages beside the bed. "Do you still love him?"

She stared at him for the longest time, myriad emotions whirling in her silvery-gray eyes. But when she spoke, her voice was firm. "No. I don't love him. But I have to find him. I have to try to get back the money he stole and . . . and . . ." She fell silent as she returned her gaze to his side.

He allowed her to administer to his injury, his mind in turmoil. He knew what she hadn't said. She had to tell Bob about the baby. But once she knew who her fiancé really was—the type of man, the things he'd done—she wouldn't marry him. She would go back to live in Masonville, to face the scorn of bearing a child out of wedlock, a child whose father was a cold-blooded murderer, a man who would soon die at the end of a rope.

He should tell her. He should tell her now. But he couldn't. He kept imagining Marlene Matlock and the things she would say to Silver. He couldn't send her back to that. Not yet.

He looked at Silver as she turned away to discard the soiled bandages she'd removed earlier. Did she really believe she was unattractive? It didn't seem possible that she wasn't aware of her unique beauty. What possible reasons could a mother have for telling her daughter that no man would ever love her, would ever want to marry her? Surely Marlene hadn't believed what she was telling Silver. The fool woman had made her daughter easy prey for a man with a few kind phrases to whisper in a gullible girl's ears.

Cass had known she was beautiful. Cass had seen how desirable she was.

The images in Jared's head were enough to drive him crazy. Rage seemed to be burning a whole in his gut. He had to think of something else. Anything else but Cass and Silver.

He swung his legs over the side of the bed. "We'd better get something to eat. I have some business to take care of before we leave Green River."

"Are you . . . are you going to see the sheriff about what happened last night?"

"Not right away. I want to see if I can find out anything on my own first." Seeing her puzzled look, he added, "I work best alone." He pulled on a clean shirt.

He couldn't tell her what was really bothering him. Cass had violated her. Winters had tried to violate her. For now, the two men had become one and the same in his mind. He didn't need help from the law for what he had to do.

Silver removed her pink dress, then sat on the bed and looked at the bloodstains. Would they ever come out or was the dress ruined? She should probably just throw it away. It had been foolish to bring it along, foolish to wear it last night, foolish to think Jared would even notice.

Her face warmed. She *was* a fool. Jared scarcely knew she was alive. She was a mere inconvenience, a necessity to help in locating Bob, a means to an end, that end being the reward she'd promised him.

Why had she told him that she had never had a beau until Bob? He must have guessed the truth long ago. He only had to look at her to know she was a spinster and always would be. Added to that, she'd admitted she didn't love Bob, that she only followed after him because of the robbery. But even that wasn't the worst of it. She had allowed him to go on believing she was pregnant with Bob's child. She'd let him believe she'd been intimate with a man she didn't love.

Compounding everything was the lingering sense of guilt that clung to her over last night's encounter with Winters. She felt dirty, soiled by his hands and mouth. Jared was right. She shouldn't have been out alone after dark. She felt a flash of indignation. If Jared had bothered to tell her where he was going, if he'd returned when he said he would, it wouldn't have happened.

She shook her head, the righteous feeling gone as quickly as it had come. No, she couldn't blame him. It was her own fault. All her fault. And Jared had risked his life to save her. He could have been killed in that alley. Even now, he wasn't out of danger. She knew he meant to even the score with Winters, and she was afraid.

She rose from the bed and began pacing across the room, from door to window to door again. She folded her hands in front of her, rubbing the knuckles of one hand with the fingers of the other, pressing so hard that the skin turned red.

What if he was killed trying to avenge her? It was her fault that her parents were about to lose everything. Was she going to be responsible for Jared's death as well? She couldn't bear to have that on her conscience too.

She had to do something.

She had to find him and stop him.

Chapter 14

Since Winters had given his name to Silver in the restaurant, it wasn't difficult for Jared to find out what he needed to know. He learned from the hotel clerk that Will Winters lived with his brother, Mike, on a hardscrabble farm a few miles southeast of Green River.

Jared rode toward the small shack, the pain in his side a grim reminder of why he was there. He stopped his horse still some distance away and studied the area. The terrain was rolling and treeless. The small patch of ground which had been plowed under seemed adequate only for growing weeds.

His eyes moved to the ramshackle house and the lean-to that served for a barn. There was a single window near the door of the one-room structure, a faded curtain hanging behind the soiled glass. A large gray horse stood in a corral, head low, tail swatting flies. A saddle hung over the top rail. One horse, one saddle—which most likely meant only one of the brothers was home. There was a dog pen at the far corner of the house, close to the corral. The hounds milled and whined, setting up a holler at the sight of him.

There was only the flutter of the curtain at the window for a warning, but it was all Jared needed. Pulling his rifle from the scabbard, he vaulted from his pinto, giving a shout to drive the horse away. Then he ran for it, diving into the cover of a ravine. He heard the shatter of glass. A bullet ricocheted in the dirt only inches behind him.

"Hold your fire!" he shouted as he leaned against the ground at his back. His fingers touched his side. It felt warm, and he was fairly sure his movements had started the wound bleeding again.

"You're on private land, mister, and you'd better git."

"I'm looking for Will Winters."

"You found him."

"We need to talk, Winters."

"What about?"

"The young lady you laid your filthy hands on last night."

"I don't know who you are, mister, but I got no quarrel with you. You just git back on your horse and ride out."

Jared checked the bullets in his Winchester, then his Peacemaker Colt. "You're wrong about that, Winters. We've definitely got a quarrel. You made it one when you pushed that knife into me. Either give yourself up and come with me to the sheriff or we can take care of it here, just the two of us. It's up to you."

"You're mighty sure o' yourself for a man who's stuck in a ditch."

Two more bullets struck the ground just above Jared's head.

Snaking along on his belly, Jared worked his way north in the ravine. He was moving away from the house but also at an angle that would eventually put him out of sight of the window. He stopped once and carefully peeked over the rim. He could still see the rifle barrel poking through the broken glass. Winters apparently wasn't smart enough to guess what Jared would do.

He moved on, inching his way through the dirt and rocks and thorns that covered the ground, ignoring the ache that had started up again in his side.

Silver descended the hotel stairs just as the man stopped before the lobby desk.

"Jared Newman's room. Which is it?" he asked the clerk.

Silver stopped still as she studied the stranger.

"He isn't in. I saw him ride out of town some time ago," the clerk replied.

"You're sure?"

"I'm sure."

The stranger frowned. "Was there a lady with him? The woman he's traveling with?"

"No, sir. He was alone." The clerk's gaze moved toward the stairs. His eyes widened when he saw Silver standing there.

Observing the clerk's reaction, the stranger turned around. His dark gaze swept the length of her, returning quickly to her face. "Miss Matlock, I presume," he said as he removed his hat and bowed briefly.

She wasn't sure how she should respond. He knew her name. He was looking for Jared. But who was *he?*

"May we talk privately, Miss Matlock? Perhaps in the restaurant?" He motioned toward the door connecting the hotel lobby to the dining room.

Making up her mind, Silver nodded and came on down the stairs, then led the way into the restaurant. She selected a table in a far corner—

secluded enough for a private conversation, yet public enough in case she felt need of assistance. She was, she thought, becoming a bit more prudent about such things.

The man held out a chair for her, then took his own across from her. He set his gray-felt bowler on the corner of the table. When he spoke, his voice was low but not threatening. "My name is Gordon, Miss Matlock. Doug Gordon. I'm a friend of Jared's. I guess you'd say we're in the same line of work."

He was dressed in city clothes, dandified rather than the hard-bitten trail look that she equated with a bounty hunter—and with Jared. He was, perhaps, as tall as she, but broad of shoulder and sturdy of build. His dark hair was swept back from his face—a pleasant face with expressive black eyes and patrician features.

"Mr. Newman isn't here now, but he should return soon," she replied, noncommittally.

Doug leaned forward, bracing his forearms on the table. "As I said, Miss Matlock, Jared and I are friends. We were together last night. He agreed to meet me at noon today for a little help on some business I'm transacting near here. It's not like him not to show up, and when I saw his horse was gone . . ."

She continued to eye him skeptically. At the moment, she wasn't ready or willing to trust anyone.

As if he understood her reticence, Doug sighed and sat back in his chair. "You're from a little town near Denver, Colorado. You hired Jared to find a missing person, Bob Cassidy by name. A gambler by profession. You've got reason to believe he's traveling west by train." He leaned forward again. "Listen, Miss Matlock, I've got a feeling something's wrong here. Now why don't you tell me what it is.''

Silver stared into the man's dark eyes and knew he was telling the truth. How else could he have known all about her if Jared hadn't told him? She knew Jared well enough to know he didn't talk much, especially to strangers. She glanced down at her hands, folded in her lap. ''Jared was injured after he left you last night. He was stabbed.''

''Stabbed?'' Doug got to his feet. ''Take me to him.''

''He's not here.'' She looked up at him. ''He went looking for the man who did it. There wasn't anything I could do to stop him.'' Her throat tightened. ''He shouldn't have gone. I think he was hurt worse than he'll admit.''

''Do you know who the man was?''

Her cheeks flushed as she remembered everything about the previous night. ''He said his name was Winters. He . . . he wanted to have supper with me, and when I refused . . . He . . . he accosted me in the alley. Jared came along just in time.'' She forced up her chin as she rose from the table. ''He wouldn't go to the sheriff. He said he wanted to handle it alone, that . . . that this was a personal matter between him and Mr. Winters.''

''I can imagine.'' Doug put his hat on his head. ''He might have overlooked a man stabbing him, but not an attack on you.''

Silver felt her pulse quicken. Had Jared told this man that he cared for her?

''No matter how bad he was hurt,'' Doug continued, ''he wouldn't let a man get away with hurting a woman.''

Her heart fell. Of course. It wasn't her honor he was out to avenge. It was womanhood in general. Jared hadn't known it was Silver in that dark alley. He had heard a woman's cry and responded to it. That's why he'd gone into the alley and that's why he was after Winters now.

But that didn't make her any less responsible for his injuries, and something deep inside told her he needed her, that he was hurting far more than he'd let on. She had to find him before it was too late.

"Mr. Gordon." She reached out, touching his arm. "Are you going looking for Jared?"

He nodded. "He'd do the same for me."

"Then I'm coming too."

"I'm sorry, Miss Matlock. I can't let you do that."

She opened her mouth to argue with him, then closed it quickly. He was too much like Jared to waste time arguing with him. "You're right. I'd just be in the way. I'll wait here. But please hurry, Mr. Gordon."

"Don't worry," Doug said to her. "Jared will probably be back with Winters before I even find out which way he rode out of town."

Hell! He was bleeding like a stuck pig. He supposed Silver had been right, after all. He should have seen the Green River sawbones and gotten the damned thing sewn up. But Jared never had taken much liking to doctors and so avoided them whenever possible. Besides, he really hadn't thought it was much of a stab wound. Little more than a scratch. More blood than anything else.

But blood loss was becoming the big concern. He knew how quickly it could sap a man's strength.

Well, there wasn't anything he could do about it until he settled this matter with Winters. Once he got back to town he would see the doctor.

Holding the rifle in front of him, he edged up the embankment. He could see the side and back of the shack now. There was a long stretch of barren ground between himself and the building, but as long as Winters was watching for him out the window, he should be safe even if he couldn't run as fast as usual.

The gray horse lifted its head, its ears darting forward as it stared toward Jared, then beyond.

Jared tensed. Suddenly, he spun around, whipping the rifle into position. A split second later, a bullet whizzed by his ear, and he returned the fire.

The man stood no more than fifty feet away. He dropped his arm to his side. His gun dangled from his index finger, then fell to the ground beside him. He stared at Jared, his expression one of surprise and disbelief. Finally, he crumpled forward, his eyes still open—and sightless.

"What's all the shootin' about, mister?"

Jared flipped onto his stomach once again. He could see Winters at the corner of the house. He'd lost the element of surprise. "Give yourself up, Winters. You haven't got anybody to help you now."

Cautiously, Winters leaned away from the house. Jared knew he must be able to see the man's body from there.

"Mike?" he shouted. "Damn it all, Mike. Answer me."

"He's dead, Winters. Your brother's dead."

There was a pause before his quarry shouted, "So're you, mister."

Winters might be right, Jared thought as another spasm shot up his side. He didn't bother to look down. He knew his shirt was bright with blood.

* * *

Silver watched the dust rising from the road ahead. She tried to stay as far back from Doug Gordon as possible without losing sight of him altogether. She refused to consider that if he was any good at his job he would surely know she was following him. And if he did know, she hoped he wouldn't take the time to try to send her back. She felt an ever-increasing urgency to find Jared.

She tried telling herself she was only worried because she had a vested interest in Jared's good health. If he was badly hurt, if he was laid up for any length of time, they might lose track of Bob, might not ever find him. She had to be certain he stayed healthy and strong so he could complete the job she'd hired him to do.

She heard gunfire in the distance. Her stomach tightened as she dug her heels into Cinder's sides. The mare shot forward, ears pressed back against her head.

There were five of them—five snarling, half-crazed hounds. They shot around the corner of the shack with teeth bared, driven by the command of their master.

Jared felled three in quick succession before the last two were upon him. He swung his rifle at the closest, knocking it away with the barrel. Even as he tightened his finger on the trigger, he felt teeth sinking into his arm. In a reflex motion, he struck the animal on the head with the rifle stock. The dog fell away, stunned. Jared didn't hesitate before jerking the rifle back into position and firing.

Out of the corner of his eye, he saw Winters appear at the side of the house even as the surviving dog lunged for Jared's jugular. The rifle fell from his hands as he grabbed the animal by the neck, holding him away as they rolled into the bottom of the ravine. In the back of his mind, he knew he was almost out of time and luck. Winters would shoot him while he was grappling with the dog.

He heard the gunfire and expected to feel the impact of the bullet entering his body—but it didn't happen. He had no more than a fraction of a second to contemplate his good fortune as he fought off the crazed hound. A second shot sounded. A high-pitched yelp split the air, then suddenly the dog stilled. Jared shoved the animal's dead weight from his chest and reached for his rifle.

Silver's blood was pounding in her temples in matching rhythm with Cinder's galloping hooves. Through panic-dazed eyes, she saw Doug leap from his saddle and fire his rifle. She saw Winters, standing in the open not far from the shack, topple forward. She heard the second shot, followed by the dog's yelp.

But where was Jared? She couldn't see Jared.

She pressed her heels into the buckskin's sides, asking for ever-greater speed. She was vaguely aware of Doug as she sped by him, but her eyes were trained straight ahead. He was there. But where?

Jared sprang up from the ravine, rifle ready. He froze as his gaze found Winter's body, then he whirled in her direction. For a heart-stopping moment, she thought he would shoot her before he realized who she was.

''Jared!'' She jerked back on the reins. Cinder sat back on her hind legs, sliding to a stop.

His shirt was torn and bloodied. Perspiration dotted his forehead, and pain was etched into his face. The sight took her breath away. She'd been right. He could have died. She might have lost him.

She slid from the saddle and hurried toward him. "Jared," she whispered again as her arm slipped around his back.

"What are you doing here?" he asked through gritted teeth.

"I had to come."

He was scowling at her, and she knew that only his pain kept him from venting the full heat of his anger. "Don't you ever learn? I told you to stay put."

"I couldn't."

"Damn it, woman!" he whispered as a grimace contorted his features. "You'll be the death of me yet." He touched the wound in his side, then looked at the blood on his fingers.

She felt herself grow cold inside. She could try to deny it all she wanted, but Jared Newman had wormed his way into her heart. She hadn't wanted it, had tried to stop it, but it had happened anyway.

She was falling in love with a man who despised her.

Chapter 15

"Sorry about not lending you a hand with your suspect, Doug," Jared said as he lay on his bed.

"Turned out not to matter anyhow," the detective answered. "I got word today my man's been found in San Francisco. I'm on my way there to pick him up now."

"It was lucky for me you were here."

"Just returning a favor. I owed you after Wichita."

Jared nodded, remembering the one time they'd officially worked together.

Doug rose from the chair near the bed. "Well, I've gotta catch a train. Sorry there wasn't that reward to share that I'd promised." He reached out and shook Jared's hand. "Hope you find what you're looking for in Virginia City."

"Thanks. I've got a feeling he won't get away this time."

"Do yourself a favor, Jare. You stay put for a couple days like the doctor said."

Again Jared nodded. As anxious as he was to be after Cass, he knew he had to be in top shape when that confrontation took place. He wanted no room for error when it came to bringing in his family's killer. He'd waited too long, worked too hard for that day to foul it up now.

Doug placed his gray bowler over his dark hair. "One more thing, my friend. Take care of Miss Matlock."

"I'll make sure she doesn't go walking alone at night again."

"That's not what I meant, and you know it." He opened the door, glancing back toward the bed. "There's something special between you two, and you'd be wise to realize it. A woman like that can make a man forget a lot of the bad he's seen. She can remind a man about what's good in life . . . like a home and children. Things you an' me don't have."

"You're crazy."

"Am I?" Doug cocked his head to one side as he took hold of the doorknob. "That woman could change your life for the better, my friend. You wouldn't be sorry."

The door closed behind Doug.

Home . . . Jared hadn't allowed himself to think about it much. But now, maybe he could afford to. With the bounty that Ted Harrison was offering for his wife's killer, he could buy back Fair Acres. He could rebuild the stables. He could fulfill the promise he'd made at his father's grave and make the Newman name stand for something in Kentucky again. Maybe he could actually have a home.

He closed his eyes and tried to envision Fair Acres the way it had been. Only it didn't come to him quite that way. Instead of his mother and father on the veranda, it was Silver he imagined. Silver with her tousled ebony hair and a baby in her arms. Could Doug be right? Could he ever enjoy that kind of peace and happiness? Perhaps . . . just perhaps . . .

Reality intruded. His blissful daydream was replaced with the memory of the string of thieves and robbers and murderers that he'd captured through the years. He kept seeing their victims. He kept seeing himself sleeping on the ground or huddled beneath a tree during a rainstorm or drawing his gun and firing.

Kentucky and the life he'd known there seemed only a dream. The hole in his side and the gun hanging in its holster on the headboard—these things were his present and his future. This was his reality. Bob Cassidy had killed the man Jared used to be as surely as he had killed his parents, Katrina, and Ted Harrison's wife. He could go back to Kentucky, but he couldn't ever go home again. And there was no room in his life for Silver Matlock.

A light rap sounded on the door.

"Yes."

The door opened to admit her. "I brought you something to eat," she said, carrying the tray across the room and setting it on the washstand near the bed. Straightening, she gazed down at him. "You look better this morning."

Her ebony hair swirled over her shoulders. Her gray eyes were alight with concern. Her mouth, pink and inviting, turned up at the corners in a half-smile. She'd never looked more beautiful to him than she did at that moment. Was it because the peaceful vision of her and Fair Acres still lingered in the back of his mind? Had Doug planted a thought that was destined to plague him unmercifully?

"I feel better." Surprised, he realized it was true, not because he was healing so rapidly but because she was with him.

She removed the napkin from over the food. "Are you hungry?"

Delicious odors filled the air.

"I am now," he replied.

She handed him a plate heaped high with fried eggs and ham. "I'll come back for your things later."

"No. Don't go." He saw the surprise in her eyes. "Stay and keep me company." He felt awkward for asking, yet couldn't help himself. He wanted her with him. "I'm not used to being idle," he explained.

"All right. If . . . if you think it will help."

"I'll eat. You talk."

"What should I talk about?"

"Anything you want. Tell me about you, about your life in Masonville. Anything."

Silver settled into the chair beside the bed. She folded her hands in her lap and kept her eyes on them. "There's nothing much to tell really. Father owned a store in Ohio before bringing us to Colorado. I was seven when we moved. I remember it was terribly exciting and rather scary, leaving everybody we knew. Mother didn't want to move, but once we were there and the mercantile was so successful, she seemed happy enough. There were so many miners going through Masonville back then, so many gold strikes. Mother always thought we were going to be richer than anyone. She was always telling Sapphire that one day we were going to move to Denver and become part of society there where we belonged. Sapphire was going to marry someone important and very, very wealthy."

"What about you? What sort of man were you going to marry?"

"Oh . . ." She gave a little shrug. "I don't think Mother ever believed I would marry. I was such a homely, gawky child, always taller than all the boys. What hope could she have of ever making an attractive young lady of me?''

Jared set his half-empty plate aside. ''You really believe that, don't you?''

''Believe what?'' She looked at him with a puzzled expression.

''That you're unattractive.''

Her silver-gray eyes, so round and wide and fringed with sooty lashes, gazed back at him, revealing far more than he cared to see. When she spoke, it was with the force of brutally honest reflection. ''Oh, it wasn't just my looks, Mr. Newman. I never could master the womanly arts well enough to please my mother. I'd much rather be riding horses or hiding away somewhere, reading a book. Mother says all those books gave me radical notions about what's proper for a young woman to do in life.''

''Like what sort of things?''

''Oh, I don't know.''

For a moment he thought she would shrug off his question, but then her eyes began to twinkle and a smile blossomed.

''Like women voting, for instance. Why shouldn't women be allowed to vote? Everyone just assumes a woman is good for only one thing—to take care of her home and family. It just isn't so. We're just as smart as any man. If I needed to, I could run the mercantile without anyone's help. I know how to keep the accounts and order supplies as well as Papa.''

''But you couldn't stock the shelves by yourself. You're not strong enough.''

''Oh, pooh!'' She waved her hand. ''I could hire men to do the hard labor, but it doesn't have anything to do with my ability to think. Why, there's no reason why a woman couldn't be a governor or even the president. That doesn't take physical strength either."

Jared couldn't stifle a laugh. "A woman president?"

Her chin tilted upward. "Go ahead and laugh, Mr. Newman, but it could happen someday. If men weren't too afraid to give us the right to think for ourselves and to run our own lives, you'd see what we could do. We would own our own businesses and serve in the government and . . . and all sorts of things."

She almost made him believe such things could happen. The fresh enthusiasm in her voice made him believe anything was possible. What a mixture of contradictions she was. Insecure and vulnerable, daring and headstrong, naive yet intelligent. But, of course, Marlene was right about this: they *were* foolish notions. A woman wasn't meant to take care of herself. She needed a man to watch out for her. Look at the mess Silver had managed to make of her life!

Enthusiastic, she continued, "I always thought I'd like to own a ranch one day. Raise horses, just like you said your family did. If I had the land and some good breeding stock . . ." The color left her face; the twinkle faded from her eyes. "Maybe Mother's right. I do have radical notions. If I didn't, I wouldn't be traveling unchaperoned with you, now would I?"

And you wouldn't be unmarried and pregnant either. He hated himself for thinking of it. Hated Cass all the more for what he'd done to her.

"It's awfully hard to be such a disappointment to one's own family. Mother had such high hopes. You must know the robbery will ruin them. They'll lose the store and house because of me if I fail to get that money back. It will be my fault. All my fault."

"It's not your fault Cassidy turned out to be a thief." There was much more he could have said about her fiancé, much more she would have to know eventually, but now wasn't the time. He wasn't ready to tell her the facts just yet, and she wasn't ready to hear them.

"It *is* my fault for insisting upon marrying him against my mother's wishes." Her chin came up again. "But then, maybe that's why I wanted to marry him. Because I knew Mother would disapprove."

"Not because you thought yourself in love with him?" he asked gently. It was unfair of him, he knew, to ask such a question, but he had to know if she'd ever been in love with Cass. It was bad enough thinking of Cass lying with her, impregnating her with his seed. But somehow, it would be worse if she'd given her heart to the sick bastard.

Silver rose from the chair and crossed to the foot of the bed. Her expression was thoughtful, then poignant, but when she turned toward him, her eyes were clear and honest. "No, I didn't ever love him. I wanted to. I wanted very much to love him because he said he loved me. But I didn't."

Relief flooded him. It shouldn't have mattered. What Silver had done in the past, what she would do in the future, shouldn't have mattered to him at all. But it did.

"Jared, there's something else I have to tell you. I'm not . . ."

He grinned, not really hearing anything she said after his name. "I'm glad you've quit calling me Mr. Newman again. I prefer it when you call me Jared."

He had a wonderful smile, and it made her forget her confession. She supposed it didn't matter if she waited a little longer before telling him she wasn't pregnant. For now, she wanted to prolong the warmth of the moment. She wanted him to go on smiling at her. She wanted to know more about Jared.

"What about you?" she asked. "You know so much more about me. Tell me about you."

His smiled faded. His eyes took on their familiar remoteness. She expected him to end their friendly exchange. But, instead, he did as she'd asked.

"I never lived anywhere but at Fair Acres. Never thought I'd leave. I had two older brothers, but they both died early in the War between the States. Their dying made an old man of my father. I was about sixteen at the time. He wouldn't let me join up after that, even though boys younger than me were going. Claimed he needed me too much. And I guess he did. I was the only son he had left. It wasn't easy trying to hold on to the farm after the war. Most of the horses had been taken by the armies—both sides—but we all worked hard, even Katrina, my little sister."

Silver noticed the way his voice softened when he spoke Katrina's name.

"She was a beauty, so full of sparkle and life. She never complained about anything." He looked at Silver. "She was a bit like you. She didn't always like what life threw her way. She just fought back as best she could."

A strange euphoria spread through Silver at the comparison, a comparison that sounded like a compliment.

"Katrina was too young to remember what Fair Acres had been like before the war, but my father always swore it would be great again. He was going to see that she had the best of everything.

Dresses and parties and . . .'' His face suddenly
darkened.

She was almost afraid to ask. ''What happened? Why did you leave Fair Acres?''

His tone was calm, unemotional. ''My family
was murdered.''

He looked at her, but she knew he didn't see
her.

''I was in town when it happened. I rode back
and found my parents first. Katrina . . . They took
their time with Katrina. She wasn't dead yet.''

For a moment, his withdrawn facade was lowered, and she saw with raw clarity his pain and
loss, the devastation of the young man he had
been. Silver held her breath, afraid to move.

Katrina . . . Lovely, gentle, funny Katrina with
her honey-brown hair and laughing brown eyes.
Seventeen and full of life. Sam Black and the Lansing brothers and Cass had ridden into Fair Acres
on that June day in 1867 and snuffed out the light
that was Katrina.

Jared found his father's slain body in the yard.
His mother, a bullet through her heart, lay in the
parlor. Katrina he found in her bedroom. She had
been raped and beaten and all her hair had been
cut off at the scalp.

Jared bathed and clothed her broken form. He
held her and begged her to hold on, not to leave
him. She wouldn't eat, didn't speak. He watched
her slipping away from him one day at a time. It
wasn't until the very end that she looked at him
with awareness, that she told him she'd recognized Sam Black, a soldier in their brother Max's
regiment. Then she told him of the man who had
raped her and then cruelly hacked off her hair.
He had a star-shaped scar in the center of his
chest. She died before she could say more.

* * *

The silence stretched interminably, and Silver knew Jared was remembering the details of his sister's death. A part of her wished he would share them with her, but mostly she was relieved that he'd kept them to himself. She knew simply by looking at him that it had been an unspeakable horror.

Jared closed his eyes. "It took her three weeks to die, and I swore I'd never stop till I found the man who had done it to her."

There was a sickness rolling in Silver's stomach. "That's why you became a bounty hunter," she whispered, more to herself than to him.

His eyes cleared, brought back to the present, and in them was reflected all the anger and hate and desire for revenge he carried with him. "There were four of them and only one remains alive. But I'll find him soon."

She stared at him. She saw the boy who had been raised in comfort, in the bosom of a loving family. She saw the son who wanted to fight in the war but who remained behind to help his parents. She saw the heartsick young man, burying his family. She saw the seeds of bitterness that had been born on that day. She saw the man shaped by long days in the saddle, long nights beneath the stars, hot summers and frigid winters. She saw the gunman and his lust for revenge.

She saw Jared, the man he'd been, the man he'd become, the man he could be.

A strange feeling enveloped her. Somehow she knew that her fate had been altered by what she had just heard and seen.

Late that night, Jared got out of bed and walked to the window. He looked down onto the main

street of Green River, his thoughts as dark as the
moonless sky. He'd been awake for hours, unable
to find respite in sleep. Ever since his conversation with Silver that morning, he had been troubled.

For six years the driving force in his life had
been revenge. Now he was close to achieving his
goal, closer than he'd ever been before. He had a
physical description of Cassidy. More than that,
he had someone who knew Cassidy well. Silver
could identify him.

Silver . . . He remembered the possibilities
Doug's comments had stirred up inside him, then
shoved them aside. He couldn't deny his attraction to Silver, but he wasn't about to let himself
act upon it. Once he'd taken Bob Cassidy into
custody and retrieved Silver's money, he would
put her on a train bound for Colorado and never
see her again. Jared had learned his lesson years
ago about loving and caring. The risk wasn't
worth it. He'd loved his family and not a one of
them was now alive. It was better not to get involved with anyone else, better not to care, for
when they were gone, the pain was too great.

Still, he couldn't help imagining what Silver
would look like lying naked beneath him, her ebony hair spreading like spilled ink across the
white sheets, her silver-gray eyes staring up at
him with wonder and desire.

His own desire flared at the image he'd conjured up. He turned his back to the window and
leaned against the cool glass.

If Silver were a different kind of woman, he
would probably find release with her for his pent-
up passions and then forget about it. But she
wasn't a different kind of woman. Pregnant she
might be, but she was a lady. Deep in his soul
he knew it, although the rest of society probably

wouldn't view it in the same light. He saw the wounded, vulnerable girl beneath the stubborn shell she wore to protect herself. He wished he could be the one to protect her from what lay ahead. He *had* to be the one to protect her from himself!

For some reason, thinking of her that way— fragile, vulnerable, unprotected—his desire to hold her, kiss her, make love to her, grew even stronger. He wondered how he would ever survive the next few weeks alone with her on the trail.

"She's pregnant, Newman," he reminded himself aloud, his tone disgusted. "And it's Cass's baby."

He returned to his bed as his thoughts moved back in time.

Jared buried Katrina beside the fresh graves of his parents, then he sold Fair Acres to his neighbor for a mere pittance of its worth, swearing for his father's sake that he would return someday to buy it back.

When he set out from Kentucky, he was green and reckless. He needed seasoning in the saddle and in the ways of the outlaw. With time, he became proficient with a gun and rifle. He learned to read the signs of the trail. He could go days with little sleep or food. Perhaps, under other circumstances, he would have become a lawman, for he had a deep-seated belief in justice. But even more than justice, he longed for the sweet taste of revenge. Serving in society's more conventional occupations of law enforcement would have meant settling in one place. That was something he couldn't do. Not until he found Katrina's killer. To support himself, he became a bounty hunter. He moved among society's outcasts, learned to

think and act and talk like one of them as first
one year and then a second faded away.

Jared arrived in the small Kansas town one day
too late. Sam Black had been hanged for stealing
horses. His partners, the Lansing brothers, had
escaped. But Jared was undaunted. With the te-
nacity of a bulldog, he followed after them. Six
months later, he turned them over to Sheriff Cooper in Denver.

The satisfaction of seeing them dangle at the
end of ropes was diminished because they had
told him nothing of the fourth man except that he
was called Cass. Cass, the man with the scar.
Cass, his sister's murderer. Three men had paid
for their crimes, but not the most heinous of them
all. Cass still roamed free to kill and destroy.

For two more years, Jared searched without
finding another clue. It was as if Cass had disappeared from the face of the earth. But Jared knew
he hadn't. Deep in his soul, he knew the killer
would tip his hand and Jared would find him.
Wherever he went, no matter who else he
searched for, he was listening for clues, watching
for faces, waiting . . . waiting.

Cass struck again in the fall of seventy-two.
With her husband blindfolded, bound and
gagged, the woman was raped and beaten. Ted
Harrison listened to the screams of his wife until
he thought he would go insane. When he was
finished with the woman, the assailant cut off the
woman's hair with a knife before slitting her
throat. Then he shot her husband and left him for
dead.

It took Jared only four days to reach the Harrison spread in Texas after hearing of the murder.
He knew only one man would do this sort of
thing. It had to be Cass. After all those years, at
last he had something to go on.

Harrison, left an invalid by the bullet lodged in his spine, offered a large reward to the man who could bring in his wife's killer alive. He had to be alive. Harrison wanted to see the scum die with his own eyes. But Harrison was little help in tracing the killer. Struck from behind, he hadn't seen the man's face. The only clue was the missing palomino stallion, a horse with very distinctive white markings, which had been stolen from the barn.

Months later, Jared traced the palomino to Denver. He was close at last. Then he rode into an ambush. A stupid mistake. Careless. The kind of thing a beginner would do. And it had cost him Cass's trail once again.

But fate—in the person of Silver Matlock—had delivered Cassidy back into Jared's hands. This time, Cass wasn't going to get away. Not this time. For Katrina. For Mrs. Harrison. For Felicity. Yes, even for Silver. Cass wasn't going to get away again.

Chapter 16

O nce they'd left Green River, Jared pushed
hard toward the west. If he was in any pain
from his injury, he didn't show it. Silver had no
doubt that he would have kept going until they
both dropped dead in their tracks if it weren't for
the horses. He didn't ask if she was tired or hungry or thirsty, but he was always aware of the
condition and needs of their mounts. Every stop
they made was for the well-being of the animals.

But Silver didn't complain. In fact, she tried not
to say anything to Jared at all. She'd hoped, after
their talk in Green River, that things would have
changed between them. She'd thought some sort
of bond had formed. She was apparently mistaken. Jared was more surly than ever. Everything she did seemed to irritate him. So she did
her best to stay out of his way.

Three days after departing Green River, they
crossed the border into the Territory of Utah. As
if trying to drive them back to Wyoming, the skies
wept down upon them for another three days.
Huge thunderheads with black underbellies roiled
before whistling winds. The cold rain ran in great
rivulets over their slickers. They bent their hats
into the wind to protect their faces from the sting-
ing wet missiles, each silently wishing they were

back in the hotel at Green River. Water soaked through their boots, drenching their feet and leaving Silver with chattering teeth. Each night they sought dry shelter without much success.

Late in the afternoon of the third day, there was a break in the clouds on the western horizon. A brisk wind widened the strip of blue until, by evening, the travelers watched a large orange sun dip behind the snowcapped mountains with nothing but an azure expanse to surround it.

"We'll camp here," Jared announced as he pulled the pinto to a halt and dismounted.

Silver slid from the saddle, then turned and rested her forehead against the mare's neck. She was so weary, and she longed for some dry clothes and a dry bed.

"Don't just stand there. We need some wood for a fire."

For six days her anger had been building up, and now it exploded all at once. "Get your own damn wood!" she snapped as she whirled around. "I've had it up to *here* with your high-handed orders, and I don't want to hear them anymore!"

His face darkened. His eyes narrowed. Dropping his gelding's reins, he moved toward her, his steps measured and slow. Silver held her breath, not sure what he meant to do. Fear and a strange expectation made her heart race in her chest. He stared down at her for the longest time. The silence seemed to stretch forever.

"You're not the only one who wants to reach Nevada," she whispered through a tight throat.

Something changed in his eyes, and her stomach tightened in response. Her anger drained from her, leaving her weak and vulnerable—and just a bit hopeful.

"You're right, Miss Matlock," he said at last. "I'm sorry."

She wished he hadn't apologized. She wished he had reacted the way he had after she'd fainted. She wished he would grab her and kiss her and . . .

"You rest," he said gently. "I'll set the fire."

A short while later, the campfire blazing and their supper started, Silver sat on a large rock, ostensibly minding the food but actually watching Jared as he tended the livestock. She realized with only mild surprise that she hadn't given a thought in days as to why she was riding across the country with this man. It felt natural to be with him, no matter what their destination. It seemed so right to be here, watching Jared as he lifted the pinto's hooves and rubbed the gelding's legs, checking for signs of stress or injury.

He straightened and their eyes met. Her pulse pounded. She pushed loose tendrils of hair away from her forehead, then fiddled with the collar of her blouse. She wished, just once, that he could see her in pretty clothes without a dusty face and mussed hair.

Her hand shaking slightly, she reached for the coffeepot and poured the black brew into a cup. "Would you like some?" she asked, holding the tin cup out in front of her. "It's hot."

"*And* fit to drink?" he asked, the hint of a grin breaking the corners of his mouth.

She knew he was trying to make amends for the way he'd been acting, and her heart responded to him. Seeking to match his teasing tone, she replied, "It's as good as yours."

"I'm sure it is." He accepted the cup from her hand. He took a long drink, then looked at her again. "You're right." This time there was no mistaking his smile. "It *is* as good as mine."

His indirect compliment made her flush with pleasure. She knew she'd come a long way in less than three weeks. They still ate better if he did the lion's share of the cooking, but her coffee was good and she could fry bacon without turning it to charcoal. Still, this was the first time he had acknowledged her accomplishments.

He continued to study her as his smile faded. The gold flecks in his hazel eyes seemed darker than usual. Perhaps it was only the reflection of the firelight, yet there seemed to be something warm and intimate in the look. She'd always found his eyes so distant, so remote, so very unreadable. But not so now.

A wave of shyness washed over her. "Why aren't we following the rail line anymore?" she asked, just to say something, anything to break the growing tension.

Jared turned his gaze west, a frown appearing on his brow. "We can make faster time this way. The rails drop down toward Salt Lake City, then come north again around the Salt Lake itself. I could be wrong, but I don't think a man like Cassidy would find much in Mormon territory to interest him. These aren't the kind of folks to go in for gambling and drinking. Unless I miss my guess, he's more apt to make a beeline toward Nevada. Lots of miners with nuggets in their pockets to be lost at the tables there." There was a pause before he added, "We want to find him before he gambles away all your money. The sooner we do, the sooner you can get back to Masonville."

She nodded without looking at him. Yes, back to Masonville. Back to being ridiculed by her mother. And she wasn't thickheaded. After spending weeks alone with this gunman, no matter what the reason, no matter how innocent their time together had been, she would be shunned by every good woman in town. And what would the fine men of Masonville think of her? She could just imagine.

Well, she didn't care. She would get back the money and see the store and house saved from the banker, and then she would make a life of her own somewhere else. She didn't need a husband to find happiness. She would never miss a man's kisses.

A sharp longing cut through her, denying her silent dismissal of her need, not for just any man's kisses. For Jared's. She could still feel his mouth upon hers. Hard and demanding. Sweet and tender. His kisses had stirred within her something she'd never felt before. Even now she longed for him to do it again.

Jared, his tin plate covered with a mess of beans, moved away from the fire and settled onto a grassy mound beneath some tall trees. Unable to resist the magnetic draw which seemed to emanate from him, Silver took her own supper dish and walked across the camp. Silently, she sat down beside him.

"We'll get an early start in the morning," he said when he'd finished eating. He set down his plate. "We've got a lot of ground to make up now that the rain's over."

"How much longer will it take to reach Virginia City?"

No matter how long, she realized, it wouldn't be long enough. It wasn't that she liked spending all day in the saddle, eating the same food day after day, or sleeping on the hard, rocky ground. It was Jared's presence she would miss.

Was she becoming a desperate old maid?

"About two weeks or a little better . . . if we don't run into any more trouble," he replied.

Two weeks. Would he kiss her again during those two weeks? She cast a surreptitious glance his way. His face was dark with a day's growth of beard on his chin and cheeks. It would feel scratchy against her skin. She watched his hands as he rolled a cigarette and placed it in his mouth. Strong hands. Quick hands with a gun. Would they be slow and gentle if he should touch her?

She looked hastily away, locking her gaze on the campfire, but she was unable to stop the train of her thoughts. Horrified—and strangely excited—she realized she wanted far more from this strange, enigmatic man than just a kiss and a caress. She had told him she was pregnant, and in truth, she understood somewhat the act of procreation. But something instinctive told her there was far more to it than she imagined. And, even more alarming and exciting, she realized she wanted Jared Newman to teach her the secrets.

Heat flooded her from her head to her toes. Certain that if she looked at him he would know what she was thinking, she rose and made her way toward the shallow brook that trickled through the cracks in a rocky outcropping.

Jared woke in the middle of the night. A breeze was rustling the trees, trees made into swaying black skeletons by a bright three-quarter moon. The air was pungent, smelling of pine and damp earth. The creek gurgled as it spilled out of the steep crag that bordered the trail.

Always alert, he listened carefully. Had something unusual awakened him? Was anything amiss? His ear in tune with the normal sounds of night, Jared heard nothing out of the ordinary— neither too much noise nor too much silence. Satisfied, he relaxed.

He rolled onto his side—and that's when he saw

her. A moonbeam had found her face, spotlighting her lovely features in a bath of white light. In repose, the strain of the journey had disappeared, and she was even more beautiful. Her mouth, full and moist, looked entirely too delectable. Her chest rose and fell in a gentle rhythm. Her blanket had slipped down, and the top buttons of her blouse had fallen open. He could see with perfect clarity the hollow between her small, rounded breasts. He imagined caressing those breasts, gently squeezing their firmness.

Her chest stilled. He knew immediately that she was awake and watching him, probably with alarm. He tore his gaze back to her face. Her lips were slightly parted, her eyes wide. And for a moment, he thought perhaps he saw the same desire burning within their silvery depths as he felt within himself.

But he gave himself no chance to act upon it. With a jerk, he rolled over and closed his eyes. Even if she did feel the same physical attraction, he would be a fool to pursue it. He had a job to do. He didn't need any complications with a woman.

Forcefully, he put Silver from his mind.

She had been so sure that nothing would make her cry again, but there was nothing she could do to stop the hot sting of tears that burned her eyes and rolled silently down her cheeks and onto her bedroll. Not even her humiliation at the church when she was left in her wedding gown without a groom had made her feel such total and utter rejection.

When she'd awakened and found him watching her, she had been overwhelmed with wanting. Her body had seemed on fire, and she'd known he could see it in her eyes. She'd longed for him to hold her, touch her, possess her. Possession. Yes! She wanted to surrender everything to him. She wanted to be swallowed up by him. She didn't understand the urgency of her need. She only knew that he alone could assuage the ache that gripped her vitals.

With a strangled groan, she turned her back toward him, just as he had done to her moments before. She swallowed the lump in her throat and brushed her damp cheeks with her fingertips, anger replacing the hurt.

It was a sickness, a fever. She'd gone too long without sleep, spent too many hours alone with the taciturn bounty hunter. She didn't want anything he could give her. So help her, she didn't.

Chapter 17

Mile after miserable mile passed beneath the horses' hooves. The icy rains that had left them drenched to the skin became fond memories beneath a relentless sun. The dust rose up in billowing clouds to blind their eyes and choke their parched throats. The high country desert crested and dipped in never-ending waves before and behind them. Always in the distance, there seemed to be the promise of some cool oasis. But always in the distance.

By the end of the next day, Silver was silently cursing Jared, convinced that he wasn't human. She'd been pushed to the limits of her endurance. Her body was tired and sore, her temper short. It was just as well that silence had reigned between them throughout the day. Whenever she recalled her feelings of the previous night, humiliation increased her anger toward the man, and she wished for the freedom to tell him just how much she loathed him.

The instant they completed the climb to the top of the hill and found the dense forest of trees, Silver reined in. "Let's make camp here."

"There's another hour of light left."

She could hear the sounds of running water. "Go on if you want. I'm staying."

"Suit yourself. You're the one who was in such a hurry to find Mr. Cassidy." He tossed the pack-horse's halter rope toward her. "I'll hunt us up some fresh game for supper. You set up camp . . . Unless you're too tired for that too." Then he rode away.

If she could have picked up something fast enough, she would have thrown it at him. And the no-good trail bum knew it too. That's why he'd ridden away so quickly, without giving her a chance to respond. He was purposefully goading her. He was trying his level best to make her angry, to wear her down. She didn't know why, but she knew it was true. He didn't want them to become friends. He didn't want them to share even polite pleasantries.

Alone in camp, Silver spent the time telling herself it was just as well. Her confused feelings for the bounty hunter could only result in more hurt and confusion. She wasn't very wise when it came to men, but that much she understood. She would be well rid of him. She reminded herself that she only had to put up with Jared for another two weeks or so. After they found Bob, she need never see or speak to Mr. Newman again. He could go his way and she would go hers. And good riddance to him!

She felt an all-encompassing fatigue, not just of body but of spirit. With still no sign of Jared, she decided to wash up. She took a towel and some soap from the saddlebags and limped off through the trees, her muscles protesting every step as she followed the sound of running water.

The cold running brook spilled over a bottom of smooth stones, wide and shallow. As Silver approached, she noticed a cloud of mist shroud-ing the rocky outcropping that rose opposite her. Curious, she waded across the stream and carefully climbed toward the top. She wrinkled her nose as she noticed the strong scent of sulphur that intruded on the fresh evening air.

And then she realized where it came from. A hot springs gurgled out of the earth, spilling in a fine spray into a bowl-shaped rock. A bath. A *hot* bath. A hot, *all-over* bath.

With a euphoric cry, Silver dropped the towel and soap and fumbled with the buttons on her blouse. The rising steam caressed her skin, causing her bared nipples to pucker. She sat on a nearby rock and tugged off her boots, then shed her skirt and underdrawers.

Finally, beneath the twilight sky, Silver eased herself into nature's bathtub.

Jared stopped his pinto beyond the ring of dancing light cast by the low-burning campfire. A quick glance confirmed what his senses had already told him. The camp was empty; Silver was nowhere to be seen. He could see the buckskin mare and packhorse tethered to a couple of trees just beyond the fire.

He nudged his heels against his horse's sides and moved forward. There were no signs of trouble, yet he couldn't help a surge of concern. She should have known better than to wander away from camp after dark. He glanced up at the sky. The black canvas of night was dotted with stars, and to the east, a nearly round moon glowed brightly as it began its trek across the heavens. At least she wasn't out there in complete darkness.

With a sigh, he dismounted. He dropped the two dead pheasants on a rock near the fire, then pulled his rifle from its scabbard. Stepping away from the fire, he paused and listened. He could hear the faint sounds of water. That's where she would be. He hadn't ridden with her all this time without learning how much she hated the dust and dirt of the trail. She would bathe in a teaspoon of water if that's all that was available. They'd been lucky to camp so often near fresh running streams.

Still, it irritated him that she had taken it upon herself to go off alone into the forest. And without a gun or a rifle. Fool woman! Didn't she realize the dangers she might run into? Wouldn't she ever learn to follow orders, to think before she acted?

Damn it, this time he was going to make sure she understood. If he had to tie and gag her every time he left camp, he was going to see that she obeyed him.

With a determined step, his way lighted by the rising moon, Jared set off through the trees.

Water spilled from the rocks above into the small pool. Silver sat beneath the shower, letting the water run over her head. Moving from beneath the spray, she reached for the bar of soap and lathered her hair, then rinsed it beneath the cascading water once again. Finally, she lay back against the smooth stone bottom and let the hot water draw out the aches and soreness from her muscles. She closed her eyes, mindless of how long she lay there.

Actually, she thought, it was even more pleasant than a bath at home, for this hot water never cooled. It was always the same temperature, continually refilled from above, then spilling over the sides, rushing to join the much cooler stream which wove through the rocky terrain on its way to the valley in the south. If it weren't for fear of drowning in her sleep, she would happily stay there all night, even if it meant wrinkling up like a prune.

Of course, that would also mean going without supper, she realized as her stomach growled. That thought made her wonder if Jared had returned yet from his hunt. And that thought made her focus on Jared.

As unwelcome as always, she imagined him bending down from his horse, his finger beneath her chin, his mouth lingering gently against her own. As the water lapped against her bare skin, she imagined his fingertips caressing her flesh. She felt a sharp tingling sensation in her womb, followed by an ache of wanting that she didn't understand.

She opened her eyes . . . and found she wasn't alone.

Seated on the edge of the rock just above her was a mask-faced raccoon. She had no trouble seeing him, for the moon had turned the night almost as bright as day. The raccoon sat up on its haunches, braced by its bushy, ringed tail. Its mouth was moving quickly, as if it were trying to speak.

"Hello," she whispered.

The animal dropped to all fours and dashed across the ledge, then back again.

"Am I in your tub?"

It sat up and gave her a withering stare.

"I'm sorry, but I was tired and it looked so very good."

The raccoon stilled, then cocked its head to one side, as if inspecting her.

Silver laughed softly. "All right. I'm leaving," she whispered as she prepared to rise.

Like a nymph emerging from an ancient forest pool, Silver stood. The water caught the silver-white light of the moon and glittered in glorious display as it ran over her pale skin, defining every curve, every plane of her body. Her ebony hair clung to her back, nearly touching the delightful rounding of her derriere.

Jared stopped stock-still, observing her moon-bathed beauty with hungry eyes. She was as slender as a reed but softly curved. Her breasts were small yet firm and perfectly formed. Her waist was narrow, her stomach flat, her hips rounded, her legs long and shapely. What a picture she made, laughing up at that raccoon, surrounded by rising steam, moonlight streaming down upon her.

He moved forward, unable to stop himself. He had to see her more closely. He had to know if she was as perfect as she seemed. He had to touch her soft flesh. He had to taste her lips.

She turned as he crested the rocky ledge. He paused, his gaze locked upon her ethereal loveliness as he laid his rifle on the ground. Her gray eyes grew round. Her mouth parted ever so slightly. Her right hand, palm toward him, lifted from her side as if to warn him away, yet she didn't speak or try to hide herself from him.

It would have been pointless if she had. She could no more have stopped him from joining her than he could stop himself. Without even pausing to remove his boots, Jared stepped into the water and gathered Silver to him as water from above showered over them both.

His hands moved to cup her face. She looked up at him with wondering eyes. Slowly, ever so slowly, he lowered his mouth toward hers. At their first touch, he felt the fires of desire become a blazing inferno.

In the back of his mind, where reason remained, he knew he shouldn't be there, shouldn't be holding her, shouldn't be kissing her. There were a hundred reasons why he shouldn't be feeling this rage of passion, shouldn't be making love to Silver Matlock. But none of them seemed to matter. He wanted her more than he had ever wanted a woman. He was consumed by the wanting.

Yet, even then, if she had protested, if she had tried to push him away, he would have stopped. But she didn't, and soon it was too late for either of them.

Had she conjured him up with her memories? The touch of his lips was better than she'd remembered it. It sent rivers of fire through her veins. It weakened her knees. It drove all power of resistance from her. She pressed the palms of her hands against his wet shirt, seeking to steady the reeling, rocking world that surrounded her.

In unison, they knelt into the warm pool, their mouths never parting. Jared's hands moved from her cheeks, sliding over the water-slick skin of her shoulders and arms, then back up, and finally stopping upon her breasts. She gasped at the unfamiliar touch, the sound muffled in her own throat as his tongue gently probed her lips. His fingers softly kneaded her nipples until they were taut.

Water leaped at her thighs, an oddly erotic sensation coupled with the nearness of his body, the touch of his hands, the taste of his mouth. An ache flared within her, urging her to draw closer to him, promising a release for the pent-up feelings she'd never before experienced or imagined.

Jared's lips moved from hers and began trailing nibbling kisses down her throat. Her head fell back, and this time her groan was audible. He traced the length of her neck to the hollow between her breasts as his hands moved to her spine, bracing her as he took a nipple into his

mouth and suckled. His teeth played lightly with
the highly sensitive flesh.

Unaware of her action, Silver wove her fingers
through his hair, holding him to her, silently asking him to continue.

Finally, he straightened. She felt him looking at
her and opened her eyes. No longer remote and
unreadable, his gold-flecked hazel eyes mirrored
her own raw desire. Her lips parted. She wanted
to speak, but there seemed to be no words to describe what she was feeling, nor did she know
what she wanted from him. Except for him to
continue. Continue until whatever was happening inside her had stilled and passed.

He kissed her again, long and powerfully, his
tongue parting her lips to dance with her own.
She closed her eyes and gave herself over to the
torrent of feelings.

"Don't move," he whispered in her ear, then
moved away.

For a while, the night air caressed her heated,
damp flesh. She thought of opening her eyes but
couldn't seem to do so. And then he was holding
her again, drawing her close against him, his
hands roaming the length of her back.

It came to her slowly that he had removed his
shirt and the bandage too. Her breasts were
pressed against the soft furring of his chest. When
his hips drew closer, she felt his hardness through
his trousers and understood—as best she could—
what was close to happening. She knew she
should stop the madness before it was too late.

"Jared . . ."

Once again, his hands cradled her face. "You're
so beautiful, Silver. Let me love you."

Beautiful . . . love you . . . The protest died on
her lips.

* * *

He could have taken her there in the pool, against the hard rock bottom, but reason asserted itself, and he knew he wanted more than a quick coupling with this woman. He scooped her up in his arms and carried her down the rocky incline, leaving her clothes and his shirt and rifle behind as he wove his way through the forest trees and back to their camp.

Gently, he lowered her onto the blankets of his bedroll, then quickly shed his boots and trousers before joining her on the ground. By the light of the moon, he feasted his eyes upon her beauty while he drew his hand slowly from her throat, over one breast, across her flat abdomen, along the outside of her thigh, then back along the inside until he reached his destination.

He heard the startled gasp that escaped her lips and was only too obliged to bring her even more pleasure.

She hadn't known . . . She'd never expected . . .

Caught in a maelstrom of feelings, she groaned. Pleasure thrummed in her veins. She felt a white-hot fire searing through her. She whispered his name again and again as his touch drove her to a heated frenzy. There was no time for fear, no room for doubt. She belonged to him. She wanted to be a part of him.

Her fingers pressed into his back as he rose above her. As he entered, there was a burst of pain. She cried out, unprepared for discomfort to intrude upon her rapture. She opened her eyes in time to see surprise register on his face.

"Silver . . ."

Her arms tightened. Her hips tensed as she pressed against him. "Don't stop," she whispered. "Please don't stop."

He gazed down at her, unmoving, his intense eyes searching for something. She willed whatever he wanted to see to be written boldly on her face. Then his mouth lowered toward hers. He kissed her, gently, tenderly, until she thought her heart might break from the yearning it stirred within her.

And as he kissed her, he began moving inside her once again. Slowly, ever so slowly. Thrust. Withdraw. Thrust. The pain faded. The fire returned. Suddenly she was moving with him, driven by a silent tempo, carried by a primal rhythm toward a shattering bliss.

She cried out his name as the unendurable ecstasy burst upon her. He echoed her cry, her name carried away on the night breeze. And then, except for the heavy breathing, all was silent.

Braced on his elbows, he lifted his head and looked down at her. She opened her eyes for a moment, then closed them again as another shudder swept through her. Never had she felt so alive, so attuned to everything around her. Their bodies were coated with sweat, and the cool night air seemed in sharp contrast. When he leaned down to kiss her, she felt the tickle of his mustache beneath her nose. Soft. Incredibly soft. But not the stubble on his face. Her own cheeks burned where his beard had scraped her skin. Yet even that felt good.

He pulled her head onto his shoulder. She brushed her hand through the hair on his chest, splaying her fingers to feel his heart beat. A deep contentment, as wonderful in its own way as the tumultuous storm that had preceded it, seemed to blanket them.

It was too wonderful to be believed. She felt truly beautiful and desirable for the first time in her life. So this was what it meant to be loved by a man. No, she thought, not just any man. She knew beyond a doubt that it could never be like this for her with anyone but Jared.

"Why did you lie to me, Silver? Why did you tell me you were pregnant?"

She didn't want to talk about it now, but she saw no way to avoid it. "Because I was desperate. I had to have your help to find him."

"I never would have let this happen," he whispered. "I'm sorry."

A sob caught in her throat. She didn't want him to be sorry. She didn't ever want to lose the joy his loving had given her.

"Shhh." His fingers wove through her hair, cradling her head against him. "Don't cry, Silver."

As his hands began to play across her flesh, her body tensed, reliving once again that moment of climax. A sigh escaped her lips as she pressed them against his throat.

His voice was husky with emotion. "I'm glad he never knew you."

Silver drew her head back and looked at him. "So am I."

He would have to tell her about Cassidy, but he couldn't do it now. Not now. Not when she was looking at him with the flush of loving on her skin, a languid passion lingering in her eyes. Not when she was lying naked in his arms, their bodies still joined, their mingled sweat drying in the night air, cooling their heated flesh.

He felt a great wave of protectiveness, possessiveness overtake him. She had given him something very special. Something she could give no other man.

Silver. Beautiful Silver. As bright and shining as her name.

He would tell her later, when sanity had returned.

Once again, his mouth claimed hers as the spark of desire returned to his loins.

Chapter 18

S ilver awoke before dawn. It was a slow awak-
ening, a sense of unreality surrounding her.
She felt deliciously warm despite the fresh morning breeze that kissed her face and ruffled her
hair. But it wasn't the breeze that she felt against
her scalp. It was Jared's breathing. She opened
her eyes to stare at the dark hairs near the hollow
of his throat.

Even as she felt a warm thrill race through her
veins, she recognized the foolishness of what she
had allowed to happen. What little of worth she
had ever had to offer a husband was now gone.
She had given her virginity to this bounty hunter,
a man hardly more than a stranger, without any
promise of a future, without any proclamations—
even false ones—of love.

Perhaps it was fitting, given the lies she had
told him. She had allowed him to believe from
the very beginning that she had done the same
with Bob Cassidy. When Jared approached her at
the hot springs, he had thought her already a
woman of questionable morals.

What would he think of her now?

Only yesterday, she had been certain she didn't
care what he thought of her. She had tried to convince herself she cared nothing for him either. But

the truth was, she was falling in love with him.
No, not falling. She was already in love with him.

But she knew the feeling wasn't reciprocated. Jared
didn't love her now and he never would. He
wouldn't allow himself to love her. She understood that about him. There was no room in him
for loving, not as long as he was ruled by the
need for revenge. He would ride out of her life as
easily as he had ridden into it. He would go on
searching for the man who had killed his sister
and parents, roaming the country, probably until
the day he died.

She couldn't bear it if he were to find out she
loved him, not when she knew that certain rejection would follow. She had to be sure he didn't
discover the power he had over her. Not ever.

She tried to slip from beneath his arm, but it
tightened around her, pulling her closer.

"Good morning," he whispered in a gravelly
voice.

Her mouth went dry. Her throat constricted.

"We need to talk, Silver."

"Not now," she managed to say. "Not like
this."

"We could both use a bath." He nibbled on her
earlobe. "Shall we go now? I'll scrub your back."

In the throes of passion, she hadn't given
thought to her nakedness, to him seeing her that
way. But now, with sanity's return, she knew she
couldn't bear it. Embarrassment poured through
her.

"I . . ." she began. "I would rather go alone."

He rolled onto his side, bracing himself on his
forearm as he gazed down at her. "We can't
change what happened between us last night, Silver."

"No, we can't change it." She closed her eyes,
unable to return his gaze.

"I told you I was sorry. If I'd known, I would have . . ."

"Please. Don't say it." She would not cry. She would not allow herself to cry. Anger was her only defense against him. "Just understand that it won't happen again."

"Silver . . ."

She pulled away from him, wrapping the blanket around her as she stood up, her back toward him. "I must have been insane to behave as I did. My mother certainly raised me better than to give myself to a common gunman. It was a tragic mistake, and if there is the slightest glimmer of a gentleman left in you, Mr. Newman, you will never again mention what happened last night. Not to me. Not to anyone."

With a haughty toss of her head, she marched off in the direction of the hot springs.

Jared watched her disappear into the woods, then rose to his feet. A matching anger flared in his chest. For one brilliant moment last night, he had hoped that what they'd shared was special, but now he knew he was wrong. Silver was right about it all. It had been a tragic mistake. If she was insane for letting it happen, he was insane for thinking they'd shared more than just their bodies.

His anger began to cool. What right did he have to be mad at her? He *was* just a common gunman. He had no home, no place to hang his hat. He had nothing to offer Silver, even if he'd wanted to—which he most certainly did not.

Grabbing some clothes from the leather bags lying near the saddle, he dressed quickly. His temper turned foul again as he pulled on his water-soaked boots. Why on earth hadn't he taken them off before going into that damned pool? Better yet, why had he gone into it at all? It would have been better for everyone if he hadn't.

Now, as if to remind him of his stupidity, he would be riding in wet boots all day.

Perfect. Just perfect.

Feeling as fragile as glass, as if she would shatter into a thousand pieces at the slightest touch, Silver sank beneath the surface of the water. She rubbed her arms, trying to wash away the lingering feel of his hands upon her—not because she hated the feeling but because she liked it too much.

However was she going to survive the days ahead?

She lifted her chin in a show of courage. She would do whatever she had to do to survive. It wasn't the end of the world. She had acted rashly, that was all. So what if she was no longer a virgin? What man had ever cared enough to propose marriage anyway? Only Bob, and he had been playing her for the fool she was. Since she would never marry, no one need ever know she was a soiled piece of goods.

She had come on this journey to save her parents from bankruptcy. She could still do that. And then she would go off on her own. Perhaps she would teach school. Old maids made the best schoolteachers. Everyone knew that.

Silver heard his approach. She backed against the far edge of the pool, her arms folded over her breasts beneath the water's surface.

As he finished his climb up the hillside, his glance flicked her way. "I came for my rifle," he said gruffly as he reached for it.

Her heart raced as she stared at his broad back, unwillingly remembering the way her fingers had gripped him, drawing him closer as he kissed and caressed her.

He turned. His face was dark, his eyes cool. "You needn't worry, Miss Matlock. You'll be safe with me until I can get you back to Masonville." He started down the hill. "Hurry up. We need to get out of here."

She waited until he was gone, then her hand slapped the water. "Damn your hide, bounty!" she whispered, her anger returning. "Damn your stupid hide!"

He should have told her the truth when she first mentioned the scar on Cassidy's chest. Every day since then, he'd meant to tell her who Bob Cassidy was. But especially after last night, once he knew she wasn't pregnant with Cassidy's child, he'd known he had to tell her. She should have the chance to return to Masonville. Jared knew they weren't following just some two-bit gambler, a seducer of women, a thief. They were following a sadistic killer, and Silver's life could be in danger.

Was it because she could identify Cassidy that Jared kept silent? Was he so possessed by the need for revenge that he would risk her life?

He glanced to his side. Silver sat erect in the saddle, her head held high, her eyes straight ahead. She had been like that throughout the day, pride stamped in the lift of her chin, the set of her mouth.

Heaven help him, he wanted her even now. He knew she was right. What happened should never have happened. And it most definitely should never happen again. But that didn't stop him from wanting her. Their lovemaking had seemed special, unique. He'd felt he wasn't just a nameless face, just another warm body. He'd felt as if he mattered to her, as if they had shared more than just passion. He was reluctant to let go of the feelings she had stirred in him.

He tore his eyes from her, returning them to the trail ahead while forcing his thoughts back to Cass. Once again he wondered how he was going to tell her the truth. He supposed there was only one way. Flat out. As soon as they made camp.

His decision made, he found no reason to delay.

"We'll make camp over there." He pointed toward a draw near a sagebrush-covered hill.

Silver nodded and turned her mare's head away from him.

"We'll have to make do with the water in our canteens for tonight. We ought to meet up with the river about noon tomorrow."

Their nightly routine was done by rote. While Jared cared for the horses, Silver started a campfire and unpacked the food and cooking utensils. Supper that night was canned beans. Jared noticed that Silver scarcely touched a bite; his own appetite wasn't much better.

Disgusted with himself for delaying yet again, he set aside his plate and looked at her across the campfire.

"We've got to talk, whether you want to or not," he said, his voice louder than necessary in the silence of night.

"I would just as soon not," she answered firmly as she gazed into the fire.

"It's not about last night, Silver. It's about Cassidy."

At last, she lifted her eyes to meet his.

"Once you hear what I have to say, you might change your mind about going after him with me. In fact, you probably should."

Silver, too, lay aside her supper plate. "I told

you last night why I lied about . . . about that. It doesn't change the fact that I need to find him and get back the money he stole."

Jared drew in a deep breath. "Silver, he's not just a thief and a gambler." Lord, how did he say it? "The man who slaughtered my family had a star-shaped scar on his chest. Bob Cassidy is the man I've been looking for for six years."

Her face lost all color.

"They're not the only ones he's killed. There were others." Avoiding the most gruesome details, Jared told her about Cassidy's victims. "I've never had a physical description of him except for the scar, because I've never found a survivor who saw his face. The only name I knew was Cass. I thought it was his first name, not short for Cassidy. I traced him to Denver this spring, but I was careless. He must have known he was being followed. Maybe I asked too many questions of the wrong people. Somehow he knew I was after him, and I rode into an ambush. He got away."

"The scar on your shoulder," she said softly. "It's a bullet wound. He shot you, didn't he?"

Jared didn't confirm or deny it. "It must have been after that that he went to Masonville. He probably tried to make himself a more respectable part of the community by . . . by courting you, the daughter of the town's leading citizens."

He longed to take her in his arms and hold her, but he couldn't let himself. Nor, he was certain, would she allow it.

"Do you think he ever meant to marry me?" She looked at him, her gray eyes luminous in the firelight. "He could have just robbed the store long before he did."

Something twisted in Jared's gut. "I don't know." His voice fell to a whisper. "But if he had, you probably wouldn't have lived long. I've told you what he does to women." He stood up and skirted the fire, stopping before her. "I think you should go back, Silver. He's a dangerous man. He'd as soon kill you as look at you."

Silver rose from the ground, her gaze steady as it met his. "You want to find him more than anything, don't you?" She didn't wait for an answer. "Well, you need me to do it. I'll know him on sight. He won't slip away from you if I'm along."

He shouldn't allow it. He should put her on the train at the next whistle-stop they came to. He shouldn't endanger her this way. But she was right. He'd already admitted to himself it would be easier to find Cassidy if she were with him. Still . . .

"This hasn't changed anything," Silver insisted.

Jared reached into his shirt pocket and withdrew the locket she'd given him. "I want you to have this back," he said as he took her hand, turned it palm up, and dropped the necklace into it. "When we're done, you won't owe me anything."

"No." Her voice sounded strangled as she drew away from him. "I guess I won't." She drew a deep breath, stiffened her spine, and lifted her chin. She held out her palm so they could both see the locket. Despite the mistiness of her eyes, her voice sounded strong when she spoke again. "But this doesn't change anything either. It's just that we're following one man instead of two. I've got to get back the money he took from my parents. You've got to find your family's killer. Nothing's changed."

Only they both knew that the previous night had changed everything.

Chapter 19

The sagebrush desert of Nevada rolled on endlessly before them. The June sun was merciless, the heat absorbed by the sandy earth, then thrown back to roast the two riders and their horses.

It was early afternoon when they saw the small homestead with its windmill. Hoping for some cool wellwater, Jared and Silver rode toward the weather-beaten house and shed.

The first shot hit the ground in front of Silver's mare. The second just missed Jared's ear. An instant later, Jared threw himself against Silver, knocking her from Cinder's back. His body covered hers as his eyes searched for cover. Then he rolled away, grabbing her upper arm as he jumped to his feet. Running, he half-towed, half-dragged her with him toward some sagebrush.

"We're only after some water," he shouted.

In response, another bullet hit the dirt, sending their horses galloping away.

Jared swore gruffly. He eased himself up to peer over the silver-green sage toward the house. The door was open a crack, and he could see the barrel of a rifle sticking out. There weren't any windows. Turning his head, he confirmed that the horses had bolted too far away for him to retrieve his rifle.

He sat down with his back toward the brush. His gaze turned upon Silver. "Can you fire a gun?"

She was breathing hard. Tiny flecks of sand clung to her pale cheeks. She shook her head. "I never . . . I never have."

"This is probably a good time to learn." He pulled the revolver from the holster strapped to his left thigh and turned the grip toward her. "Just pull back the hammer and look down the barrel into the sight, then pull the trigger. Don't use it unless you have to. And make sure it's not me you're pointing at before you shoot."

He'd added his last words intentionally, and they served their purpose. He saw a spark of anger in her gray eyes. A spot of color returned to her cheeks.

"I'm sure I can manage it, Mr. Newman."

"Good. Now stay put." He drew his remaining Colt from the right holster, checking the chambers out of habit, although he knew they were full. Then he moved toward the edge of their cover.

"Jared . . ."

He glanced back at her.

"Be careful."

This wasn't exactly the best moment to be thinking how long it had been since a woman had said anything like that to him, since a woman had been concerned for his safety, so he shoved the thought away as he gave Silver a curt nod. Then, crouching forward, he sprinted toward another clump of sagebrush.

Darting from cover to cover, he made an arc toward the back of the house. No more shots were fired, although he was certain whoever was inside must have seen him making his way around. Was he headed for an ambush?

There weren't any windows in the back of the one-room house either. The only way in or out was through the front door. Taking a chance that there was only one person inside and that he couldn't be seen any longer, Jared ran toward the building. He pressed himself up against the board siding, slowing his breathing so it couldn't be heard. Then he inched his way around the side and toward the front.

When he poked his head around the front corner, he glanced toward Silver's hiding place. He could see the top of her ebony hair and wanted to yell at her to get down, but he didn't dare.

The door was still open, the rifle barrel still visible. Sliding sideways, he moved toward the door. There was no sound from inside, no indication that his presence might be suspected. A sixth sense told him he wasn't dealing with an outlaw but with a very frightened human being.

It was a chance, but he took it. He holstered his revolver, then reached slowly toward the rifle barrel poking through the opening. As his fingers closed around the metal, still warm from the recent shots fired, he jerked upward and outward. Then he spun and kicked the door with his boot, knocking it open with a crash. In an instant, he had the rifle turned upon its owner.

The boy, knocked to the hard-packed dirt floor when the door flew open, stared up at him with a startled expression. Jared glared at him a moment, then made a quick survey of the room. The lad was alone.

"Stand up," Jared ordered.

The boy obeyed, brushing off the seat of his pants as he did so.

"Why were you shooting at us?"

"You were trespassin'."

"Where's your folks?"

The boy's mouth clamped firmly closed.

Grabbing the boy by the scruff of the neck, Jared propelled him outside into the daylight. "It's all right, Silver," he called without taking his eyes from his captive.

He was a wiry lad of about ten or so years. His hair was a deep chestnut brown and badly in need of a trimming. Dark brown eyes looked out from a dirt-smudged face.

"What's your name, boy?"

Brown eyes turned upon the ground.

"You might as well start talking." Jared's temper was growing short. "I mean to have some answers."

Silver arrived at his side. She glanced at the boy, then at Jared, then back at the boy. "Was *he* shooting at us?" she asked.

"Yes. Says he doesn't like trespassers."

"Let go of him, Jared," she said as she knelt before the boy. "You're frightening him."

Frightening *him*? Ha! The kid was as tough as rawhide. For crying out loud, he'd just tried to *kill* them!

"Jared, let go," Silver said, more firmly this time.

With a sound of disgust, he released his grip on the back of the boy's neck and took a few steps back.

With a handkerchief from the pocket of her leather skirt, Silver wiped the dirt on his face. "You must have a very good reason for shooting at two complete strangers. Why don't you tell us what it is?"

The stubborn chin began to quiver. The defiant look in his eyes disappeared behind welling tears. "I thought . . . I thought you might be him."

Silver used the falling tears to wipe away a little more of the dirt on the boy's cheeks. "Who?" she prompted gently.

The boy hiccuped over a sob.

Silver put her arms around the boy and drew his head to her shoulder, her fingers stroking the chestnut-colored hair. Jared felt his anger fade as he observed the tender act of the woman toward the child.

"There now," Silver said as she held the boy away from her, once more rubbing his cheeks with the handkerchief. "My name is Silver Matlock, and this is Jared Newman. We're on our way to Virginia City. We saw your windmill and were hoping to find some fresh water in your well." She stood, causing the boy to look up at her. "Now you know all about us. How about telling us about you? Starting with your name."

He sniffed and wiped his nose on his sleeve. "Dean."

"Dean what?" she asked.

"Dean Forest."

"And where are your parents, Dean?"

The boy cocked his head slightly to one side as he looked up at Silver, once again fighting back tears. "I buried 'em in the barn. It was the only place where the ground was soft enough for me t'dig." Dean's jaw tightened. The tears disappeared. His fists clenched at his sides as he turned toward Jared. "I'm gonna find him someday. I'm gonna kill him for what he done."

Silver stared down at the two mounds of dirt in the center of the musty-smelling shed.

"Who did this, Dean?" she heard Jared ask.

"I never saw him before. He just come in and shot 'em."

Silver turned her gaze upon the boy. His voice

no longer sounded young and frightened. It sounded old and full of hate.

"Where were you?"

"I was here, in the barn, doin' my chores, takin' care of the horses 'fore supper. He came here first an' tied me up. I didn't get a good look at his face 'cause it was already gettin' dark, but I'll remember his laugh til the day I die. When I got loose, he was gone. Took both the horses and left." Dean knelt in the dried manure and straw that covered the dirt floor of the barn. His fingers stroked the closest mound. "He cut off all of Ma's pretty hair," he said, his tone puzzled and confused. "Now why d'ya suppose he had t'do that?"

"Cass," Jared whispered, the name sounding like a curse.

A violent pain ripped through Silver. She turned and fled the pungent scents of the barn, but not in time. Just outside the door, she fell to her knees and emptied her stomach. Her eyes watered and her throat burned. She groaned, but she felt more like screaming.

"Silver . . ." Jared's fingers closed around her arms.

"It was him. Bob did this," she croaked. "He killed Dean's parents for two horses. He murdered them and then left them for that boy to bury by himself. What kind of man is he?"

His grip on her arms tightened, but he made no response.

She wiped away the traces of sickness from her mouth, then straightened and looked into Jared's eyes. "I didn't realize til now what you were telling me about him. Oh, dear God, he killed your sister and how many others, and I . . . I . . ." She shuddered at the thought of Cassidy touching her, kissing her. It made her want to retch again.

"Let's get you inside out of the sun," Jared said, an unusual gentleness in his voice.

He helped her to her feet, then, with an arm around her waist, guided her toward the ramshackle house. He settled her onto a wooden stool, took a bucket from the sideboard, and went back outside. Minutes later, he returned with the bucket full of fresh water.

"Drink this," he said as he handed her the dipper.

She did as she was told, glad to rinse away the taste of bile that remained.

"She all right?" Dean asked from the doorway.

"I . . . I'm fine." Silver hung the curved handle of the dipper over the outside of the bucket.

Jared turned around. "Have you got any other family around these parts?"

Dean shook his head.

"How far are we from Elko?"

"'Bout a day's ride by horseback," the boy answered. "Longer by wagon."

"We'll take you with us that far. We'll find someone who can watch out for you."

Dean stuck the tips of his fingers beneath the waistband of his britches. "I ain't leavin' here. I can take care of myself."

Jared's expression hardened. "I'm not arguing with you, boy. You can either come sit on the packhorse with reins in your hands or I can truss you up and toss you over it like some of our supplies. Either way, you're going with us."

Silver paused beside Dean's bedroll and gazed down at the sleeping boy. His hair had fallen over his forehead, covering one eye. She tenderly pushed it back.

Poor little fellow. So young to have seen so much.

She felt her stomach lurch again. She rose slowly, her hand pressed against her abdomen, as if to keep it from reacting as it had earlier in the day, but she couldn't shake the lingering sickness.

Somehow what Jared had told her about Cassidy hadn't sunk in until she'd seen Dean run his hand over his mother's grave. Perhaps it was because she'd been in such turmoil over the night she'd spent in Jared's arms. Or maybe it was because she'd felt a twinge of hope when she'd learned Bob Cassidy was the same man Jared had been searching for these past six years. It meant that when they reached Virginia City Jared's search could be over. He would no longer have to tramp around the country, looking for Katrina's killer. He would be free—free enough, perhaps, to love a woman.

But the truth about Cassidy had hit her square in the face at the Forest homestead. She couldn't think only of what finding him could mean between her and Jared. She had to face what sort of man she'd nearly given herself to. She had to take a long, hard look at just how desperate she had become to gain acceptance from her mother. She had been willing to marry a man she didn't love, didn't even like much, just to overcome her mother's criticisms.

She wanted to scream and rail against the world. She wanted to go back and change the past. She wished she'd never set eyes on Bob Cassidy. She felt unclean from just having been near him. When she'd thought he was merely a ne'er-do-well gambler, a simple thief, getting back the money he'd taken had seemed enough. But it wasn't enough any longer. She wanted to see him punished for what he'd done to this boy's family and to all the others.

She turned, her eyes finding Jared.

And to his family, too.

But unlike Dean, Jared wasn't a boy in need of a mother's care. He was a man and she loved him with a woman's heart.

Silver walked across the camp and sat down on the ground beside Jared. "He's sleeping," she said.

"Poor kid. I was sorry I had to get tough with him."

"We couldn't leave him there."

"I wish I knew why Cass got off the train," he said, more to himself than to her. "There has to be a reason. I don't even know if he's still headed for Virginia City."

"At least we're not as far behind him as we thought we were. We're actually on his trail now instead of just hoping to reach Virginia City before he goes elsewhere."

Jared tossed a stick into the campfire. A shower of sparks erupted into the night. "I'm not going to let him get away again. Not again."

"We'll find him," Silver whispered. "We've got to."

Jared's eyes captured Silver's gaze. He raised a hand and tenderly touched her jaw, stroking the flesh close to her ear. "I should leave you in Elko with Dean."

"I'm not staying behind." Her throat felt tight. "We've been through it all before."

"It's not safe. He knows I've been following him. If he sees us together . . ." His voice drifted away.

"I have to get the money back in time to pay the mortgage. I can't stay behind and wait and wonder." She reached up and covered his hand, pressing his palm against her face. She wanted him to kiss her. All her good arguments about why she shouldn't love him were forgotten. She just wanted him to hold and kiss her, to make love to her again beneath the stars, to make her forget.

Jared pulled his hand free before rising and taking a few steps away. "Listen, Silver. You were right about me the other day. There's not much of a gentleman left. I've lived too hard and seen too much. If you keep tempting me this way, you'll find yourself sharing my bedroll again, and I don't think that's what you want, because that's all there'd be. When I've found Cassidy and taken him in for the reward on his head, I'm going back to Kentucky. Alone."

She felt as if he'd kicked her. Was that what he thought? That she was looking for a husband? Couldn't he see what she felt for him? No, of course he couldn't see it. And she didn't want him to.

"Don't worry, bounty. I don't *want* to go anywhere with you once we find Bob."

He'd been intentionally cruel, but it was the only way he could keep himself from crushing her to him and tasting once again the sweetness of her lips.

Damn! He would lose his edge if he kept thinking about Silver that way. He had to focus on Cassidy alone. Catching that cold-blooded killer had to remain the most important thing on his mind.

"You know who killed my ma and pa, don't ya?"

Jared swiveled on the heel of his boot.

Dean was standing just a few feet away, glaring at him with hostile eyes. "I heard you talkin'. You know who done it, don't ya? You know who killed my ma and pa."

Looking at the boy, he decided Dean deserved the truth. "Yes. I've been on his trail for a long time. He's killed before."

"You the law?"

"No."

"Bounty hunter?"

Jared nodded.

"I'm goin' with ya."

"Sorry, son. I've got my hands full as it is."

"I ain't your son." Dean stepped forward. His hair had fallen back over his forehead, nearly obscuring one eye. His hands were balled into fists at his sides. "And I ain't stayin' in Elko. You leave me there, I'll just come after you on my own. I gotta right t'see him swing for what he done."

It was a little like seeing himself six years before, Jared couldn't help thinking. He hadn't been a boy like Dean. He'd been a young man, twenty-two years of age, when he'd found his family murdered. But he recognized the hate in those dark brown eyes. He recognized the lust for revenge. He'd felt it all before. He'd been living with it for six years.

"Maybe you do," he replied, "but you're not going."

Dean shot him one more angry look, then turned away. "You just try'n stop me."

Silver stood. "You could be a little more understanding," she said in a soft but accusing voice. "He's been through a lot."

Jared felt himself grow cold with an icy rage. He didn't dare even look at her. He didn't need to be reminded of what the boy had been through. He already knew. He'd felt it all before himself.

"What do you want me to do?" he asked. "Take him along? Expose him to danger too? Don't I have enough problems having *you* with me without adding a kid to boot?"

"Well, if we're lucky, you won't have me with you much longer," she snapped back.

Muttering a blue streak, Jared walked off into the dark.

Chapter 20

"I reckon Lucas Feldt would take in the boy. He's got himself a lot o' land an' can always use a hand with the chores. His missus is kinda sickly and not much help around the place no more. Don't know how long he'd be willin' to keep him, though." The sheriff leaned back in his chair. He rubbed the day-old whiskers on his chin. "How'd you say you come by him, Mr. Newman?"

"His folks died about a week before we got there. We couldn't just leave him out there all alone, so we brought him with us this far. But we can't take him any farther. We've got quite a ways to go yet."

"Where you say you're headed?"

"I didn't."

The sheriff eyed the double holsters. "Don't wanna tell me, huh? You got any reason for that?"

Silver recognized the expression in Jared's narrowed eyes and could tell he was losing his patience.

"No reason," he responded. "We're on our way to Virginia City."

The sheriff's gaze shifted to Silver, then to Dean. "Mighty hot crossin' on horseback. Most

218

folks take the train these days. You an' the missus oughta think about takin' the next train through." He leaned forward, placing his elbows on his desk. "How'd your folks die, boy?"

Dean shook his head.

"Can't you talk?" When Dean didn't reply, the sheriff turned his head toward Jared once again. "Not gonna be easy findin' anyone to take in a dumb mute. Even Lucas Feldt's not likely t'want him if'n he can't talk."

Silver bristled as she listened to the scruffy old man behind the desk. What kind of representative of the law was he?

"Why don't you folks take yourselves over to Maddie's across the street. She sets out a right good meal. I'll check around an' see what I can come up with for the boy. He don't look too terrible strong. Kinda thin if you ask me. And if he don't talk . . ." He shook his head.

Silver clasped Dean's hand and pulled him outside. Another second in there and she would have told the sheriff just what he could do with himself.

As soon as Jared joined them, she turned on him. "You can't mean to leave Dean with that man," she said indignantly. "Or anyone else he could find. They'd just be looking for a spare field hand. Hasn't he been through enough already without being turned into free labor?"

Squinting, Jared looked up at the noon sun. He rocked back on his heels, then rolled forward again. Finally, he glanced down at Dean. "You mean to follow us if we leave you here?"

The boy nodded.

"I thought so. Then I don't suppose there's much point in wasting time looking for a place for you to stay."

Silver let out a sigh of relief.

"It's not 'cause I want t'be with you, ya know,'' Dean said. "I'm just comin' along t'see that man hang."

Jared pulled his hat low on his forehead. "I know." He stepped down from the boardwalk and gathered his pinto's reins in his hands. "I want to check at the station, see if Cassidy bought himself a ticket here."

Suddenly it occurred to Silver that Jared hadn't told the sheriff that the Forests had been murdered or that they suspected who had done it. As they rode through town, she asked Jared why.

"Because there's no warrant for Cassidy. Because there's no proof yet that he's killed anyone. Even Dean didn't get a good look at him. If we tell the law what happened, we could be held up here for days and Cass could get away. I'm not letting that happen again. *I* know he's guilty, and I'm going to be the one to bring him in."

Looking at him now, his handsome face set in hard lines, his brow drawn tight in a frown, his hazel eyes filled with hate, she wondered if the tender man who'd made love to her really existed or if she'd only imagined him. Had she ever seen him smile, heard him laugh, or had she dreamed them up?

I've got to be out of my mind.

It wasn't the first time he'd thought it, and it probably wouldn't be the last. Not only was he traveling with a woman while trailing Cassidy, but now he'd taken on a scrawny orphan.

At least he could be thankful for one thing, he thought as he dismounted in front of the train station. With Dean around there was no chance of seducing Silver again.

Jared stepped up to the ticket window. "I'm looking for a friend of mine who might've caught a train west within the last week or so. Tall, blond, blue eyes. Have you see him?''

The clerk's eyes ran the length of Jared. ''What you want him for?''

''Like I said, he's a friend.''

''Sorry. Ain't seen any strangers out of here this past week. Just local folks.''

Jared tugged at his hat brim. ''Thanks.''

He stepped outside, his glance taking in Silver and Dean as they waited with the horses. He didn't know whether he was glad or not that Cassidy hadn't taken the train out of Elko. It could mean they were right behind him and had a chance to catch up with him. Or it might mean he wasn't headed for Virginia City anymore. If he'd taken off in another direction, they wouldn't even know it. They were too far behind him. It wasn't like they were hot on his trail and could read the signs of where he was going.

And there was another matter. There could be only two reasons why Cassidy wasn't traveling by train any longer. Either he was headed somewhere off the line or he'd lost all his money and couldn't afford the price of a ticket.

Jared looked at Silver again. If Cassidy didn't have the Matlocks' money, she would be along for no purpose. He might be exposing her needlessly to danger.

Silver's brows lifted in a silent question.

''No, he wasn't here,'' he answered as he stepped forward to take his horse's reins. ''Let's go.''

Wordlessly, he led the way out of town.

Jared pushed everyone to the limits of their endurance over the next couple of days. He stopped at every whistle stop, every dusty little town they came to. He questioned clerks at the train stations and bartenders in the saloons. Nothing. No one had seen the good-looking blond gambler. Once again, he seemed to have disappeared.

Jared scarcely spoke to his two companions. He didn't want to acknowledge that there was a strong possibility they had lost Cassidy, that he'd changed directions on them, that he wasn't headed for Virginia City after all.

Lord, he was tired. Tired of the endless miles. Tired of the two-bit saloons. Tired of the dirt and the hunger and the heat. Tired of carrying a gun and always being ready to use it. Tired of the hate that ate at his soul. Tired of what he had become.

The fire had burned low, the coals white-hot. Dean and Silver were both asleep. Jared wished the same were true for him as he leaned against his saddle, smoking a cigarette.

Silver sighed softly and rolled over.

She was so beautiful. He still found it hard to believe that she didn't realize what she could do to a man with just a smile or a glance from those silvery-gray eyes. Those eyes. That's what had gotten him into this trouble in the first place. Her eyes and the memory of Katrina.

Are you sure this was what I was supposed to do, Kat?

That confirmed it. He *was* crazy. It wasn't enough that he imagined Katrina would have wanted him to help Silver. Now he was asking her questions—and expecting answers!

He tossed his cigarette into the fire, then lay back and closed his eyes, but Katrina's image wouldn't leave him. And now she was joined by his parents. They seemed to be looking at him with great sadness.

I'm doing this for you.

But was he? Perhaps, when he first started out, it had been for them, but now, wasn't it because he didn't know what else to do, how to stop what he'd started?

If there is the slightest glimmer of a gentleman left in you . . . That's what Silver had said to him. And he knew there wasn't. What made him think he could ever go back to Kentucky, to Fair Acres, even if he had the reward money offered by Harrison? What made him think he could go back and be accepted by those genteel people who had once been neighbors and friends? He wasn't even sure he could sit at a table with a white tablecloth and silver candlesticks and eat fancy foods without making a fool of himself. He'd forgotten how to make idle conversation, how to dance with a lady in a dressy ball gown.

His fingers touched the cool metal of his Colt revolver. Violence. That's what he knew. That was all he knew anymore. He'd become so inured to it, it was second nature. Like the time that boy had called him out on the streets of Dodge. He could have refused. He could have turned and gone into that saloon and ignored the brat. But he'd been surrounded by members of Charo's gang, and he couldn't let their leader think he was a coward. So when the boy had gone for his gun, Jared's instincts had taken over. He'd shot him. Just some stupid kid trying to make a name for himself, and Jared had ended his life in an instant.

Maybe that was the day he'd known he could never go back. He'd become no better than the criminals he tracked. He thought like them, acted like them, lived like them.

He looked at Silver once again, and a longing stirred within him that had nothing to do with physical desire. He allowed it to linger only a moment before he drove it ruthlessly into a dark corner of his heart. He might as well face the truth.

He would never be good enough for Silver. He would only end up hurting her by association. He was what he was—a bounty hunter—and that's what he would be until the day someone like Cassidy got lucky and plugged him with a bullet through the heart. He couldn't allow her or anyone else to stir up feelings for things that couldn't be. He had no room in his life for sweet longings—or for Silver Matlock.

"Jared, we've got to stop and rest. Look at Dean. He's about to fall out of the saddle. He's exhausted. We all are."

Jared's gaze was harsh and as unrelenting as his tone of voice. "I warned you it wouldn't be easy. If you and Dean can't keep up, you can stay behind."

"For heaven's sake," Silver shot back, "at least take pity on a little boy."

Her words had the desired effect. Jared slowed his pinto to a walk, then looked around for some shade beside the river they'd been following for a number of miles.

"Fifteen minutes," he said as he dismounted.

She longed to come back with a sharp rejoinder, but she managed to keep silent. Jared had been sour enough for the past few days without her adding fuel to the fire. And it was odd, too, because there were times when she caught him looking at her and felt he might truly care for her. It always stirred a burst of hope in her heart, which was only crushed again later when he made it clear he wanted no part of her.

She shook her head. It was pointless to try to figure Jared out. She'd just better get down from the saddle and stretch her legs while she had the chance.

She dismounted, flipped up the stirrup, and

loosened Cinder's cinch. Then she turned toward Dean and the packhorse. The boy was still in the saddle. His chin was dipped forward, touching his chest. He appeared to be sound asleep.

She walked over to him, raising her arms to his waist. "Come on, Dean. You'd better lay in the shade over here for a few minutes."

He mumbled something as he slid into her waiting arms. He was heavier than he looked, and she stumbled backward beneath his dead weight.

"Give him to me before you fall down." Even as he spoke, Jared lifted the boy away from her. With one hand, he pulled a rolled blanket from the back of the packhorse, then carried Dean toward a tree that grew beside the river.

Silver watched as he dropped the blanket on the ground before carefully setting the sleeping boy on it. Just as she had done in the past, he brushed Dean's hair away from his face. The gesture offered her a brief glimpse at the tender side of a hardened man, and her heart squeezed in response. What might he be like if he had children of his own?

She turned, seeking to banish the image from her mind. She moved toward the water and squatted near the edge. For a long time, she stared at her distorted reflection in the shallow river. Jared with a child of his own . . . Jared with *their* child . . . The longing was unbearable.

Quickly, she filled her cupped hands and splashed her face, washing away the trail dust along with the unwanted thoughts. Then she filled her hands once more and took a long drink. When she rose and turned around, she found Jared standing close by. Her pulse quickened in response to his nearness.

He reached out and wiped a drop of water from

the tip of her nose. ''You're pretty when you're all wet,'' he said softly.

She couldn't have stopped herself, even if she'd wanted to. She lifted her arms to circle his neck and drew down his head so she could kiss him, offering him her heart with her lips.

But he didn't accept it. He took hold of her wrists and freed himself from her embrace.

''Jared,'' she whispered.

He shook his head, then turned and walked away.

Chapter 21

It happened so quickly she had no time to prepare. One moment, she was riding along the narrow trail on a hillside, the next Cinder was rearing on her hind feet. With the mare's shrill whinny still ringing in her ears, Silver tumbled into the draw far below, coming to an abrupt halt as she hit the bottom. She felt a sharp pain in her head at the same moment that the wind was driven from her chest. Then everything was blessedly black.

Needles of pain shot up her leg as she returned to consciousness. She opened her eyes to find Jared bending over her.

"Don't move," he cautioned.

She felt his hands moving lightly over her, checking for injuries. She felt bruised all over, but the pain in her leg was excruciating. She tried to sit up.

"I said don't move."

She grimaced as she propped herself on her elbows. "It's my ankle," she said through gritted teeth. "My right ankle."

"I'd better take your boot off and have a look."

When he lifted her foot off the ground, a wave of dizziness sent her spiraling toward the black pit once again. She lay back on the ground, closing her eyes, and dug her fingers into the dirt as he removed her boot.

"Wiggle your toes," Jared told her.

It hurt but she managed to do so. Frowning, she opened her eyes again and looked at Jared. He was frowning too.

"I'm no doctor, but I don't think it's broken. You're not going to get that boot back on, though. It's swelling fast." He carefully lowered her leg to the ground. "Dean, you'd better bring the horses down here. This will have to be our camp for the night."

The boy nodded and took off at a run.

"If you can stand to ride tomorrow, we ought to be able to make Winnemucca before nightfall. We'll have a doctor look at your ankle there."

"We can't afford a doctor. It's just a sprain. I'll be all right."

Jared wore a humorless grin. "We'll see how you feel about that in the morning. For now, we'd better try to make you comfortable."

"What made her spook like that? It all happened so fast, I didn't see anything."

"Rattler."

"Where's Cinder now?" Silver twisted and tried to look up the steep incline. Her head throbbed in response to the sudden movement.

"Long gone, I'm afraid." He looked up the hillside. "I'd better go help Dean find her and bring down the other horses. Will you be all right?"

"I'll be just fine. It's just a little sprain."

Jared rose above her, his eyes staring into hers. Finally, he nodded. "We won't be long."

As soon as he was out of sight, Silver let out the groan she'd been holding in. The pain was worse than anything she'd ever felt before. She'd taken her share of tumbles and spills as a child, come home with skinned knees and scraped elbows more than just a few times, but she'd never had anything hurt quite like this. Still, she couldn't let Jared see how much pain she was in. He was always looking for some reason to leave her behind and continue the search on his own. This just might prove to be the excuse he needed.

Tears burned the back of her eyes as hopelessness overwhelmed her. She had less than sixty days now to find Bob Cassidy and get back the money he'd taken. Less than sixty days to redeem herself in her mother's eyes. Less than sixty days to keep her father from losing everything he'd worked to build. She wasn't so naive that she didn't know Cassidy could be anywhere by now. He'd left the train for some reason. And, as Jared had said, he might not even be going to Virginia City. If he wasn't there, all was lost.

Try as she might, she couldn't stop the tears from spilling over.

What a mess she'd made of it all. Not only had she left her parents facing financial ruin because of her foolishness, but here she was, out in the middle of nowhere, in love with a man who didn't know it and couldn't understand it if he did. And she'd given herself to him like some common trollop. What was to become of her?

She heard a sound and opened her eyes. Dean was coming down the hillside, leading the packhorse. Jared was nowhere to be seen.

"Your mare took off. Jared's gone after her," he said.

She sniffed and wiped the tears from her eyes.

"Hurts pretty bad, huh?"

"I'm all right." She attempted a smile.

"You got some cuts on your face."

"Do I?" She reached up and touched her cheek, wincing when she found a scratch.

"Here. Let me." He pulled a rag from his back

pocket, then poured water from the canteen onto it before kneeling beside her. "You don't have t'feel bad about cryin', ya know. Pa always said women had a right t'cry when things got hard. He said menfolk had t'take care of 'em as best we could." He carefully dabbed at the blood and dirt on her face. "There." He leaned back on his heels. "I didn't hurt ya, did I?"

"No, it didn't hurt. Thank you."

Dean cocked his head to one side and frowned. "How come you're travelin' with him? You his woman or somethin'?"

"No." Jared's woman. She wished . . . "No," she said again. "I hired Mr. Newman to find someone for me."

Dean's voice lowered. "This Cassidy? He kill someone o' yours too?"

"No." She drew in a deep breath. "He stole some money from my parents, but he didn't' hurt anyone."

"Pa always said Ma was a right handsome woman an' we was lucky to have her with us. Ma, she always wanted a home, someplace to settle in, but Pa liked to move around. When we come to Nevada, she said this was where she was goin' t'stay. Said she wasn't movin' agin and he would have to bury her right there." His voice cracked.

Silver wished she could reach out and touch him, but he was seated too far away. He was trying so hard to be tough, not to show that he was a hurting, lonely little boy.

"There weren't no call for him t'hurt 'em. He could've just taken the horses an' let my folks live."

"I don't think he needs a reason to kill, Dean," she whispered, feeling once again that sweeping sickness. "He would have killed my parents, too, if they'd been home when he stole the money." It wasn't until she spoke the words that she realized just how true they were. Cassidy would have killed them all if he'd needed to.

"I wish I could kill him myself," Dean said, his voice filled with anger.

So much hate in one so young. And what about her and Jared? Each of them was on a journey for revenge. Three people, so very different from each other, bound together by their search for Bob Cassidy, each wanting recompense for something he'd taken from them.

She wished there were other ties to bind them together. She wished it with all her heart.

There were only a few coins left in Jared's pocket after he paid for the hotel room. If Silver's injury kept them in Winnemucca more than a couple of days, they would be broke.

He walked outside and helped her from her horse. He didn't set her down on the walk as she expected. Instead, he carried her inside the hotel. It was his chance to hold her in his arms without her knowing just how badly he'd been wanting to do just that. She leaned her head against his shoulder, and he could feel her warm breath on his neck. Despite the trail dust, he could smell the faint fragrance of lavender. He was tempted to bury his face in her hair and breathe deeply.

She made a little sound in her throat, and he knew she had sensed his growing tension. He hurried his steps up to the second floor, Dean trailing behind with a couple of saddlebags. He stopped in front of the door with the number four at eye level. Without him asking her to, Silver reached out, turned the knob, and pushed the door open.

The room was small but clean, the bed covered with a patchwork quilt, the window hidden behind bleached muslin curtains. There was an oval rag rug in shades of blue on the floor. A cherry-wood dresser with a mirror stood against one wall, a washstand with pitcher and bowl against another.

As Jared set Silver on the bed, he said, "I only had enough to pay for one room. Dean and I can sleep on the floor."

Even as she nodded, he knew they were both wishing there wouldn't be a young boy present in the room.

"I'm going to check around town, see about a doctor."

Silver grabbed his wrist before he could move away. "We can't afford a doctor," she insisted. "It's just a sprain. If I can rest, it'll be as good as new in no time."

He knew she was right about the money, but he wished it were otherwise. He wanted to assure himself that her injury wasn't more serious than it appeared. Reluctantly, he agreed. "All right. We'll see how you feel in the morning."

She smiled at him, as if thanking him for agreeing with her this once. It reminded him how often he did just the opposite of what she wanted. He pulled his arm free of her grasp.

"I'm still going out to ask some questions, see if anyone's seen Cass. Dean, you bring up the rest of the supplies, will you? Take care of Silver if she needs anything."

"I will," the boy answered.

He was going to have to do something about money, Jared thought as he descended the narrow stairway. Silver would need a couple of days' rest. It was tempting to use that as an excuse to leave her and the boy behind, but without any money, what would they do then? Jared couldn't just desert them, and there wasn't any way to pay for a train ticket back to Colorado.

He glanced down the dusty main street of Winnemucca. He removed his hat, wiping his sleeve across his forehead, then replaced the hat with a firm tug, the wide brim shadowing his eyes. He'd start with a few questions at the train station, then he'd find a poker table. He'd fed them more than once that way. He could do it again. He started walking.

What had begun as a trading post in 1850 had grown into a fair-sized town with the coming of the railway. Winnemucca had the typical false-fronted stores and saloons, most of them unpainted, all of them faded by the hot desert sun and cold winter winds. The main street was wide to facilitate turning wagons. A few of the buildings had raised boardwalks. It was just another town, like a hundred others he'd passed through.

The clerk behind the counter at the rail station looked up from beneath his green visor. "Help you, sir?"

As he'd done numerous times before, Jared described the man he was seeking.

"Your name wouldn't be Newman, would it?"

Jared tensed. "Yes. Why?"

"Got me a telegram here for you. Come with instructions that you'd be askin' about a man fittin' the description you just give me." He handed Jared an envelope.

"Thanks." Jared turned away as he ripped the paper and pulled out the telegram. He scanned quickly for the sender's name. It was from Doug Gordon.

He went back and read more slowly.

. . . *Three murders . . . in jail in Silver City, Idaho . . . could be Cassidy . . .*

Cassidy in jail? Was there a chance it was him? But Doug couldn't be sure. The man was unknown in the area and had refused to give a name.

Jared turned back toward the clerk. "Does the stage to Idaho come through here?"

"Sure does. San Francisco to Boise City up in Idaho Territory and vicey versey."

"Where can I find out about the schedule?"

"Right here. You're in luck if you're headed north. Next one through'd be round six o'clock tonight. Boards outside and across the street."

"Thanks," Jared said, then left the station.

He had to find out if Doug's telegram was right. And if it was Cassidy, he wanted to be sure he didn't get free to kill again. Of course, Jared would also like to be the one to haul Cassidy back to Texas. Jared wanted that reward money. Maybe with enough money, he could change his life, become a respectable part of society again. Maybe he could put the past behind him. But he had to have the means to start fresh. And only the bounty on Cassidy's head would do that for him.

He jammed his hand into his pocket, fingering the few remaining coins. There wasn't enough for a second night at the hotel, let alone the fare for a stage ride. Yet the stage would be at least four days faster than he could make the trip on his own.

He paused in front of the hotel, his gaze falling on the horses tied at the rail. He stared at them for a long time before making his decision.

It was well past eight o'clock and still he hadn't returned. Silver was growing worried. She'd sent Dean to find him about an hour ago, and even he wasn't back yet.

Dropping her legs over the side of the bed, she tried to stand. Her ankle protested mightily. Frustrated, she sat down as shafts of pain shot up from her ankle into her thigh.

The door opened, and she looked up hopefully. It was Dean.

"Couldn't find him anywhere," he said. He looked at her foot where it rested on the floor, then glanced down at his own feet, his hands shoved deeply into the pockets of his overalls. "The horses aren't out front anymore."

"They must be at the livery." Silver tried to stand again, this time bracing herself on the washstand and keeping the weight off her foot.

Dean's voice was very soft. "I checked. Cinder an' the pinto are there." Now he looked up. "Man said he bought the packhorse from Jared."

Silver dropped back onto the bed as cold dread swept through her. "He sold the packhorse? But . . ."

"The man said he seen Jared get on the stage outta town."

"He's gone?" She couldn't believe it had happened like this. Not like this. Just leaving them in this strange town without a word.

"We gonna wait for him?" Dean asked.

Wait for him . . . Of course, he'd left his pinto there. He had to be coming back. She let out a soft sigh of relief, but her anxiety soon returned. Where had he gone and why had he left without telling her? How long would he be away? He'd said himself there hadn't been enough money for two nights in the hotel. If he was only going to be gone overnight, he could have taken his pinto; he wouldn't have sold the packhorse and taken the stage.

The truth was painfully clear. He had left them stranded with no money. He'd probably gone to Virginia City without them. He'd found a way to get there faster, and he'd taken it. He'd left them without so much as a by-your-leave or a backward glance.

She'd thought him capable of a lot of things, but not this. Never this. He had betrayed her in the worst of all possible ways. She could have forgiven him anything else but this.

She drew her injured ankle up from the floor, propping it high with an extra pillow and blanket. She forced her voice to sound calm and unconcerned. "Let's get some sleep, Dean. We'll worry about what to do in the morning. If you're hungry, there ought to be something to eat in the saddlebags."

"I ain't hungry," the boy replied.

She could hear the disappointment in his voice and knew he shared the betrayal she felt. He had begun to look up to Jared. It was Jared who was going to find and capture the man who'd killed Dean's ma and pa. He had betrayed Dean as much as Silver.

She closed her eyes against the terrible ache in her breast. Never again would she trust a man. Never again would she give into the wanting that Jared had stirred up within her. Never again would she let her heart rule her head.

Never again . . .

The stage bounced and rocked on its leather springs, jerking its inhabitants from side to side. Holding onto the side panel of the coach, Jared stared out the window. The setting sun was casting a red-purple hue across the desert floor, making the sage look like bushes of fire.

But Jared wasn't thinking about the colorful sunset or the pungent sagebrush or even the rough ride of the stagecoach. He was thinking about Silver, wondering how she'd taken the news when the blacksmith had delivered his note and the remainder of the money. There should have been enough for food and for several more nights at the hotel. Before she needed more, he would be back to Winnemucca.

Oh, she wouldn't be happy with him for leaving without talking to her, but he'd known she would try to go with him to Silver City if he'd given her a chance, and he couldn't wait for her ankle to heal before he left. Perhaps leaving her a note was a coward's way out. Still, that had seemed his best option. There wasn't anything she could do about it now anyway. She would just have to wait for his return.

Jared leaned back, drew his hat down over his face, and sought slumber. It was going to be a long night. He might as well try and rest. Tomorrow, if he was lucky, he would be looking at Bob Cassidy behind bars.

Chapter 22

Leaning on Dean, Silver entered the livery stable. She waited a moment for her eyes to become accustomed to the dim light. At the back of the building, she could see the red glow; she could hear the roar of a bellows and the clang of metal as the blacksmith pounded the iron shoe against the anvil.

Throwing back her shoulders, she moved forward. "Excuse me, sir," she said, her voice drowned out by the noise.

The smithy kept hammering away.

"Excuse me," she hollered.

Still no reaction.

Impatiently, she reached out and touched the man's shoulder.

He jumped up, swearing, and turned upon her with his hammer raised, as if ready to strike. His eyes widened when he saw her, then he lowered his arm slowly to his side. "What're you doin', sneakin' up on a man like that?"

"I didn't sneak up. I've been talking to you for the past couple of minutes."

The blacksmith's eyes flicked to Dean before returning to Silver, starting at her feet and making a slow trip up her length. "What can I do for you?"

"I . . ." She tried not to think about what she was doing. It would hurt too much. "I hear you buy horses."

"Sometimes." He set aside his hammer, then wiped his hands against his leather apron. "What you got?"

She had spied Cinder as she approached the blacksmith, and she turned toward that stall now. "The buckskin mare. She's mine. I need to sell her if you're interested."

The man's face was darkened by soot and reddened from the heat of the fire. He was about the same height as she was but would have tipped the scales at more than double her own weight. His eyes seemed rather small in his large, square face, showing entirely too much white around them. She didn't like the way he'd been looking at her since she came in, and she doubted he had a decent, kind bone in his body. She hated the very idea of selling Cinder to him, but she didn't see that she had any choice.

"She's yours?" he asked, his tone suspicious.

Silver leveled him with her most authoritarian glare. "I was traveling with Mr. Newman, who brought in the three horses. I believe he sold you our packhorse. The pinto, I presume, still belongs to Mr. Newman. The buckskin is mine, however, and I should like to discuss a fair price for her."

The blacksmith drew his arm beneath his nose as he sniffed. "I don't do a lot o' tradin' in horses," he said as he walked toward the stall holding Cinder. He leaned against the rail and peered at the mare. "She probably makes a pretty good mount for a woman."

"Yes, she does," she said as she followed him, still leaning on Dean.

" 'Course, we still don't have us an overabundance of the female persuasion 'round these

parts. Not them that has time to go ridin', anyway."

"She's a good saddle horse. I've ridden her all
the way from Colorado without her coming up
lame or giving me any kind of a problem."

"Musta had some problem. My guess is she
throwed ya." He turned a piercing glance her
way.

"We were startled by a rattlesnake. It was entirely my fault that I lost my balance." She wasn't
going to let this riffraff find fault with Cinder.
"Perhaps you can recommend someone else who
would be interested in buying her."

"Don't get your nose in the air, little lady. I
never said I wasn't interested in buyin' the
mare."

The blacksmith grinned as he watched the tall,
slender woman limp out of his livery stable. The
last two days had been most profitable. He'd purchased two horses at low prices, knowing he
could double the money when he took them out
to the Anderson place. Better yet, he had paid for
the buckskin mare with the money Newman had
left for Miss Matlock. The mare actually hadn't
cost him a nickel of his own money.

It had worked out even better than he'd
thought it would. Now he wouldn't have to worry
about what story to tell Newman. Miss Matlock
would be gone, and he could let Newman think
she'd taken the money he'd given her.

Sometimes, he was just too darned smart. Yes,
sirree. Too darned smart.

I should have taken the money and bought a
ticket on the eastbound train for home.

That's what she was thinking as she and Dean
stepped from the station platform onto the west-

bound train. Using the money her father had given her—the money she'd kept so safely tucked away in case of an emergency—plus the money she'd obtained from the blacksmith for Cinder, Silver had purchased two tickets for Virginia City, territory of Nevada.

She didn't have any idea what she would do when she got there. She certainly wouldn't know how to go about finding Bob Cassidy or what she would do if she *did* find him. She only knew she wasn't going to give up so close to their destination. And if he wasn't there and never did come? Well, at least she would have tried.

Silver sat down in the passenger coach. The seat was hard. But, she reminded herself, at least we don't have to ride in the immigrant car, and this is a far sight more comfortable than taking a stagecoach.

She hoped Jared Newman was miserable, wherever he was.

Dean shoved the saddlebags they'd brought with them beneath their seats, then sat beside her. Was she doing the right thing to bring him along with her? she wondered. What if she were taking him into danger? He was just a boy. What right had she to drag him around the country?

And yet it would have seemed wrong to leave him behind—as Jared had done to her.

No, Dean belonged with her now. She placed an arm around his shoulders. When the boy glanced up at her with a quizzical expression, she offered a reassuring smile. He returned it, then continued his curious study of the passenger coach and the people around them.

Silver, on the other hand, turned her gaze out the window, wondering once again just what she was going to do when they reached Virginia City. If she found Bob Cassidy, she would figure out some way to get back the money, but if he wasn't there . . .

No, she wasn't going to think like that. He had to be there. He just had to be. She hadn't come all this way through the rain and dust and heat to be disappointed. She hadn't sold her beloved mare for a fraction of her worth only to fail yet again. Cassidy had to be in Virginia City, and she was going to find him.

Jared stepped out of the Silver City jail. He was disappointed but not surprised to find that the prisoner and suspect of three murders wasn't Cassidy. The man had, indeed, fit the physical description—tall, blond, blue eyes; even, Jared supposed, handsome—but he didn't have a scar on his chest nor had he been in Colorado in recent months. Jared had confirmed that with the sheriff. The man had been right there in Idaho all the time.

Jared placed his hat on his head, then stepped down from the boardwalk and started across the street toward the nearest saloon. He needed a drink, and then he was going to find himself a cheap room for the night. The southbound stage wouldn't be through Silver City until the next afternoon.

Leaning against the bar, watching as the bartender poured the golden brown whiskey into a squat glass, he found himself wishing the stage was there now. He was anxious to get back to Winnemucca. Or, to be more accurate, back to Silver.

He couldn't help wondering how her ankle was doing. Was she walking around on it now? And was she still angry at him? He didn't doubt that she'd been furious when the blacksmith delivered the note, but she should have cooled off by this time. He'd seen her temper flare often enough since meeting her to know she could calm down just as quickly. She was generally pretty fair-minded and rational, although he wasn't about to admit that to her.

He caught himself smiling as he reminisced about the past few weeks, each scene that flitted through his mind centered upon Silver. Strange how he didn't mind having her along anymore. It felt right to be with her.

Why didn't he just admit it? He missed her. He'd been away from her for only a couple of nights, yet already he felt like a part of him was missing. How had this happened to him, Jared Newman, outcast, loner, bounty hunter? How had he ever let a girl like Silver get under his skin? It wasn't a very smart thing to do. It wasn't very smart at all.

His smile faded as he recalled their night of lovemaking. Guilt assailed him. She'd been a virgin. True, she had lied to him, made him think she was experienced in such things. But still he couldn't shake the guilt. He'd been brought up to believe a man behaved differently toward a lady. It was one thing to sow one's wild oats with a woman of lesser morals and more experience; it was entirely another to take a virgin outside of marriage. He could almost hear his father lecturing him about such things, the two of them closed up in his study at the back of the house.

He motioned to the bartender for another whiskey, then tossed it down the back of his throat.

Hellfire! He couldn't believe he was letting it get to him this way. She had been as willing as he. There hadn't been any professions of love or false hopes of a future together. It wasn't as if he'd promised to marry her or give her a home.

She could have turned him down. She could have said no.

Jared turned away from the bar and walked out of the salon with quick strides. He needed that bed and a good night's sleep. He was tired. That's all that was wrong with him.

But sleep didn't help. Silver's image stayed as clear as ever in his mind. Not just Silver on the night they'd made love, her pale flesh glowing in the moonlight, but Silver mumbling sleepily in the morning, Silver brushing Dean's hair aside, Silver trying to cook over the campfire. He pictured her in her wedding dress as she raced toward him along the boardwalk, gray eyes snapping with fury even as they welled with tears. He saw her in her leather skirt and simple blouse, her wide-brimmed hat set securely over her blue-black hair, her thick braid bouncing against her back as they cantered the horses across the desert. He saw her sleeping in the chair beside his bed, her pink gingham dress covered with dried blood. He saw her crying and laughing, cursing and whispering.

Get a hold of yourself, Newman, Jared thought the next morning as he paused outside the hotel. He was beginning to act like a moonstruck youth. Or worse, like a man falling in love.

He touched the butt of the revolver riding against his right hip. This was reality. This was his life. He wasn't about to let himself fall in love with some woman just because he'd bedded her. Besides, loving was too risky. Getting close, loving someone else, only left you lonely and hurt when they were gone.

He'd better remember that next time he thought of Silver.

Chapter 23

A feeling of helplessness swamped Silver as she gazed along the main street of Virginia City. She hadn't imagined it would be so big. A continuous line of roofs stretched for a distance of five miles or so, and more spread out on either side, rising up the mountain on her right and downward on her left. She'd been told thirty thousand people lived in Virginia City and Gold Hill, but it seemed like even more. Dust filled the air as horses and wagons moved constantly along the thoroughfares. The sun baked the arid mountain terrain, scorching the flowers planted by women hoping to bring a little color to this corner of the world.

Silver grasped Dean's hand firmly within her own. "We'd better find a place to stay," she said, trying to sound sure of herself.

How on earth would she find Cassidy even if he was there? she wondered as they moved along the uneven boardwalk. There must be dozens of saloons and gambling dens and nearly as many hotels. It would take her days to search out each and every one.

She thought of the small horde of money she possessed. How long would it last? The prices she'd seen thus far seemed exorbitantly high. If

245

she turned around now, she would have enough to purchase tickets back to Colorado for both her and Dean. But only if she did so right away.

She paused on the boardwalk as a wagon lumbered past them. Her gaze was caught by the stoop-shouldered man holding the reins. His bald head was bare, his bushy brows drawn together in a frown. His wife, her face dour and bleak, sat beside him on the wagon seat. The buckboard was piled high with what was obviously their worldly possessions.

She thought of her parents being thrown out of their home. Where would they go? What would they do? Would they wind up someplace like this with no money and no hope? She couldn't let that happen to them, no matter what she had to go through. She couldn't back out now.

Bolstering her courage, she began walking again. As they approached a dress-making shop, sandwiched between a dry-goods store and a drugstore, a buxom woman carrying a parasol stepped through the doorway onto the boardwalk. The violet parasol with its white lace edging hid the woman's face from view, but it was the gown that captured Silver's attention. It had been a long time since she'd seen anything so lovely.

The violet silk dress had a trained skirt, trimmed with four scalloped flounces, each surmounted by a band of black velvet ribbon. The overskirt and waist were a lighter shade of violet faille, trimmed with white lace and black velvet ribbons and bows. The sleeves of the bodice were long with lacy cuffs. The woman's hands were covered with matching violet gloves.

The woman turned toward Silver as she switched the parasol to her other shoulder. Silver glimpsed the curls of blonde hair beneath the white chip bonnet, trimmed with light violet rib-

bon and yellow and purple pansies, before looking at the woman's face.

She had the face of an angel, every curve, every
angle perfection. It would have been difficult to
guess how old she was. She might be twenty; she
might be thirty-five. She was beautiful, no matter
her age.

The woman's light blue eyes were friendly as
she met Silver's gaze. She inclined her head
slightly. "Good day," she said in a voice that
seemed almost musical.

"Hello." Silver realized she'd been staring and
felt herself blush.

Now the woman smiled. "You look lost. May I
help you find something? Or someone?"

Silver took a deep breath. "We just arrived and
we're looking for a place to stay. Someplace af-
fordable," she added hastily.

Laughter escaped the woman's cherry-pink
lips. "There is no such thing in Virginia City."
She held out a gloved hand. "Miss Corinne Duvall."

"I'm Silver Matlock. And this is Dean."

"How do you do, sir," Corinne said as she
shook the boy's hand. Her eyes shifted back to
Silver. For a moment they seemed to assess the
tall, ebony-haired girl. "How long do you intend
to stay in Virginia City, Mrs. Matlock?"

"I . . . I'm not sure . . . And it's *Miss* Matlock."

With another thoughtful look the woman perused Silver. "Miss . . . Yes. Then I assume you'll
be looking for suitable employment as well as a
place to stay?"

"Yes . . . I . . . yes."

"Come with me, Miss Matlock," Corinne said
in a voice that allowed for no argument. With a
hand lifting the front of her skirt just enough to

reveal the toes of her violet walking shoes, she turned and led the way toward a black buggy tied in front of the dry-goods store. "Just put your things in the back," she said as she stepped up into the buggy, her every movement graceful.

Silver stopped abruptly. "Really, Miss Duvall, we can't impose. You don't even know us. We can't put you out."

"Nonsense. I remember what it was like, arriving here with no friends or family. Get in. I'm more than glad to help."

Feeling as if she'd been swept down river by a strong current, Silver obeyed.

As soon as Dean had climbed into the back, settled between their saddlebags and Corinne's packages, Corinne lifted the reins and slapped them against the horse's rump, and they took off at a smart jog.

"What do you mean, she's not here?"

The hotel clerk glared at Jared. "Just what I said. She paid her bill and left."

"Where did she go?"

"It's not my business, mister, to be askin' the guests where they're going. The lady and the boy just carried their bags out, and that's the last I saw of them."

Jared checked his anger. "Thanks," he mumbled as he turned toward the door.

"Mister!" the clerk called after him.

Jared turned around.

"She did leave some things behind. Said they were yours, if you came back for them. I put 'em in the storage room behind the kitchen." He pointed.

"Thanks," he said again. "I'm going to check on my horse. I'll be back for my things later."

Jared walked swiftly toward the livery stable.

His eyes swept the street, as if he expected trouble at every turn. There had to be a reason for Silver to suddenly leave Winnemucca. Was she in danger? Had Cassidy shown up here?

He paused inside the livery doorway. "Crandon!" he shouted.

The blacksmith stepped out of a stall, a pitchfork in hand. His eyes narrowed when he recognized Jared. "I wondered if you'd be comin' back."

"Why?" He looked quickly down the row of stalls on his left until he found the familiar black-and-white head poking over the rail. The pinto nickered at him as he turned his attention back to the blacksmith. "Why'd you think I might not be back?" he repeated. "I told you I would. You didn't think I'd leave my horses, did you?"

The smithy shrugged as he set aside the pitchfork. "I didn't know what to think after that Miss Matlock come in and sold me her mare."

"She *what*?"

"Sold me that mare o' hers."

"Where is the mare?"

"Outside. I got me a buyer comin' by t'look at her."

Something wasn't right here. Jared knew it. He'd left Silver enough money to hold her until he got back. She wouldn't sell Cinder without a very good reason. He knew how much the horse meant to her.

He stepped toward Crandon. "Why did she sell you the buckskin?" His voice was low, harsh. He looked down at the burly man, who was about six inches shorter than he was.

"Don't have any idea."

Jared's fingers closed around the collar of the blacksmith's shirt and drew him closer. "I want to know why she sold you that horse." But he already had a strong suspicion. Silver had never gotten his note with the money. She'd thought he'd left her and Dean stranded there with nothing.

"I don't know, I tell you." Crandon managed to pry Jared's hands free of his collar, then stepped back a pace or two.

"I don't have the time, Crandon, or I'd settle this with you right now. Just get my horses—the pinto *and* the buckskin—ready. You give me no grief, and we'll forget that you stole from me." He leveled a deadly gaze on the blacksmith. "But if any harm comes to Miss Matlock because of this, I'll be back. You understand me?"

Normally, the blacksmith might have had an edge over the tall, lanky bounty hunter. After years of wrestling animals, hammering iron, and pumping bellows, he had arms as thick as tree limbs and hands that could grip like a vise. But there was something in Jared's tone which must have warned him that this time he couldn't win.

He swallowed hard. "I'll have 'em ready in a minute." Then he hurried into the corral at the back of the stable, rope in hand, and returned moments later with Cinder.

Damn! Jared swore. Why did this have to happen? With insight from the heart, he knew that desertion would hurt Silver more than anything else. She'd been rejected often enough in her life. And if there was anything he didn't want, it was to hurt her.

Now he had to find her and tell her.

Corinne Duvall's palatial home sat on the hillside overlooking Virginia City. It was an enormous red brick structure with white shutters at the windows and a white veranda around three sides. Rosebushes twined around the narrow columns on either side of the front steps. Here, at last, a gardener had succeeded in producing colorful flowers and a patch of green lawn.

The moment Corinne stopped the buggy, the front door opened and a short, slight Oriental man hurried toward them.

"Thank you, Chung," Corinne said as he helped her down from the carriage. "Please take Miss Matlock's things to the blue room." She glanced toward Silver. "Come with me, dear."

Silver stared up at the three-story house before her and wondered what she was doing there. All she'd done was ask for directions to an inexpensive place to stay, and now she was at Corinne Duvall's home. Not just a home—a mansion!

Dean's hand gripped hers, causing her to look down at him as he took his place beside her. She could see her own awe mirrored in his eyes. Judging by the small ramshackle abode she'd found him in, she guessed he'd never seen anything close to the likes of this. Silver had seen similar mansions in Denver, but she'd never been invited inside.

Squeezing Dean's hand and giving him a brave nod, she followed Corinne.

Chapter 24

The beautiful blonde was waiting for them just inside the front door. She had leaned the handle of her parasol against the wall, a panel of violet silk balancing on the shiny parquet floor. She had removed her gloves, laying them one on top of the other on the dark mahogany table near the front entrance. She was looking into the mirror as she freed the perky bonnet and lifted it from her yellow curls. Patting her hair, she turned toward Silver.

"I love hats, but they can get tiresome," Corinne said. Then she waved a carefully manicured hand toward an arched doorway. "Let's get comfortable, shall we, and you can tell me all about yourself."

Silver's hand tightened around Dean's as she followed the woman into a large parlor. There were fireplaces with elaborate fire screens at both ends of the room. To her right was a white grand piano, its curved edges trimmed with gold paint. A white fur rug lay beneath it. Several groupings of chairs stood about the high-ceilinged room, and plenty of light spilled through the glass windows, their heavy brocade drapes pulled open and tied back.

Dominating everything else in the room, above

the far fireplace mantel, was an enormous portrait of Corinne Duvall. Silver felt herself drawn to it. She freed Dean's hand and walked across the room.

"Quite good, isn't it?" a voice said near Silver's shoulder.

She turned to look at Corinne.

"Maurice was in love with me when he painted it. You can tell. He was kind to me."

"But it looks just like you," Silver said, her eyes returning to the portrait.

"When I was young, perhaps. No more." Corinne moved away.

Silver continued to stare up at the painting in its gilded frame. The artist had painted his subject in a yellow strapless gown with a daring plunge at the bodice. There was something about the look on Corinne's face as she gazed at the artist that made Silver feel warm, almost embarrassed, as if she'd just walked in upon an intimate moment between lovers.

Silver turned around.

Corinne was seated on a white-and-gold brocade sofa. She gestured toward a companion piece set not far away. "Please sit down."

"Miss Duvall, I really can't impose . . ."

"Everyone calls me Miss Corinne."

"All right. Miss Corinne, I appreciate your offer to help us, but I don't know why you've brought us here. We simply needed a hotel for the night . . ."

"This is a very rough-and-tumble town, Silver. People are getting rich and getting poor with equally incredible speed. We like to think we're a civilized city, equal to anything back east, but the truth is, we have more than our share of drunkards, outlaws, and cutthroats in Virginia City. It's not the safest of places for a young, attractive, single woman." Once again she motioned toward the nearby sofa. "Now sit down and tell me about yourself," she said in her no-nonsense voice.

Overwhelmed, Silver obeyed. "There isn't much to tell really. I'm from a small town in Colorado, near Denver."

"And what brought you here?" Corinne prompted.

She hesitated, not certain what to say.

"Ah . . . I see. A man." Corinne stretched an arm across the back of the sofa as she reclined against the side cushion. "And you think he's here in Virginia City. Is he the boy's father, this man?"

Silver shook her head.

Corinne's mouth curved in an angelic smile. "I don't mean to pester you, Silver, and I pride myself on being a good judge of character. I like you. I would like to help you, if you'll let me."

"Help me. But I don't know . . ."

The blonde raised a hand. Her eyelids fluttered shut a moment, then opened to reveal a commanding look. "When I came to Virginia City, I was a penniless orphan. To survive, I worked in a saloon and . . . *entertained* the men. It wasn't a very pleasant existence. But I was smart and I was lucky, and I managed to change my life for the better." Corinne straightened on the sofa. "There are lots of reasons for young girls to end up in a place like Virginia City. I try to keep a few of them from going through what I went through."

Corinne *was* older than Silver had at first thought. She could see it now. For a moment she caught a glimpse of something in the woman's face that said she had seen too much, lived too hard, to be young any longer. And then it was gone.

"I have no intention of prying into your private

affairs, Silver. I only mean to help out while you're here. I would like you to go to work for me.''

"Me? Why? You know nothing about me.''

Corinne waved a hand, flicking away her protest as meaningless. ''I know that you are tall and beautiful, and I suspect that limp is only temporary. A sprain, perhaps?'' She didn't wait for Silver to confirm or deny her assumption. She glanced toward Dean, who still stood just inside the parlor doorway. ''And I know that you are kind. I suspect this boy is no relation of yours. You're far too young to be his mother. You've simply helped him out of the goodness of your heart. Am I right?''

Silver had no chance to answer before the servant, Chung, appeared in the doorway carrying a silver tea tray.

"Ah, my afternoon tea. Thank you, Chung. You'll have some, too, won't you, Miss Matlock? Such a civilized practice, tea in the afternoon.''

Chung set the tray on the low table between the sofas, then bowed sharply toward his mistress and left.

Feeling as if she were being swept before a gale-force wind, Silver asked, ''But what would I do for you, Miss Duvall? I've worked in my parents' mercantile store, but I . . .''

"Miss Corinne, remember?'' She leaned forward and poured tea into a delicate china cup. She offered the cup to Silver, then poured her own.

A clock chimed in the entry hall.

"My goodness,'' Corinne said, her eyebrows arching in surprise. ''I had no idea it was so late. Chung . . .'' she called, rising from the sofa. When the man appeared, she said, ''Show Miss Matlock to the blue room and then draw her a bath. And I think the boy would like that little room on the third floor. The one on the north side." She started from the parlor in a swirl of violet skirts. "I'll see you at supper. We dine at six-thirty sharp."

Silver let the steam rise around her face as she leaned back in the tub. She still wasn't sure what was going on with Corinne Duvall or what exactly she was supposed to do, but for the moment she was going to enjoy the bath as it soaked the soreness from her muscles.

With a lazy glance she took in the opulence of the bathing room with its thick rug, ornate molding, gilded mirror, and multicolored bottles of sweet-smelling bath salts and perfumes. She'd never seen anything like it and certainly wasn't sure what she'd done to be enjoying it.

Finally, the water cooling, Silver stepped from the bathtub and wrapped herself in the plush towel. She pulled the ribbon from her hair and allowed it to fall down her back. She would have loved to wash her hair, but the thick ebony tresses would never dry before suppertime.

She opened the adjoining door to the "blue room," as Corinne had called it. And blue it was, from the paper on the walls to the Persian rugs on the floor to the bedspread to the curtains. All in varying shades of blue, from the delicate hue of a robin's egg to the vibrant color of an indigo bunting.

And when she looked for her clothes where she'd left them on the bed, she found instead a blue gown that was every bit as lovely as the violet silk Corinne had worn. Silver picked it up, her eyes wide. She couldn't accept it. She would have to refuse. But—she glanced quickly about the room—she had to wear something when she went to find Corinne, and her own clothes were missing.

If she had any sense, she thought as she slipped

into the soft undergarments left beside the gown on the bed, she would find Dean and get out of this place. Corinne Duvall was obviously some sort of eccentric—or worse. Perhaps she kidnapped young women and boys and sold them into some sort of slavery, shanghaied them to China even. Or perhaps she . . .

Get a hold of yourself, she silently scolded as the blue gown settled around her, a perfect fit. This isn't a bad novel you're living in. Miss Corinne doesn't strike me as a crazy villainess. You might as well hear her out. You haven't the slightest idea how to go about finding Bob, and you don't have an abundance of money with which to take care of you until you do. Maybe Miss Corinne can even be of help. She must know lots of people in Virginia City.

From somewhere in the house, she heard the chiming of the quarter hour. Perhaps she should leave the room now. She had no idea how long it would take her to find the dining room.

Even as she contemplated it, she heard a door close—and then another and another and another. Muted voices and soft laughter filtered into the room. Curious, she hurried forward and opened the door a crack just in time to see several young women descending the stairway to the first floor.

Confused and slightly alarmed, her fantasies of kidnapped maidens returning to haunt her, Silver turned from the door. She crossed the large room once again, returning to the bedside where she slipped her feet into the blue satin slippers that had been left for her. Once again, they were a surprisingly good fit. Then she picked up the gold-inlaid hairbrush on the dresser and began brushing her hair until it gleamed. She tied it back at the nape with a blue hair ribbon.

Butterflies were whirling in her stomach when

she opened her door for the second time. Voices floated up from below, happy, girlish sounds. Silver followed them as she walked down the staircase and moved across the parquet floor toward the back of the mansion, her way lit by several chandeliers in the windowless entry hall.

The door to the dining room stood open. The voices and laughter were louder now. Silver stepped forward, stopping beneath the transom, her gray eyes surveying the room.

They were arrayed in a spectrum of colors, no two the same. There must have been close to twenty of them, ranging in ages from twelve or thirteen to perhaps twenty-five or more. There were redheads and brunettes, golden blondes and strawberry blondes, and plenty of hair in varying shades of browns. Jewelry glittered at their throats and on their earlobes and fingers. They smiled and laughed and hugged one another as they milled around the long table covered with a white cloth. Fine china and crystal sparkled in candlelight shed by the candelabras.

A thrumming started up in Silver's head. The pain throbbed at her temples and just behind her eyes. She didn't know if she'd ever felt so confused and disoriented in her life. Perhaps she was having a dream, and when she woke up, she would find herself back in Winnemucca, Jared watching over her and asking how her ankle was doing.

No, she thought as she lifted her chin. Jared wasn't anywhere around. He had left her without a thought, not caring what happened to her. She would have to figure this all out on her own.

Squaring her shoulders, she stepped into the dining room.

Chapter 25

Each girl had a story of her own, some exciting, most sad. As the sumptuous meal was served by Corinne's servants, Silver heard bits and pieces from each of them as they were introduced. It took her a little while to comprehend what each of them was saying, but finally she understood.

Corinne Duvall, who at one time had been forced into prostitution to survive and who later rose to wealth and power in Virginia City, had saved each of them from a fate similar to her own, a fate which usually had a much different ending. In return for a place to stay, plenty of good food, and pretty clothes, the girls worked in Corinne's Rainbow Saloon, serving drinks, entertaining the customers with songs, talking with lonely miners. But one thing was strictly forbidden. There was no fraternization with men except in the parlor in Corinne's home, an activity which was strictly chaperoned.

Silver listened, absorbing the information, as her eyes moved around the table. If the young women in that dining room had one thing in common, it was beauty. She'd never seen so many perfectly sculpted faces, rosy mouths, or pearl-like complexions. If beauty was a prerequisite for being there, Silver thought, she was most certainly out of place.

Supper finished, the women rose in unison, their voices still gay. Silver started to follow after them, planning to seek the safety and quiet of her room, but Corinne's cultured voice stopped her.

"May we speak a moment, Silver?"

She turned toward the woman who was still seated at the head of the table. "Yes?"

Corinne motioned toward the vacated seat on her right. "Sit down, please." She gave Silver a moment to do so. "I presume you understand about my saloon. We allow no fighting, no troublemakers, and the girls are off-limits to the men, except as pleasurable company for the evening. It's a safe environment for these young women as long as they choose to stay. Many of them meet men who later come to court them here at the house. We've seen a number of them married in the parlor. I would like you to stay if you wish."

"Miss Duvall . . ."

"Corinne."

Silver nodded. "Miss Corinne, you don't know why I came to Virginia City."

She waved a hand. "Everyone here has a story to tell. You heard parts of them tonight. It doesn't matter, as long as you're willing to live by the rules." She raised a finely arched eyebrow. "Are you?"

"Yes, but—"

"Then it's settled." Corinne began to rise.

The words sprang from her lips before she could stop them. "But everyone here is so beautiful. I just don't belong."

The woman's blue eyes widened, then perused Silver with ruthless scrutiny. Finally, a gentle smile curled the corners of her perfect mouth.

"You truly believe that, don't you?" she asked softly.

Silver couldn't reply. She was too mortified by the words she'd already blurted out. It had sounded as if she was fishing for a compliment. Worse still, she didn't want to force a comparison with the other young women who lived there.

Corinne stood and took Silver's hand, drawing her from her chair and across the room to a gold-backed mirror above the fireplace. "Look at yourself, my dear."

Silver did. She saw the way she towered over the petite Miss Duvall. She saw the long, narrow face dominated by large gray eyes. She saw the slender figure with breasts too small, her only curves made by the bustle beneath her skirts. Her black hair, when compared to her hostess's yellow curls, seemed so grim and lifeless.

"Good heavens," Corinne whispered, "you still don't see. You are a classic beauty, my dear. Look at those fine, high cheekbones and your flawless skin. And your eyes. There are men who would kill just for a moment to gaze into them. And your mouth. Like a promise of wild honey."

Silver shook her head, disbelieving.

"Look at the way you hold yourself, tall and proud despite yourself. Don't be ashamed of your height, Silver. You're lucky. You have a better view of the world than someone like me."

As Corinne continued, ticking off one point after another—the lush ebony-blue of her hair, her soot-colored eyelashes, her high, firm breasts, her narrow waist—something miraculous happened. The gawky youngster and the skinny spinster who had always gazed back at her from every mirror began to fade from view, replaced by another young woman, a stranger to her. The hair, the eyes, the mouth were all as Corinne had described. Her mother's voice, echoing in the recesses of Silver's mind, tried to drive off the stranger, tried to bring back the spinster, but she refused to let it happen. Not yet anyway.

"All right," she said in a low, uncertain voice. "I'll stay with you. For a little while, at least."

"Of course. Just while you need to. Now come. The carriages are ready to take us to the Rainbow. We don't want to keep the customers waiting."

Jared's body was weary beyond belief. He knew he couldn't push the horses as hard after today without breaking them down. He would have to go easy or he'd find himself afoot.

He stared up at the sliver of moon overhead. She would be in Virginia City by now. Had she gotten enough from the sale of Cinder to cover not only the train fare but also a hotel room? Were she and Dean eating all right? Was Cassidy in Virginia City? Had he seen Silver? Was she safe?

He rolled onto his side, setting his jaw. He'd never get any sleep if he kept thinking about her. Fool female! Didn't she know him better than to think he'd just leave her like that? Couldn't she have figured out what had happened?

Damn fool female! She could drive a man crazy. If he ever made it back to Denver, he was going to strangle Rick Cooper.

Maybe he would get lucky and he'd never even see her again.

Dear God, keep her safe. Please, keep her safe until I can find her.

After Silver's experiences in Black Hawk and Laramie, she knew about saloons. They were rough board floors, brass spittoons, green felt card tables, and smelly cowboys and miners. They were scantily clad women with painted faces.

They were smoke-filled, small and narrow, and noisy with off-key pianos banging in the background.

The Rainbow Saloon wasn't any of these things.

Silver stood in a corner, her gaze sweeping once again around the spacious room. The floors were as smooth and shiny as those in Corinne's own home. Elegant curtains cloaked the ceiling-high windows that lined the street-side wall. The felt tables were in every color of the rainbow rather than the usual emerald green. Colorful wallpaper decorated the walls. The smooth wood pillars and railings and wainscoting were all painted white. Crystal chandeliers hung from the ceiling, matching lamps along the walls. Waitresses in simple pink or blue or lavender gowns with white aprons and caps took orders for drinks; there was no bar or bartender in view. The music that played softly in the background was elegant, refined—out of place for other saloons but not for the Rainbow. Corinne's girls, as Silver mentally called them now, were scattered around the room, talking with men in secluded corners or watching behind them at the gambling tables.

Her attention shifted to the male customers. They weren't all wealthy gentlemen in fine suits as one might expect in such a place, yet even the least well-dressed were clean and tidy. Long hair was swept back and beards were freshly groomed. They spoke respectfully to the girls, their smiles hopeful rather than leering.

Throughout the evening, Corinne had moved around the Rainbow like a queen in her own throne room, giving audience to those fortunate enough to gain her attention. Her angelic smile could leave the toughest of men speechless.

Of course, it wasn't just Corinne's presence that kept the peace within her saloon. There were sev-

eral muscular young men in black evening suits
stationed at key points in the immense room, their
arms clasped behind their backs as their eyes sur-
veyed their surroundings, always watching for
signs of trouble. At the first indication of drunk-
enness, a flash of anger, or an indiscretion toward
one of Corinne's girls, the perpetrator was po-
litely, firmly, and promptly whisked from the establishment with scarcely another person aware
that it had happened.

If Bob Cassidy was in Virginia City, Silver
thought, this was where he would come. It was
difficult for her to assimilate that the Cassidy who
could kill and mutilate women was the same Bob
who dressed with flare and patronized fine res-
taurants. Yet she knew it was true, and she knew
she'd found the place to be if she was to meet up
with him in this town. She just had to be patient
and wait for him to show up.

The curtains on the stage at the back of the saloon parted, accompanied by an announcing cre-
scendo from the piano. A small, dark-haired girl
with a bronze complexion and round brown eyes
stepped forward, her hands folded in front of her
sun-yellow gown. The crowd grew quiet as she
began to sing, the sweet strains of the aria filling
the room.

"Remarkable voice, hasn't she?" Corinne
whispered near Silver's ear.

She turned, surprised by the woman's sudden
appearance at her side.

"Maria has the talent to be a great singer some
day, with the right training. She was traveling
with a little show and being abused by her man-
ager when she came to me. I don't expect she'll
be with us much longer though. Already there
have been a number of inquiries from theatrical
agents looking for new talent. When I've checked

them out thoroughly and am assured of their le-
gitimacy, I suspect she will be leaving us."

She acts like a doting mother, Silver thought as
she watched Corinne.

The woman's blue eyes were filled with pride,
her gaze locked on Maria. There was also a glimmer in the corners which looked suspiciously like
tears.

When the song was finished, Corinne turned
toward Silver. "So, what do you think of the
Rainbow?"

"I would never have imagined it in a hundred
years," Silver answered truthfully.

"Come. You've stood here and watched the evening's activities long enough. Let me introduce
you to a few of our regular customers. I'll walk
slow so you don't tax your ankle."

Silver opened the door to the bedroom, allowing a streak of yellow light to stream in from the
hall. Dean was nestled on his side in the bed,
sound asleep. He frowned as the light touched
his face but didn't awaken.

She tiptoed across the room and knelt beside
the bed. Her fingers brushed the hair on his forehead, more out of habit now than because it had
actually fallen across his face. He mumbled something unintelligible before rolling onto his other
side.

Silver tugged the light blanket up over his
shoulders, then rose and bent forward to kiss his
temple. He looked well-fed and comfortable and
that, in turn, made her feel she had done something right for a change. She hadn't been mistaken to buy the train tickets and come to Virginia
City. She hadn't been wrong to bring the orphan
with her.

With one last glance at the sleeping boy, she

left the bedroom and descended the stairs to the second floor, quickly making her way to the blue room. She was tired and ready for sleep.

Upon opening the door to the bedroom—which she had already begun thinking of as hers—she found the bedside lamp lit and a pretty new nightgown lying across the bedspread. She smiled, no longer surprised by the clothes that seemed to appear out of nowhere. She shed the blue silk gown, placing it carefully across the back of a chair, then slipped the sheer nightgown over her head, enjoying the feel of the cool fabric as it slid over her skin toward the floor.

Removing her hairpins, she promised herself that she would enjoy another long bath in the morning and this time get to wash her hair. And then she was going to investigate Virginia City, perhaps buy some new clothes for Dean with her dwindling cash.

She crawled into bed, slipping beneath the cool sheets and the fluffy comforter, her head resting on a down-filled pillow. She closed her eyes, reveling in the luxury. This wasn't a cheap hotel or a bedroll under the stars or the hard seat on a moving train. She was lying in a beautiful room on the most comfortable mattress she'd ever believed could exist. Perhaps she should pinch herself to see if it was real.

She sighed, feeling happy and content. Her body relaxed as she drifted toward sleep.

I wonder where Jared is now?

No, she didn't want to think of Jared.

I wonder if he'll go back for his pinto.

Oh, please. She wanted to sleep. If she kept thinking of Jared, she wouldn't be able to.

What would it be like to have him make love to me in a bed like this?

Warmth spread through her as a gnawing want

began in her vitals. Self-consciously, she touched her breasts, trying to stop the tingling sensation that was torturing the nipples. Instinctively she knew that only Jared could really assuage the building need.

I hate you, bounty. I hope I never see you again.
Her body knew it was a lie.

Chapter 26

Morning sunlight flooded the second-floor solarium where Silver reclined on a lounge. Her satin-and-lace negligee spilled over the brocade couch and onto the floor where a fat, long-haired cat had curled up for its morning nap. The rest of the house seemed just as lazy as the feline. She hadn't heard a single sound since she had followed Nissa into the solarium thirty minutes before.

Just as that thought dissipated, the rattle of dishes came from outside the door. Carrying a coffee tray, Chung hurried into the room, nodded to the two young women, set the tray down on the table, and left the parlor.

Silver stared after him, then turned to Nissa. The pretty Swedish girl with nearly white hair and eyes of icy blue was only two or three inches shorter than Silver. Perhaps that was why the two had been drawn to each other from the moment they met. They each understood what it was like to be different.

"You know," Silver said thoughtfully, "I've been here for four days now, and I've yet to ever hear Chung speak. Why doesn't he? Surely he can. He understands English well enough when it's spoken to him."

"No one told you?" Nissa replied, her words rounded and rolling. "Chung has no tongue. Someone cut it out when he worked for the railroad."

"How awful!"

Nissa's voice dropped to a whisper. "Miss Corinne says there was a young woman he loved who was raped by some white men. She starved herself to death out of shame. When Chung demanded justice for the crime, he was punished instead."

Silver couldn't think of anything adequate to say. She simply shook her head to indicate the sorrow and pity she felt.

"Nissa, Silver." Maria bounded into the solarium. "At last I have found someone who is not so lazy. Everyone else is still in bed and the day is half gone. I am going shopping. Want to come?"

Nissa shook her head. "I cannot." She glanced at Silver. "I have some letters to write. Mama, she has written twice since I last answered. No, I had better stay in today."

"I'll join you, Maria," Silver replied, rising to her feet. "Dean needs some new britches, and I don't think that's something Miss Corinne keeps in stock with all her pretty gowns."

Maria's laughter, bright and boisterous, filled the room. "I think you are right, Señorita Silver. Dean is the only *niño* to ever live here."

Where Nissa was tall and fair, Maria was petite and dark. Nissa's speech rolled with the cadence of the Swedes while Maria's was sprinkled with words from her native Mexico. Silver found the girls and their accents charming.

"Give me a moment to get dressed, and I'll meet you out front."

Several hours later, her arms loaded with packages—all except one belonging to Maria—Silver stepped through the doorway of the Golden Emporium. Behind her she could hear Maria's rapid chatter as she shared gossip with the proprietress of the store. Silver decided to unburden her arms before going back inside to retrieve Maria.

She turned and began walking beneath the awnings that shaded the uneven boardwalk, headed toward the horse and buggy tied two stores away. She'd taken no more than a half-dozen steps when she abruptly stopped and leaned against the building at her back, feeling as if the wind had been knocked out of her.

His white hat had a broad brim, shading his eyes from view, but his smooth-shaven jaw with its small, white scar was easily visible. He sat straight in the saddle, guiding the sorrel mare down the center of the street. Sweat darkened the animal's neck and haunches and formed a white lather around the edges of the saddle blanket. The man's light-colored suit was covered with a fine layer of dust, but despite his travel-weary appearance, there was an aura of power about him.

When Bob Cassidy turned his head in her direction, she quickly ducked behind the pile of packages in her arms. She held her breath, wondering how soon it would be safe to look again. Finally, she lowered her cover in time to see him turning a corner.

He was there. She'd seen him. She'd found him. He was actually in Virginia City. The excitement lasted only a brief moment.

The shaking hit her suddenly and without warning. What if he'd recognized her too? What if he suspected why she was there? What if he did to her what he'd done to Jared's sister and to that woman in Texas and to Dean's mother?

"*Amiga?*" Maria's hand touched Silver's shoulder.

She jumped, a scream strangled in her throat, the packages scattering in all directions.

"*Amiga*, what is wrong? Are you not well?"

Silver knelt and began picking up their purchases. "No. No, you just startled me."

"You are as white as Miss Corinne's cat. You stay here. I will get the buggy and take you home."

Silver nodded. She wanted to get back to the mansion on the hill. She wanted to hide in the safety of the blue room. Later she would have to think of a plan for getting her money back, but right now, she wanted only to rid herself of the frightening images stirred by her first sight of Bob.

As she waited, she glanced nervously toward the spot where he'd disappeared moments before. She didn't want him to come back and discover her there. She didn't want him to know she was in Virginia City until she'd had a chance to think things through, to formulate a plan. If she acted prudently, there was no need for her to be in any danger. He knew the money was hers. Surely she could get it back from him.

"Are you sure you feel up to working tonight? You still look pale." Corinne's smooth fingertips stroked Silver's forehead.

"Truly, I'm fine," she answered. "If you don't mind, I'll eat in my room while I gèt ready, but I really feel quite well. I don't know what was wrong with me this afternoon. It was probably too much heat or too much excitement from shopping with Maria." She smiled, doing her best to convince Corinne.

"Well . . ." Corinne rose from the mattress

where she'd been sitting at Silver's side. "I'm not sure I should let you."

"I want to go, Miss Corinne. I'm supposed to be working for you, aren't I? Besides, I enjoy it. Please."

A slight narrowing of her blue eyes said better than words that Corinne still wasn't convinced, but at last she nodded. "I'll have Chung bring up your supper."

"Thanks. I'll be ready."

After Corinne left the bedroom, Silver lay back against the pillows and closed her eyes. It would have been so much easier to agree to remain within the safety of this house, to pretend she'd never seen Bob Cassidy. But staying in hiding wasn't really an option.

As she'd lain in bed that afternoon, she'd known she couldn't take the chance that Cassidy would simply pass through Virginia City on his way elsewhere. She had to make sure he stayed there until she could get her money back and see him safely behind bars. So far she hadn't been able to come up with a plan that would accomplish either of those things. She would have to settle for just making him stay in Virginia City, and the only way she saw to do that was to let him know she was in town. She would have to talk to him, convince him she still cared for him. She had no idea if she possessed the necessary acting skills, but she was determined to give it a try. She'd known the first time she saw the Rainbow Saloon that he would go there if he was in Virginia City. She had to be there when he arrived.

She shuddered at the thought of that confrontation. She kept seeing Dean kneeling over his parents' graves. She kept hearing Jared telling her the things Bob Cassidy had done. He was a ruthless, demented killer. No one was safe when he was around.

How she wished she could just go to the sheriff and be done with it, but she knew it would be a waste of time. Bob Cassidy walked free because no one had ever survived to point the finger of guilt at him. Without that girl in Central City to identify him, the one Jared had told her about, Bob would remain free. She couldn't let that happen, but how was she to stop it?

If Jared was there, he could tell her what to do. "But he *isn't* here," she scolded herself aloud. "You have to do this on your own."

Silver tossed back the bed sheets and dropped her feet to the floor. Clothed in a white corset and jaconet petticoat, she padded barefoot across the room to the dresser. She removed silk stockings from the drawer, then sat on a nearby stool and carefully pulled them over her feet and legs.

She paused, the petticoat still pulled up to mid-thigh, and stared into space. Wouldn't Jared be surprised if he could see her now, surrounded by so many feminine trappings? The plain blouse and split leather skirt were packed away in the bottom of a drawer. The weathered boots were tucked into the back of the wardrobe. Every day now, she dressed in gowns nearly as fancy as the one she was to have been married in. It had been so long since Jared had seen her in something pretty and feminine instead of covered with trail dust, dirt streaking her cheeks. She wished he could see her in one of these pretty silk dresses.

Wasn't it strange how people could change? She'd always preferred the simpler clothes. Her parents had given her plenty of attractive dresses and riding habits, yet she'd always liked her split skirt and boots best of all. So much easier for riding astride, for escaping the disapproval of others.

She rose from the stool and went to stand before the full-length mirror. It still surprised her to glance at her reflection and not see what her mother had always told her was there. She still expected to hear the teasing of her schoolmates. She couldn't quite believe that she had grown into all the long angles and bean-pole appendages which had made her childhood such a torment.

You're so beautiful, Silver. Let me love you.

Her face burned hot as she recalled Jared's words. Had he really thought her beautiful?

You needn't worry, Miss Matlock. You'll be safe with me until I can get you back to Masonville.

No, any woman would have served his purpose, and she had been handy. He was a hard, driven man, used to getting what he wanted when he wanted it. And he'd known just the right words she needed to hear to make her a willing participant.

She fingered the locket at her throat. *I want you to have this back. When we're done, you won't owe me anything.*

She wished she could hate him. She wanted to hate him. She'd tried to hate him. But more than anything, she wished he were here, holding her in his arms and telling her she was beautiful.

She closed her eyes and imagined his callused fingers stroking her cheek, her throat, her breasts. She could feel him cradling her in his arms, holding her close against his broad chest with its soft mat of curly hair. It seemed an eternity since she'd last seen him, though it had been scarcely more than a week. Why wasn't his memory fading? Why didn't his image leave her be? Why did she have to love the shiftless, no-good bounty hunter? Why couldn't she have fallen for a short, bespectacled, balding banker who would go off every day to his boring little job and come home every night, safe, dependable—and alive.

Silver swallowed the lump in her throat, blinked away the burning in her eyes. She had no time to act like a helpless female or make desperate wishes. Bob Cassidy was in town, and she had to get back what he'd taken from her. No matter what the reason, Jared had deserted her, and now she would have to face Cassidy on her own.

Chapter 27

He liked the way women smelled, with or without perfume. He imagined he could smell them even before he entered the saloon—a room full of beautiful women. That's what he'd been told about the Rainbow Saloon. It had the most beautiful women in the whole territory.

And Bob Cassidy liked beautiful women. He liked the way their hips moved when they walked. He liked the soft plumpness of their breasts. He liked their soft voices and the tears they shed so easily. He liked almost everything about women, especially the way they felt beneath him.

He was grinning as he pushed open the fancy white doors. He was remembering the last woman he'd been with. She'd never even screamed. Not once. But she'd been a fighter. What a ride she'd been. He rubbed his jaw where she'd struck him just before he'd sunk the knife between her ribs.

"Welcome to the Rainbow Saloon, sir. May I take your hat?"

She was a pretty, dark-eyed girl, little more than a child, yet there was something sultry and unchildlike about her. He wondered if she . . .

Cassidy's smile broadened. "Thanks." He handed her the Stetson.

"The show is about to start." She waved a hand toward a curtained stage along the back of the saloon.

"Where do I get a drink?" he asked, not seeing a bar.

"Just ask one of the girls in the white aprons. Enjoy yourself, sir."

"Thanks. I'm sure I will." He smiled at her again, then walked away.

It was good to be back in civilization, he thought as he looked around. Whoever owned this place must have plenty of class as well as money. He looked forward to meeting her. It had to be a woman. Few men would be clever enough to think of a place like the Rainbow.

He took a chair near the end of the stage, then let his eyes roam around the room once again. Everything he saw was rich and sumptuous— especially the women. He'd never seen so many beautiful . . .

He nearly choked. It was impossible. No two people could look so much alike. Yet it surely couldn't be her. It couldn't be. Not here in this town, in this place.

But it was.

She glanced up and their eyes met. For a moment, Silver didn't move, didn't bat an eye, just stared at him. Then she whispered an apology to the gentleman she'd been talking to and started across the broad sweep of room that separated them, moving slowly with the vaguest hint of a limp.

Her black hair was gathered onto her head in a cluster of soft curls. Gems sparkled on her delicate earlobes. Her gown was a dusky shade of rose. It had a low, square bodice, edged with pointed lace. He noticed the perfection of her skin across her collarbones, imagined the milky whiteness of her breasts just hidden from his view. The bustled skirt accentuated her narrow waist; the long faille train made her seem even taller and more regal than ever.

A bolt of desire streaked through him. He'd always thought she was beautiful, and he'd been tempted to bed her before the wedding. If that damned deputy or bounty hunter or whoever he was hadn't shown up in Masonville, three days before the wedding, breathing down his neck, he would have married her. He'd married before when it was convenient. When it wasn't convenient any longer, he'd simply ended the marriage in the most expedient way.

Silver prayed that her terror didn't show on her face. She'd known he would come to the Rainbow, but she hadn't expected him quite so soon. No, that wasn't true. She had expected him, but she'd still *hoped* it wouldn't be tonight. She didn't feel ready to face him just yet.

"Hello, Bob." Her voice was soft and quivered ever so slightly, but her eyes never wavered from his. "What are you doing in Virginia City?"

"I was about to ask you the same thing." His bold gaze traveled the length of her, returning slowly to her face.

"It wasn't easy for me in Masonville after you left. So, I thought I'd give myself a new life." She slipped into the chair beside him. "Why did you do it, Bob? Why did you leave like that?"

He shrugged and offered an apologetic smile. "I guess I'm a bachelor at heart. I found I couldn't go through with it." He reached forward and grabbed hold of her hand.

Revulsion shot through her. Instinct demanded she yank her hand free, but she quelled it with steely determination.

His smile faded slightly. His eyes took on a hooded appearance. "I'm beginning to think I was gravely mistaken to have left you behind."

She'd always thought him handsome and was amazed to discover he still was. It surprised her that the evil lurking beneath the suave, debonair exterior didn't show through. How could he appear so charming, so charismatic when in truth he was immoral and corrupt? His ability to disguise the truth frightened her more than ever, and she wished herself someplace else, anywhere but seated so close to him.

She allowed him to hold her hand just a moment longer, then extracted it with a smooth motion, not jerking away as she would have liked to do. "Did you have to rob the store as well as make me a laughingstock?"

His expression plainly stated he was about to deny her accusation. Then he laughed. "I had no choice. I needed the money." He waved his hand at her fancy attire. "It's obvious you didn't miss it. You've done quite well for yourself in a short time."

"It's just a job, but I'm not starving, thank you." She saw no reason to tell him that without Corinne she was virtually penniless, but she certainly couldn't let him think she had struck it rich. "Be that as it may, the money you took belongs to my parents. I want it back."

Cassidy's blue gaze sent a chill down her spine. She felt as if she were able to look inside him at his soul and, having done so, discovered he had none. She pushed such thoughts from her mind. She couldn't let him see that she knew who and what he was. She had to convince him that she was the naive, foolish girl he had left standing at the church in Masonville.

"You loved me once, Bob, and I . . ." Her voice

fell to a whisper. The lie would scarcely clear her throat. "I still love you. Please don't make me bear the shame any longer. My parents will lose their store if I don't send them the money. Perhaps that's why we've met again. So we can rectify what went wrong, so we can be together again. If you'd let me try, I could teach you to love me once more."

He leaned forward, and for one terrible moment, Silver thought he might try to kiss her. She knew she couldn't continue the charade if he did so. She would run screaming from the room. The thought of his lips upon hers made her ill.

As if he'd thought better of it, he drew back. "You tempt me, Silver, more than you know. But the money is another matter. I couldn't return it even if I wanted to. It's gone. I lost it."

"I don't believe you!" she exclaimed without thinking. She almost blurted out that she knew he'd been winning in Laramie but stopped herself in time. "You're an experienced gambler. *You* don't lose."

"Ah, Silver," he said with a laugh, "you're priceless."

The piano announced the beginning of the entertainment, saving Silver from revealing her desperation. Cassidy turned toward the stage as the curtains were drawn open, revealing three of Corinne's songstresses.

"Excuse me," Silver whispered as she rose from the chair.

His congenial mask dropped momentarily. "You're leaving?" Displeasure chilled his voice.

"I have things I must do. I work here, after all." She steeled herself, then reached out and touched his shoulder ever so briefly. "You're staying in Virginia City for a while, aren't you? We'll have time to talk again?"

Cassidy nodded.

"Good. Then I'll see you soon. I'm here every evening."

She turned, sweeping her long train out of her way, then walked sedately away. No one would have guessed at the turmoil exploding inside of her. She wanted to knock the chairs and tables out of her way and get out. Not just out of that saloon, she realized, but out of that city. But she didn't do what she wanted. Instead, she retreated with grace and style, nodding to the customers who glanced her way, speaking with the few of them she knew until she was across the vast length of the room.

She found Corinne in her small but well-appointed office in the back of the saloon. She told her she wasn't feeling well and wanted to leave. Corinne must have believed her. One look at Silver's face, and she called for the buggy to take the girl home.

Jared walked along the boardwalk from the livery stable toward the hotel. He considered asking around about a black-haired beauty or a fair-haired gambler, but with the exception of the saloons— a good place to look for Cassidy—businesses and shops were closed for the night. It would be tomorrow before he could locate Silver. Besides, he thought, it would be better to wait. Something warned him he would need to be fresh and alert to survive what was coming, and after all these years, he'd learned to trust his instincts.

He heard a medley of sweet voices singing. He stopped and turned in the direction of the song, looking across the street at a massive brick building, its awning and supporting columns all painted white. No sign announced the name of the establishment. An opera house, perhaps?

A buggy, pulled by a trotting horse, came down the alley next to the building, then turned the corner and moved quickly past him. He caught a glimpse of rosy pink skirts flapping in the breeze created by the moving buggy. He wondered what had caused the woman to leave so quickly while the show was still in progress.

In fact, he found himself questioning everything. His five senses were on full alert, attuned to anything out of the ordinary. A sixth sense told him he was close to Cassidy. His heart told him he was about to find Silver.

He drew a deep breath, let his eyes rove over the brick building across the street, and licked his dry lips as he thought about a drink to cool his parched throat. Then he turned and began walking toward the hotel the liveryman had recommended.

First thing tomorrow, he would find Silver. He would satisfy himself that she was safe, and then he would turn his full attention to Cassidy.

Silver dropped her clothes on the floor before crawling into bed and curling into a ball, a pillow hugged tightly to her chest. She shook violently, as she had earlier that day. She wanted to cry but didn't seem to have the energy. She felt frightened and helpless.

Bob Cassidy was in Virginia City, and there wasn't anything she could do about it. He was a thief, a rapist, a murderer, and he walked the streets free and protected, no one knowing what kind of fiend he really was.

The money's gone. He lost it.

How could she help her parents now? Should she simply leave and return home the same failure she'd been when she left? Even *more* of a failure than when she'd left.

Where are you, bounty? If you were here, you could do something.

The thought was accompanied by a familiar flash of anger, driving off the fear for the moment. Her shaking quieted as she envisioned Jared in her mind—tall, bronzed, gun belt strapped to his hip, hat pulled low over his eyes. She remembered the lightning speed with which he could draw his gun. She remembered the way he could dart across a stretch of ground while under fire.

He'd used her and left her. He was everything her mother had said a bounty hunter would be. She'd given herself to him without hope for returned affection. Yet she couldn't help thinking she would be safe if he were there.

He'll come. He has to come. You'll see.

She'd been fooled by a man before. There was no reason to believe it would be different this time. Jared hadn't made any commitment to her. He'd tried to make it clear from the first that he didn't want her along, even more so when he knew the gambler she followed was also the murderer he'd been seeking for years.

He'll come. He won't let me down.

She touched the locket at her throat, knowing he had once carried it in his shirt pocket, held it in his hand. Somehow, it made her feel close to him. Close and safe.

At last, she slept.

Chapter 28

"Can't miss it," the clerk had told him as he'd headed for the door. "Sets up there on the hill like a palace or somethin', flowers everywhere. Don't know how that Chinaman gets 'em to grow for Miss Corinne like that."

The fellow was right. The house did look fit for royalty, Jared thought as he rode his pinto up the hill, leading Cinder behind him.

"If she's as purty as you claim, Miss Corinne more'n likely got hold of her 'fore she could get into trouble." That's what the man at the hotel had told him when he'd first started asking questions. "Can't say as I've ever heard of her takin' in children, though. Big town. Guess your woman and the boy could be anywheres b'now."

But Jared had asked directions and been told how to find the house, and now here he was.

A circular drive brought him to the hitching rail in front of the veranda. He dismounted and tied the horses, then stepped up into the shade of the porch. He removed his hat, raking the fingers of his other hand through his hair.

The air was still and already growing warm. In the distance, he could hear the sounds of the mines—ore cars rolling on tracks, the grind of heavy chains, the rumble of wagons, the pounding of picks—but there on the hillside, except for the chirping of birds, everything was silent. There was an aura of peace and serenity about this place, something not usually found in a mining town.

Just who was this Corinne Duvall, he wondered, and why would she want to take Silver in?

He rapped sharply on the door.

From the corner of his eye, he saw a lace curtain flutter at the window. He would have sworn he heard giggling behind the beveled glass. He turned his head, but the curtains dropped back into place. At the same moment, the door opened.

A slightly-built Oriental man, clad in a pair of baggy pants and a black shirt, stared up at him. Jared waited for him to speak, but the man continued to watch Jared in silence.

Finally he said, "I'm looking for a Miss Matlock. Miss Silver Matlock. Is she here?"

He was ushered in with a wave of the Chinaman's hand. He paused in the entry hall and waited while the door was closed behind him. Then he followed the short fellow into a large, elaborate parlor. His eyes were instantly drawn to the enormous portrait at the far end of the room. He walked toward it, captured by the look of love on the subject's face. It reminded him of Silver the night they'd . . .

"Chung tells me you want to speak with Silver."

He turned toward the melodic voice. It was the woman in the portrait, just as beautiful as the artist had portrayed. She was wearing a morning gown of sunshine yellow, something light and breezy with plenty of froth around her neck and wrists.

"I don't believe I've ever seen you at the Rainbow before."

"The Rainbow?"

She motioned for him to be seated, and she did likewise. "My saloon. It's why the gentlemen usually come calling. But not you?"

Jared realized he should have asked the hotel clerk more questions. It was just one more indication that he was becoming lax. If he went on thinking about Silver instead of paying attention to details, he was going to get himself killed.

"No. I've never been to your saloon." He sat in the proffered chair, setting his hat on the nearby table. "I'm a friend of Miss Matlock's and was told she might be here."

"Ah." She raised a brow, her expression thoughtful. She said something beneath her breath, something that sounded to Jared like, "So you're the one." But then she gave a breathtaking smile and offered a hand toward him. "I'm Corinne Duvall. And you are?"

"Jared Newman."

"A pleasure, Mr. Newman. Silver is here, but she isn't up yet. She was ill yesterday."

He jumped up from the chair. "Silver's sick? Where is she?"

"Calm yourself, Mr. Newman. I'm sure it's nothing to be alarmed about. Simply a summer cold. I'll see if she's up for company." Corinne rose gracefully and moved toward the door. "I'll send Chung with some coffee. I won't be long."

Silver stirred, the light rapping working through her sleep to touch a strand of consciousness.

"Silver, may I come in?"

She groaned and rolled onto her other side, pulling the pillow over her head.

"Silver?" The voice grew louder as the door

opened. "My dear, you have company down-stairs. Are you feeling up to a gentleman caller?"

Her stomach tightened, and she felt herself growing cold. There could be only one person who would come to see her. Only one man who knew her name and might presume to come call-ing. She just couldn't face Cassidy again so soon, not even if it meant she was a coward.

"No," she said. "I don't want to see anyone."

Corinne stepped beside the bed and pulled the pillow from Silver's face. She touched her fore-head with cool fingers. "Perhaps we should have the doctor in. You haven't a fever, but you do look unusually pale. I'll tell Mr. Newman you're not well enough for visitors."

"Mr. Newman?" Silver shot upright. "Jared's here?"

Corinne turned around, one delicate eyebrow raised. "In the parlor."

Her heart was racing a mile a minute. He'd come. He'd really come. She'd thought he might, hoped he would, and now he was there. He hadn't deserted her. He was there!

"Silver, I do believe you've gotten back some of your color." Corinne's voice sounded teasing.

She flushed a deeper shade as she threw aside the blankets and dropped her feet to the floor. "Don't let him leave. Tell him I'll be down shortly. Keep him here for me, Corinne. Please."

Corinne was smiling broadly now. "I wouldn't think of letting him get away," she said as she swept from the room.

Jared's here! Jared's here!

She pulled the dresses from the wardrobe one at a time.

Which one? Which one?

Why was she acting so crazy? He'd left her in that miserable hotel with no money, just disap-

peared without a word, and now she was going
to rush down and welcome him back.

She stilled. No, she wasn't going to welcome
him back. She had a few choice words to say to
Mr. Newman, and then she was going to tell him
she'd found Bob Cassidy. *She'd* found him—and
without Jared's help!

He was being observed from the doorway.

Jared turned in his chair and met the curious
gazes of two girls. They couldn't have been more
than thirteen years old, both of them wearing
morning gowns similar to the one Corinne Duvall
had worn, except the colors were different. Were
these her daughters?

He dismissed that notion the moment it came
to him. One of the girls was obviously a mulatto.
She had skin the color of coffee and cream. Her
eyes were a rich brown, fringed with thick black
lashes. Her mouth was generous. She was probably less than five feet tall but already developing
a woman's curves.

The other girl, much the same height and build
of her companion, had riotous red hair, thick and
curly. Her complexion was inordinately pale except for the splash of freckles across the bridge of
her nose and her cheekbones.

"Hello," he said to them.

They giggled.

So it was those two who had watched him at
the front door. Perhaps they could tell him what
Silver was doing there. "Join me for some coffee?" he offered.

They looked at each other with an air of con-
spiracy, then broke into grins before entering the
room side by side.

Jared stood. "I'm Mr. Newman. I've come to
see Miss Matlock. Do you live here too?"

The redhead opened her mouth to reply but was cut short by Corinne's reappearance.

"Idonna. Helene."

They jumped and turned toward the woman.

"Can you explain what you're doing here?"

"No, Miss Corinne," they answered in unison.

"Then I believe you had best excuse yourselves and return to your room. We'll talk about this later."

"Excuse us, Mr. Newman," they each mumbled. Then they scurried from the parlor, heads hanging.

Corinne turned and watched them hurry down the hallway and up the stairs. Once they were out of sight, she faced Jared.

He was scowling. "They weren't bothering me."

"I'm sure they weren't, Mr. Newman," she replied calmly as she moved toward him. "But they know the rules."

"Rules?"

"None of my girls are allowed to be unchaperoned with a gentleman caller. It's for their own protection. But those two . . ." Her smile was tender. "They are much too young to entertain gentlemen at any time. When they're sixteen will be soon enough."

Jared shook his head, still confused. He wasn't sure whether to like this woman or suspect her of some ulterior motives. "Just exactly why *are* those girls living with you, Miss Duvall? And where is Silver?"

"She'll be here presently. In the meantime, let's sit down. Oh, good. Chung brought the coffee. I could use some myself." She settled onto a sofa. "Chung is the most remarkable man. I have two maids who help with the housework and a wonderful woman to do the cooking, and, of course, there's the groom to care for the horses. But Chung truly runs everything. Did you see the gardens? They are his creation.''

"Beautiful," he mumbled, resuming his seat. "About those girls . . .''

Her blue gaze hardened. ''Mr. Newman, just what are your intentions toward Silver?''

"My inten—''

"You seem very anxious to see her, and she certainly didn't try to hide the fact that she knew you. But I don't want to see any harm come to her." She eyed the guns on his thighs.

His anger began to boil. He kept it from his voice as he replied, ''I assure you, I have no intention of harming Silver. But I would like to know just what's going on. What are Silver and those girls doing here?'' He rose from the chair and took a threatening step forward. ''I'd like to know why some half-wit hotel clerk says any beautiful, single girl would most likely end up in this place on the hill.''

Corinne Duvall tilted her head back to look up at him, but she seemed not the least bit alarmed by his anger. In fact, she appeared to be amused.

"Well?'' he snapped, incensed by her calm reaction. ''How 'bout some answers.''

"Hello, Jared.'' Silver's voice came softly from the doorway.

Jared's tirade died in his throat as he spun around.

She was wearing an elegant red silk gown with plenty of flounces and drapes and lace and bows. He was no connoisseur of ladies' clothing, but he didn't have to be. Never had a gown been so beautifully displayed as the one which adorned Silver Matlock's body. She looked like royalty, framed by the archway, holding her slender form erect, her head high, her expression sure and proud.

"I didn't know if I would ever see you again," she said as she moved gracefully toward him, accompanied by the soft swish of silk skirts.

He was surprised to find he could still think, still speak. "Your limp is almost gone."

"I heal quickly."

"Silver, I . . ."

She turned toward Corinne. "May we have a little privacy, please?"

"You know the rules," Corinne answered, "but I shall withdraw across the parlor."

Jared longed to put the woman totally from the room, forcibly if necessary. Instead, while she walked toward the doorway, he took hold of Silver's elbow and propelled her over to the fireplace mantel beneath Corinne's portrait. "I want to know what's going on here," he demanded in a stage whisper.

"Nothing is going on. I work for Miss Corinne and live here with the rest of her girls."

"What kind of *work?*" His anger had returned as quickly as it had disappeared moments before.

Her gray eyes sparked, warning him of her own temper, but he was too frustrated to take heed.

"Answer me, Silver. What kind of work?"

"What do you care what kind of work it is?" came her retort. "You left me in Winnemucca to fend for myself and certainly didn't care what I'd have to do to get by."

"That's not true. I—"

Silver pulled her arm from his grasp. "Don't lie to me, bounty. You don't owe me anything, remember? You returned my locket. We're square with each other."

"Silver—"

"I don't even need you to find Bob. He's here

in Virginia City. I've seen him. I've talked to him."

He grabbed her arms, pulling her toward him. Her head snapped back, forcing her to look up at him. "You *what?*" He was staring hard into her gray eyes, but he was aware of Corinne rising to her feet, sensed her alarm.

Once again, Silver jerked free of him. "If not for him, you wouldn't be here now. You wouldn't have cared what happened to me or to Dean. Would you?"

"That's not—"

She slapped him. It was what she'd been wanting to do from the moment she'd learned he had left them in that hotel in Winnemucca.

Her voice was a breathless whisper. "Get out, Mr. Newman. I'm no longer in need of your services." She stepped away from him. "He doesn't have the money. It's gone. My parents have lost everything." She stared at him in silence, the slap still seeming to echo against the high ceiling of the parlor. "So have I," she added.

Jared picked up his hat and placed it on his head. "You're wrong, Silver. I left a note and money for you in Winnemucca. I was gone only a few days. When I got back, I followed you here to Virginia City."

She shook her head.

"I followed *you*, not Cassidy."

Why did he go on lying? He was the bounty hunter. He didn't need her help. He could find Cassidy on his own.

"I brought Cinder with me. She's tied up outside."

With that, he spun on his heel and left.

Cinder?

She heard the door slam and still she couldn't seem to move.

Cinder? But she . . .

Silver broke free of the spell that had kept her frozen in place. She rushed to the front door and tore it open. She was too late. He was already riding away from the house. And there, just as he'd said, stood her buckskin mare, tethered to the hitching post.

I followed you, not Cassidy.

Could it be true?

Corinne's fingers closed around Silver's shoulders. "You'll see him again, my dear."

"I don't think so. I . . . I said some terrible things."

"Never mind what you said. If he loves you, he'll be back."

Silver's throat felt tight. "But he doesn't love me," she whispered, fighting the burn of tears.

"You think not?" Corinne chuckled softly. "You have much to learn, my dear. Now, come back inside. You need your rest."

Chapter 29

Jared, I was wrong and I'm sorry. Please meet me at the Rainbow Saloon tonight. I think Bob will come in again.

Silver

Jared received Silver's note that afternoon. By the time the Rainbow Saloon opened its doors for the evening entertainment of gambling and song, he knew everything he could learn about the saloon, Corinne Duvall, and the girls she employed and housed. It hadn't taken him long to acquire a grudging admiration for a woman who had come up the hard way, yet whose heart was apparently in the right place. She was rich—and getting richer, judging by the success of the Rainbow—but she used her wealth to make sure others didn't suffer as she had.

Jared was grateful that she'd made a place for Silver.

"Good evening, señor. Welcome to the Rainbow Saloon."

"Thanks."

The girl gave him a coy glance. "I am Maria. Are you interested in a game of chance or would you maybe like to sit and talk?"

"Is Silver here?" he asked as his gaze moved around the large saloon.

"Sí, she is here." Maria pouted. "I will find her for you."

"No." He stopped her. "Don't bother. I'll just go sit down and see what goes on around here."

The dark-haired beauty brightened. "You would like some company, no?"

"No."

She sighed. "As you wish, señor. But please, you must check your *pistola* before you go in."

Jared removed his gun belt and holster without protest. He'd known that was a requirement of the Rainbow Saloon and had prepared for it. He had a Sharps four-barreled derringer hidden in his boot. With a nod at the pretty Maria, he made his way to the farthest and dimmest corner he could find. He sat with his back tight against the wall and left his hat pulled low over his forehead. Then he waited.

It was still early. There were a couple of older men playing cards, a few more—miners judging by their clothes—standing near a roulette wheel. Footlights burned brightly across the front of the curtained stage. Piano music came from beyond the velvet curtains. The Vienna Waltz. One of his mother's favorites. A strange choice for another saloon but not for this one.

He ascertained that Silver wasn't one of the half-dozen young women in the room, then focused his attention on the front door, studying the men as they came in, their numbers increasing as the hour grew later. And as more customers arrived, more lovely young women in colorful gowns appeared. Finally, Silver was among them.

She was wearing a gown the color of limes, with matching green ribbons in her hair. As he watched her talking with those around her, returning smiles, he realized there'd been a change in her since they had first left Denver together. It was a subtle change, yet unmistakable. There was an air of confidence about her. It added to her beauty.

He was enjoying looking at her, remembering all the different ways he'd seen her—in her wedding gown, mad as a wet hen; with dirt smudges on her nose and cheeks; on horseback in a rainstorm; asleep in a chair, his dried blood staining the pretty pink gingham; naked in a mountain hot springs, her gray eyes seductive, her face flushed with passion. And he loved every single image because he loved her.

He loved her. It was a strange discovery. Yet maybe not so strange. Maybe he'd known it for weeks.

He loved her.

The realization didn't bring him any joy. It only complicated things. He had no business being in love. It could endanger both their lives. He'd already seen the way his attraction for her had eroded his attention to other matters, matters that could mean life or death.

Besides, he argued internally, he had nothing to give her. He had no place in his life for loving a woman. No place for a woman period. And she'd certainly made it clear that she wanted nothing to do with him. Could he blame her? From her point of view, it must seem he'd used her, taken her virginity without promises of love or marriage, then deserted her. If she'd ever felt any tenderness toward him, he'd killed it by now.

But she had sent him the note, had asked him to be there. Perhaps . . .

He saw the smile fade from her mouth, saw the infinitesimal tightening of her jaw. He followed her gaze to the man at the door and knew he was

looking at the man he'd been seeking for six long
years.

"Is there something wrong with me, señor?
Perhaps I have a wart on my nose?"

Cassidy glanced at the pretty Mexican girl, not
understanding what she could mean. She had a
flawless beauty—and certainly no warts.

"The men only seem to ask for Silver tonight,"
she explained. "At least, the most handsome
men."

He stared across the room at Silver. "The men
like her, huh?"

"*Sí*, but she does not seem to care for you any
more than the other *hombre*."

The girl was right. Silver had already turned
her attention back to the men around her, giving
him not even a wave or a word of welcome.

Cassidy ground his teeth. He didn't like to be
ignored. He was used to receiving admiring
glances, flirtations. Of course, he didn't mind a
woman who could put up a good fight at the right
time either. But he hated to be ignored.

Was she trying to pay him back for not giving
her the money he'd taken from the mercantile?
Did she think she could punish him for not marrying her? If she did, she was greatly mistaken.
Her female games wouldn't work with him. He'd
made up his mind that she was going to be his
woman. He'd left something unfinished in Masonville, and he wasn't about to leave Virginia
City until he'd made her his—and his alone.

From beneath a veil of sooty lashes, Silver
watched Cassidy's approach. She fought against
the desire to flee. She'd made up her mind before
coming to the Rainbow that she was going to help
Jared. She didn't care that Cassidy claimed to be

broke. She wanted to see Jared take him back to Central City where his victim could identify him to the law. She wanted to see Cassidy punished for the things he'd done.

But she hadn't counted on Cassidy arriving before Jared. She'd thought she would have a chance to talk to Jared first, find out what she could do to help him. She'd been so sure he would come as soon as he got her note.

Maybe he didn't care if she was sorry. Maybe he was still angry with her. Maybe he would never forgive her for slapping him. Corinne was wrong. He didn't love her.

"Silver, I'd like a moment with you."

The sound of Cassidy's voice caused her heart to skip a beat. She lifted her head, meeting his gaze, and forced herself to remain composed. She was on her own. Jared wasn't there to advise her. She would have to depend on herself. "Of course, Bob. Excuse me, gentlemen." She rose from the table.

Cassidy took hold of her elbow and guided her toward the stage. He pulled out a chair from a small, round table. She could feel his eyes on her as she stepped past him. It made the back of her neck tingle. She settled into the chair and folded her hands in her lap. Cassidy sat across from her.

Find out where he's staying. Then you can tell Jared . . .

"You look beautiful, Silver."

Stay calm. She squeezed her hands and tried to quiet her racing heart. "I was hoping you would come back," she said in a breathless voice.

"I thought about what you said last night. Perhaps it is fate that brought us together again."

"It is." She leaned forward. "I know it is."

"I'd like to see you alone." He glanced around the saloon. "Outside of this place."

Silver's insides were twisted into knots, but she managed to keep the turmoil from her voice. "Miss Corinne's rules are very strict. We are allowed gentlemen visitors at the house, but there is always someone else present."

"I want time *alone* with you, Silver."

Now. Now was her chance. It might never come again. Her heart pounded against her rib cage until she thought it might break free. Her palms were perspiring. She lowered her voice to a whisper. "Tell me where you're staying, Bob. I'll try to slip away later."

"At night?" His blue eyes were suspicious. "You'll come to my hotel room?"

"Don't you understand?" She dropped her gaze to her hands, glad she didn't have to look at him while she told her lies. "I love you. I'll do anything to win you back. Anything."

"I'm at the Grant Hotel."

She felt a sudden panic—what if she couldn't find Jared to tell him what she'd learned?—and looked up at him. "If I can't make it tonight, you won't leave, will you? You won't leave without telling me?"

He grinned, revealing his straight white teeth. "Don't worry, Silver. I'll be around. I promise."

His words sounded more like a threat than a promise, but she managed a facsimile of a relieved smile. "Why don't I get you something to drink?"

"I'd like that."

She hurried toward the serving area beyond the stage and through a set of swinging doors. She could have found one of the waitresses, but she needed a moment to pull herself together.

Cold rage possessed Jared. He didn't move, scarcely bothered to breathe. It was him. Cass.

After six years of searching, looking, listening, waiting—it was him. Through narrowed eyes, he memorized everything about the man, from the pale color of his blond hair to the patrician lines of his face to the tiny scar on his jaw to the fancy suit he wore. This was the man who had raped and beaten his sister, the one who had hacked off her hair with a knife. This was the man who had left her to die by inches, ending not only her life but Jared's as well.

Nothing had prepared him for Cassidy's appearance, not even Silver's description. This man—this ruthless butcher of women—looked every bit the refined gentleman, moneyed and educated. Coop had been right. Jared could have walked past Cassidy in the street and never known it. It took all his will to keep from pulling the derringer from his boot and shooting the bastard in cold blood—and to the devil with the law and Harrison's reward.

He tensed as he watched Cassidy cross the room toward Silver. His gaze flicked to her face. She seemed composed, controlled, but Jared sensed her underlying fear. Did Cassidy feel it too? Did Silver even understand the sort of man she was dealing with? Just knowing him put her life in jeopardy. He should have done something to stop this meeting. He never should have let her talk to Cassidy again.

Silver had joined Cassidy at a table near the stage. She was leaning forward, talking softly, and he was grinning at her in a possessive manner. Jared's hand touched his thigh where his holster should have been. He frowned, clenching his jaw. He couldn't bear this much longer. He wanted to stalk across the room and pull her away from that table. He wanted to see Silver as far away from Cassidy as he could get her. But he couldn't do it. Not yet. He couldn't alert Cassidy to his presence in Virginia City.

Suddenly, Silver rose from the table and hurried toward a pair of swinging doors behind the stage. Jared relaxed slightly. Now that Silver was out of danger, he could concentrate fully on his prey.

"Please, Maria," Silver whispered as she peeked out between the doors. "Tell the gentleman that I've been called away. Tell him I'll see him tomorrow."

"You are wanting him to come to Miss Corinne's?"

"No!" Silver answered quickly.

Maria shook her head. "You will have trouble if Miss Corinne finds you are arranging to meet with this man elsewhere." She grinned and shook her head. "Perhaps I will keep him company this night."

"Maria, you mustn't."

"You have *two* men asking for you and do not want this one. Why shouldn't I be friendly?"

Silver turned around. Her hands gripped Maria's arms. "*Two* men? Who was the other?"

"He is over there." Maria pulled free, jerking her head to one side as she rubbed her arms. "In the corner."

The blood began to pound in Silver's ears. He'd come. He'd received her note and he'd come.

"Never mind, Maria," she said as she pushed open the doors before her.

She walked boldly toward Cassidy. She needn't be afraid any longer. Jared was there.

When she reached the table, she tried her best to look disappointed rather than relieved. "I can't get away tonight," she whispered, "but I'll send you a note tomorrow telling you where and when." She glanced toward the entrance. "I think you should leave before Miss Corinne gets suspicious. She doesn't like us to favor one gentleman over another."

Cassidy's eyes narrowed as he rose. He took her hand and lifted it to his lips. "I'm counting on tomorrow," he replied softly, gazing at her over the back of her hand.

She fought the urge to wipe away his touch on her dress, instead folding her hands demurely before her. "Good night, Bob."

Silver stood very still as he made his way through the crowded saloon. The moment the door swung closed behind him, she whirled toward the dark corner. But Jared wasn't there any longer. He was standing within arm's reach.

Chapter 30

"What the hell do you think you're doing?"

Silver grinned at him. He could yell at her all he wanted. He was here. That's all that mattered. "Helping you."

"Helping me?" Jared's eyes widened. "Helping me how? By risking that scrawny little neck of yours?"

"But Jared, I—"

He took hold of her arm and propelled her back into the corner where he'd spent most of that evening. "I don't want you talking to him again. Do you understand me?"

"Yes," she replied breathlessly. "I understand." She wondered if *he* did. "Jared, I found out where he's staying."

"The Grant Hotel."

Some of the wind went out of her sails. "You knew?"

"He's not trying to hide. He's registered under his own name."

"I thought . . ." She let her voice trail off. She'd been so certain she was being of great help to him.

Jared's fingers tightened on her arm as he drew her closer to him. The anger had disappeared from his face. "I know you want to help, Silver, but the best thing you can do is stay away from Cass. I don't want you in danger when I take him prisoner."

"And what about the danger *you're* in? He knows you. He's tried to kill you before. What if he saw you tonight? What if he recognized you? Your life is in danger, too." Until she'd spoken the words aloud, she hadn't acknowledged that Jared could die. Now she realized how fragile their time together had become.

"This is what I do, Silver. This is how I live. I know what I'm doing."

She gazed up into his darkly handsome face. "I won't be sent away."

"Silver, be reasonable. You—"

"I don't want to be reasonable." Her voice turned husky with restrained emotions. "There isn't anything reasonable about my being with you, about my trying to find Bob, about my coming to Virginia City. It may not be reasonable, but it's what I've had to do. Just as I have to be with you now." Her fingers cradling his face, she raised on tiptoe and kissed him.

Jared's arms wrapped tightly around her as his mouth took possession of hers. There was something almost desperate in the way he held her, and she knew in that instant that he sensed the aura of evil that lingered in Cassidy's wake.

"Silver." Corinne's voice was low, but there was no mistaking the command in that one word.

Jared released Silver's mouth but kept his arm around her waist as they turned to face the woman.

Silver's heart was still hammering in her breast, and her voice shook when she spoke. "You needn't tell me I've broken the rules, Miss Corinne. I know. I'll come for my things in the morning."

"Silver, please think—"

"I have to go with him," she answered in a small voice, turning her head to look up at Jared. "I *must* be with him."

Did he feel the same way? Did he understand her urgency to be alone with him, to be lost in his arms? Did he sense that only their love could protect them from the danger that swirled around them, seeking to destroy them?

Yes, he felt it. Jared wanted to claim and possess Silver, as if holding on would save her, keep her safe from harm. All his arguments against loving her seemed pointless now. He had to be with her.

With scarcely a glance in Corinne Duvall's direction, Jared escorted Silver out of the Rainbow Saloon, pausing only long enough to retrieve his gun belt at the door.

Silver's head was spinning. As Jared pushed closed the door to his room, she wound her fingers into his shaggy brown locks and drew his mouth to hers. The sense of desperation hadn't abated as they'd hurried along the boardwalk toward the hotel. It had seemed to increase with each step. She was frightened—frightened of what lay ahead—and only the safety of Jared's arms could take that fear away.

Jared broke their passionate kiss and stepped away from her, leaving her alone in the darkness of the room. She heard the scrape of a match, saw the sudden flare of light. She turned and watched as he lit the oil lamp, then turned it low before replacing the chimney. As he walked back toward her, gray shadows dancing along the walls, his gaze seemed to sear her flesh, boldly stroking where his hands had yet to touch.

His fingers closed around her arms as he stopped before her. An almost painful throbbing began at the juncture of her thighs. Her breath caught in her throat. She swayed forward as he lowered his mouth to hers.

His tongue danced along the sensitive skin of her lips, causing them to tingle. With a little gasp, she opened her mouth, allowing him entry. The intimacy of the kiss made her heart race. She grew courageous, darting her own tongue into his mouth, running it over his teeth, sparring briefly with his tongue before withdrawing once more.

She felt a thrill as his fingers deftly freed the tiny buttons up the length of her spine. Only once before had she known his touch upon her flesh, yet she yearned for it with every fiber of her being. She longed to be rid of the cumbersome gown and corset. She longed to feel the hair of his chest against her breasts, to see the stark contrast of his sun-bronzed skin against the whiteness of her own.

I love you, Jared.

Did she say it aloud? She wanted to. She meant to. But the words wouldn't form. The most she seemed capable of was a groan somewhere deep in her throat as he pushed the sleeves down her arms, peeling the bodice away to reveal the lace and satin of her corset, her breasts swelling above it.

Her own fingers fumbled with loosening his shirt from his trousers, fought with the clasp of his gun belt. She hadn't time to be surprised or appalled at her own forwardness. She only knew that she wanted him unencumbered and free to make love to her.

With haste, their mouths still eagerly devouring

the other, they continued to disrobe until the lime silk gown mingled with the faded brown of his trousers, the ribbons from her hair lay beside the Colt revolvers and holster, green slippers flopped beside leather boots. And then two bodies fell upon the bed, limbs entwined.

"What is it you do to me, my sweet Silver?" he whispered near her ear.

I love you, she mouthed, but no sound came with it except another groan as he ran his hands expertly over her bare skin.

He brushed the tender flesh of her thighs with his fingers, caught the areolae of her breasts between his teeth, teasing until they were taut. He stretched his lanky body alongside hers, and she felt the hardness of his desire pressing against her. Her own wanting increased.

She rolled toward him, her fingers sliding along his chest, weaving through the dark hair. Then, with a sudden flash of courage, she began to explore his long, hard body just as he explored hers. Her excitement mounted until she thought she might explode.

Silver cried his name. He shifted, rising above her on the bed, and then they were joined. Elation burst through her as he drove deep inside. She grasped his back, holding him ever closer as they rose rapidly toward a rapturous peak. There was no time for tender words. They shared an urgency neither had known before.

And then she did explode, just as she'd thought she might. There was a great shattering, followed by indescribable spasms. She writhed and arched, seeking to be ever closer to him even as she thought she could bear no more.

Jared's thrusts quickened. She heard him whisper her name, then suddenly he stiffened, drawing her hard against him as he drove deep. His movements wrought another shattering pleasure.

And then they lay limp, exhausted, their panting breaths the only sound in the tiny hotel room. Jared's forehead rested on the bed beside her ear. She could hear his rapid breathing, feel the way he propped himself on his elbows to bear his own weight even while remaining close to her. Sweat trickled between her breasts—hers? his? theirs?

Jared rolled onto his side, taking her with him. Their legs and arms were still entwined, their bodies still joined. The room was stifling hot, yet he couldn't bear to part from her. Not just yet. He had wanted her too long, imagined this moment too well to relinquish it so quickly.

He kissed the tip of her nose. "You're beautiful."

"So are you."

He chuckled. No woman had ever accused him of being beautiful before. Unshaven and trail-weary much of the time, he didn't imagine any woman had ever thought him beautiful either. No woman except Silver.

"Jared . . ."

Her eyes were sultry, the color of a stormy sky at dusk. He felt a tightening in his belly just looking into them.

"I love you," she whispered.

There was a pain in his chest. He wanted to echo her words, but he couldn't allow it. They were too different. He could never offer her a proper life. He wouldn't be good for her, no matter how hard he tried to change.

With a sigh, he rolled away and dropped his legs over the side of the bed. He braced his hands against the edge of the mattress as he sat up. "I shouldn't have let this happen again."

"Neither of us could have stopped it from happening," she said as she ran her fingers along his spine.

She was right. Nothing could have stopped him from making love to her. But he could stop himself from ruining Silver's life. He couldn't tell her he loved her. He couldn't pretend there was any hope for a future together. "Listen, Silver," he began gently. "Taking Cass in has to come before . . . before anything else. We've got to concentrate on getting him back to Colorado." He would ride out of her life for good once they reached Masonville, but he wasn't going to argue about it now.

He felt the bed dip, then rise as she left it. He heard her moving about and knew she was gathering up her clothes and dressing as quickly as possible. He waited, expecting to hear the door open as she fled his presence.

"We'd better discuss the plans for catching Bob."

He twisted on the bed to look at her. She was seated in the chair, her hands folded in her lap, her hair caught back with the ribbons once again. Except for the flush of color on her cheeks and a look of heat in her eyes, not even he would have guessed what had transpired between them only minutes before. She looked as if she had just arrived for an innocent visit with an elderly aunt.

Jared turned away. His pants and shirt lay on the floor not far from her feet. He suspected now that she'd left them there on purpose to gain an advantage, but he wasn't going to fall victim to her tricks. He rose from the bed.

Silver held her breath as he came toward her— broad of shoulder, hard and lean, undeniably male, and gloriously naked. Her heart quickened, her blood warmed. It took every ounce of restraint she could muster to remain sedately seated in her chair when what she wanted was to throw herself into his arms and make him return her love.

He stepped into his trousers and slid them up his muscled calves and thighs, then over his tight buttocks. He reached for his shirt and slipped his arms into the sleeves. As he buttoned the front, he turned his hazel eyes upon her.

"I don't want your help, Silver. If I'm worrying about taking care of you, Cass could get away. Or he could use you to protect himself. You could get hurt."

"Why don't we go to the sheriff? I know there's no warrant, but Bob admitted to me that he stole the money from the mercantile. I can tell the sheriff that. And there's that girl in Central City. She can identify the scar on his chest. Surely the law would hold him until he could be identified as the man who attacked her."

"You still don't understand. I've got to take him back myself."

"Because it's personal," she whispered to herself, remembering the way he'd spoken those words back in Green River. Her chin rose with determination. "All right then. You'd better tell me your plan. How are we going to take him prisoner without bringing in the law, and what do we do with him once we've got him?"

"I don't suppose it would do me any good to try to send you back to Corinne's?" He scowled at her.

"Not a bit. I couldn't go back if I wanted to, not after leaving the Rainbow with you."

"And you intend to stay here."

She shrugged. "I haven't anywhere else to go."

Jared walked over to the lamp and turned it up, flooding the room with light. When he turned around, he was wearing that all-too-familiar frown. "You win this time, Silver. We'll work together. But we don't share a bed. We keep our minds on our job. And you do every last thing I tell you to do without question. Agreed?"

Silver nodded. "Agreed."

I don't have to share your bed, Jared Newman, to prove I love you. You can deny me all you want, but I'm going to go on loving you. And you're going to love me too before we're through. You'll see.

Chapter 31

Silver walked up the drive. She paused in front of the house and stared up at it. She had stayed there only six nights, but already she felt a great affection for everyone who lived within its brick walls. Corinne had befriended her when she was in need. She was sorry to have betrayed the woman's trust, but she could have done no differently.

As if she'd been watching for her, Corinne appeared in the doorway. "You've returned," she said as Silver climbed the steps.

"I've come for my things."

Corinne watched her with great sadness. "I hope you're not making a mistake, my dear."

"I'm not. There's so much you don't understand."

"We often think like that when we're in love." The woman shook her head as she turned and entered the house, followed by Silver.

"Corinne, I . . . I have a favor to ask. May we sit and talk a moment?"

With a nod of her head, Corinne led the way into the parlor.

When they were both seated, Silver continued. "I've never told you what brought me to Virginia City or why Dean is with me."

Corinne looked as if she would interrupt, as if she might say it didn't matter.

Silver spoke quickly. "I hired Mr. Newman to find someone. Jared is a bounty hunter. I've been traveling with him for some time now. The reason isn't important. Besides, it's Dean I want to talk to you about. We found him along the trail. His parents had been murdered, and we couldn't leave him on his own, so we brought him with us. Mr. Newman and I became separated in Winnemucca, but now we have to move on. I want you to keep Dean with you, help find a family for him. Will you do that?" She leaned forward in her chair. "I know I've disappointed you, leaving with Jared as I did, but it was something I had to do. He . . . he could be in danger because of me. I have to be with him. But I can't risk taking Dean. Please say he can stay with you for now. With all your friends, surely you can find a good family who will give him a home and . . . and love him."

"It was never my intention to take in young girls like Idonna and Helene, let alone orphan boys." Corinne rose from her chair and walked toward the portrait above the fireplace. "What do you think, Maurice?" she whispered. As if she sensed Silver's curiosity, she glanced back over her shoulder. "Maurice was my . . . benefactor. He took me from the wretched saloon where I made my living and cleaned me up and gave me food and beautiful clothes. He tutored me, taught me to read and how to speak properly, instructed me on fine foods and wines. He built this house for me." She waved her hand at the room. "And he wanted nothing but my love in return. When he died, he left everything to me."

She turned once more toward the portrait, her eyes revealing a great sadness. She lifted her hand and touched the gilded frame, saying softly, "So many times he asked me to marry him, and so many times I turned him down. I didn't think I could be a proper wife to him. I couldn't give him children. He loved children so very much, but I knew I couldn't ever bear him a child.''

Silver rose and moved toward Corinne, her eyes upon the painting. ''He painted this, didn't he?''

''Yes. Maurice had great talent.'' With a quick motion, she wiped away the tears from her eyes, then faced Silver. ''I will keep Dean myself. I have grown rather fond of the boy . . . And it would please Maurice.''

Jared, his hat brim pulled low on his forehead to shade his face from view, stepped into the spacious lobby of the Grant Hotel. His eyes swept the room. There was a gentleman seated near the window. He held a folded newspaper in one hand, a smoking pipe in the other. Another man, accompanied by his wife, stood before the desk. The clerk stared down his nose as he observed the guest signing in. A bellboy stood to one side, his arms laden with luggage.

Through an arched doorway, Jared could see tables covered with white linen cloths. Waitresses in crisp aprons and caps bustled about the restaurant, serving breakfast to hungry customers.

Jared entered the restaurant and, as was his custom, selected a table in the corner. He sat in a chair with his back to the wall. When the waitress came, he ordered coffee.

''Is that all, sir?'' she asked.

''That's all.''

The look on her face plainly stated that she knew his sort. He would demand plenty of refills but wouldn't order anything to eat. Unfortunately, she had him pegged.

He fastened his eyes on the stairs leading to the second-story rooms and settled in to wait. There wasn't any hurrying a thing like this. Patience and an alert eye were two important traits of his trade, and Jared had them both.

"I ain't stayin' here."

Kneeling on the floor before him, Silver didn't know that she'd ever seen a jaw with a more stubborn set than that of this ten-year-old boy. "Dean, you must stay with Miss Corinne. I can't take you with me where I'm going."

"Mr. Newman's back, an' you've found my ma's killer. Ain't that so?"

She didn't answer.

The boy jammed his hands into his pant pockets as he took a step back from her. His chin jutted forward; his eyes narrowed. "You can leave me, but I ain't stayin'. I told you I'd see him dead, an' I mean t'do just that."

Silver stood up. She felt helpless dealing with this boy, perhaps because she understood what he was saying. But she knew she couldn't let him go along. She and Jared would have enough trouble just dealing with Cassidy once they had him in custody. Dean needed a family to love him, not to be dragged across the country with a bounty hunter, a single woman, and a cold-blooded killer.

"You'll do as I tell you, Dean Forest. Haven't I seen to your welfare since we met? Now it's time you showed some appreciation by doing as I tell you. You'll stay with Miss Corinne. I'm not deserting you. I just want what's best for you."

"You said yourself you've taken care o' me. Why ain't you what's best? Why can't I stay with you?"

"Because I said so," she snapped back at him. "And that's all the reason you need." With those words, she spun around and left his room on the third floor.

She didn't stop to say good-bye to anyone else. She'd already said her farewells. If she stayed a moment longer, she would find herself crying—which was silly. She'd scarcely known them long enough to cry at their parting. Still . . . She swallowed back the welling tears and hurried out the front door.

Cinder was tied to the hitching post. Silver swung onto the horse, throwing her right leg over the saddle. She was strangely soothed by the familiar feel of her leather skirt and comfortable boots. She'd loved the fancy clothes Corinne had given her, but she loved these too. Jared had seen her both ways, made love to her both ways. The clothes didn't matter to him. He thought she was beautiful no matter what she wore. She knew that in the most secret part of her heart, and it made her glad.

She nudged Cinder's sides, and the horse trotted down the hill toward town. She wondered if Jared would have returned to the hotel yet. A blush warmed her cheeks as she remembered the passionate moments they had shared in his room the night before. He was determined it wouldn't happen again, but Silver understood, perhaps better than he did, the unique bond they shared. He wouldn't be able to go on denying it forever. Once they took Bob Cassidy prisoner and returned him to Colorado, there wouldn't be any reason left to deny his love for her.

Cassidy . . . A cold chill washed over her. If only Jared wasn't so determined to catch the man himself. If only he would turn Cassidy over to the law and let them take care of him. But she understood why Jared couldn't do that. It wasn't for the bounty he had mentioned. It was the need for revenge. How did she free him from the hate?

She glanced down the long, narrow street. Jared had set off this morning to wait for Cassidy, to find out what he was up to in Virginia City. He wanted to make sure Cassidy had no close associates who would miss him if he suddenly disappeared. After that, they would lure him out of town and take him into their custody. It sounded clean and simple. She shouldn't even be worrying. Still . . .

"Silver!"

She drew back on the reins, bringing the mare to a quick stop even as her eyes met Cassidy's. Terror paralyzed her. This wasn't part of Jared's plan. She wasn't to have seen Cassidy again.

He stepped down into the street. "I was just on my way back to the hotel to see if your note had arrived." He took hold of Cinder's bridle. His gaze ran over her attire. "What a change from last night."

She saw his eyes flick to the saddlebags behind her before returning to her face. She couldn't deny that she was dressed for travel. What was she to tell him? Where was she going? She had to think of something. There was no escaping him now. He was holding onto Cinder's reins, his cold blue eyes curious.

Think! she told herself.

Cassidy held a hand toward her in silent invitation to dismount. "Walk with me."

"I really shouldn't. Miss Corinne . . ."

His fingers closed around her arm. He gently pulled her from the saddle, then tucked her hand into the crook of his elbow, pressing it against his side. "The devil with your Miss Corinne. Neither of us has any intention of your returning to work for her. You made it clear you wanted to be with me. Why not begin now?''

Her ears were buzzing. She felt cold despite the warm summer morning.

"Come with me to my hotel. We'll have coffee and talk."

If she refused, he would become suspicious. But would that matter? How had Jared intended to lure him out of town? Did she have any part in it? She couldn't seem to recall. Everything Jared had told her was jumbled up in her head. Nothing made any sense.

Cassidy was already walking, drawing her along with him. She turned her head to look at him. She thought of Dean's mother, of Katrina and all the others. She had to pull herself together. She had to stop this man so he couldn't hurt anyone else. She had to think. Jared had warned her she could be in danger. She couldn't let everything fall apart now just because she was caught unprepared.

Drawing a steadying breath, she forced herself to smile at him. "All right, Bob. I wouldn't mind a cup of coffee."

His first thought when Silver appeared in the restaurant doorway was, *What is she doing here?* Then Cassidy stepped up beside her, his hand taking hold of her arm. Jared's whole body tensed. His breathing slowed. His eyes narrowed. He lowered his head so that his hat brim shielded his face.

She was smiling—too brightly. Her chin was up in that now-familiar attitude of courage and stubborn pride. Her eyes held a slightly glazed look. He felt her terror from across the room, and it nearly drove him insane.

Minutes ticked away as the couple was served

coffee and pastries. Cassidy seemed always to be touching Silver—on the hand, on the knee, on the cheek. She scarcely moved. Her replies to his conversation appeared to be mostly monosyllables.

At last, Cassidy rose from the table. He held out his hand toward Silver. Jared saw her flinch, saw her eyes widen, saw her face pale. Inside, fury exploded. The desire to kill Cassidy with his own hands became uppermost in his mind. Only years of training kept him still. If he moved too soon, Silver might get caught in the middle. She could be hurt, maybe killed. If he moved too soon, he might never accomplish what he'd come for. He waited—and the waiting was agony.

She couldn't pretend any longer that she wasn't frightened. As Cassidy's fingers closed around her arm and he drew her up from her chair, her stomach convulsed. The room swirled around her.

"Wait," she croaked. "I'm not feeling well." She tried to sit back down.

His fingers bit into her arm, keeping her on her feet. His voice sounded concerned, but beneath his controlled expression, she sensed his displeasure and impatience. "Then we should go directly to my room so you can lie own. Come along, Silver."

"Bob, I . . . I've never . . ."

He grinned as he pulled her closer to him. "I understand," he whispered. "And it gives me great pleasure to know I'm the man you waited for."

She couldn't go with him. She had to find some way to extricate herself. She had to—

He was there, watching. She couldn't see his face. In fact, it looked as though he could almost be napping, so relaxed was his body as he leaned on his forearms over the table. But she knew he was watching, knew he was prepared to act.

Jared was there. Everything would be fine. She cocked her head coyly to one side and offered Cassidy what she hoped was a timid smile. "Do you suppose we might go for a ride first? It's . . . well, it's so early in the day."

Cassidy appeared to mull over her suggestion. "Perhaps you're right. We might find someplace more pleasant . . ." He leaned forward; his voice grew soft and intimate. "Someplace more private for what I have in mind."

Inside, she recoiled from the picture his words suggested. Outwardly, she nodded.

"I'll hire us a buggy."

"I'll wait here for you."

Cassidy shook his head and began leading her from the room. "Nonsense. You might change your mind while I'm away. I want to keep you with me, my dear Silver. I promise you an afternoon you'll not forget."

She longed to glance over her shoulder to see if Jared followed, but she kept just enough wits about her to stop her from doing so. She could only pray he knew what was happening and would follow.

Chapter 32

He stopped the horse in a meadow surrounded by scrub pine and firs, miles from anywhere. The only sound was the buzz of an occasional insect, the whisper of a hot breeze through the long grass. Cassidy pulled some blankets from the back of the buggy and a picnic basket he'd asked the hotel to prepare for them. Then he turned and offered his hand to Silver.

Her face was pale, her eyes rounded. He could feel her fear. It excited him to see her this way. Already desire was pounding in his loins. But he mustn't rush her. He had all afternoon to enjoy her sweet innocence. She could scream to her heart's content and not be heard by anyone but him.

"We'll picnic beneath the trees," he told her.

He wasn't the least bit hungry and had no intention of wasting time with food. The only appetite he intended to satisfy was purely sexual. But he didn't want her to know that. Not just yet.

As he spread the blankets on the ground in the shade of a pine tree, Silver stood off to one side, her hands clenched tightly in front of her. He was aware of the way her eyes darted around the meadow. There was no place for her to run, no place to hide. He smiled to himself. Maybe a game of chase might be fun. He was quick on his feet. She had no hope of escape.

He faced her. "Come here, Silver," he commanded in a low voice.

"Bob, I—"

"Come here." His excitement was increasing. It was time to remove some of her clothing, time to get a closer look at the treasures in store for him.

There was a sudden change in the look on her face. He didn't like it. The fear seemed to have vanished. Well, he knew how to put the fear back where it belonged. He took a step toward her.

"Silver, I said come—"

Cold metal touched his skin right behind his ear. "You take another step, and you're a dead man."

Cassidy froze in place, but his eyes were still locked on Silver. Now he understood what the change had been. Relief. She'd been waiting for this man.

"What's going on, Silver?" he asked through gritted teeth.

She stood a little taller, her shoulders back, her head up. "We're taking you back to Colorado."

A slight quiver remained in her voice, reminding him of what could have been.

"What for? There's no proof I stole that money from the mercantile. Are you so desperate for a husband you have to kidnap me?"

The man's voice came from behind him. "You're not going to be anybody's husband, Cass. Now turn around. Nice and slow. Get your hands in the air."

He obeyed. He saw the terrain slip past—the green meadow, the squatty pines, the majestic firs— and then he was facing the man with the gun. "*You!* How did you find me? I thought you were—"

"Dead? Your aim was a little off, Cass. I was

careless to ride into your trap, but you were stupid not to make sure I was finished.''

"Who are you? You're not the law. What do you want with me?''

"The name's Newman." His eyes narrowed. "Jared Newman. And all I want is to see you hang.''

Cassidy didn't often feel fear. He knew how to create it in others, but he rarely felt it himself. But now he did. Looking into those hate-filled hazel eyes, he thought he could see himself swinging at the end of a rope. And this was the man who meant to see it happen.

He remembered the first time he'd known someone was looking for him. It was freezing outside. A blizzard had raged for days, and Cassidy had settled in Denver to wait it out. An acquaintance had mentioned a man who had been asking about the palomino he'd been riding since he came up from Texas. Cassidy hadn't tried to find out why. He'd simply led the man into an ambush and shot him. He'd thought that would be the end of it.

His throat felt dry and scratchy. "Why?" he asked. "Why have you been following me?''

"You know why," Jared answered.

"You don't have anything on me, mister. I'm just a gambler who likes to move around the country. There's no law against that.''

"Silver, get the handcuffs from my saddlebag.''

Cassidy stared hard at his captor. "You've got no grounds to hold me. As soon as we go back to town, the sheriff will turn me loose. You know that." He couldn't keep a grin from curling the corners of his mouth.

"Yeah," Jared answered. "I do know that. Turn around and hold your hands behind your back.''

He did as he was told. He had nothing to worry about. He'd let them take him into the sheriff. He'd be free in short order.

He heard the sickening thud a split second before the pain exploded in the back of his head. There was a flash of light, then a flood of darkness. He was out cold before he hit the dirt.

"Give me those cuffs," Jared ordered briskly without looking at Silver.

He didn't dare look at her. If he did, he would forget what had to be done. He would want to spend the rest of his life holding her, making sure she was safe from harm.

He felt the cool metal touch his outstretched hand. "Thanks."

"He stopped me on my way back to the hotel," Silver offered. "I didn't know what else to do. He insisted I go with him." She paused a moment. "He wanted me to go to his room. That's why . . . that's why I got him to bring me out here. So you could follow."

Once Cassidy's hands were captured safely behind him and his mouth was firmly gagged, Jared rose and turned. "You did right," he admitted reluctantly. "Now you're going to have to do something else. You'll have to stay here with him until I get back."

Her eyes rounded. "Where are you going?"

"I've got to go back for our things. You and Cass both need horses to ride. I'll have to turn in this hired buggy."

"Of course." Her voice was low and quavery-sounding. "I should have known. I didn't think."

Jared took a step toward her. "You could go back to Corinne's."

"No." Her denial was sharp and sure. "I'm staying with you."

He didn't argue with her. He couldn't. If he remembered clearly, he'd never won an argument with her yet. Not since the day she walked into his hotel room and handed him that locket.

The ground seemed to have grown harder after ten nights with a bed to sleep in.

Silver opened her eyes to find a cloudy, pewter-colored sky overhead. She sat up, pursing her lips as she bent backward to relieve a crimp in her spine. As she straightened to a more normal position, she found herself staring into a pair of icy blue eyes.

His back against a tree and his arms handcuffed around the trunk behind him, Cassidy watched her with undisguised hatred. Her mouth went dry, and she glanced quickly around in search of Jared. He wasn't anywhere in sight.

"You're going to be sorry you did this, Silver."

She wished Jared hadn't removed Cassidy's gag when they made camp just a few hours ago. The sound of his voice made her insides quake.

"I'll make sure you regret it," he added.

Silver rose from her bedroll. She brushed at the dust on her skirt, refusing to look at the captive. "You won't be able to make anyone do anything. Not once the law gets through with you."

He laughed sharply. "The law's got nothing on me. I'm just a gentleman gambler who jilted a spiteful young woman."

Jared's appearance at the top of the ridge silenced her reply. He moved in that loose-limbed gait of his as he walked down the side of the hill, his arms laden with firewood. He glanced at Silver, then dropped the wood beside the fire before turning to face the other man. He wore the inscrutable mask Silver had seen so often before. Cassidy could have been no more than an irritating fly buzzing overhead for all the emotion Jared revealed. "How's your head?"

Cassidy ignored the question. "What's your part in this, Newman? Who are you?"

"I'm a bounty hunter."

"A bounty hunter? You fool! I'm not a wanted man. How long have you been wasting your time following me?"

Jared took a step toward the prisoner. His face was still impassive. "Six years."

Silver noticed the trickle of sweat inching its way down Cassidy's forehead. She saw the nervous tick begin in his left eye.

"You've got the wrong man, Newman. You must think there's some reward on my head to follow as hard and long as you have, but you're wrong. I'm not accused of any crimes. How'd you find me? My face isn't known."

There was a slight tightening in Jared's jaw. "It wasn't your face that's known. It's the scar on your chest. Your victims don't tend to forget it."

"What victims?" the prisoner challenged. But his voice faltered and the tick by his eye worsened. "I'm telling you, there isn't any—"

"Like the saloon girl you tortured in Central City. You remember Felicity, don't you? She didn't die, Cass. She's waiting to testify against you. And what about the little orphaned boy you left out in the middle of nowhere in Nevada. Did you think he'd ever forget you or what you did to his ma and pa? Or how about the husband in Texas who had to listen to his wife's screams. Did you think he wouldn't remember your voice?" The unconcerned facade dropped away as Jared knelt before Cassidy, their faces only inches apart. "My sister didn't live long enough to see you hang, but she lived long enough to let me know what you did to her." With a swift motion, he ripped open the front of Cassidy's shirt, revealing the star-shaped scar. "She told me about *that.*"

An alarm sounded in Silver's head as she sensed Jared's fury. In that instant she knew he was very close to committing cold-blooded murder. She stepped forward and placed a hand on his shoulder. "Help me start the fire, Jared," she said softly. "I'll make some coffee."

He turned his head toward her. For a moment, she saw only hate within his hazel gaze. She knew he didn't even see her, so blinded was he by his own rage.

"Jared . . ."

Slowly, recognition returned.

"The fire, Jared. Help me start the fire."

Once more, he looked at Cassidy, then he stood and took a step backward. "Don't try to escape. I won't hesitate to stop you any way I can. I think I might enjoy it." His meaning was deadly clear.

If it hadn't been for Silver's presence that morning, he would have killed Cassidy. He would have strangled the life from him with his bare hands—and enjoyed every second of it. If he'd ever doubted the truth of what he'd become, that moment had proven it once and for all.

He glanced behind him, looking past Cassidy to where Silver followed in the rear. She saw his look and offered a weary smile. Jared nodded briskly and turned forward, his eyes on the slate-colored horizon. It had threatened to rain all day, but as afternoon turned into evening, still no rain had fallen. He hoped the wet weather would hold off altogether. Rain would only slow them down, and he wanted to be rid of Cassidy as soon as possible.

He felt a kind of sickness in the pit of his stomach. The search for revenge was nearly over. And then what? What would he do when he no longer had that driving force in his life?

I love you.

He could still hear the way she'd whispered the words.

I love you.

A tragic sense of loss weighed down upon his shoulders. No matter how much he wanted to succumb to those words, he knew that he couldn't. He had to save Silver from her own blindness. She couldn't see what a destructive companion he would be, but he could. She didn't know the things he'd done, but he did. She deserved much better than the man she thought she loved.

At least he could do something for her before he rode out of her life. He could give her the money to pay off the mortgage. He couldn't kid himself any longer. He wouldn't be going back to Kentucky, no matter how much money he had. But he could do something good with the reward Ted Harrison was offering. He could help Silver's family.

Yesterday afternoon, when he'd returned to Virginia City to retrieve their belongings, Jared had sent a telegram to Ted Harrison, telling him to meet them in Denver in late July. He'd sent another to Rick Cooper, asking him to go to Central City to talk to Claudette and Felicity at the Crystal Palace. He wanted Felicity ready to identify Cassidy as soon as they got there. With luck, they'd be in Denver in four weeks.

Just four more weeks. That's all the time he had left with Silver.

Chapter 33

The first quarter moon, resembling one-half of a pie topped with whipped cream, hung suspended above the eastern horizon as she sat on her bedroll. The supper fire was already dying. Hot coals were turning from red to white.

Silver turned her head toward the west. Jared was standing with his back toward her, his stance nonchalant, yet she sensed an underlying current of tension emanating from him. In the five days since they left Virginia City, she'd often found him looking behind them. She'd wanted to ask him why, but couldn't seem to do it. Jared had erected an invisible barrier that kept her at arm's length without him saying a word.

"What's eating him?" Cassidy asked from behind her.

She ignored him. She had found that to be the best solution over the past few days. She never knew, when Cassidy spoke to her, if he would be trying to convince her of his innocence or warning her that he would get even for her part in it. Either way, he frightened her. She had a terrible feeling that the worst was not yet behind them. She wished she could at least find comfort in Jared's arms, but even that was denied her.

And something *was* eating Jared, just as Cassidy had said. It was time she found out exactly what it was. Wearily, Silver pushed herself up from the bedroll and walked across the camp. "What's wrong?" she asked softly as she drew up beside him.

"We're being followed."

"Followed?" She looked back along the route they'd traveled that day. She saw nothing but rolling country, sagebrush, and trees.

"He's been following us from the start."

"Who?" she asked.

"I don't know. I thought it was just coincidence at first, but no more. He's staying the same distance behind no matter how fast or how slow we travel. He even stops when we do. It's time I found out what he wants and who he is."

Jared spun around and returned to the center of camp. He bent first to check the handcuffs around Cassidy's wrists. Apparently satisfied, he rose again and headed for the horses. In a matter of minutes, he had his pinto saddled and bridled.

As he swung into the saddle, he glanced at Silver. "Keep a sharp eye out. If anything moves, including him"—he pointed at Cassidy—"shoot first." He pulled his Winchester from the scabbard and tossed it to her. "If it's me coming, I'll let you know." He rode off into the night.

Silver held the rifle away from her. He knew very well that her skills as a marksman made her cooking seem like sumptuous cuisine. She couldn't actually shoot someone, even if they . . .

"If you'll free me, I'll make sure you're protected." Cassidy's voice was as smooth as molasses.

She turned to look at him. "You must think me a great fool," she replied as she pulled the rifle into position. She might not be able to shoot

straight, but she didn't have to let anyone know
it in advance, especially not Bob Cassidy.

"How'd you get tied up with that bounty
hunter anyway?"

"I hired him to find a thief. But that's all I
thought you were. I realize now I didn't like you
much. I was just too stupid to know it. But I never
thought you were a killer."

"How can you believe it, Silver? We loved each
other."

She turned her back on him, unable to face
what she'd nearly done to herself while trying to
be what her mother wanted her to be. "We never
loved each other. Never."

Silver sat down on the blankets, positioning
herself so she could see Cassidy out of the corner
of her eye without looking directly at him. She
cradled the rifle in her arm with the business end
pointed at the prisoner. Her right hand rested on
the stock.

Staring off into the night, watching for Jared's
return, she realized that loving the bounty hunter
was the one thing she'd truly done without any
outside pressure. She'd spent her life trying to be
what her mother expected her to be or, failing
that, doing her darnedest to be the very opposite.

Somewhere in between was the real Silver.
Could that be the woman Jared might love?

Jared dismounted and left the pinto. He moved
forward without a sound, his Colt in his hand.
Whoever was following them wasn't very smart.
He hadn't even attempted to hide the campfire. In
fact, he had a royal blaze going, lighting up the
area like a torch. By now, every Indian and white
man for miles around knew his position.

Jared paused behind a clump of sagebrush and
peered into the camp. He could see the form be-

neath a blanket not far from the fire. Didn't the fool know he was so close to the light he'd never be able to see danger approaching from out of the dark?

Moving stealthily, he stepped into the camp. Keen eyes watched the blanket for the slightest movement, for any indication the person below might be awake and watching. There was none.

With a swift motion, Jared grabbed the blanket and jerked it away. "Don't mo—" His command died in his throat. "Dean!"

The boy sat up, terror written across his face as he grappled for the revolver stuck beneath the saddle he'd been using for a pillow.

Jared grasped his hand. "Dean, it's okay. It's me."

The sleep-induced confusion cleared, followed by a look of wary anger.

"What are you doing here, son? Silver told me you were staying with Miss Corinne."

"I ain't stayin' behind while you take him in. I got a right t'see him hang for what he done."

Jared recognized the boy's lust for revenge. That feeling had been his sole companion for years. "You shouldn't have come after us alone," was all he said as he rose to his feet.

"I can take care o' myself." Dean jumped up too. "I managed t'keep up with you without no problem, didn't I?"

"So you did." He glanced toward the lanky sorrel tied nearby. "Where did you get the horse?"

The boy let a lengthy pause elapse before answering. "I borrowed it from Miss Corinne."

"Saddle, revolver, and supplies too? Very generous of her."

"I'll pay her back."

Jared nodded. He knew Corinne Duvall hadn't

given these things to a young boy and let him ride out onto the desert alone—and he knew that Dean knew he knew it. He'd taken everything and stolen off into the night. But there wasn't any point in belaboring the issue now. "You bet you will. I'll see that you do."

Their eyes met, Dean's rebellious and stubborn, Jared's hard and unwavering.

"I ain't goin' back," Dean whispered.

"You would if we were any closer to Virginia City," Jared responded. "But there's no time for it now. Get your gear and come on. Silver will be wondering what's happening."

She heard them first, then saw their silhouettes as they rode toward camp.

"It's me, Silver," Jared shouted as she rose from her blanket and leveled the rifle.

She only had a few moments more to wonder about the identity of the second rider before the moonlight lit his face.

"Dean! I don't believe it," she cried as she dropped the rifle and hurried forward. She couldn't help but be glad to see him. Their parting had been so angry, and she hadn't wanted it to be that way. "What are you doing here?"

He didn't return her smile. "I told you I wasn't gonna stay behind." His gaze flicked to Cassidy. "I told you I'd see him dead," he said in a low voice.

Dean slipped from the saddle and walked slowly across the camp. Cassidy watched with a bemused expression. The boy stopped a few feet away from him and just continued to stare.

"What do *you* want?" Cassidy finally snapped at him.

"I wanna see you hang."

Cassidy grinned. "Bloodthirsty little bastard, aren't you?" Then he laughed.

With an angry cry, Dean jumped forward and kicked Cassidy in the stomach as hard as he could. And then he kicked him again and again.

Stunned, Silver couldn't seem to move, but Jared rushed forward and grabbed the boy, hauling him away beneath one arm.

Cassidy gasped for air as he bent forward as far as his bound arms would allow. When he looked up, his eyes swept the other three, stopping on the boy. "You keep him away from me. He's crazy."

"He only did what I've wanted to do for weeks," Silver said without a trace of compassion in her voice. "It's not nearly as bad as what you did to his folks. It isn't even as bad as you deserve." She turned away, put her arm around Dean, and led him across the camp.

Jared watched as Silver laid out Dean's bedroll next to her own, then tucked the boy in for the night.

"You shouldn't have left Miss Corinne's," she said to him, "but I'm glad you're all right. I've missed you."

Dean remained silent, but there was a suspicious quiver in his chin.

Silver leaned forward and kissed his forehead. "Close your eyes and get some sleep. We get an early start."

"He laughed like that when he tied me up." Dean's voice was choked with tears. "He laughed like that when he killed my folks.'

Silver gathered the slight lad in her arms and hugged him close, smoothing his hair and murmuring platitudes. Finally, she laid him back on the ground, dried the tears from the corners of his eyes, and pulled the blanket up beneath his chin. "Go to sleep now. It'll be all right."

He looked up at her for a moment before nodding his head and rolling onto his side as he pulled the blanket over his face.

She's good with children, Jared thought as he watched.

As if sensing his observance, she turned her head and met his gaze. She smiled gently, then rose and came toward him.

"I think he'll sleep now," she whispered.

"He shouldn't be here," Jared said gruffly.

"I know. But he is, so we might as well make the best of it." She placed her fingers on his forearm. "Besides, he probably does have a right to see justice done, and maybe the courts will need his testimony. He's one of the few living witnesses."

"He said himself he didn't see Cassidy's face clearly."

"He remembers him," Silver said as she glanced back at Dean. "He remembers more than he should." Her own voice caught.

Jared didn't think about what he was doing as he drew her into his embrace. He held her in silence for a long time, enjoying the feel of her hair against his jaw, the way each small breath she took pressed her breasts against his chest. "You need some sleep yourself," he said softly near her ear. "Come on." He guided her toward her own bedroll. "Get under that blanket."

She twisted toward him within the circle of his arms and tipped her face up. Her eyes seemed to glitter in the light of the quarter moon. Or could it be tears rather than moonlight?

"I'm no good for you, Silver Matlock," he whispered, then pressed his lips against her hair.

She pulled her head back, tilting her face up so

she could look into his eyes. "Why?" The lone word couldn't be heard, but he saw her mouth the question, saw it repeated in her eyes.

"I'm not much better than he is." Jared jerked his head toward Cassidy. "I wanted to kill him with my bare hands. I wanted to watch him die, slowly and painfully." He held up his hands and stared at them, as if he could see the destruction they could bring.

"But you didn't, Jared. Don't you see? That's what makes you different. No matter how badly you wanted to, you didn't do it."

"I've killed before. I've done things . . ." He felt himself breaking up inside. He couldn't tell her. He couldn't ever tell her what he was, what he'd done.

Her hands lifted to frame his face. "I've seen the man you really are, Jared Newman. The man inside is good and tender and caring." One hand slid down to touch his chest. "I've seen the love you've hidden in your heart. I'll wait until you see it too."

"Don't wait, Silver."

Before he could forget himself and kiss her, he turned and walked away.

Chapter 34

The strain was beginning to tell on all of them. They covered forty miles or more each day, stopping only for the sake of the horses. They stayed away from towns and the rail line. Their food consisted of whatever fresh game Jared happened to find, supplemented with hardtack and beans, and even those supplies were running low. The temperatures soared into the nineties and higher, sweltering heat during the day that chilled quickly after the sun went down.

The journey would have been hard enough on its own without the added unpleasantness of Cassidy's presence. For Silver, it was especially so. She didn't like the way he always seemed to be watching her. Often she found him grinning, as if he had a special secret that pleased him no end. He seemed to forget that *he* was the prisoner. She wanted to ask him what he found so amusing but managed to refrain. She didn't want to give him the satisfaction of knowing he bothered her. He complained constantly—about the heat, his sore muscles, not being allowed to shave. His suit, once dapper and crisp, was layered with dirt. His hair was oily, his face covered with a scraggly blond beard. It was hard to believe this was the same man who had come calling with flowers and poetic-sounding words. Now, whenever Jared was out of earshot, he spewed forth foul language in a constant barrage.

Dean cut Cassidy a wide berth, although he often stated aloud—to no one in particular—how much he was going to enjoy seeing "that man" hang. Silver tried to tell the boy he shouldn't hate so much. The desire for justice was well and good, but his obsession with Cassidy's death would benefit no one. Dean ignored her.

After the night Dean joined them, Jared had retreated behind that familiar remote facade of his. Silver had hoped he would find another opportunity to put his arms around her, to hold her, perhaps to kiss her, but he hadn't. And, to be honest, by the time they made camp each night, Silver was too tired to pursue a casual conversation, let alone anything of a more personal nature.

It was late in the afternoon of their tenth day on the trail when Cassidy's mount began to limp. Jared found a small stone imbedded in the frog of the bay's hoof.

"It's a bad bruise," Jared said as he lowered the animal's leg. "We'll have to take it easy on him for a few days." He glanced around. "We'll make camp here."

Silver breathed a sigh. Their campsite was in a mountain pass with trees and a nearby stream instead of the interminable desert and sage. She knew more desert lay beyond this respite, but she meant to enjoy it—and the early stop—while she could.

Jared managed to shoot a couple of quail for their supper. Silver roasted the birds over the fire and saw the men fed, then slipped away to the stream for her first bath in days.

The icy water elicited a tiny shriek as she

slipped into the stream. If she lay flat on the
smooth rocks that lined the bottom, the water almost covered her completely, but she couldn't
stand the cold for very long. She scrubbed herself
clean, soaping her hair twice. Then she doused
and scoured the clothes she'd worn for several
days before laying them across some rocks to dry.
With any luck, there would be enough daylight
left to do the job. She rubbed her damp, goose-
pimpled skin with a blanket, then dressed quickly
in her lone change of clothes, after which she sat
on a boulder and combed out her hair.

She wasn't surprised when she heard footsteps
behind her. She knew it was Jared. She had
known he would come to check on her if she tar-
ried long.

"It'll be dark soon," he said.

"I'm nearly finished."

He drew closer. "We'll have to do some walking, give the horses some rest. Could add several
days to our journey."

Her head was tilted to one side as she ran the
comb through the thick black tresses. "I don't
suppose it makes much difference now. Without
the money . . ." She shrugged. She'd come to
terms with it. She could only go back to Masonville and try to cushion the blow for her parents
when it came.

Jared lit a cigarette as he leaned against a tree
at his back. "I've been meaning to tell you something. I'm not sure how soon Harrison will pay
his reward, but I mean to give you your share.
Maybe it'll be in time."

Her hand stilled in midair, then lowered to her
lap as she turned to look at him. "You've only
mentioned the reward in passing. What will you
do with it? Is it very much?"

His gaze caressed her face as he tenderly studied her eyes, her mouth. "Yes, Silver. It's very much. I thought it would be enough for me to go back . . ." He stopped abruptly, tossing his cigarette into the water. "There's plenty to help your parents," he said, then walked away.

There was a terrible pain in her chest as she watched him go. Why wouldn't he tell her he loved her? Why did he have to go on being so stubborn?

Cassidy's gaze moved back and forth between Jared and Silver. He was right about those two. If they weren't lovers now, they had been in the past, and now there was something amiss between them. If he had any hope of escape, this was what he must use. He wasn't sure exactly how he could use it, but if he bided his time and watched, the right moment would come.

And when it did, he meant to make Silver regret her part in all this. Newman he would just kill and be done with it, but Silver . . . He had plans for Silver. He would keep her with him for a while, and she would curse every moment she remained alive. Cassidy knew how to make a woman feel that way. He was very adept at it. He smiled to himself as he contemplated just a few of the tricks he knew.

He rolled over, but it was impossible to find a comfortable position. At night, Newman allowed him to have his arms cuffed in front. A sturdy chain secured him to the nearest tree—when one was available. Otherwise, Cassidy found himself trussed up like a calf for branding, arms and legs tied with ropes.

His thoughts returned to the bounty hunter. He wondered, as he'd wondered before, which girl his sister had been. Could it have been that pretty blonde in Wichita? No. Newman had a Southern drawl, a drawl that said money despite the influence of western slang that cropped up occasionally. Perhaps his sister was that girl with the curly auburn hair in New Orleans. No, he didn't think she was the one either. Which one had it been?

He lifted a brow as he considered the possibilities. Had he killed so many he couldn't remember each one? Usually just hearing them scream and beg for mercy was enough. Unless they got a good look at his face, of course. Then they had to die. Or, sometimes something just snapped inside of him, and he knew he didn't ever want another man to look upon them, to touch their bodies, to feel the lust and desire he'd felt. The first one had been his wife, Mary Ruth. He'd caught her flirting with that Confederate captain. She should have known he wouldn't stand for such a thing. She'd belonged to him.

He thought he'd been so careful, thought there was no way anyone could trace him down, could ever suspect him of having a hand in anyone's death. Apparently, he'd grown careless through the years and left a few eyewitnesses. Newman said he'd been following him for six years. Six years!

Why hadn't he made certain Newman was dead when he had the chance? He should have gone back, should have checked. He'd gotten too sure of himself and now the mistakes were catching up with him.

He'd made another one when he left Masonville the way he did, but he'd panicked when he saw Newman passing through town just three days before the wedding. He should have realized Newman didn't know he was there, that it was merely coincidence. He should have stayed and married Silver, then quietly left town with enough of his father-in-law's money for their honeymoon. He could have gotten rid of the girl in good time.

Cassidy ground his teeth. He didn't like making mistakes, and he'd made a number of them. But he wasn't going to continue making them. Next time, he'd make sure the bounty hunter was dead.

But not Silver, he thought as he glared across the camp. *Not right away.*

Silver he meant to enjoy.

"You don't have any choice, Jared," Silver said as she squinted into the late-morning sunlight. "We can't go on with a lame horse."

"I don't like it."

"You've said it yourself. If we keep going, he'll be ruined in a day or two. Then what will we do? We won't have anything to trade."

Jared turned toward Cassidy, and Silver's gaze followed. A strong, narrow chain went through the cuffs on the prisoner's wrists, then was wrapped around a tree and closed with a padlock. The chain secured Cassidy to the tree while still allowing him some small measure of movement. Jared had told her he'd used this method of holding prisoners many times. He'd assured her it would be impossible for Cassidy to break free.

Jared looked at Silver again. He was scowling in that dark, threatening way of his. "Don't remove those cuffs. Not for any reason. No matter what he tells you. Do you understand me?"

"I won't. I promise. We'll be fine."

"You've got plenty of water and enough food for the day. I should be back around nightfall."

"We'll be fine," she repeated.

They didn't have any choice and they both knew it. They couldn't take Cassidy anywhere near a town, and without another horse, they would be slowed to fifteen miles a day, twenty if they were lucky. And Jared was the only one who could go into town and make the trade. Silver couldn't. Even she realized she would be safer here than out alone on the trail. At least here she knew who the enemy was—and he was chained to a tree.

"Go on," she chided gently. "You'll never be back if you don't get going."

Jared's hazel eyes studied her for a long time. It was difficult to keep from looking away from his intense perusal, to keep up a front of bravery and confidence, but she managed somehow. Finally, with a deep sigh, he turned and swung up onto the pinto.

"Keep the rifle handy," he said before riding out of camp, Cassidy's lame horse followed behind him.

Silver watched until he'd disappeared from sight. A warm breeze whispered in the treetops. Normally, she liked the sound, but today she thought it had a terribly lonely feel to it. She'd tried to let Jared think she could get along just fine without him, but the truth was she was more than a bit nervous.

As if sensing her feelings, Cassidy said, "We'll be lucky if he's able to make a trade today. He might not even be back until tomorrow."

"He'll be back." She straightened her shoulders and lifted her chin. "He said he would. He will be." She turned toward the prisoner. "I'll fix our lunch."

"Wouldn't mind something to eat." He slid his back down the tree as he sat down. "Kind of nice, havin' you all to myself this morning. Where's the boy?"

"Dean's trying to catch some fish." She wished he'd quit talking, especially about how nice it was to be alone with her. She didn't think it was nice. She hated it. Even with him tied to that tree.

"You don't expect me to stay in this same spot all day, do you? A man needs to stretch his legs"—his grin was more like a leer—"and take care of a few other private matters."

"Sorry. You'll just have to do the best you can."

"Afraid of me, Silver? You could hold the rifle on me, just like Newman does." He chuckled low in his throat. "I'd promise not to go far."

"I'm not afraid of you." She turned her back on him, not wanting him to see the apprehension in her eyes. She *was* afraid of him. She'd seen too clearly the evil that lurked in his eyes, heard the wickedness spill from his mouth. She would be a fool not to fear him. But she couldn't let him see it. Somehow she knew he would use her fear against her.

She glanced down the trail where Jared had disappeared only moments before. He wouldn't have left her if he'd thought there was any danger. She would just ignore Cassidy's comments and concentrate on frying up some of the venison left over from last night's kill.

Cassidy remained chatty as she worked over the campfire, preparing the meal. He talked about little, inconsequential things, as if they were good friends spending the day together in the country. He certainly didn't sound like a murderer being taken in to face the hangman's noose. She almost didn't realize what he was saying, his voice was so unconcerned and casual.

"You know, Silver, there really isn't any evidence against me. I never killed anyone. I'm a bit of a reprobate, I suppose, and my profession isn't looked at with high regard, but I'm not a bad man. No jury is going to find me guilty of mur-

der.'' He smiled as she looked over at him.
''You'll see. We'll about kill ourselves getting to
Denver, and I'll be free within a few days. A couple of weeks at most. They'll never convict me of
any wrongdoing.''

''They'll convict you,'' she said firmly—even as
she began to wonder if he could be right. He
sounded so sure of himself.

''And if they don't,'' Dean added from the edge
of their camp, ''I'll kill you myself.''

Silver saw Cassidy's smile fade as he looked at
the boy. Cassidy's eyes were the color of ice—and
about as warm. Even though he wasn't looking
at her, she felt chilled to the bone.

Dean turned away and held up a string of fish.
''Want 'em for lunch or are they our supper?''

''It'll have to be supper. The venison's ready
now.''

Jared guided the pinto down the mountain. If
he remembered from the last time they were
through this way, there was a small town in the
valley to the north. He should be able to reach it
by two o'clock. With any luck, he'd be able to
trade for a sound horse and be back at their camp
by suppertime. The bay was a prime piece of
horseflesh. With just a week's rest, he'd be as
good as new. But Jared couldn't give the gelding
the time he needed to heal. They'd never gone
above a walk the past two days, and Cassidy had
either walked as well or had taken a turn riding
Dean's sorrel, but the bay's limp had still worsened. It was clear that they couldn't continue at
that pace.

He tried not to think about leaving Silver and
Dean alone with Cassidy. He'd known it was their
only choice, but he hadn't liked making the decision then and he liked it even less now. True,

Cassidy was immobilized by the handcuffs and the chain, but what if something went wrong? If only he could be sure Silver would be safe.

He asked the pinto for more speed, but it still didn't seem fast enough.

Chapter 35

D ean joined her in the shade of a dark green pine. He sat cross-legged on the ground amidst the dried pine needles and pungent-smelling pinecones. His brows were drawn together in a frown. "Do you think he's right?"

"Who?"

He jerked his head toward Cassidy. "Him."

"About what?"

"Is he goin' t'get off like he says? Ain't they goin' t'believe me when I tell 'em what he done?"

Silver patted his knee. "He's just trying to convince himself." She hoped she was right. She remembered the way Cassidy had threatened her, saying he'd get even for her part in all this. If he walked free, he would do as he'd sworn. She was sure of that.

"I ain't goin' t'let that happen. If he gets loose, I'll shoot him myself. If I have to follow after him like Mr. Newman's been doin', even if I have t'do it the rest o' my life, I'll see that he pays for what he done to my ma and pa. I swore it on my ma's grave."

Silver looked at the boy's face. Carved into its childish features were the hate and determination of a grown man. It saddened her heart. Dean

347

should be carefree at his age, not saddled with an oath of revenge.

"I'm sure you won't have to worry about that," she said softly. "This will be over for all of us very soon."

Dean scrambled to his feet. "It would've been better if we'd just shot him in Virginia City an' been done with it. Then we wouldn't've had t'worry about him gettin' away." With another hateful glance toward Cassidy, he turned and sauntered off into the woods.

Silver glanced up at the sky. She wished the sun were lower. She wished Jared would return.

She closed her eyes and immediately summoned up a vision of the bounty hunter. Lord, how she loved him. Why couldn't he admit that he felt the same? It would all be so simple if only he would admit it . . .

He wasn't going to make it back before dark. The horse trader, a crafty old buzzard, had dickered for what seemed an eternity. Jared had known he would eventually make the trade, but the fellow was enjoying himself too much to be rushed. Jared hadn't had a whole lot of choice. He'd just had to wait it out.

Now he was pushing the pinto harder than he should. Lather was glistening on the gelding's black-and-white neck and around the edges of the saddle. He eased back on the reins, but his own impatience soon had him nudging more speed from the weary animal.

He's promised Silver he would be back before nightfall. He didn't want to break his promise. Something told him it was important.

Cassidy shouted and struggled to his feet. He shook one leg, then the other. "Ants! I'm crawling with ants!'' He swore as he tried to bat at his pantlegs with his bound hands. ''Get me out of here!''

Rifle in hand, Silver stepped cautiously forward. She was half-expecting a trick, but he was telling the truth. The small, biting creatures were swarming around the base of the tree. His boots and legs were covered with them, and they were rapidly spreading up his hands and arms—even to his neck and face. Already they had made their way under his clothes and were biting him without mercy.

Half-crazed with pain and fear, he was straining against the chain, jumping up and down and pulling at his clothes. ''Silver, help me!'' he shouted. ''Help me! They're all over me. Oh my God, get them off of me!''

Silver turned and ran back across the camp. She set down the rifle and picked up a saddle blanket, then raced back to him. Mindful to keep enough distance between them, she swung the blanket against his legs and feet. Even as she did so, she felt as if the ants were beginning to swarm up her legs as well.

''That's not doing any good. Look at them,'' Cassidy cried. ''They're everywhere!'' He cursed again as he desperately swatted his arms and legs, and clawed at his neck, which was already turning red and swollen from the bites. ''You've got to get me away from them. I'll go crazy!''

Silver dropped the blanket as she backed away. What was she going to do? She couldn't leave him there. She rubbed her arms, shuddering with revulsion as his screams continued to pierce her ears. She turned to find Dean watching from across the camp. He almost seemed to be enjoying Cassidy's misery.

''Dean, you're going to have to help me.'' She

hurried toward the saddlebag, where she knew Jared kept the spare set of keys.

"Mr. Newman said not to let him go, no matter what. You told me so yourself."

"I can't leave him there. The ants are biting every inch of him. If we don't do something, he'll go crazy."

"So let 'em bite," the boy replied spitefully.

Silver spun around to look at him, the key in her hand. "Dean Forest, listen to you. What if it was you over there? Even *he* deserves a common kindness, no matter how else we feel about him."

He looked suitably ashamed.

"Now help me. I can't do this alone."

"Mr. Newman ain't gonna like it," Dean grumbled as he moved forward.

"He'll know we didn't have any choice." She glanced over her shoulder at Cassidy. He was continuing to curse and shout and swat at the ants. She couldn't stand listening to him and not help. If she was the one under that tree, covered with ants, she would go crazy. She shuddered at the thought. She had to help him. She took a deep, steadying breath. "We've watched Jared do this every morning and every night. We'll do it just like he does. I'll keep the rifle on him while you slip the chain through the cuffs. Then we'll just walk him to another tree."

It sounded simple enough. She'd seen Jared do it a dozen or more times already. There'd never been a bit of trouble. She had the rifle, after all, and Cassidy's hands would still be cuffed. What possible trouble could he be?

"You stay behind the tree," she reminded Dean as she picked up the rifle. With the barrel of the Winchester, she pointed to the opposite side of the camp. "We'll move him over there."

Together, they walked toward Cassidy.

"It's about time," he snapped as they approached. "Get me the hell out of here."

"Go on, Dean," she said softly, then leveled a steady gaze on her captive. "We're going to move you to that tree over there, but if you make any trouble, I'll shoot. Do you understand me? Just one wrong move and I shoot."

"All right, damn it. All right. Just get me out of here."

"Dean." Silver nodded when the boy looked at her from beyond Cassidy's right shoulder.

The chain slid around an inch or two until Dean had the padlock in hand. She could hear the click as the key turned in the lock. Once again Dean looked at her, and once again she nodded. She raised the rifle and pointed it at Cassidy's chest, her finger on the trigger.

The chain separated, and Dean began to tug it slowly through the cuffs. But Cassidy wasn't waiting. He gave his arms a quick jerk and broke free. He danced off to the side, cursing and swatting. Silver's heart was racing as she watched him. She tried to move with him, to keep the rifle leveled on him.

"Hold it," she ordered. "Get over to that tree over there. To your right."

He shot her an angry look but moved in the direction she indicated, his arms still moving madly from side to side, swiping at his legs. Dean followed with the chain and padlock.

"Put your wrists against the tree," Silver told him, echoing Jared's usual commands. "Dean, toss him the chain. All right, Bob. Pick it up. Slowly."

It was going just as it was supposed to. Cassidy had done everything as instructed. She was the one with the gun. He was the one with his wrists cuffed together. So how could anything go wrong?

She wasn't sure exactly how it happened. Dean swung the chain out. It landed at Cassidy's feet. Cassidy leaned down and picked it up, dropping the end between his wrists. It was just as she'd seen it done before. Only this time Cassidy made a sudden move. He pulled his hands into the air, jerking on the chain, causing Dean to stumble forward. Silver didn't hesitate. She pulled the trigger. The rifle exploded with a powerful kick, knocking her backward. By the time she'd steadied herself and was looking down the barrel once again, Cassidy's arms were on either side of Dean's head and the links connecting the handcuffs were pulled tightly against the boy's throat.

"Put down the rifle, Silver."

She was shaking with fear, but she didn't lower it.

He tightened his hold on the boy's neck. She heard a tiny squeak of air.

"Put it down. I'll kill him."

"Next time I won't miss," she responded. "I won't miss again."

"But the boy'll still be dead. You can kill me but it won't bring him back." He jerked again on the handcuffs.

Dean's fingers came up to his throat. He tried desperately to pry the chain away as he gasped for breath. His face turned a bright red. His eyes seemed to bulge in their sockets.

"Do it, Silver, or it'll be too late."

Feeling an icy terror seeping through her veins, Silver lowered the rifle.

Jared knew something was wrong before he entered the camp. The fire was still burning. He could see Cassidy's shadowed form beside the

tree, and from just above the cover of under-
brush, he could see the edges of the other bedrolls. It seemed everyone was asleep. Yet his
instincts told him something wasn't right.

He dismounted slowly. Even the pinto seemed
to sense something. The gelding nickered softly,
ears thrust forward, neck arched.

"Easy, boy," Jared whispered as he drew his
Colt.

He walked slowly, silently toward camp. His
eyes darted about, checking for any strange
movements, any hint of danger beyond the light
of the fire. It wasn't until he was nearly within
the camp itself that he could see the bedrolls
clearly. They were empty.

And then he knew what else was wrong. Cassidy was beneath a different tree.

His heartbeat quickened as he stepped toward
the prisoner's still form. "Cass?" he said, sweeping the camp with his gaze once again. "Wake
up." He reached down and jerked the blanket
away.

His heart slammed into his chest with alarming
force. It wasn't Cassidy. It was Dean—bound,
gagged, and cuffed to the tree. There was a cut
along his temple, the blood now dried and crusty.
When he first looked at Jared, it was with stark
terror. Then, as recognition occurred, he mumbled and fought against the bindings.

"Dear God," Jared whispered, "what happened?" He knelt and hurried to free the boy.

Dean spit the gag out of his mouth the moment
it was loosened. "He's got Silver," he croaked.

"How long ago?"

The boy shook his head. "I don't know. He hit
me an' knocked me cold." His arms freed, he
lifted fingers to tenderly touch the bloody spot at
his temple. "It was still light."

"How did it happen?"

"It was my fault. We were movin' him 'cause there was ants. They were all over him, an' Silver said we couldn't just leave him there. I reached too far forward. He got the cuffs 'round my neck, and . . . I'm sorry, Mr. Newman. It was my fault."

Jared rose and turned his back toward Dean. "I told her not to move him, no matter what." Why hadn't she listened to him?

Three, no, four hours. Cassidy had at least a four-hour head-start. And he'd had some of it in daylight.

With quick strides, Jared moved toward where he'd left the horses that morning. He hunkered down and peered at the ground. It was too dark to see. It was too blasted dark.

He got up again and moved through the brush, looking for clues, even just one that would tell him which way Cassidy was headed. But it was useless. Despite the moon, he couldn't make out any signs. The tall trees cast deep shadows, hiding any tracks from Jared's well-trained eyes.

"Cassidy!" he shouted suddenly, his voice echoing through the mountain terrain. "Cassidy!" He slammed his fist against a nearby tree. "Damn you, Cass. I'll find you. I'll find you!"

If he hurt her, if he harmed one hair on her head . . .

A cry—as if from a caged wild animal—was torn from his chest. He dropped suddenly to his knees, letting his head fall forward as impotent fury overwhelmed him.

"God, don't let him hurt her," he prayed. The words were nearly choked back by the welling agony in his throat.

A small hand touched his shoulder. He looked up to find Dean, his cheeks streaked with tears, his face pale and frightened, standing beside him. "She . . . she'll be . . . be okay," he stuttered over his sobs.

Jared grabbed the boy behind the neck and pulled him down beside him. He hugged Dean's thin frame against his own broad chest, seeking to draw comfort and assurance from his presence—and perhaps giving back a small measure of the same. "I know," he whispered. "We'll get her back. She's going to be okay."

"Do we . . . do we go now?"

"No." Waiting for daylight. It was one of the hardest things he'd ever had to do. Even now, Cassidy could be torturing or killing Silver. But if they tried to follow and chose the wrong way, he might never find them. "We'll leave at first light."

It would be the longest night of his life.

Chapter 36

Silver swayed in the saddle. She feared that at any moment she would tumble toward earth. Pain still shot tiny needles from her jaw where he'd struck her, and her right eye felt swollen. She was cold, too, dressed only in her blouse and skirt. At the moment, she would welcome the sun, although she knew she would be despising it later when the heat blasted down upon them. But mostly, she was weary beyond measure. Throughout the night, he had kept them moving without respite.

He knows Jared will be right behind him, she thought.

Another wave of dizziness swelled and crashed over her. She sank her fingernails into the leather pommel. She didn't dare let her fatigue get the better of her. She didn't want to stop. She would be safe only as long as they kept moving. If she should force him to stop, there was no telling what he might do to her. She kept imagining the abuse this madman could mete out before dispatching his victims.

Jared will come. He'll find me.

But would he come in time? Or would he find her bloody, mutilated body?

She glanced ahead at Cassidy's back, at his red

neck still swollen from ant bites. Her stomach sickened at the thought of his hands on her body, touching her in places only Jared had known. He wouldn't be gentle. He would hurt her. He would delight in causing her pain. She would rather die than feel him invading her body. She would rather die.

She imagined Jared, finding her, burying her as he had his parents and sister. She felt his utter devastation and knew she wouldn't rather die. She would rather live. She had to live.

Jared.

She concentrated on the eastern horizon. The sky had lightened quickly, yet the sun still hadn't shown its golden head. Had Jared made it back to camp last night with the new horse? Had he been able to find their trail yet? Was he even now close behind them?

Hurry, Jared. I'm so frightened.

The rope bit into the tender flesh of her wrists, and she felt the warm trickle of blood before she saw the crimson streak stain the leather tooling of the saddle.

"We'll rest here," Cassidy said as he reined in the sorrel. He dismounted and walked back toward the buckskin mare, his stiff movements indicating to her that he was still suffering from the insect bites. He grinned up at Silver. "If I untie you, will you behave yourself?"

She nodded, not trusting herself to speak. She wasn't sure her legs would hold her once she was on the ground, but she needed badly to empty her bladder. She watched as he loosened the rope that bound her wrists to the saddle horn. Fresh pain ignited as the cool morning breeze hit the raw flesh. She sucked air between her teeth, then pressed her lips together.

"Come on. Get down." He grabbed her arm and pulled her from the saddle.

She fell to her knees but struggled quickly to her feet and backed away from him. All her senses were alert for his first attack. She would fight—until the last ounce of strength had left her body. She wouldn't give up. She wouldn't give in. Never.

He seemed to read her mind. "Not yet, my love." His grin widened as he laughed. "Later, when we have lots of time." With a jerk of his head, he added, "I'll even give you some privacy. You haven't the strength to go far. There's some bushes over there."

She turned and stumbled toward the bush. He could have kept her tied, kept her close to him, and she knew she would rather have died than drop her skirt in his presence. She took longer than necessary, as long as she dared, all the while thinking that every moment she delayed brought Jared that much closer.

When she returned to the horses, her legs still feeling rubbery beneath her, Cassidy held out a canteen. "Drink. We won't have time for food for a while."

As she lifted the canteen to her parched mouth, she saw him watching the mountainside they'd just descended. He was watching for Jared. He was scared. She felt better knowing it.

"Thanks," she whispered as she returned the canteen.

Instead of taking it from her hand, he reached out and touched the bruise on the side of her face. "It's a shame I had to do that," he said. "The swelling hides your pretty eyes. From now on, you do as I say and maybe I won't have to hit you again. You remember that."

Silver dropped the canteen. She was quaking

inside, but she wasn't going to show it. "I'll remember." She grabbed hold of the saddle horn
and placed her left foot in the stirrup. It took every
bit of strength she could muster to pull herself up
and astride Cinder, but she did it. She didn't want
Cassidy touching her; she didn't want anything
from him if she could help it.

Cassidy wasn't taking any trouble to cover his
tracks. That either meant he wasn't worried about
Jared catching up with him or he didn't know
much about hiding out in the rocky mountain terrain. Jared couldn't be sure which it was. Cassidy
had ambushed him once before, but that was because Jared had grown careless. He wouldn't
make the same mistake twice.

He kept the pinto alternating between a canter
and a fast walk and spared no time for conversation with Dean. He knew the boy understood that
if he fell behind Jared would have to leave him
and come back later. And he knew that was exactly what Dean would want him to do. Dean was
as worried about Silver as Jared was.

Again, he mentally berated himself. He should
never have left Cassidy behind with Silver. It had
been too great a risk. There were too many things
that could have gone wrong. He should have
taken the extra keys with him. He never should
have let her know where they were.

His eyes swept the trail up ahead as panic clam-
ored in his chest.

He hadn't yet told her he loved her. He had to
weave his fingers through her hair, stare down
into those round, gray, wondering eyes. He had
to kiss her sweet lips. And then he had to tell her
he loved her.

If any harm came to Silver, it would be his own
damn fault. He'd left her with that killer and

trusted her to obey his orders. He should have known better. When had Silver ever obeyed without argument, without question, without asserting that mind of her own? And he'd give anything to have her with him now, arguing and causing him grief.

He fought back the fear born of desperation. He couldn't give in to it. He couldn't even think about Silver and how much he loved her and what it would do to him if he lost her. He couldn't think of anything now except following Cassidy's tracks.

They ate the last of the jerky and washed it down with cold mountain water. Silver tried to eat slowly, to savor every bite. She knew it might be a long while before she ate again.

She was seated on an outcropping of rocks beneath the shade of a dark juniper. Cinder grazed on sparse clumps of grass nearby. Behind her, she could hear Cassidy moving about. She twisted to look at him. He was staring back down the stretch of trail they'd climbed during the course of the afternoon.

Several times that day he'd changed direction suddenly. He pretended to know where they were going, but she guessed they were lost. And he wasn't happy with the amount of ground they'd covered. He'd yelled at her often enough, telling her to hurry, threatening her if she tried to hold them back. She'd always denied his accusations but had continued to do anything she could to slow them down.

As she watched him, he began to pace from side to side. His movements were quick, jerky. She could see the sweat beading on his forehead. His shirt was stained with damp circles beneath his arms. He cursed as he moved, one moment his knuckles resting on his hips, the next flailing the air.

She realized in that one heart-stopping moment that Bob Cassidy was teetering on the brink of insanity. He was capable of anything for any reason. Logic would have nothing to do with his decisions.

His blue eyes impaled her as he strode toward her. He grabbed her by the hair and jerked her to her feet. "Get mounted." He shoved her toward her horse. "Now."

Tears of pain sprang to her eyes, but she held them back as she pulled herself into the saddle. She refused to cry in front of this man. She turned, looking down the rugged mountainside. Jared was out there. She knew it. She could feel him. He was coming for her.

And Cassidy knew it too.

"His horse has lost a shoe." Jared's fingers moved over the sandy mountain soil. "The hoof is cracking. Could pull up lame. Might slow him down." He rose stiffly, then bent backward, working out the soreness in his muscles.

Dean held his hat in his hands. Grain filled the deep crown, and he was holding it out to the horses, feeding first one, then the other. "How far you figure we're behind them?"

"Two hours, maybe a bit less. They're not stopping to rest very often, but we're moving faster. I don't think he knows where he's going. That's good. Uncertainty is good."

Dean shook the traces of grain and the horses' slobber from his hat, then placed it on his head. "I'm ready when you are."

The boy's shoulders drooped and his eyes were ringed with dark circles, but he hadn't complained. Jared remembered how much Silver had hated the trail, especially at first, but she'd never complained either. She'd been as tenacious as Dean was now.

How was she holding up? Cassidy wasn't giving her much rest. She had to be tired. But at least Cassidy couldn't harm her while they were riding. Jared wished he could find some comfort in that knowledge, but it didn't help much.

Jared stared up the trail. *Hang on, Silver.*

"All right," he said as he strode toward his gelding. "Let's go."

"Lie down," Cassidy ordered, his hand pressing on her shoulder.

He didn't have to push hard. Silver's weary legs crumpled beneath her. Under the wool blanket, the sandy red soil was hard, but it mattered little to her. She was just glad to be down from the saddle.

The sun had barely dipped beyond the western horizon when Cassidy stopped. Even now, the heat of day lingered and the sky was light. True darkness wouldn't come for hours for already the full moon was a promise in the east.

With a sigh, she turned on her side, resting her head on her jacket which Cassidy had allowed her to pull from her saddle pack. Since her wrists were still bound tightly together, she couldn't put it on, but she would be able to draw it over her shoulders as the night cooled. For now, she still felt hot and sweaty, and was covered with a gritty layer of dust. She could taste grains of sand and dirt in her teeth. She longed for a drink of water but decided not to ask. The less attention she called to herself the better.

She stiffened, her breath catching in her throat. Cassidy had spread his own blanket next to hers. Even now he was stretching out behind her. Suddenly, his arm was thrown over her as he drew himself up tight against her back. His fingers stroked her breast for a moment, then slid to her waist.

Terror dug its icy claws into her throat. She threw her arms up, but he quickly pinned them in front of her, chuckling softly.

"Not yet, my dear Silver," he whispered in her ear. "I know what you're expecting from me, but it's not quite time. I promise I won't disappoint you much longer. But tonight I need some sleep, and I must know if you try to get away." His voice deepened. "Don't try. I warn you, love. Don't try."

She'd sworn to herself that she would fight him to her last breath, but she found herself unable to move. An ocean of helplessness was washing over her, and she didn't know how to roll back the tides.

His hand slid to her abdomen. He pressed hard against her skin. "You won't try anything, will you?"

A shudder racked her body. "No. I won't."

"Good."

She lay still, listening as his breathing steadied, feeling the rise and fall of his chest against her back. She felt violated wherever their bodies touched. She wanted to push herself away from him and run screaming into the mountains.

No, she thought, giving herself a mental shake. She couldn't give in to hysteria. It might be just the excuse he needed to make him follow through with his threats. She had to stay calm. She had to have all her wits about her when Jared came. She had to be ready to act quickly. No matter how vile she found Cassidy's nearness, she had to get some sleep. She needed her rest even more than he did.

Jared was coming.

Chapter 37

Silver awakened suddenly. Cassidy's arm still clasped her to him. His breathing was slow and even.

What had awakened her?

She opened her eyes and perused the mostly open ground. The moon had nearly completed its arc across the heavens. Its soft light was already fading. There was no breeze, no sounds of scurrying nocturnal animals. Their horses stood nearby, heads hanging low as they slept, tails moving slowly from side to side.

What had awakened her? she wondered again.

And then she knew. Jared was there. He was out there. He wasn't just following, trying to find them. He was there now, watching her in the waning moonlight.

Excitement coursed through her. Should she try to roll away from Cassidy? Should she try to get up and run?

"If you move, I'll kill you." She felt the cool steel of the rifle pressed against the back of her skull.

He knows Jared's there, too.

"Get up nice and slow. Don't try any quick moves."

She hesitated.

"Now!" He jerked the rifle, knocking her head forward. Then he took hold of her loose, tangled hair and pulled her head back toward him.

She sat up, sliding onto her knees, then stood. Without moving her head, she tried to see Jared, but there was no one in sight. The ground was so barren. The nearest trees and brush were a good fifty yards away. Was he there, crouching and watching even now?

Cassidy obviously thought so. He was walking backward, pulling Silver with him, the rifle still touching the back of her head.

At any moment she could be dead. She might not live to hear Jared say he loved her. She wanted to hear those words. She wasn't going to let Cassidy keep her from it.

"You think I'm going to let him take you back alive?" he whispered harshly. "You think I'm going to let him have you at all? You're wrong. Even if he tries to shoot me, you'll be dead first. It's me or no one."

"Then I'd rather it was no one," she answered, surprised to hear the strength in her voice. "I'd rather be dead than have you touching me."

His fingers bruised her arm. "You're probably going to get your wish."

Her heart thundered against the wall of her chest. Blood pulsed in her ears until she could scarcely hear. She couldn't think. He was going to shoot her. Any moment now, she would feel the bullet exploding inside her head. She wasn't ready to die yet. She'd only just found what made life worth living.

She forced down the rising panic. If he was going to shoot her, he would have done so by now. He needed her for protection. He might kill her as soon as they reached cover but not yet. Not quite yet. She still had time to think of something.

Jared peered down the barrel of the rifle. Cassidy was holding Silver square in the line of fire. He couldn't take the chance. But Cassidy was edging further and further away, driving the horses—still saddled—before him. The open area separating Jared from Cassidy and Silver was growing. He was running out of time.

"What do we do?" Dean whispered.

Jared didn't look at the boy. He could hear his own fears echoed in the small voice. "Don't move. Not a muscle," he answered in a monotone. "No matter what happens, you stay here. Understood?"

Instinct told him Dean nodded in response, but Jared never took his eyes off Cassidy and Silver.

"I know you're out there, Newman," Cassidy shouted. "Throw down your gun and show yourself."

Jared didn't move.

"I'll kill her. You know it and she knows it and I know it. You let us ride out of here without any trouble, you don't follow me any further, and I'll let her go."

"You're a liar, Cass," Jared shouted in return. "That's something else we all know. You let Silver go first, then we'll talk."

"You're not the law. You know damn good and well that I'll probably be loose in a few days. There's nothin' to hold me. There's no proof."

"There's plenty of proof, and I'm taking you in."

"What am I worth to you, Newman? You must need me alive or you'd have killed me back in Virginia City when you had the chance. What's the reward they're offering? Hell, I'll get the money myself and pay you off. I've got friends. I can get the money. I'll double it.''

If Cassidy would just take one wrong step, Jared might be able to stop him before he reached cover. But he was moving with great care, keeping himself sheltered behind Silver's body.

''How much, Newman?''

''Five thousand, Cass. Seeing your face is worth five thousand to Ted Harrison. You remember Harrison. He has that big spread down in Texas. You shot him in the back when you were done with his wife. Well, he's waiting to get a good look at your face, and he's ready to pay for the privilege.''

There was an insane note in the burst of laughter. ''Five thousand! Then you can't kill me, can you, Newman? I was right. He wants me alive. You can't kill me.''

Jared steeled himself against the rage that flared inside him. Cassidy was right. He wasn't worth a plug nickel dead. Given the chance, Jared could wound him, disarm him. It would mean five thousand dollars.

But a wounded Cassidy could still harm Silver. A wounded Cassidy was still a dangerous one.

Five thousand dollars.

Suddenly, Silver lost her footing. She stumbled, then fell to her knees. Cassidy jerked on her arm but not quickly enough. For that brief moment, he stood alone and exposed.

Five thousand dollars meant nothing.

Jared pulled the trigger.

Silver felt the bullet whiz past almost at the same instant she heard the gunfire. For a split second, she expected to feel the pain of death. Then Cassidy's hold loosened and he fell back from her. The rifle clattered to the ground.

She turned around, staring down at him. He lay face up, his eyes wide but unseeing. She didn't want to look at the flow of blood running from the small hole between his eyebrows, but she couldn't seem to pull her gaze from it.

Then she heard footsteps running up behind her. She whirled around just in time to be gathered into the safety of Jared's arms.

"I knew you were coming," she whispered. "I knew you'd find me."

Jared's hands cupped the sides of her face, forcing her head back so he could stare down into her eyes. His left hand slipped forward to tenderly touch the bruised and swollen skin on the right side of her face. "He hurt you."

"Only that," she assured him. "Nothing more."

"When I saw he'd taken you—"

"I knew you would come," she said again.

"I thought I'd go crazy. I never should have left you alone. I should have known you couldn't follow orders."

And once again. "I knew you'd come."

"He could have shot you."

"You shot him first."

He kissed her, sweetly caressing and tasting her mouth, a lifetime of loving promised in the touch of his lips. "Why did you let him loose, even for a moment?"

"He was covered with ants. I couldn't just leave him like that. I—"

"You promised you wouldn't."

"I had to."

"Why are you always so stubborn?" He offered another gentle kiss. "Look what happened."

"I'm sorry, Jared. You've lost the reward because of me. I didn't know it was so much. I'm so sorry."

"Do you think it's the reward I'm thinking about?"

His arms tightened around her, pulling her against his chest, his hands moving up and down her back. He twined the fingers of one hand through her hair. There was no longer anything gentle about the way his mouth claimed hers, plundering, possessing.

She melted willingly into his embrace. She needed to feel him, feel every part of him. She needed to convince herself that she was alive and in his arms. She pressed herself against his length, felt the beat of his heart against her breast.

He withdrew slightly and stared down into her face. She understood the hunger in his eyes. He needed the same assurances she did.

Then, with only five whispered words, he made the world a safe and joyous place to be. "I love you, Silver. Forever."

Jared placed the last large rock on Cassidy's shallow grave. He glanced toward the horses where Silver was waiting with Dean, her arm around his shoulders. Then he stood, his back toward the woman and boy, and stared down at Cassidy's resting place.

He felt strange, knowing his six-year quest was at an end. The hate, the lust for revenge—they were gone now. He'd done what he'd set out to do. The future spread before him, and he felt free to explore it.

This was what you wanted, wasn't it, Kat? he thought. Not for me to help Silver. Not for me to kill Cass. You wanted me to be free again.

He'd imagined once before that his sister was smiling at him. This time, he was sure of it. She was smiling because he was free. And he knew that with his freedom came hers as well. After six years, Katrina could truly rest in peace.

He turned around. Silver smiled gently, her beautiful eyes filled with understanding. His heart swelled with joy.

Thanks, Kat, he thought.

And then he walked into the arms of his future.

Chapter 38

Masonville was dry and dusty, the dirt of the main street packed hard and baking beneath the August sun. A few horses stood outside the Mountain Rose, their tails flicking at persistent flies, their heads hanging low. Laundry had been strung up to dry behind the Mitchell home, and the Pearson boys were splashing in a tub of water while their mother rocked her new baby in the shade of the side porch.

The small town looked mighty good to Silver.

Still, as they approached the mercantile, anxiety balled in Silver's stomach. How were her parents going to receive the news she brought with her? She'd selfishly refused to think of this confrontation during the journey home. She'd wanted to think only of Jared and their love. But now she couldn't avoid it any longer. She would have to tell her mother and father that all was lost.

She glanced toward Jared, riding on her left. He met her gaze and offered a reassuring smile. He was with her, the look seemed to say. What more could she need? *Nothing*, her own smile replied.

She turned her head, glancing to her right this time. Dean was also watching her. His eyes were

371

filled with their own share of uncertainty, and it was her turn to offer some encouragement with a confident nod.

They reined in their horses in front of Matlock Mercantile. Silver stared up at the bold lettering across the false front. It seemed a lifetime since she'd last looked upon it. Maybe it had been a lifetime. She had certainly been another person.

The door was flung open, and her father stepped outside. "Silver!" he cried.

Her trepidation vanished as she vaulted from the saddle and flew into his waiting arms. "Papa. Oh, Papa, it's so good to be home." She buried her face against his burly chest.

"We've been worried about you, daughter," Gerald whispered near her ear.

She stepped back from him and looked into his faded brown eyes. She saw tears glimmering there and felt her resolve not to cry weakening. "I haven't brought good news. I . . . I wasn't able to get the money back, Papa."

"You're home safe. That's all your mother and I wanted."

Jared had dismounted, and he stepped up onto the boardwalk at that moment. Gerald released his hold on Silver's arm and offered his hand to the younger man.

"Thanks for bringing her back safe and sound, Mr. Newman."

Jared nodded.

"Papa, there's something . . ."

The door opened once again.

"Silvana," her mother said as she hurried forward. "Thank God, it's my Silvana. You've come back. Gerald, I told you our girl wouldn't let us down. I told you she'd get back in time." Marlene wrapped Silver in a tight hug.

Silver looked at Jared above her mother's graying head. How could she have ever thought his eyes were cold and remote? She could so easily read the tenderness there.

She freed herself from Marlene's arms and moved to stand beside Jared. "I'm back, Mother, but without the money. Bob lost it all before we found him."

"What? You mean . . ." Her mother's complexion turned ashen. "I knew it," she whispered. "I knew you wouldn't be able to do it. All these weeks and—"

Silver drew a deep breath as Jared's arm slipped around her back, his hand riding on her hip. "Mother, before you say any more, you may as well know Jared and I are going to be married."

"You can't mean . . . Silvana, he's a bounty hunter!"

"Yes, I do mean it," she interrupted, her voice strong, her head high. "And I don't care whether you approve of his profession or not— or whether you approve of him or not, for that matter. I love you, Mother, but you can't run my life. I was going to marry Bob for all the wrong reasons, because I wanted to prove to you that I wasn't the failure you always made me think I was. I'm marrying Jared for all the right reasons. Because I love him and because he's a good man and he loves me. I want to spend the rest of my life with him."

Marlene pressed a hand against her breast and looked as if she were having trouble breathing.

"I think we'd better all go inside," Gerald interrupted. "I don't know about you, Marlene, but I'd like to get to know our future son-in-law a little better. How 'bout some lemonade, everyone?"

"Wait, Papa. Before we go in, there's one more thing." She pulled away from Jared's embrace and turned toward Dean. She motioned with her hand for him to dismount and join them. When he'd done so, she faced her parents once again. "This is Dean, and once Jared and I are married, we're going to adopt him. Dean, these are your new grandparents."

"Well, I'll be." Her father's mouth broke into a broad grin. "You are full of surprises, my girl."

She looked at her mother. "Can you accept us, Mother? Just like this—Jared and Dean and me as a family?"

Time seemed to stop while she awaited her mother's response. The air was heavy, hot, and still.

There was a telltale glitter in her mother's dark blue eyes. "You're my daughter," she said softly. "You needn't be so angry with me. I love you, Silvana. You don't appreciate what I've tried to do for you. I've only ever wanted what was best. I've tried to guide and help you. You haven't always taken my advice, but I understand that's my cross to bear. If this man . . ." She glanced at Jared, then back to Silver. "If this man is who you want, then I will, of course, accept him. And the boy too." Her voice sounded condescending, but it also revealed her hurt and disappointment.

Poor Mother, Silver thought suddenly. She'll never know the joy of loving someone else more than herself.

Jared stepped forward and put his arm around Marlene, drawing looks of surprise not only from the older woman but from Silver as well. "We're going to do everything we can to try and save this place for you, Mrs. Matlock. I promise."

Silver's throat tightened. She knew he understood how her mother felt about him, yet he didn't hold it against Marlene. He was prepared to care for her mother as if she were his own. It was one more reason for Silver to love him so very much.

"Yes. Well. Let's go inside," Gerald said once again. "It seems we have plenty to talk about."

The wedding was a quiet affair held in the Matlocks' front parlor with only the family present. The bride wore a simple but attractive gown of pale pink and a garnish of rosebuds in her hair. The groom looked handsome, although slightly uncomfortable, in a dark suit, white collar, and necktie. The bride's mother wept softly throughout the ceremony. The bride's father beamed with joy. Sapphire and Dan Downing stood up with the couple. Dean, with the proprietary air of an older cousin, kept an eye on the two Downing boys.

"You may kiss your bride," the minister said with gentle authority.

Jared gathered Silver in his arms. He stared down into her beautiful face and knew that no other man had ever been as lucky as he was. Time and again, he'd tried to reject this woman's love, but she hadn't let him succeed. He was thankful she was so blasted stubborn.

He paid the knocking on the door no heed as his lips claimed hers. His wife. She was his wife. For now and always.

"Jared?" His father-in-law's hand touched his shoulder. "There's someone here to see you. Says it's important."

He turned, Silver still wrapped in his arms. "Coop, what are you doing here?"

Rick Cooper grinned as his eyes flicked from Jared to Silver and back again. "I could ask the same. Shouldn't you let a friend know when you do something like this?"

Jared shrugged.

"Can I talk to you a moment?" the sheriff asked.

"Sure." He looked down at Silver. Her gray eyes looked worried. He kissed the tip of her nose. "I'll only be a minute."

As soon as Jared turned his back toward Silver, he frowned. He couldn't imagine what had brought the sheriff up from Denver. He'd already told him everything about Cassidy's death. The matter should have been closed. He followed Cooper out onto the porch and closed the door behind him.

"What's up, Coop?"

"Not what you think, my friend," the sheriff answered. He reached into his breast pocket. "Mr. Harrison stopped by to see me before he left Denver. He asked me to give this to you." He pulled a slip of paper from his pocket and held it out toward Jared.

Jared took it. His eyes widened. "But this is a bank draft for five thousand dollars."

"That's right."

"But I didn't bring Cassidy in alive. He doesn't owe me . . ."

Cooper placed a hand on Jared's arm. "Didn't seem to matter to him. He wanted you to have it. Said you'd earned it."

Jared stared at the draft a moment longer, then turned toward the door. "Excuse me, Coop."

"There's trouble of some sort, isn't there?" Marlene whispered as she twisted a handkerchief in her hands. "I knew it. I knew something would go wrong if you married a man like—"

"Be quiet, Mother," Silver said sternly. She was just as afraid as her mother that something was wrong, but she wasn't going to let Marlene say anything against Jared, no matter what.

But something was most definitely wrong. The longer she waited, the more convinced she was. Why else would Rick Cooper have ridden all this way? He was Jared's friend, true, but he hadn't known about the wedding so that wasn't why he'd come. Did he need Jared to find a criminal for him? Jared had said he was going to give up bounty hunting. He'd talked of heading north into Montana and homesteading, starting a cattle ranch, raising a family. But she knew money would be in short supply, especially at first, and Jared's reputation would follow him. This wouldn't be the only time he was asked to take a job, and although she hoped he would refuse such offers, it would be hard to turn down the money he could earn. But did he have to make that choice so soon? Was her husband going to be leaving her before they'd even had a proper honeymoon?

The door opened and Jared strode inside, a big smile on his face. He picked her up in his arms and spun her around several times. Her head flew back. Her hair broke free of its pins and spilled down her back. His loud whoop echoed through the house. He was grinning from ear to ear as he set her down and then kissed her soundly.

"Jared, what on earth?" she asked breathlessly when he released her.

"This!" he shouted, his grin getting even bigger. "This is what." He held out a piece of paper. "Look at it."

It wasn't the size of the draft she noticed so much as the sense of relief that flowed through her. And in its wake came a joy to match his own. He wasn't leaving. He wasn't going to buckle on his gun belt and ride away. Her face broke into a smile that rivaled the one Jared was wearing.

"Mr. and Mrs. Matlock," he said, turning toward his in-laws, "we have the money to pay your mortgages. You won't have to leave your home or give up the store."

"Jared?" Silver whispered as her smile disappeared.

Marlene gasped and fell against her husband. "Where do you suppose a man like that got the money to do—"

Looking at his daughter's anxious face, Gerald snapped, "Not now, Marlene." His voice sounded stronger and more sure than it had in years. "Just sit down and be quiet."

Stunned, Marlene did as she was told.

Silver wasn't even aware of her parents' words or actions. "Jared . . ." she said again as she touched his arm, bringing his gaze back to her. She looked up into the face she'd grown to love so very much. "You don't have to do this. That money . . . you talked once of going back to Fair Acres. You could with—"

"Fair Acres belongs to the past," he said softly as he embraced her. "I let go of it when I let go of all the hate. We'll build something better, you and I."

"But it was important to you once. With that reward—"

His arms tightened around her. She could feel his heartbeat against her breasts. She could read the love in his eyes.

"Nothing is as important as you, Silver. You're the only reward I'll ever want or need."

Jared saw his love returned in her beautiful eyes of gray and knew the words he'd spoken were true. He'd collected the best bounty of all . . .

His bounty of Silver.